MW00659318

BEACON OF VENGEANCE

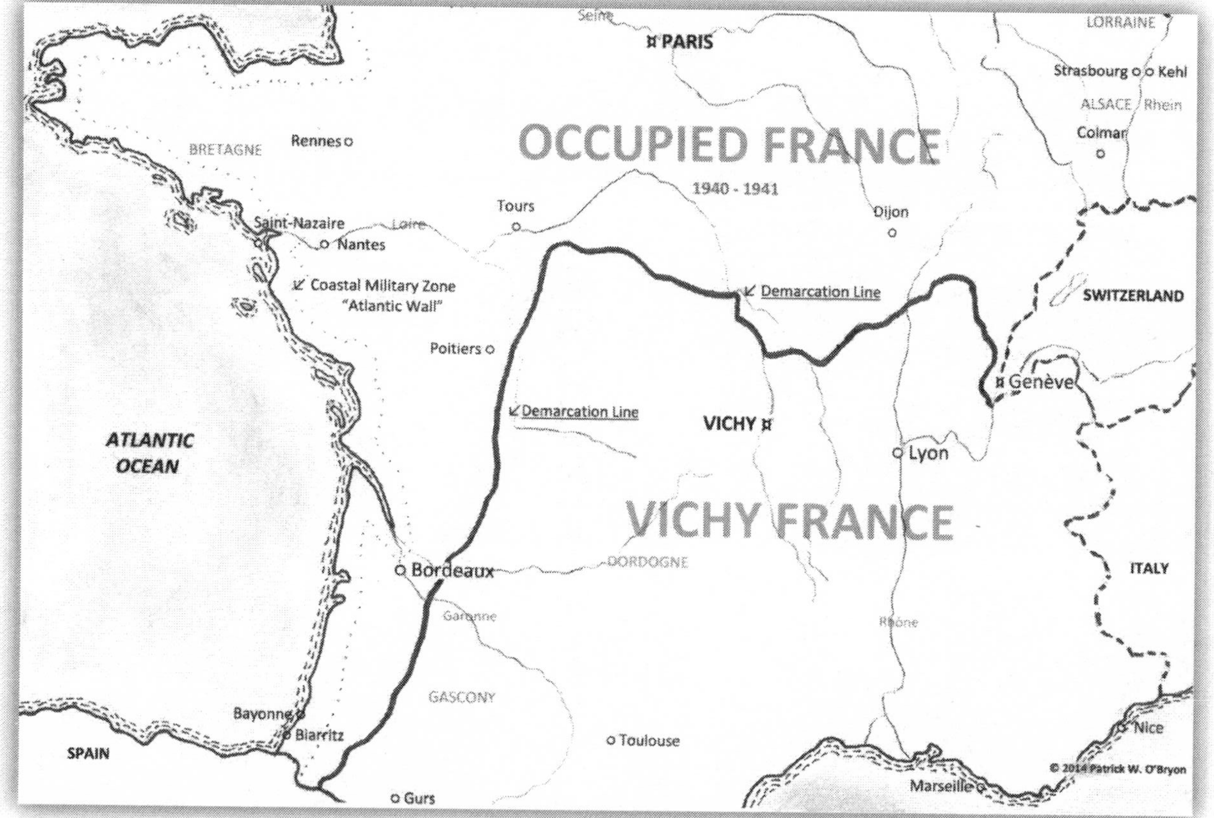

OCCUPIED FRANCE
1940 - 1941
VICHY FRANCE
PARIS
Seine
LORRAINE
Strasbourg
Kehl
ALSACE
Rhein
Colmar
BRETAGNE
Rennes
Tours
Dijon
Saint-Nazaire
Loire
Nantes
Coastal Military Zone
"Atlantic Wall"
Demarcation Line
SWITZERLAND
Poitiers
Genève
Demarcation Line
VICHY
Lyon
ATLANTIC
OCEAN
Bordeaux
DORDOGNE
ITALY
Garonne
Rhône
GASCONY
Bayonne
Biarritz
Toulouse
SPAIN
Nice
© 2014 Patrick W. O'Bryon
Marseille
Gurs

BEACON OF VENGEANCE

A NOVEL OF NAZI GERMANY

Patrick W. O'Bryon

Brantôme Press
NAPA, CALIFORNIA

Publisher's Note: This is a work of fiction. Names, characters, places, and incidents are a product of the author's imagination. Locales and public names are sometimes used for atmospheric purposes. Any resemblance to actual people, living or dead, or to businesses, companies, events, institutions, or locales is completely coincidental.

Cover Design by G. S. Prendergast
Book Layout ©2013 BookDesignTemplates.com
Author Photo by Ashley Urke Photography
Photos of Florentine Ring by Leonard L. O'Bryon, Jr.

Beacon of Vengeance/Patrick W. O'Bryon. -- 1st ed.
ISBN 978-0-9910782-3-3

To Dani

CONTENTS

Tangle within tangle, plot and counter-plot,
ruse and treachery, cross and double-cross,
true agent, false agent...incredible and yet true.

—Winston Churchill

LE PRÉLUDE

1938 - 1940

CHAPTER ONE

Kehl, Germany
12 November 1938
4:33 a.m.

The fury of the blast left René no time to react. An incoming Mauser round pierced the fuel tank of their launch and his comrade took the brunt of the explosion. Uwe's body struck René with mind-numbing force and both men flew out over the lagoon. René felt the searing heat and was momentarily blinded by a flash which shredded the fog, and then came impact with the water. Once he regained the surface the shattered hull was in flames, burning fuel and oil slicked the surface, and Uwe's mutilated body bobbed face down in the choppy wash.

His fellow fighter had paid the price for shielding his friend and leader. A brief check confirmed what René instinctively knew—Uwe was a raw mass of blood and seared skin, and dead. One arm was missing. The signature thatch of coarse blond hair hung loosely from his head, and the curve of the flayed skull glowed dully in the flames from the wreckage. Large wooden splinters protruded from the flesh of his neck and back, forcing René to think fleetingly of mariners' deaths in the days when cannon balls wreaked havoc on the tall sailing ships.

There was no sound. Or rather, only an incessant humming which filled his head, blocking all ambient noise. René could not tell if the firefight ashore was still ongoing. He treaded water and looked toward the docks, but the fog had gathered again, leaving only diffuse pinpoints of light along the row of warehouses and a brighter glow from the Water Police patrol boat which had been their undoing. René was sapped of energy, resting on a floating hatch cover and cursing the loss of his comrade as the current drew the mangled body away from his raft. He wondered if he had permanently lost his hearing, the constant buzz in his ears a distraction as he calculated his odds and those of his friends ashore. He wondered if he had been concussed again, if he would spend months recovering as he had after the brutal beating by von Kredow that had changed his life. His thoughts came so slowly. He was unaware of the cold.

Time passed, leaving his mind to drift. Then he sensed a subtle variation, a rhythmic thrumming approaching across the water, and he abruptly remembered they might search the wreckage. He forced his dulled mind alert. The inverted hull, no longer aflame, bobbed several meters away as it drifted toward the Rhine. He left his hatch cover to breaststroke over to the shattered wreck and he dropped below the water to resurface under the capsized keel. A two-handed grip on the ragged framing above his head gave his weak right leg a rest, and there he waited. The backwash slapped against the hull as a passing craft slowed nearby, although the ringing in his ears and the dampening shield of the hull allowed little sound to penetrate. And then the vessel accelerated at open throttle, leaving his shelter bobbing violently in its wake.

He would swim to rejoin his comrades, with luck still rescue his friends. He thought of Erika and that little boy he had carried on his arm, and of Ryan. *If I still have comrades to save,* he thought. He left the hull with a determined stroke toward the distant lights dimming and flaring in the shifting mist. His hearing had barely improved, but once again he sensed the throb of a vessel approaching and rapidly gaining speed. He knew it must be the police gunboat, and in a hurry. He submerged to let it pass.

❖

She knew she had lost. Erika cradled Leo, his face buried at her chest, and fought against the numbness, both mental and physical. She imagined springing from the bench, Leo still in her arms, and plunging overboard to join Ryan in death. She knew the future held no promise for her or her son. She would sink beneath the waters and not fight the pull of life, and this brutal ordeal would be over. But then she thought of Leo struggling to live, and she let the thought go. As long as she was still sound of mind and body, she *could* fight. As long as Leo was with her, she would not surrender, *would* fight. She hugged her three-year-old closer and rocked him gently. *But we will both still die*, she thought.

The SS policemen out on the deck tended to the wreckage of Horst's face. It no longer mattered now what happened to him. She had seen his jaw shatter as the bullet struck home, the spray of blood and bone and flesh backlit in the glare of the searchlight. It had felt good. He had paid the price for destroying the future of the boy in her arms, for the death of her parents, for her torture and rape. Should he live, his face would be a horrific mask exposing him to the world, his mutilated features an indelible mirror of the monster within. Should he die, the world would be a better place.

Ryan had been so strong at the end, so certain of their success and escape to France. Only two hours earlier they had relaxed in the shack, sensing an end to the terrifying flight from Berlin, letting down their guard, and she had seen the happiness in his eyes when she revealed that he was likely Leo's natural father. He had been a good man, a decent man, and she fought back tears, picturing his drop into the dark waters, the loathsome Pabst dragging them both beneath the roiling surface. *Ryan won't be back to save us this time, despite his promise.* The tears finally broke loose, and she sobbed, pulling silent Leo ever more tightly to her. She wished she had the toy bear to offer her son as comfort, but Bruno lay abandoned on the deck of the motorboat which followed in their wake.

Horst lay unmoving on the stretcher, his head a swath of bandages. His moaning had ceased, and the medic remarked on the inordinate amount of morphine it had taken to calm his agony. Little did he know that Horst had routinely injected the pain killer.

The young policeman hovered over the captives, his machine pistol alert. He no longer tried to comfort her with assurances that the Reich would look after her son once she paid the price for assaulting a high-ranking Gestapo official. She had read Horst's protocol, knew what the state planned for all Jews like her. If her husband did not manage their deaths beforehand for having "tricked" him into marrying a Jewess, they would certainly still disappear into a concentration camp to ultimately perish there. But Erika would never go willingly.

❖

René found the Gesslinger docks in shambles as he climbed to the loading platform and limped ashore. Downed SS soldiers lay on the gravel near the gate where his men had dragged the bodies. He dispatched the sole survivor—badly injured with a gut wound and unconscious—with a quick slip of his pocket knife. The attack had commenced as planned, but the loss of Uwe and the failure to achieve their principal goal meant a devastating defeat. The police launch was away, and with it Ryan, Erika and the boy. His other fighters were unscathed, a miracle in itself. He found them consoling one another over René's own presumed death.

The dockside shack had its own story to tell. The table displayed tools of torture. Ryan's overcoat and Erika's handbag still hung on the hooks. René noted where his friend had suffered, the burned ropes and scorched wood of the chair arm, the cut ties which earlier had bound Ryan's feet. Blood splatters streaked the floorboards, and the stench of burned flesh still permeated the shack. He doubted his friend could have withheld his secrets—few men could in the face of such cruelty—so the Lone Ranger network was likely exposed to the Gestapo. There was no sign of Hugo Gerson, but René sadly guessed his fate, as well.

He sent his men home, warning that they were compromised and suggesting they too escape to France. His remaining boats were at their disposal. He burned with fury, but knew his job had just begun and fought the blinding rage which would render him ineffective.

René gave his mother no choice. Jeanne was in tears and resisted, but he helped her into her coat, grabbed her handbag and some family documents, and had his man escort her to the waiting Opel. She insisted on taking an album of photographs of her early married years. He quickly changed to dry clothing and gathered a few basics. Long ago he had stashed French francs at the Kehl home, for he had known this day would surely come. Within half an hour the family estate would sit abandoned, and he and his mother would be across the river before the new day fully dawned. They would head for her ancestral home south of Colmar in Alsace, take a few days to recover, then assess their situation and decide the future fight.

❖

Erika expected that soon now some official would step in and seal their fate. Her mind raced as the gunboat headed upriver toward the police docks in Kehl. The long railroad bridge passed overhead in the fog, carrying others to the safety they had sought in France. The muted lights of the town beckoned as the launch made a sweeping curve toward shore.

The Water Protection Police station was understaffed—*Horst's welcoming party at Gesslinger Shipping must surely have depleted their resources,* she thought—so some confusion reigned. The ambulance awaiting their arrival quickly whisked Horst away, its siren pointless in that pre-dawn hour when no one braved the streets without official permission. Horst von Kredow, her sadist husband, the man she once believed she loved, the man who was destined to make her future in the new Germany, was out of her life at last.

Her guard placed handcuffs on her wrists, the cold metal raw against the welts left from Horst's rape barely twenty-four hours earlier. It now seemed an age, an epic series of events which had taken all from her but Leo, clutching at her arm. They were placed in an interrogation room and told to expect the Gestapo shortly, and she knew she would soon lose Leo. He would go to an orphanage, at least until word got out of her Jewish heritage, or until Horst tracked them down. She would now face interrogation far more brutal than anything she had yet endured. *There is no future in this new Germany,* she thought.

The sleepy-eyed sergeant behind the desk—obviously resentful of the interruption in a swing shift normally devoted to dozing—insisted the woman give an official statement. He called for the key to her cuffs and placed it in his breast pocket. Despite her damp clothing, disheveled hair and makeup long missing, he still ran his eyes the length of her body and managed a lecherous smile, appreciating both her looks and her discomfort. Leo clung to her bound hands.

"Now here's a nice piece of ass to grace our station," he said. "Don't worry—we'll get you out of that damp clothing as soon as possible, for your own good, of course. But first, I need a name." Erika eyed the desk, the pen holder, the brass fire extinguisher affixed to the wall to her right, barely visible past the man's head. She quickly returned her gaze to the sergeant. His stubble and mustache carried remnants of something white and powdery and recently eaten—confectioner's sugar, perhaps. The fatigued eyes revealed nothing beyond the obvious leer, but his words made her decision easy. She remained silent.

"*Mutti, ich muss Pipi machen*." Leo, pressing against her leg, looked up imploringly. He hadn't uttered a word since the shooting on the river, but now the immediacy of his need brought him back.

"A toilet for my child," she said, a mother's demand, not a request.

"It can wait. He won't be coddled where you're headed." The sergeant chuckled.

"*Mutti*, I need to go, I need to go now!"

"Remove these cuffs and I'll take him to a toilet, or you'll have a real mess to deal with. Your man there can stand guard."

"The cuffs go nowhere, and you'll stay right here even if you piss yourself, my dear. As for your brat—" he gestured to the guard, "—Corporal Mannheimer, get this kid to the shitter and make sure he does his business."

The young policeman nodded and put a hand on Leo's shoulder. "Let's go, kid."

"*Mutti?*"

"It's fine, Leo, go with the man. I'll be here when you come back, don't worry." Leo saw the truth in his mother's eyes, and though hesitant to leave her, nature called too strongly and he allowed himself to be shepherded into the hallway.

The sergeant returned to the typewriter. "Again, what's your name?" Erika stayed mute, staring at the desk. "Listen closely, madam, we'll get it out of you eventually. Would you prefer the Gestapo way, or our way?" She said nothing. "Very well, you fired upon and grievously wounded a high-ranking SS officer before witnesses. The reason for your action?"

She finally spoke: "He deserved to die."

He looked at her with impatience and began to type, a finger of each hand tapping at the keys. He only got as far as "deserved." The heavy bronze eagle in her bound hands met his skull, and Erika heard the crunch and felt the give and knew she had aimed true. The sergeant loosed a grunt and a fart and his head fell over the rank of type bars as blood poured from the head wound. She returned the eagle to its roost at the center of the desk, the talons gripping the swastika now glistening red. The sergeant's two fountain pens lay scattered across the surface, the spilled ink forming sinuous patterns as it mingled with blood from his crushed temple. The scroll of paper in the typewriter was now saturated; no name or mention of her relationship to Horst would ever be noted. The machine itself sat half hidden by his drooping head, as if he were searching within for his missing consciousness. Erika withdrew the key from his pocket and freed herself of the restraints, then pulled the fire extinguisher from its wall bracket and positioned herself behind the hallway door to wait.

She glanced over at the fallen sergeant and realized her error. Though the young policeman would not see her empty chair as he came through the door, he would immediately spot the slumped body of his sergeant. She forced the unconscious man upright, positioning his elbows on the desk, his forearms over the machine. She wiped the blood from her hands on his uniform jacket, then concealed herself again behind the door, the bulky brass canister at the ready. She heard Leo's voice in the hall and then they were outside, just beyond the door.

Leo entered first, the guard on his heels. "*Mutti*, I'm done. This man is nice." A few steps beyond the threshold and the corporal would see her empty chair. She brought the extinguisher down on the back of his head and he slumped to the ground.

The boy turned in amazement: "But *Mutti*, I said this one is nice!"

❖

The ringing jarred René as he shut the house door, perhaps all the more so because his hearing now slowly returned despite the persistent dull buzz in his head. He knew the Gestapo never phoned first, just arrived at the doorstep unannounced and in force. It had to be one of his crew, so he picked up the receiver and recognized the voice of Erika.

"It's me, René. Please hurry!"

CHAPTER TWO

Karlsruhe and Berlin, Germany
December 1938

Horst von Kredow set the chess board aside on the clinic bed, careful not to disturb the ivory and ebony pieces. As always, he found himself to be a worthy opponent. The young and buxom nurse had just entered to change his facial bandage before giving the daily sponge-bath, and he imagined strapping her face-down to a gurney and exposing those firm buttocks to his pleasures. Yes, he was feeling his old self again.

Another man would have suffered mental and emotional trauma in the wake of the damage done by the bullet. The projectile had pierced his chin from below, shattering the left side of his jawbone before pulverizing teeth and shredding gums and tissue. Though the cheekbone suffered, his eye socket and vision escaped unscathed. Horst knew to endure the discomfort and recovery with his dignity intact, pleased that his ability to manage pain had always far exceeded any typical man's.

"Bring me a mirror." His calm voice threatened rather than soothed. She had shown her revulsion at first removal of the bandage to clean the sutures. "I want to see exactly what you are seeing."

"But, sir…the doctor said you must wait."

"Bring me a mirror—right now. This face belongs to me, not some doctor."

She hurried off to check with her superior, knowing she would find a mirror no matter the physician's response.

The previous weeks had passed in splendid drug intoxication, a morphine drip in his arm to still occasional bouts of escalating pain. He had drifted in and out of consciousness, using any opportunity when clear-minded to plan what he would tell Heydrich about the disastrous turn of events. A Gestapo subordinate had already briefed Horst in general terms. The Jew-bitch had managed to escape Water Police custody, and his Gestapo spies across the Rhine had reported a woman of Erika's description with a large, limping German and a small boy at the Strasbourg train station.

The nurse reappeared with a hand mirror and Horst regarded his face, evaluating the damage from every angle. Reassuring the patient was standard nursing practice. "It will get better, sir."

The right side of his face was untouched, strong, and perfect. The left half was still purplish and swollen after two surgeries to correct the damage, but he was proud to be a wonder of German reconstructive surgery. Small screws held a stainless steel prosthesis in place, a slim glistening structure which replicated his strong original jawline. He opened his mouth to admire the handiwork. The surgeons had also artificially reconstructed his cheekbone. He used his tongue to explore for the thousandth time the smooth surface of the metalwork and the gap left by missing molars.

He would only chew on his right side, but externally, once the swelling was gone, his face would be stunning in its impact.

The fine dueling scar that had shaped his adult life remained in all its pallid glory. He stroked its length with his fingertip, amazed to touch it once again without fear of wrenching pain. Remarkably, as the level of morphine in his veins had diminished he learned that the neuralgia that had caused his decade-long *tic douloureux* was gone. The bullet somehow tore away the disturbed nerve damaged by René Gesslinger's blade in the academic duel. With it went the debilitating attacks which had left him convulsed in pain and unable to maintain self-control without medication.

He would never smile again—too much damage to facial musculature—but he had relegated the smile long ago to the realm of weakness. Consider Ryan Lemmon, who bared his teeth mindlessly at the drop of a hat.

"Splendid, just splendid," Horst handed the nurse the mirror, his new face the perfect mix of cruelty and beauty, a mask hiding nothing. He grabbed her ass as she turned to leave. Hard.

❖

In the week following the incident on the Rhine, when Horst had still been deep in the morphine drip, Reinhard Heydrich had sent flowers to the hospital room along with a handwritten card. A young SS lieutenant had come down from Berlin to deliver both in person.

My dear Horst,

It is with great sadness that we learn of your unfortunate accident. Come see us again as soon as you are able. The Reich needs its best men.

Sincerest wishes for a full and speedy recovery from

Your Reinhard

He could picture his mentor seated at that grand desk in his formal office, surrounded by rich red carpet and flanked by scarlet flags. Heydrich, head of Reich internal security and intelligence services, Horst's protector, who had brought him close to the highest echelon of power, to Himmler and ultimately the Führer himself.

Horst's story would have to be solid. The card made no mention of Erika and Leo, so Horst assumed Heydrich might not know the true course of events. If he handled this well, his future in the Gestapo could still be secured. His first thought had been to pull some attractive Jewish woman and a small boy from one of the detention camps, stage an auto accident, and then claim his family had perished on a week-end getaway. He thought to blame his own injury on that same crash which he somehow miraculously survived.

Though powerful enough within the Gestapo hierarchy and intimidating enough to quash the truth, he knew that a report of his gunshot wound would have already reached Berlin. Knowing Heydrich, Horst suspected people in the clinic were keeping an eye on him without his knowledge—he was privy to too many secrets to be unattended while under the influence of anesthesia or drugs. A ludicrous thought, considering that his established dependence on morphine was no secret to Heydrich.

Without his "dagger" Klaus Pabst to investigate what was already known at Berlin Gestapo headquarters, he had to rely on less reliable sources, so he called Peter Brenner down from Kassel to visit him in the private clinic room. Brenner had been the third leg of his Marburg triumvirate alongside his first lieutenant Pabst, always ready to do what was necessary for the good of the Nazi cause. And for Horst's future. Peter greeted his old university friend and leader with a firm handshake after carefully securing the door and moving a chair bedside.

Horst skipped any platitudes and launched right in with instructions. "First off, find out exactly what was reported or even rumored." Horst absent-mindedly ran his tongue along the slick inside surface of the jaw prosthesis, his tongue not yet accustomed to that slippery metallic bit. "Berlin is one big gossip mill, and many would discredit me given half a chance, so preemptive action is a must."

"Consider it done, Horst." Peter had registered shock at the damage to his friend's face, but realized immediately that the shooting had done nothing to affect his leader's critical facilities and temperament.

"Let's use a propaganda technique our Dr. Goebbels applies so well—"If you tell a lie big enough and keep repeating it, people will eventually come to believe it." Our story is as follows: my beloved Erika and dear little boy were kidnapped by the Alsatian brute René Gesslinger and died by his hands."

"In Kehl?"

"No, kidnapped in Berlin, and then killed near Kehl, clear? And not a word about the American, right?" Horst forced himself to show patience. He longed for Klaus Pabst's instant grasp of any situation. "Now pay close attention, Peter—'Monsieur' Gesslinger, furious at our disruption of his network of Bolshevik spies and saboteurs, brutally snatched my family from my home and brought them under threat of death to Kehl. My son's governess never saw who hit her, so there won't be any questions from that end."

Peter nodded in agreement as he confirmed the fictional account. "First off, this story will back up any official reports already posted which mentioned three fugitives, so I can easily discredit any rumor of an American being involved. We have only the one criminal, this "Frenchman" Gesslinger who stole your warrant badge when he kidnapped your wife and child, and he alone caused the mayhem on the Koblenz train."

The report to Berlin would make sense coming from Brenner, since Kreisler and Fischer had the agents out of Kassel he had assigned to pursuing the fugitives. They had given their all to the task. "My second agent Fischer died from his injuries, as well, you know."

Horst shrugged and moved on without responding. "In fact, include that Gesslinger used my prescribed morphine to subdue both my wife and child."

"Nice touch, Horst."

"Now let's get to his motivation: he took Erika and Leo as leverage to get the Gestapo off his back. We tracked them down to the docks where his gunmen attacked with overwhelming force. The bastard fled into the fog and night, only to drown my family in the Rhine before slipping into France."

"And your injury?"

"Klaus and I pursued the fugitive onto the river, shots were fired from both sides, Klaus was lost to the river and I took a bullet meant for him." Horst touched his scarred cheek, marveling again at the lack of sensation after years of neuralgia. "As simple as that."

"What of the Water Protection Police? They will have filed a report."

"All copies now destroyed, and sadly, the gunboat captain and his two men also met later with an unfortunate accident, gunned down on the police docks. We assume a retaliatory action by Gesslinger's dangerous crew of misfits."

"Understood, Horst. Any other loose ends?"

"Here's what we've got: it appears that someone bashed in the head of the duty sergeant at the station that night, and a young policeman was left unconscious. The corporal's injuries were insignificant, but sadly someone gave him the wrong medication and he lapsed into a coma. No further brain activity. Obviously we hold our "Frenchman" responsible on all counts."

"Nicely handled, Horst. I'll see that Berlin finally has the full story of the day's events."

"One more thing, Peter. Minor but important."

"Yes?"

"Since you couldn't leave your Kassel duties immediately I had to rely on a local man to handle what couldn't wait. I'm afraid we now must tie up that loose end, as well." Horst scribbled a name and location on a pad and handed it to Brenner.

"*Zu Befehl*, Horst. Consider it done. Now you get some rest and know I'm there for you, as always." Peter returned the chair to its place on the wall and shook his friend's hand. "And Horst, will I join you in Berlin, now that we've lost Klaus?"

"Trouble at home, Peter?"

"No, sir, all's fine, and Hedy and the boys are doing well. I'm just anxious to be of greater service. After all, it's been a while, and you lead a much more interesting life than I'll ever see in Kassel."

"Count on it, Peter, count on it. Once back on my feet and with Heydrich satisfied, I'll call for you."

❖

Peter Brenner left with a smile, but once outside the room, he hesitated, the door handle still in his grip. Seeing Horst again had been a blow, the changes to his friend's face unsettling. The handsome Germanic features which had made him a Teutonic ideal as they won adherents to the Nazi cause in Marburg in the early days were now a distant memory.

As always, Peter accepted unflinchingly the tasks assigned to him. Any true soldier obeys his leader without question in honor of the greater good. The severity of the actions he would undertake next caused him little concern, even though the targets were not Bolsheviks or Jews or faggots but rather fellow police officers. The Reich had few men as great as Horst. It made no sense allowing a few lesser men to threaten such a leader's survival. And by fulfilling his duties as a true soldier now, Peter knew he would finally assume the role he had always envisioned, a place beside their leader that Horst had first given to Pabst.

An attractive nurse waited in the hallway, distracted, some unknown concern reflected in her eyes as she waited for permission to enter Horst's room. She might not even realize what an honor it was to serve and care for such an important and powerful man of the Reich.

Don't you worry, lovely Fräulein, your patient's doing just fine. Our leader is back.

❖

At Gestapo headquarters on Prinz Albrechtstrasse the high window in Reinhard Heydrich's back office stood ajar. The draft of frigid air fought a losing battle with the clanging radiator beneath the sill. Berlin lay under the pall of an early January storm. Sheets of icy sleet and occasional rain forced vehicles to a crawl, and pedestrians bent to the wind with their hat brims down and collars up, umbrellas straining to the breaking point. Inside, the muffled rumble of traffic penetrated the stuffy office.

Von Kredow's superior, overseer of the secret police services of the Reich, rose from behind the immaculate desk to shake hands. "You're looking your old self again, Horst." Heydrich's closely-spaced, pale-blue eyes scanned every new scar and facial distortion, missing nothing.

Heydrich lies with grace, thought Horst. He could read revulsion on the tall Gestapo leader's face, the look of someone unable to fully appreciate how well this new mask would serve his purposes. "Thank you, sir. It's taken a while, but I'm fit again and ready for duty."

"My deepest condolences on the loss of your wife and son. No man should bear such a burden."

"A horror beyond words, Reinhard." Horst accepted Heydrich's offer to sit, his demeanor suitably subdued under his great loss. "But we all must suffer for the cause, and this tragedy has given me new focus."

"Forgive my indiscretion, Horst, but the bodies of your loved ones? Were they found? An appropriate ceremony and interment to honor their sacrifice would be fitting."

Horst remained momentarily silent, his eyes downcast. He had caught the hint of suspicion in his leader's look. "Sadly, no. I'm told they likely washed ashore on the French side, but too much time had passed to know for sure." He pressed a hand to his forehead, shielding his eyes.

"This murderer, this Gesslinger—you know his whereabouts?"

"Most likely Alsace—his family ties are there—though I've no recent updates."

"I can only assume you wish to be free of duties here in Berlin to pursue this matter to the end?"

Horst despised that high-pitched voice, so disconcerting in a leader of Heydrich's stature. "Thank you for your understanding, sir. I *am* committed to avenging the suffering my family endured."

He could hear the dismissal in Heydrich's words, the desire to move things along.

"Understood, Horst. We've seen some preliminaries from various stations. I ask only that you—once sufficiently strong to handle it, of course—prepare a thorough report of this action for the record. For the moment, your man has filled us in. Brenner, is it not, head of Kassel station?"

"Yes, sir. Brenner's a good man, known and trusted since university."

"Then consider yourself on provisional attachment to our Baden station, subject of course to my recall to Berlin at a future time. You'll have free rein until you've wrapped up the case down there."

"But, Reinhard…our plans for the Jews, my protocol…"

"Sorry, Horst, but I need you free of all distractions. You're of lesser use to me with this crime and tragic loss clouding your mind. The proposals for the Jewish question need time, so your efforts are better utilized elsewhere."

Horst sensed how the wind now blew. He had neared the summit. His protocol for elimination of European Jewry would have established his name—his dedication and insight—in the minds of Himmler and the Führer. Did Heydrich perhaps fear him? His brilliance? But all that was now lost, at least for now. He would have to prove himself anew, but first he would find the Jew-whore of a wife who had cost him his well-earned rise to the top, and she would pay a steep price for her treason.

Heydrich swiveled toward the window, then rose to stand over the overworked radiator, allowing Horst time to collect himself. Horst sensed his mentor was uncomfortable looking directly at the static mask of his subordinate. Observing the foot traffic on the street below, Heydrich continued: "Report only to me, as always. Make arrangements for any visas and identification papers needed. You'll find a decent network of our people across the border, and our Reich-friendly French colleagues will be glad to help you run this treacherous criminal to ground." He turned back to face Horst. "However, I will certainly call upon you in the future. Your work has always been exemplary, and I'm sure we'll work side-by-side again soon."

"Thank you, Reinhard. I deeply appreciate it. And if I might, I'd like Brenner to join me. My right-hand man—you'll recall Klaus Pabst—fell to this bastard Gesslinger, as well. Brenner and I'll track down this criminal and make him pay for my loss."

"For our loss, Horst…for our loss. Your Erika was indeed a beautiful angel, and I'm sure your son would have made the Reich proud." Horst remembered Heydrich ogling his Jew-wife's long legs at Party functions, and knew any thoughts of her remained less than angelic.

"Thank you, Reinhard."

"And Horst?"

"Yes, sir?"

"Might I suggest using your time in Alsace and France to connect with our friends over there. Alsace and Lorraine will certainly find their rightful place in the Reich soon enough. Any groundwork you lay, any connections you establish with our fascist allies across the Rhine will be useful as we move westward. The Reich needs room to grow, and that growth must come soon."

"Consider it done, once I've buried this Gesslinger."

"I trust your judgment." Heydrich extended his hand. "And now, if you'll excuse me, Horst, other matters demand attention."

"Of course, sir. Thank you for your time and your support."

"Just know you have my heartfelt condolences on your tragic loss." He lowered his eyes in sympathy. "We must be ever vigilant in rooting out these enemies of the state."

Horst saluted and withdrew as an aide waiting in the antechamber shut the door behind him. He went upstairs to the office he hadn't seen in over a month, ever since that fateful day when Klaus Pabst had revealed Erika to be a Jewess and a traitor. Whether Heydrich knew more of the matter than he had revealed was of little importance. Horst was on his own, a man with a mission and carte blanche to use the Gestapo to accomplish his goals. He would destroy Gesslinger. And the Jew-bitch. And have that bastard Lemmon licking the shit from his boots.

CHAPTER THREE

Paris, Occupied France
14 June 1940

Artillery to the north and the distant crump of explosions on the outskirts of the city alarmed her many times during the long night. Memories of finding her way home through the crowded streets made sleep difficult. Everyone knew the *Boches* would reach the city center by morning light and that the war was lost. "They're coming! They're coming!" had echoed for hours.

Ever since the rapid fall of Belgium just weeks before, the government had assured them the German army was starving and ill-equipped, that it would take little to bring down the Huns. A valiant military response would put the enemy on the run. But the rumors of a counter-offensive and the incessant propaganda boasting of imminent victory had all proved a sham. Now greasy, roiling clouds on the horizon announced the enemy's arrival as fuel storage tanks north of Paris burned out of control and the frightening sirens of the Stuka dive bombers whined through the filthy clouds. A pall hung over the awakening city. Marita drew aside the blackout drapes and stepped cautiously out onto her balcony.

A gentle rain of fine soot slowly coated the metal railings and the tree leaves below the terrace. The usual birdsong was missing, the feeder with its stale crusts left untouched. Even the winged creatures had taken flight from the coming danger. Rumor was that Paris was now an open city, the government on the move to Tours, and no attempt would be made at defense in the hope that the advancing army would spare the ancient city further devastation. The throngs in the streets below pulsed with desperate hope and crushing despair.

Enough was enough. She returned to her living room and drew the drapes, shutting off much of the clamor rising from the street. Another cigarette in hand, she paced the Oriental rug, then poured herself a Cognac and downed it. "*Je m'en fous,*" she said aloud, "it's breakfast time, after all," and poured herself a second.

❖

Around midnight, after her family joined the surging stream of refugees, she had made her way home through the crowded streets. At first many motorized vehicles had clogged the narrow rues and broad boulevards, their horns urging aside the less fortunate on foot. Under the dim glow of the streetlamps automobiles and farm trucks rolled through, burdened by mattresses and fully-laden trunks and baskets. Heavy furniture and household goods covered every available surface, and some passengers took to the running boards to make more room for personal possessions. Motorcycles carried impossible loads yet somehow stayed upright, their headlamps casting bluish beams in the smoky pre-dawn air.

The citizens of the great city joined the trudging refugees from the north in ever greater numbers, an exhausted, relentless parade of sorrow and numbed anger. Marita had never witnessed such a crowd. *Paris will surely be empty soon,* she thought. The few remaining vehicles now moved at the same sluggish pace as the foot traffic, but still the horns blared and bicycle bells clanged. The people came relentlessly with their peasant carts and baby carriages, refuse wagons and hand carts, all filled to overflowing. A hearse moved through the crowd, small children peering from behind the black curtains. Peasants drove livestock before them—cattle, pigs, sheep and goats, and others led horses or mules burdened with cages of squawking chickens and cooing pigeons. To reach her apartment Marita had followed an ox-cart piled high with household goods and *grand-mère* sitting unceremoniously atop on her rocking chair. Dogs ran freely in the sea of legs, yapping at all the excitement, dodging citizen and peasant, army deserter and released lunatic, nun and priest, even the occasional *gendarme*, concerned only with saving his own skin.

Marita would remain in Paris come what might, but for the moment she was relieved to know her parents and her sister Marie were already well ahead of this massive exodus. With a head start on what must have become a mob of millions fleeing south, they would surely have reached the train station and be heading safely out of the city toward a new life overseas. But the separation had been anything but smooth.

"Sheer folly, Marita—can you even imagine what they'll do to you?" Her father's raspy voice betrayed hours of argument. Her mother remained silent as was her way, lost in her own thoughts as she packed traveling clothes in a suitcase. "Marie, convince your little sister," he said at last, "perhaps she'll listen to you."

"Do come along, Marita; without you they'll die of worry before we're out of the city." Marie smiled weakly at her younger sibling and business partner, going through the motions, knowing her words were wasted.

"Tell you what," conceded Marita, both sisters knowing the lie, "the three of you get to the Gare de Lyon; leave right now—it's just past eleven and things will only worsen with all the refugees. Take any train south—bribe someone if you have to—just get out of here. I have to get to the club to shut everything down and empty the safe; we'll need every franc for the ship passage once we get to Marseille. I'll follow any way I can, and we'll rendezvous down south."

"And how do you propose finding us in a strange city?" Her father glared, knowing his daughter all too well. "You know they could rape you, or even kill you, which is most likely." Her mother's face expressed shock at his language, but she turned back to packing, distractedly shoving aside the first over-stuffed case and opening an empty valise.

"First of all, I know these *Boche*s. They've been frequenting the club for years now, and we know how to ply them with drink and keep them happy, right Marie?" Her sister wanted nothing more to do with the argument and turned to help their mother pack. "After a day or two they'll be lining up at the door for champagne and to squeeze a few firm breasts again." Her mother gasped but said nothing, shaking her head in disgust at Marita's candor. "But second, in answer to your question, Papa, leave a letter for me *poste* *restante* the moment you get to Marseille, main post office. I'll check daily when I arrive—just tell me where you're staying and I'll find you."

"Maman, leave it be now." Marie sighed, exhausted by everything. "You're packing far too much for any of us to carry. We'll buy new things in Provence, just wait and see." Their mother surveyed the room, taking in all that was to remain behind. She reached for a framed portrait of the girls still in pig-tails, still innocent, and added it to the bulging suitcase before storming from the room with a handkerchief at her eyes.

"Marita, just listen to me." Her father bent down to look her in the eye and spoke softly. "My father told me what the Huns did here in '70. They starved us out—we'd already eaten the rats, you know. I simply can't leave my daughter to such brutality!" He turned away to hide his tears.

"Papa! Please don't worry; I know what I'm doing, so trust me."

He turned back. "Then we'll all stay to face them, and that's final."

"We've been over all this before. My American friend made it clear three years ago—these Nazis will wipe out all the Jews, and that means Maman. And Marie…and me, too, if they find out. So I'll be right behind you. Ryan stole proof of their plans from Berlin way back then."

"For all the good it seems to have done." Marie shook her head. She remembered well the handsome American with the resonant voice and broad smile who had enthralled her little sister for years. "What became of him, anyway?"

"We lost contact." Marita lowered her eyes, momentarily lost in thought, then shook her head of memories and moved on. "But the fact remains—none of us is safe here," she gave her sister a knowing glance, "so the three of you need to get going, and now!"

Her father merely scowled.

"Come on, Papa, do you think I have a death wish?"

"I assume that's rhetorical?"

"I promise I'll join you when I can, even if it's not till Palestine."

"Marita, you've always been the best at working truth to your advantage. I actually love that about you… proof of an agile mind when used with good intent." He dropped to the couch, his hands dangling between his knees and addressed his words to the carpet. "You'll follow along all right, but only when it suits you." For a long minute he remained sitting, thinking. "But I know words are wasted now and time's short, and it's up to me to look after your mother and sister, so we'll leave without you." He rose again to hug her, kissing the top of her head. "Be safe, my little Marianne, be safe."

It had been years since he had used her given name. He turned abruptly and left to find his wife. She heard him blow his nose once out of sight.

"Here, take this—you'll need it," Marita handed Marie a thick envelope. "It's most of the cash from the office safe and most of my savings, too. You have all your valuables?"

Marie nodded and patted the pocket of her coat. "I just knew you had already taken what you could from the office. But what'll you live on without this?" Marie reached for her sister's arm and drew her close. "You need to think of yourself for once now."

"The club will make that up in no time, and we've got good inventory to make it several weeks. Besides, I've held out enough to get by without this." She put an arm around Marie's waist. "Just keep them both safe, leave that letter for me in Marseille telling where you've headed, and get out of France. And do it quickly. Ryan knew this was coming, and I've known for some time what I must do."

There had been no long good-byes, just hugs all around and a final slow shake of the head from her father as he conceded her the victory. She felt the lump of sorrow in her throat as her family joined the sad migration down the dark street, three more refugees hoping to escape before the worst arrived.

❖

By morning the last straggling fugitives were gone from the city when the first German scouts appeared, handsome young men in field-gray uniforms on motorcycles, gunning their engines in sorties up the broad avenues and narrow rues. Next came the armored columns boasting impressive machines of war, and then at last the marching rank and file soldiers in splendid well-cut uniforms, their shiny boots pounding the Parisian streets to the strident martial airs of the brass bands, their bodies and faces fit and healthy. Nazi photographers and film makers recorded it all for posterity and propaganda.

Many café owners lowered their shutters and hid inside, while others swung doors wide to welcome the conquerors with offers of free drinks. Wehrmacht vehicles plied the streets, scattering leaflets announcing that Italy had joined the war against France. There was no raping and pillaging, for Hitler and Goebbels had ordered best behavior. The whole world watched, and the Nazis would show everyone they weren't really barbarians. Besides, they would need the French economy to support their martial goals elsewhere and wanted cooperation from the populace.

By afternoon rain began to fall, tears dampening the great city. And Marita also wept.

❖

Aging and scattered, Geneviève Pateu had known Marita's parents for years, had watched the girls grow and mature, and had suffered along with her mother when both young daughters had thrown propriety to the wind to dance in the cabarets and later own a night club. The Pateus had always occupied the ground-floor flat just below Marita's parents' apartment. Monsieur Pateu had survived the Franco-Prussian war and the Great War, only to awaken one night spewing blood across the sheets and perish within minutes from a burst artery. He left Madame to look after Frou-Frou their Persian cat and dispense the neighborhood gossip. With the great exodus as the Germans took Paris she had herded the furry beast into an old bird cage and joined the procession south, and as luck would have it, she encountered Marita's family at the Gare de Lyon.

A week later she showed up at Marita's door to share the story of their exodus with no commiserating preamble to soften the blow.

"My dearest Marita, I must tell you that your sweet family is gone."

"Yes, I know. I saw them off myself."

"No, my little one, they are dead. The *Boches* killed them all."

Marita shook her head uncontrollably from side to side in disbelief. "But no! That's not possible—how can that be? Are you certain?"

"I'm so sorry, Marita, yes, all three perished."

Marita grabbed at the doorway to steady herself, then slid to the threshold. Madame Pateu helped her back to her feet and led her inside to the couch, then went to the kitchen to prepare tea while Marita sobbed. When the old woman returned with a tray in hand, Marita found the strength to ask for details.

"No seats were available at the station. In fact, many trains sat idle on the tracks, their crews gone. And people shoved and pushed and even fought with fists to find any place on board. It was a madhouse, and your dear father refused to participate, so the four of us tramped out of the city on foot at first light. The tedium was indescribable, step by step, kilometer at a time, no food, no water, just horrible."

"But, Madame Pateu, what happened to my parents, what of Marie?"

"I'm getting to that, my dear. Have patience with an old woman—it's all so horrible to relive."

"Of course, Madame Pateu." Marita could barely force words through her tears. "Please go on."

"We left the outskirts of the city and were into the country when your distraught mother complained of her sore feet. Marie did her best to console her as your father marched ahead. The wealthy ones pushed forward in their automobiles, honking and furiously yelling at us to get out of their way."

"My family, Madame Pateu?" Her eyes were so swollen she could barely see the wrinkled visage of the old woman. "What of my family? Please!" She came close to screaming.

"Yes, my dear, I'm getting there. One fancy car tried to drive around us refugees and became stuck in a ditch, and the people robbed them of their food and possessions until those wealthy types were no better than the rest of us and joined the procession on foot. There were many soldiers as well, hiding in the crowds and carrying no weapons."

"But, Madame… my family. How did they die?"

"I'm almost there, Marita, but do know that I did all I could for them." Now the older woman was also sobbing.

"I'm sure you did, Madame Pateu." She steadied herself, forced the question yet again: "Tell me what happened."

"They came from the north at our backs, those airplanes with their infernal whining sirens and their machine guns and bombs, trying to mow down everyone, civilian and soldier alike. We all fell to the ground and covered our heads, or ran—those of us able to run, of course—to the roadside ditches for shelter, but they strafed the road and there was blood everywhere, possessions everywhere, and the dead. And then they circled round and came at us again. I stumbled and fell and a man dropped atop me and I couldn't move. Then the planes were gone and I dragged myself free and saw the man had a hole in his forehead, and I went to find your dear parents and they lay crumpled together and your father held your mother in his arms, rocking and moaning. And then he died, too, but of a broken heart, I'm sure, since I saw no wounds." She blew with great force into her lace-trimmed handkerchief. "I'm so sorry, my dear Marita, so very sorry. I did what I could, but I had to go look for Frou-Frou."

They sat on the couch shoulder to shoulder and cried softly. Finally Marita reached over and took the old woman in her arms and held her close. "And Marie? What became of my sister Marie?"

"I looked for her along the road, and then there she was, leaning against a tree and staring at the sky, and I ran to speak with her. Your beautiful sister...the plane had taken her legs and blood was everywhere. I said a prayer for her and closed her eyes. And then I looked for Frou-Frou's birdcage, and my dear kitty cried pitifully but was safe. And many were turning back and others were forging on, but Frou-Frou and I decided to walk back home."

"Those dancer's legs…those dancer's legs." Her loss piercing deep into her heart, Marita loosed a plaintive wail.

They sat a long while. The tea remained untouched. And then Madame Pateu excused herself and kissed Marita and left to feed her cat.

Marita's stubborn will had forced her family to leave the city. The decision had felt so right and proven so wrong. In wishing to spare them she managed to condemn them all to a horrifying death. She left her apartment to wander about aimlessly in the silence of her parent's empty flat, and she cried until no further tears would come. Hours later she returned home, determined to fight the enemy who had destroyed her family using whatever tools it took, acknowledging she would carry the burden of guilt forever.

CHAPTER FOUR

Berlin, Germany
23 July 1940

The maître d' of the Hotel Kaiserhof in Berlin discretely confirmed Rolf von Haldheim's identity before guiding him to a private booth in the rear of the restaurant. The fussy, balding man cast a stern eye on each of his waiters as he moved through this dining establishment most favored by the Nazi elite. An aide in Kriegsmarine uniform standing in front of a curtained table pulled the drape aside to reveal Admiral Wilhelm Canaris, idly stirring a half-consumed martini.

Rolf immediately recognized the somewhat short, gray-haired man with the intense blue eyes. This brilliant, cultured, unreadable Chief of the Abwehr, the Reich's military intelligence arm, was said to be at constant odds with the *Sicherheitsdienst*, the intelligence wing of the SS and the Nazi Party. Rolf had worked with the SD for half a decade. In fact, many suspected the Admiral's files held damaging information on Heydrich and Himmler that kept both powers at bay and permitted Canaris a free hand in his operations.

"*Herr Sturmbahnführer*, thank you for coming." They shook hands. "Please join me." Rolf slid into the booth across from his host. "A cocktail?"

"A martini would suit me just fine," Rolf said.

"Word has it you favor champagne," Canaris smiled and signaled his aide, "much like our dear English friend, Mr. Churchill." He emptied his drink and signaled the junior officer before returning to his guest.

"I do enjoy *Sekt* on occasion, but a decent gin martini is hard to beat." Rolf felt at ease, back in the genteel company of the upper class and away from the crassness and venality of his Sicherheitsdienst colleagues. "May I ask to what I owe the pleasure of this invitation, Herr Admiral?"

"All in good time, Major, all in good time. Allow me first to learn a bit more about your recent experiences. I do have a proposition which may grab your interest, but first we must see if we find one other *sympatisch*."

Having given the waiter the drinks order, the aide hovered outside the booth again. Canaris flicked his fingers and the curtains closed to provide them privacy. "Tell me about your family."

Rolf hesitated, startled by the unexpected question and unsure just how much the Admiral already knew. *A test of commitment to the Reich?* He chose honesty, for surely a man at the top of the intelligence field had done his due diligence before hosting a meeting. "I now believe my parents are no longer among the living. The von Haldheim clan is of venerable and aristocratic stock— over a thousand years' commitment to Germany—but my parents crossed the wrong people in '38 and disappeared."

"My heartfelt condolences, sir. Such tragedies were not uncommon then, and sadly still occur today. Newly-found power is seductive, *nicht wahr*? We servants of the Third

Reich may share a common goal, but no consensus on how best to achieve it."

A wary Rolf offered a formulaic response: "Thankfully we have our Führer to guide us."

Both glanced up abruptly as the aide drew the curtain aside. He set down two cocktails and just as quickly withdrew.

"Yes, of course, but our beloved Führer—being such a busy man—cannot possibly keep track of everything his loyal followers undertake." The latent sarcasm in the admiral's words was as strong as Rolf's first sip of his martini. "So we are forced to regulate our own actions, at least insofar as we can." He took an olive between his teeth and withdrew the toothpick. "Which provides considerable latitude in interpreting our assignments, don't you think?" Canaris toasted his companion and both drank. "Now tell me about your current assignment with the Sicherheitsdienst."

Rolf knew of the bitter turf war between the SD and the Abwehr, and also knew the need for discretion. He harbored no love for his current bosses. Life had been hell in the SD after his parents' disappearance into the Sachsenhausen concentration camp, their ultimate fate unknown. His longstanding connections within the Nazi Party had yielded no answers. In fact, his personal inquiries had come to an abrupt halt with orders to drop the matter accompanied by none-too subtle threats of expulsion from the Party. And perhaps worse. Despite the loss of family wealth he had maintained his own investments and annuities which enabled the luxurious lifestyle he required. But his income stream already showed strains of weakening as the war took its toll in the homeland. Shortages of every kind were becoming more apparent daily, and—much to Rolf's personal disappointment—getting hand-made British shoes or a custom-tailored suit from Savile Row was now only a dream. "In all candor, things haven't been easy within the SD. Mistrust rules."

"The nature of our business. Suspicion, distrust, ruse upon ruse."

"I would like to think that—within our own ranks, at least—we can find some degree of trust."

"Have your assignments inspired you to trust?" Canaris didn't wait for an answer. "Without betraying confidences, what can you tell me about your recent work in the east?"

With the Blitzkrieg of September 1939, Rolf had accompanied a Waffen-SS division into Poland, and by summer of 1940 he was in Krakow under orders to help stabilize the local populace. The occupation authority was setting up a forced-labor camp in the right bank district of Plaszow, and Rolf became involved in helping fill the barbed-wire confines. A number of helpful Polish citizens stepped forward to aid in the suppression of dissidents and the elimination of the Jewish threat. Rolf followed orders, helped quash resistance, and witnessed gut-wrenching executions and families torn apart by war. He returned to Berlin a sobered man. But in spite of his unflinching service, his superiors within the SD hierarchy had still eyed him with suspicion—his parents' "sedition" always tainting some file—and he found himself ever more excluded.

So when invited to meet at this well-known restaurant on the Wilhelmsplatz, he had arrived filled with curiosity and a touch of dread. Now one of the most powerful men in intelligence was vetting him personally, but to what purpose? Rolf was well aware that his personal rank in the intelligence services did not warrant an invitation to drink with this inscrutable Reich leader. So he replied with caution: "Routine desk matters now that things in Krakow and Poland have settled down. Nothing of particular note; just sorting reports on the Jewish situation there."

"Please, let's not speak cavalierly of the 'Jewish situation.' I was at Bedzin in September '39 to witness our SS troops herding hundreds of Jews into a synagogue and setting it afire." He finished his martini in one long draught. "These mass executions of the Jews, this singling out of Polish aristocracy and Catholic clergy for extermination—we have nothing there to be proud of."

Rolf realized he had either found a kindred spirit, or might be stepping into a trap. "I was equally shocked by what I saw in Krakow, Herr Admiral." He lowered his voice and shook his head. "Horrifying."

Canaris idly rolled the stem of his empty glass between two fingers. When he spoke again, his mood had abruptly lightened. "Then you wouldn't mind a change of pace? Something a bit more to your tastes...Paris, perhaps?"

"Paris?" Had he misheard following such talk of inhumanity and barbarism?

"Let's be frank, Herr von Haldheim." Canaris regarded him with heavy-lidded eyes, and Rolf noted he had stopped using his SD rank. "I know a great deal about you, and I appreciate what you bring to the table. I also knew your late father quite well, and although we didn't always see eye-to-eye, we did share certain beliefs on what is best—and worst—for our nation. That's why I thought you might be of value in achieving *my* goals for our beloved *Deutschland*."

Rolf didn't miss the Admiral's emphasis on the word "my." He recalled a rumor that on more than one occasion Canaris had referred to his fellow Nazis as "sheep."

"I'm flattered, sir, but in all candor, my father and I didn't always see eye-to-eye on everything, either."

"None of that matters now. What does matter is whether we can work past any differences and accomplish something of value to help Germany survive and prosper. Our work in the Abwehr is somewhat different from those more regimented efforts done on your current side of the fence, and I personally favor giving my operatives plenty of autonomy."

"That would be a pleasant change of pace."

"I speak in all candor. Your Sicherheitsdienst is saddled with shortsighted direction—it lives in fear of independent thought…much like its parent, the SS. We of the Abwehr see a broader picture, and know there are many means to achieve our goals. I value education and good breeding. I want wolves, not sheep. My personnel, left to their own devices, accomplish so much more than those who live in dread of some bourgeois overseer hampering their creativity and stealing their accomplishments, all to rise higher in the Party's favor. Am I making myself clear?"

"Yes, sir, very clear indeed."

"And you are interested in what I have to offer?"

"Without a doubt, Herr Admiral."

"Good. Now on to a personal matter—we've done our homework, so I am aware that you enjoy cabarets, night clubs, music halls. And certain other distractions. Paris would be a good match. It also comes to my attention that you may well—forgive me if I use an expression favored by our friends across the Channel—'bat for the other side.' "

Rolf took a quick sip and smiled benignly despite the tension in his gut.

"All that means nothing to us…to me. Your stultified SD leadership may rant and rave about 'degenerate behavior,' as they call it, but I'm after results, and personal preferences remain your own as long as they don't compromise our mission, is that clear?"

"Indeed it is, sir." Rolf exhaled. His sexual inclination had been a constant burden, for discovery by the SD would have been his end. Now Canaris, reputed 'Knower of All Things,' knew this, as well. And yet he claimed disinterest. It was becoming obvious why this powerful man was considered untouchable.

"Good. Then we're clear on that. In fact, your inclination toward the less sober-minded side of life interests me, because it suits the assignment I'm considering." He drained his glass. "Nuts?"

Rolf declined the condiment tray the admiral had slid across the table.

"So, first things first, are you ready to jump ship, to join us at the Tirpitzufer?"

"*Jawohl*, Herr Admiral, "and with pleasure." Rolf set down his glass. "But may I be as upfront with you as you've been with me. My SD efforts amount to little of real value, and my file carries the taint of my father's transgressions, whatever they may have been. And I'm sure you know my military experience was merely a brief stint in the last war and then mustered out after a gas attack which left me somewhat myopic. I'm afraid the soldier's life and military matters weren't my cup of tea, despite the value they carried for my late father, 'the Old Major'. "

"None of that matters. One of the advantages of my position is making field promotions at the drop of a hat. A word from me and you can be a Wehrmacht major with all the benefits of military rank and influence and none of the drawbacks. Sound good?"

"That sounds excellent to me, sir."

"So we will now have another drink and explore a few options, and tomorrow I'll pull a few strings."

The admiral called for his aide, who called for the waiter, and two fresh martinis appeared within minutes.

CHAPTER FIVE

Occupied France
1940

Despite all they had endured, René and Erika had been lucky. Unlike most refugees, they arrived in France with financial strength and a well-established connection to the Alsatian community. The gracious reception from the caretaker Rothe family, who had preserved the fortunes of the estate with the passing of Jeanne's parents, smoothed the transition. Charles Rothe had risen from poverty and trained in oenology under her father's mentorship. He had never forgotten the debt owed this long-established family. Under Charles' vintner skills—and despite economic trials across Europe—the finely-crafted wines in the distinctive dark-green bottles always drew a premium price.

By winter of 1938, René and Erika found the vines bare but the family coffers heavily laden. Upon arrival René had quickly retreated to the office to review the company books. With relief he found plenty of resources to carry them through the coming months and years. Should the Reich fail to collapse of its own recklessness and inner depravity, and France remain their home for an extended period, finances would not become a problem.

Through mid-summer of 1939 the new-arrivals ran a station for Jewish families driven from the Reich, providing food and clothing and arranging passage to Marseille. There the immigrants hoped to board steamers bound for Tel Aviv. Word spread among the newly-arrived Jews in Strasbourg that the Gesslinger estate near Colmar was a safe if temporary haven on the route south.

But Erika and René knew word would also reach foes not satisfied with keeping persecution of Jews a purely Third Reich matter, so they used money and connections to acquire forged identities. The papers carried the family name of "Dalfert" with residency in Lyon. With this proof of French citizenship in hand and substantial funds transferred to a Lyon bank, the couple prepared for that certain moment when a snitch would surface, intent on shutting them down.

It hadn't taken long. Already in that first winter at the family estate came news of round-ups and interrogations to the north in Strasbourg by an intimidating German. Refugees arriving in Colmar spoke of his frozen facial features and a vicious dueling scar on the left cheek. Those with the misfortune to see him in person called him "*le Masque*," and reported he sought Erika by name. He appeared to work hand-in-hand with French police, and local fascists were promising bribes or protection should anyone reveal Erika's whereabouts.

She knew immediately that *le Masque* could only be Horst. Shaking with both fury and fear, she recounted to René for the first time the details of the cruel torture she had undergone at her husband's hands. While his mother Jeanne took charge of Leo and put him to bed, René sought to reassure Erika, taking her hand in his, later holding her close on the couch until early morning. With the first rays of the sun she was again resolute. The catharsis that came with finally sharing her suppressed fears left her more determined than ever to master her frightening situation.

For René the catharsis was of a different nature. During the long night at her side he finally acknowledged to himself his love for this intriguing woman. His earlier support came from a natural desire to help those in need and from a responsibility he had assumed on behalf of his friend Ryan, who gave his life to save this beautiful mother and her small child. But during those long months sharing common challenges and fears she had become so much more to him. His only care now was to spare this strong and intelligent woman further suffering and help Erika and Leo achieve some semblance of happiness in a tumultuous world.

One evening a month later, a friend at a service station in Strasbourg phoned to warn of a black Gestapo Citroën, just refueled and seeking directions to their Colmar vineyards. They would have at most an hour. In the darkness of the gravel drive René closed their Renault's trunk on the getaway luggage, had Leo sit beside Jeanne in the back seat, and climbed up the stairs to see what delayed Erika. He found her kneeling before the safe in the home office, carefully stacking bundles of francs in a valise. He hesitated at the threshold, struck by her courage in the face of any adversity.

Erika glanced to the doorway. He knew she recognized the obvious love in his eyes. She handed the valise up to him, placing her hand on his forearm and moving closer. "You do know I love you, don't you?" She kissed him softly on the lips. "Well, don't you?"

Stunned, he dropped the bag and took her in his arms. "Then you should marry me."

Erika laughed as he swung her in a great arc. "I shall, but first put me down. If we don't get out of here now I'll never prove to my new husband just how much I love him."

❖

From that moment she wished nothing more than to share her fugitive life with this bear of a man whose strength and will protected the persecuted. Protected her and Leo.

Erika had recognized early that her choice to marry Horst von Kredow back in 1934 stemmed from a desire for worldly adventure, for escape from the constraints of small-town life. She had fallen for the Gestapo star's powerful demeanor and obvious strength, overlooking his lack of warmth, of heart. That choice had proved deadly, had led to the death of her parents and almost cost her child his life. And in choosing the Nazi, she had abandoned any future with the brilliant but carefree Ryan Lemmon, a dashing charmer disinterested in any long-term commitment and off to a teaching position in the American Midwest. She had raised the son borne of their brief romance under the adverse, hate-filled rule of the sadistic Horst, finding in Berlin the glamor and social prestige she had sought, but at the cost of self-determination and at great physical risk to herself and her son.

When the harrowing flight from Berlin brought her back to the arms of the American, she again briefly dreamed of another life. A life with a gentler, kinder man who would risk all to protect the child she loved. But then the Rhine had dragged Ryan to his death, and only René, the faithful university friend who had come to their aid, had remained behind. And with every day spent together over the months that followed she had seen in the burly Alsatian a mix of what had always appealed to her most in the other two men who had most influenced her life—the strength of will of her strong but malicious husband, and the loving compassion of Ryan Lemmon.

René could be her husband in name only. Still legally married to Horst, she would never see a divorce as long as that sadist lived. But in her heart he would be everything, and for the first time in her life she knew she was truly doing the right thing for Leo and for herself.

❖

The winter of 1939-1940 proved unusually brutal. The infirm and elderly perished in their frigid homes when supplies of heating fuel failed to arrive. The wretched cold buried itself deep and refused to surrender its grip, and some even wondered if God were punishing France for waiting out the Germans. "Let's go fight the bastards and get it over with, not sit on our asses!" Yet the French army felt secure manning the Maginot Line "certain" to keep the Germans at bay. Hadn't it worked just fine so far? Wasn't it clear the *Boches* were too afraid to attack? So the *drôle de guerre,* "the phony war," limped along, and people cursed the cold and the war and the army, but mostly they cursed the Germans.

Fleeing Colmar, Erika and René had holed up in a working class neighborhood of Lyon and became involved with Socialists furious with the discredited Third Republic. The group blamed the past incompetence of the nation's liberal leadership for encouraging the growing call for a fascist government modeled after Germany's. René listened to hours of debate but found too much emphasis on angry articles in the newspapers and noisy street protests and too little willingness to take on the thugs who terrorized otherwise peaceful street demonstrations. René was ready to break a few fascist heads and dearly missed the rough-and-tumble river life and the successes of his old "Lone Ranger" network. A fighter when threatened, his experience in Nazi Germany had shown he thrived on danger, but opportunities to make a difference in France still eluded him.

By early spring they abandoned Lyon and moved further westward as the undercover agents of *le Masque* nipped at their heels. Every move demanded a new uphill battle to win local support. René's egalitarian views and determination won him comrades with like-minded political and social views. Erika earned trust by dispensing free medical care to poor families. She helped with difficult births and obtained medicines out-of-reach for all but the wealthy.

Many they encountered were suspicious of the slender German woman of obvious breeding, but her warm heart soon softened theirs, and she was pleased her studies at the Marburg women's clinic were finally doing others good. The happiness and gratitude of her "patients" brought tears to her eyes as she recalled her physician parents lost to Nazi terror. In the end, René and Erika inspired loyalty despite their German heritage, and left behind supporters anxious to throw pursuers off their trail.

When rumors of Horst von Kredow's relentless pursuit of his Jewish wife began to resurface, René and Erika packed the family up and moved on. Jeanne, feeling her age and exhausted by a life in constant motion, phoned her elderly cousin Brigitte and within a week they arrived at her farmstead outside Morlanne in the far southwest region of Gascony. Leo immediately felt a connection with all the animals and seemed to relax for the first time. Seeing her son run and laugh with abandon brought Erika joy, but René complained almost immediately of vegetating in some backwater of France far from where they could make a real difference.

After only a few quiet weeks in the country, word came that the "phony" war, the "*drôle de guerre*," had finally turned real. Rumor fell upon rumor, conflicting stories filled the newspapers, but one thing was certain—the discredited Third Republic would soon fall to the German invasion. The government leaders in Paris closed up shop and fled. The first haggard refugees straggled into Gascony, starving and exhausted, telling of hundreds of thousands if not millions of others who had abandoned northern France as the armor of the Third Reich overran their homeland. The mass exodus of civilians had eventually dispersed when confronted by limited food and fuel and local resentment. Few country folk were willing to share their own supplies and shelter the strangers.

Most fugitives returned to the cities, villages and farms they had abandoned in fear. The national government had moved first to Tours, and then the Germans forced it farther southwest to Bordeaux before an armistice finally brought the war to a standstill. Millions of French soldiers disappeared into *Boche* prison camps. The spa town of Vichy became the new, centrally-located French capital. Although France officially maintained self-rule, she found herself divided into occupied and "free" zones, her conquerors would dictate the terms of continued existence, and French fascists and reactionaries hastened to assume a guiding role in implementing the new order.

Erika and René found themselves in the Occupied Zone. By chance, their last move had placed them within the more tightly-controlled coastal region along the "Atlantic Wall." Their forged papers gave them residency in the back yard of a Waffen-SS battalion stationed outside Bayonne near the seaside resort of Biarritz. Here at last they saw opportunities to actively fight the Nazi tyranny with quiet acts of sabotage. Local partisans gathered to learn how a bit of sand or a handful of metal shavings in the gearbox of a vehicle could hamper the *Boche* occupation, how communication lines could easily be disrupted with a snip of shears, and how organized work slowdowns and "mistakes" in deliveries and engineering could cost the enemy valuable time, energy and resources. René made contacts dockside, finding camaraderie with those accustomed to the river and the sea and anxious to confound the occupying forces.

But the personal risks increased daily as ever more locals learned of René and Erika's activities, and soon they got wind of strangers frequenting local bars and inns seeking a broad-shouldered German with a limp and a long-legged blonde with a young son named Leo. They found themselves backed into the geographic corner of France and their pursuer unrelenting and ruthless, and they knew their days of freedom might be numbered.

CHAPTER SIX

Loire Valley, Occupied France
11 August 1941

The flight had been long and cold, but now young Devon Whitaker dropped the woolen blanket from his shoulders as he approached the "joe hole." Strong crosswinds and turbulence had made the passage even rockier. The constant thrum of the Bristol Mercury engine created a sympathetic vibration in his head, so he barely heard the flight sergeant shout "ten minutes out." The enlisted man tapped him on the shoulder and pointed to the small light staring from the forward cabin wall. After hours of red it had finally turned to yellow. Devon checked the straps of his parachute once again. He watched the man trip the hold-downs at the hatch and shuddered in anticipation despite himself.

Devon's assignment for MI6 had been clear, and also clearly difficult. Once on the ground he was to hide his gear and stow the wireless in a well-noted spot until he or another operative could put it to good use. He would contact an established and well-trusted way station for escaping British pilots and POWs, a farmhouse near Tours. From there he would follow the underground railway south, ostensibly trying to escape the Occupied Zone and seek further help in nominally neutral Spain on his way to Gibraltar or Lisbon.

In reality, his task was much more challenging and dangerous. MI6 had recently learned that several fugitives had gone missing along this escape route. Somewhere lurked a double-crossing partisan or a Gestapo plant, waiting to trap the unwary fugitive and surrender him to the SS. The last agent British intelligence had put in the field to unmask the traitor had also disappeared. So Devon was here to give it a second go, to play the hapless refugee, seeking to draw forth the treachery and root out its source.

He thought of Trish, and wished himself luck and speedy success.

The Westland Lysander banked sharply to circle over the drop zone. The engine throttled back and silence reigned as the plane entered a glide, and the flight sergeant moved the hatch cover aside. The black abyss beckoned with a howling wind. Then the damned light was green and it was time to go and go quickly. He dangled his feet at the edge, said a quick prayer, and let himself drop into the prop wash. The static line did its trick and he felt the jerk and the chute blossomed above him, an exhilarating carnival ride.

He pulled down on the lift webs and the chute steadied, the plane was gone, and the earth approached in the darkness below. He spotted three flashes from a torch and knew his reception was waiting. In the distance, unexpected anti-aircraft fire pitted the sky and searchlights pierced the heavens, but he was happy for any diversion to draw attention from his small plane and its descending cargo.

As his booted feet raced toward the ground he felt a sudden gust drag him off course and a large farm machine rose toward him, spotted too late to veer aside. The impact slammed him into something unforgiving and doubled him over, deflating his lungs and hurting like hell before he tumbled several meters to the ground. For a few moments he lay unmoving beside a threshing machine of some sort. Once he found his breath, a quick survey found all limbs intact, his forehead bleeding profusely, and an aching certainty that he had broken—or at the very least bruised—several ribs.

Where the hell's my guide? The flashlight signal had been clear enough. The man had to be around somewhere. Devon's eyes were adjusting to the dark, the sky glowing faintly brighter than the deep shadows around him. He knew time was of the essence. He had to move out quickly to avoid capture, since his drop plane may have been spotted.

With effort and some reluctance, Devon pulled himself upright, and a stabbing pain jolted through his chest. He drew only the shallowest of breaths. He cautiously unzipped the camouflage jumpsuit and removed his crash helmet, and tore a strip of shirttail to wrap his bleeding forehead. Every move cost excruciating pain, but he gradually paid it less mind. *Shock settling in,* he reasoned—*all the better.* As practiced many times, he gathered the silk of the chute and tied it off with the cords, then peered toward a distant hedge row. He crouched below the line of the crop and scanned the dark field. Nothing moved. He waited long minutes, knowing someone might be observing him. Finally, painful step by step, he crossed the field in a low crouch, unwilling to show his silhouette to the sky, tediously hauling the bundled chute and jump clothing and the small suitcase with the wireless.

Devon nearly missed the body. It lay face down in the irrigation ditch just meters from his feet. With effort he turned the man over to reveal a dark slash against the white of the throat. Half-buried in the mud of the trench glowed an Ever Ready. He turned off the flashlight. He had no choice but to continue.

Long minutes passed before he reached a small wood near a country road. Alert for any movement around him, he used the collapsible shovel to bury the transmitter. The excruciating task demanded a quarter hour and left him drenched in sweat, but now he felt ready to move on at last. Someone had betrayed his mission before it ever began. Someone was waiting out there for him.

I should never have stolen your heart, Trish, nor you mine.

Devon knew to hurry. Once on the road he checked the markings on a kilometer stone, a benchmark to the hidden wireless. He cautiously followed the long row of evenly-spaced trees pointing south. His worker's garb was caked with mud. His chest ached, and every breath drew stabbing pain. The first priority was finding a local willing to help. Priority two, and not necessarily in that order, was to survive long enough to complete his mission.

A twig snapped behind him. He had been moving attuned to his surroundings, so the crack shattered the still of the night, and he gripped the pistol tucked at his waist. With the rush of the assault came a guttural oath growled in the heat of rage: *"Espèce de salaud!"*

Devon knew to expect the butcher's knife plunging around his neck, and his adrenaline surged as he reacted as trained. The dead partisan's entry wound had been at the left carotid, so Devon knew the assault would come from behind with a weapon in the attacker's right hand. The agent ducked to his left while seizing the man's wrist and used the attacker's momentum to propel the assailant into the ditch beneath the tree line. Devon cringed in pain and reached again for his pistol, but the handgun had disappeared during the attack. Instead he dropped atop the downed man's chest, pinning his knife hand to the ground. The stench of the man told him this was no trained assassin, but rather an unwashed peasant, insane and murderous, and inept in the use of weapons.

"Who the hell are you?" Devon whispered through gritted teeth.

"Who the fuck cares, *connard?*"

A lifetime of farming had given the man incredible strength compared to Devon's weakened state. He felt his energy ebbing and knew he couldn't outlast this enraged farmer.

"I'll slit you prick to gullet and bleed you dry before you bastards steal another pig!" The threat was a low growl in the assailant's throat.

My God, thought Devon, *he's no Gestapo thug—he's killing us over poaching.* But killing all the same, and Devon had neither the patience nor stamina to convince a berserk peasant that black market pork was far from his mind.

"*Putain de merde,* you've got it wrong, monsieur! Stop struggling and let me explain!"

"Explain this!" With a violent jerk, the assailant wrenched his knife hand free and swung with sudden momentum, forcing Devon to reel back. The blade had yet to complete its arc and did little damage. But the brutal blow from the butt of the knife sent agonizing waves clear to Devon's spine, amplifying the damage done by the parachute landing. In a last desperate lunge, he twisted the peasant's blade and buried it deep in his attacker's chest. A froth of blood gurgled from the man's lips, and Devon collapsed atop him, forcing the last breath from the assailant's body.

Bloody fucking Christ, he thought as he finally rolled off, struggling for breath, *now we're both done for.*

CHAPTER SEVEN

Paris, Occupied France
11 August 1941

The loathing gnawed at his gut, forcing Ryan Lemmon to take deep breaths to still the tension. He braced his hands on the edge of the conference table and allowed the incessant drone of the negotiations to wash over him. The leather band of his watch only partially covered the pale scars at his cuff, and the stench of burning flesh rose again in his mind, memories of the searing pain. Without self-restraint—and armed SS guards stationed at either end of the room—he could easily lunge over and throttle the man.

Across the table stared Richard Kohl, former head of German and Austrian Affairs at the State Department in Washington, ousted for ties to the German-American Bund. Here sat the same despicable bastard who destroyed priceless intelligence which cost Ryan so much anguish, photographic evidence stolen by Erika that might have saved innocent lives had it ever reached the right hands in Washington. He cast a smug grin in Ryan's direction.

Ryan could still picture Kohl's manipulation and bigotry back in '38, as he disputed the very existence of that remarkable information. His boss at State had shown his true anti-Semitic colors, driving Ryan from Washington and into a deep spiral of depression which had plagued him for years.

Only word of his German friends' internment in a holding camp in France had brought him back to intelligence service barely two months before. His life had found new meaning. Ryan would now fulfill a promise made to Erika von Kredow in their deepest moment of despair—he would save her life and that of their little boy.

Now the malicious man's smirk reflected in the polished walnut conference table of the Hôtel de Crillon. His hair was thinner three years later, his eyeglasses thicker along with the belly straining against his vest. No longer forced to radiate geniality, his eyes glared cold and aloof. His lapel sported a swastika pin, and at his side sat the SS colonel heading the German delegation. The Third Reich and the American government working hand-in-hand for the mutual benefit of all—welcome to the Department of State's emerging Special War Problems Division.

Ryan shot a glance at his brother Edward, if only to measure his reaction to their former boss. Ed appeared to be taking it all in stride, just part of the job. His gaze appeared fixed on the German colonel now speaking and he seemed to ignore Kohl altogether.

The chief American delegate signaled an aide to pass the brown-leather portfolio to his counterpart on the other side. The man dutifully carried the file around to the German aide, who then spread out the contents before the Nazi colonel. Carefully-typed sheets listed the names, identities and last-known location of American citizens who had disappeared in the wake of the German *Blitzkrieg*. Many had gone missing as the Wehrmacht charged into battle, first into Poland and Eastern Europe, then a year later into the Netherlands and Belgium on the way to France. And now, barely twelve months had passed since Paris had fallen to the Reich juggernaut. But they heard no talk in this meeting of common people, no mention of suffering masses or prisoners of war. Here the concern was for powerful businessmen, scientists, even university scholars, influential people of political, commercial, or strategic importance to each respective government or its commerce. Two records of names, one common goal.

The SS colonel turned the pages slowly and methodically, as if he might recognize one of the many names spread out before him. "Your list is complete?"

"Let's say it's a good beginning. Other names will surface in the coming months, but this gives us a solid starting point. Our people are already working on your roster of German citizens caught outside the Reich who may be having difficulty returning home."

As a neutral negotiator, the United States was acting as an intermediary between the Allies and the Germans in this exchange endeavor. All parties tacitly expected that this neutrality would have a short fuse. America had proven its support for the Allied war effort through the recently-enacted Lend-Lease policy passed by Congress. Ships, armaments and war materiel were underway. Even if America eventually became an active combatant, the need for some existing diplomatic mechanism to repatriate certain important citizens was recognized by both parties at this Paris meeting.

"As you're aware, war takes a serious toll. Many disappear without a trace, but we'll certainly do our best to track these people down." He squinted through his monocle at the American embassy officer, then removed the signature page and slid the portfolio to Kohl on his right. "We'll be obliged to strike from your roll any enemies of the Reich or known criminals."

"Understood, but we're in agreement that both our governments are committed to repatriating any innocent citizens who've found themselves, through no fault of their own, in harm's way."

"*Aber natürlich.*" The colonel removed the cigarette from its holder and carefully wiped the mouthpiece on a linen napkin. He used his gilded fountain pen to sign with a flourish alongside the American official's signature and looked up. "For the moment, I believe our work here is done. I'm told that, to get this program rolling, you've already brought us a valued German citizen anxious to return to the Reich?" He removed the monocle from his eye.

The American embassy officer turned to Edward, who nodded. "Yes, Mr. Lemmon here will make the arrangements for the transfer of Mr. Goldblum later this afternoon. Meanwhile, allow me to express the appreciation of the U.S. government for this cooperation. We're confident it will be of mutual benefit in the coming months—" he pushed back his chair, "and perhaps years." Those seated around the table rose to shake hands.

The colonel nodded in agreement and the guards stood to attention as he reached across the table to the embassy official. Edward smiled tightly as he shook the hands of both the German officer and his former boss.

Ryan held Kohl's gaze but did not offer his hand.

"Doctor Lemmon, how nice to work together again, if now from opposite sides of the table." He dropped his outstretched hand. "And once again to find the able brothers working side-by-side—truly touching." Kohl offered another insipid smile. "Now, shall bygones be bygones? Why allow past differences to hamper a mutually-rewarding mission, right?"

Ryan turned abruptly on his heels, clutching his briefcase tightly to restrain the fury in his hands. He headed toward the door, leaving Ed to follow and the bastard Kohl chuckling to his back. *Kohl in bed with the Nazis—the last straw.* A quick glance at his watch. With this travesty of an organizational meeting finalized, Ryan could now turn to undoing the damage of years past. Time to help old friends. Old enemies could be handled later.

The SS guards saluted smartly as the American delegation left the conference room and headed for the lobby. The wide hallway glowed with Sèvres porcelain vases holding freshly-cut flowers, proof that money still flowed to the conquerors and their collaborators. A porter manned either side of the wrought-iron gates at the entry. One asked Edward whether to bring around one of the official sedans parked below. Ed shook his head brusquely and took Ryan by the elbow, steering him off to the side of the landing. He reached for a fresh pack of cigarettes and offered his brother a smoke. Ryan declined, a pipe his usual preference.

"So you knew this was coming all along?" Ryan was pissed.

"This business with Kohl?"

"Hell yes! What else?"

"I knew he was now working their side, but didn't expect to find him here. He's supposed to be in Berlin. Had I known he would be here, you can bet I wouldn't have invited you along." Ed placed a hand on Ryan's shoulder. "God knows, we can't risk another international incident with you in the middle, brother." He spit out a shred of tobacco before returning the Lucky Strike to his lips.

"Kohl's yours to deal with from here on out, Ed—I see him again, I throttle the man." Ryan stared across the broad Place de la Concorde toward the Seine and absentmindedly took out his briar and tobacco pouch.

Ed took a long moment before responding. "Wouldn't have it any other way, brother. Your own plate is full." He struck a match. Ryan bent forward to accept the light and nodded his thanks. They stepped down the staircase fronting the Crillon and strode out across the imposing square, almost devoid of traffic despite the midday hour.

❖

Ryan's grand old Paris was no more, and the closer he looked, the more disappointed he became. So much had changed since he'd left the French capital almost three years before. The stunning architecture and lovely ironwork remained the same, and familiar monuments complemented a pearlescent summer sky. The glorious Arc de Triomphe shone far down to his right, the Eifel Tower rose skyward across the Seine, the gilded statues on the Pont de la Concorde, even the expansive breadth of the Place itself with its fountains and soaring Egyptian obelisk—all the same, and yet so very different.

Brilliant scarlet banners hung limply along the boulevards, swastikas distorted to random slashes of black on white. He remembered how bold and festive the flags had first appeared against the gray stone and low overcast of Berlin. Here they appeared gauche draping the architecture of the French capital. Where once smartly-dressed crowds of strolling Parisians lent culture and polish to the Champs-Élysées, now field-gray uniforms and polished jackboots evoked discord, resignation, and intimidation. Parisian class and feminine couture had surrendered to military chic, and the loud laughter and jesting of soldiers on leave seemed incongruous in this city once known for its genteel manner. Step carefully around approaching Germans or you might get a kick in the ass.

They passed cafés crowded with Wehrmacht officers, their polished boots extending into the aisles. Waiters in long, white aprons moved amongst them, keeping their demeanor obsequious. The men chatted and smoked over coffee and cake, a tableau suggestive of Ryan's last days in Berlin. The coffee was real. He had already heard that other Parisians now drank a weak grain substitute. They passed an old man stooped into the gutter, rescuing cigarette butts abandoned half-smoked by the conquering heroes. Along the Seine the newsstands flashed headlines boasting of Wehrmacht successes and forecasting a speedy victory against the Bolshevik hoards. A tall green advertising column and the walls of a nearby *pissoir* were plastered with warnings against terrorist activity. The brothers stopped before a large poster as Ryan translated the call to victory. Bold signs on street posts directed the German occupiers to troop clubs, field hospitals, casernes and canteens. Paris had become an odd dreamscape, its backdrop familiar but the foreground surreal in a sea of uniforms.

And the traffic—bicycles and canvas-enclosed bicycle-taxis advertising *Vitesse-Confort-Sécurité*, their tinny bells jangling as drivers pedaled their way through the streets; horse-drawn carriages once again the norm after the occupying force outlawed French-owned private automobiles; the rare German staff car or Grosser Mercedes barreling along the broad avenues; a distant police siren, and then another. An occasional delivery vehicle spewed smoke from its wood-fired *gazogène* engine. And military trucks with swastika-bedecked hoods rolled from the city laden with French foodstuffs and commercial goods bound for the rail yards and Germany. Paris, spared massive destruction by her quick surrender, now offered citizens little but constant surveillance and increasing deprivation.

The brothers strolled through the Tuileries gardens and past the Louvre, crossing the Seine at the Pont Neuf. They opted for the right bank of the Isle-de-la-Cité. Ryan set aside his disgust at having seen Kohl in the knowledge that a reunion with Erika, Leo and René was at most a couple of days away. How very much the four of them had suffered three years before in that valiant attempt to escape her sadist husband and his Gestapo. Ryan had given them up for dead and nearly consumed himself with self-recrimination, and now within days he would guide them to freedom. He dreaded waiting another day for the train to Vichy, but their itinerary was subject to the slow-turning wheels of diplomacy. Thank God that was Ed's calling, not his. He felt an incessant itch to be done with this changed city but knew nothing would happen without the official sanction of the Vichy Interior Ministry.

An embassy inquiry with the French authorities had already confirmed that his friends were still in Gurs. Happily the camp sat east of the demarcation line in what was designated—sometimes ironically—the "free" zone. For all Ryan knew, Horst's plan for the annihilation of European Jewry might already be instituted in the occupied regions, and Ryan found himself racked again by the unending self-blame. If only Erika's stolen evidence of the Nazi's criminal intent had gone to someone other than Kohl. No telling how far implementation of that despicable protocol had already progressed now that Hitler's troops were victorious on all fronts.

The French persecution had begun immediately following the armistice with seizure of Jewish property by the new Vichy government. The new anti-Semitic laws emerged without coaxing and with fervor even the Germans found surprising. Few Frenchmen cared enough to consider the injustice. Some Jewish merchants placed their medals and citations from the Great War in their shop windows, hoping to win favor for their earlier valiant service to France, but to little avail. Just months earlier six thousand foreign-born Jews had received orders to report to gathering centers in Paris, where the authorities shipped them off to Beaune-la-Rolande, way station to the German concentration camps. It was only a matter of time before the police would come knocking at the doors of the established and wealthier Jewish families in France. Perhaps then there'd be some outcry.

That very morning consular officials had described to Ed and Ryan the despicable state of the French internment camps, sharing reports of starvation, disease, and numerous deaths. Unlike a German concentration camp with brutal guards and barbed wire several meters high to prevent escape, Gurs had first housed Spaniards escaping Franco's retaliation at the end of the Spanish civil war. Fearing detrimental effects on the local economy and populace, local French authorities detained the political refugees in quickly-constructed camps. Following the armistice, the new Vichy regime released many of the Spaniards to make room for foreign and Alsatian Jews shipped west after the Reich annexation of Alsace and Lorraine. Living conditions at Gurs appeared to be deplorable, although mail got through and some foodstuffs were available, especially to those with money. Rescuing his friends from that horror couldn't come soon enough. He worried about their state of health from living in such pestilence-ridden conditions, but arranging their release would have to wait a while longer.

"Face it, Ryan, you'd better be prepared for the worst." Ed recognized the intense concern on his brother's face. It had recurred often as they made their way to Paris. "Even a few months in such a despicable camp can wreak havoc, especially on a child, and they've been in there for at least six months, based on your friend's last note."

"Where can I take them for immediate medical help?"

"Back to Vichy if they aren't fit for travel to Marseille. I'll be in the new capital for about a week, then it's back to Paris for me. At least there we can have the embassy doctor treat any immediate health problems."

"Now you've really got me worried, brother."

"Tell you what—bring them to Vichy no matter what, okay? Healthy or sick. Marseille is the best route out of the country, but at least we'll know they're okay. Once they've passed muster you can take them south and out of France. Then rejoin me in Paris."

They crossed the tree-framed square, the impressive cathedral of Notre Dame rising up before them. Ryan had hoped that at least this one landmark would recall the untainted Paris of the recent past, and he wasn't disappointed. The splendid façade and triple portal remained as they had for centuries. In this spot, at least, Paris remained Paris.

Ed hoped to distract Ryan from his immediate concerns, anything to forestall the deep melancholy which had plagued his younger brother so frequently since his last days in Europe. He couldn't recall the last time Ryan's face had lit up with that trademark smile. "Pretty magnificent, just as you described it." Ed scanned the massive gothic towers of the cathedral. "I think I just saw Quasimodo up there."

Ryan played along: "You can't still be referring to Kohl—at least the ugly Quasimodo had a tender heart." Ryan wouldn't burden his brother further with his personal worries.

They tried the main entrance, but an armed guard rebuffed them, declaring a contingent of high-ranking German officers had first claim to the French cultural landmark. "Come on, Ed—let's head around to the gardens in back. The view of the flying buttresses from the Pont St. Louis is fantastic."

"Sorry, Ryan, that's it for me today. I'm due back at the consulate—transfer paperwork to complete and hands to shake, as always—but do continue your rounds. Perhaps you'll still find a bit more of that old Paris you're missing."

"I appreciate your accompanying me this far. Needed the distraction. Just seeing that bastard again really set my teeth on edge." Ryan watched the newly-arrived Wehrmacht officers enter the cathedral unmolested. "You'll actually have to work hand-in-hand with Kohl?"

"That's what Foreign Service is all about. You can't pick your bed-fellows—you only hope they're not overly infested with vermin."

"Well, say the word and I'll gladly crush that particular louse." His face brightened. "As for me, it's the subway to Montmartre."

"Ah, your little Miss Lesney? Ed's heavy eyebrows lifted. "Some things never change."

"I do owe Marita a quick visit, Ed. She tried her best to cheer me up when I was at my lowest. The least I can do is make sure she's doing all right with her cabaret. Perhaps there's some help I can offer."

"Just don't let that 'help' keep you overnight. And use protection." Ed laughed. "One surprise kid's enough, unless you plan to make an honest woman of this dancer of yours." During the Clipper flight to Lisbon Ryan had revealed that he was likely Leo's father.

"Never fear, brother, I've learned my lesson well."

"Train leaves at nine in the morning, and I'm told tickets these days are rarer than a perfectly-seared *steak au poivre.*" Edward gave a throaty chuckle at his own way with words. "But just in case you *don't* make it back to the hotel tonight—it's Gare de Lyon, eight-thirty sharp, out front, and no excuses. I'll bring your bag from the hotel should we not meet before then."

With a dismissive wave Ryan headed off toward the Châtelet Métro station. With luck, Marita would already be in her office above *la Chatte bottée,* preparing for the evening's revelry. If not, he would drop by her apartment just a few blocks from the night club. Her welcome would be warm either way, and he began to feel better about himself again for the first time in years. Once Erika and Leo were safely at the American consulate in Lisbon, he would be ready to take on his new assignment, and Marita would make a great first contact in Paris.

He fought his way down the crowded steps into the Métro, lined up to purchase a ticket at the booth, and finally passed through the turnstile. A rush of cool air drew him into the dampness of the labyrinthine complex, a welcome escape from the city's heat. The corridors were packed elbow-to-elbow with sweaty, harried commuters. From below came the screech of metal on metal as the cars made their constant stops to disgorge and take on passengers.

Ryan followed signs on the white-tiled walls toward the platform showing the end station Porte de Clignancourt. Armed metropolitan police, bored and smoking, gathered on the train-level landing, and German uniforms formed pools of field-gray in the mass of drably-dressed Parisian passengers. The French faces were pallid and drawn, cheeks sunken and eyes hollow. The Germans appeared pink-cheeked and well-fed.

A train rolled in and the doors slid open. The Wehrmacht soldiers rapidly occupied the red-lacquered first-class section where they rode at no charge. Ryan stepped into the green of second and reached for the overhead bar. The car filled quickly. Several riders glanced his way before moving on, while others found places beside him. He felt conspicuous with his well-cut suit and nourished look.

As the doors began to close, a man in a herringbone jacket with loosened tie suddenly leapt aboard, fedora pulled so low that only a neatly-groomed, graying mustache appeared beneath the brim. He worked his way through the car to find standing room at the far end, and Ryan followed the stranger's progress. Years living in a secret police state had taught him to be curious and ever vigilant, and old habits were surfacing again. He recognized his own suspicious nature, for there was undoubtedly nothing unusual about the man.

The train slid into the darkness, and Ryan smiled in fond memory. Ceramic wall signs announced each station as they entered, halted, then rolled on, reminding him of earlier, carefree days when he had known these subway routes by heart. Here in the maze of tunnels beneath the city, Paris felt like home again.

It was good not to have phoned Marita in advance. She was truly in for a surprise.

CHAPTER EIGHT

Paris, Occupied France
11 August 1941

Marita slid one leg slowly across his hip to press insistently against him. His eyes remained closed as he feigned disinterest. Her finger traced a line from his belly up his chest, and her tongue circled his nipple in the lightest of caresses. He hardened beneath the pressure of her thigh. In one move she straddled him, and he surrendered at last, his eyes opening and his wide smile showing appreciation for the lovely woman above him, her dark hair falling unbound to frame her pale face. Her flushed breasts betrayed arousal, should any doubt still linger. None did. She guided him with her hand and once again they moved in unison.

Marita knew his attention was divided—always so much on this man's mind—so she proceeded slowly, manipulating him with agonizing restraint until he focused solely on her. She admired the flexing of his muscles in response to her movement, and his hands followed the curve of her hips and waist to gently knead her breasts and tug at her nipples until she moaned softly.

She lowered her mouth to his ear. "*Lentement, mon amour, toujours lentement.*" *Slowly*, she whispered, knowing he was near. He slowed, and then she surprised him by moving with abandon, tossing her long hair from side to side until they both surrendered. Marita gasped at the deep waves of pleasure, relishing that rare moment when worries and the hunger in her belly briefly ceased. He drew her close and kissed her lips and chin and neck, then pulled her into the cradle of his arm.

She would have loved to remain there, to savor the warmth of the moment. Instead she sat abruptly upright in the tousled sheets and looked about for clothing lost in the passion of their reunion. She dried her thighs with the corner of the sheet, then slipped on panties and fastened her garter belt, rolling one crumpled stocking into place before searching for its missing partner.

"Where'd it land, *mon Cher*?" Her eyes searched the bed and floor in the near blackness. She lit a cigarette, took one quick puff and stuck the Gauloises between his lips.

"I'm supposed to encourage you to leave?" He took a single drag and buried the butt in the ashtray. The dim evening sky filled the room with a diffused glow.

"It can't have gone far." She bent to peer beneath the bed before shoving aside the pillows to find the missing silk. Sitting on the edge she drew on the fine material—so difficult to acquire now, even on the black market. Pointing her leg in a dancer's pose, she slowly rolled the stocking to her thigh and clipped it to the garter, then fended off his attempts to cup her breasts, to pull her back to him.

"*Ça suffit*," Marita said. "Enough already, I must put things in order for this evening's guests. And you—what's on your agenda tonight, now that you've had all you want of me?"

"Certainly all you *offered*, but not all I want." He rolled from the bed and moved to the window, his silhouette framed in the moonlight. The blackout drapes had remained open upon his unexpected arrival, and the darkening city spread out in the distance. What little man-made illumination remained suggested a romantic Paris of centuries past rather than fear of danger coming from the skies.

She felt herself respond again at the sight of his muscular body against the soft light. He strode to the chair where he had tossed his clothing and pulled on an undershirt. Before dressing further, he grabbed his hat, set it atop his head at a jaunty angle, then turned and saluted her, his lingering tumescence saluting, as well.

Marita laughed out loud at the ludicrous yet appealing sight—a striking figure of a man, for all intents naked, his military cap incongruous without the full uniform of a *Wehrmacht* lieutenant. *Truly a beautiful specimen of a Boche, this lover of mine.*

❖

Ryan ascended from the Métro stop into a remarkably quiet scene. The last rays of the sun had left both Boulevard de Clichy and Rue Pigalle in deep shadow. Only an occasional pedestrian was still out and about, and the street was almost free of vehicles of any kind. The loss of most internal combustion engines when the occupation government outlawed private vehicles had rendered the city nearly mute.

Evening approached, and the lines before the food shops wouldn't reappear until hours before sunrise. France was now on Reich time and everything opened while all was still dark. Parisians rose well before dawn to pursue rumors of butter or cheese just in from the country, or of eggs, even whispers of beets or fresh meat. Housewives bribed concierges to pass the night in hallways and porches near shops, just to be early in line. Ration coupons changed hands, deals were made, honest folk cheated.

In many Parisian neighborhoods household pets had already become rare, and cats and sewer rats were now at a premium. Hamsters were the new balcony livestock. Many citizens of Montparnasse already made do with one daily meal in the soup kitchens rather than starve before the family hearth, and few shops remained viable at all, since little sold on any market not black. The Reich was sucking all nourishment from the teat of a defeated France.

Night had yet to fall, so clubs and cabarets remained closed. Stage doors opened only to showgirls heading to dress or undress, as the case might be. In another few hours the wealthy, the well-connected, the gangsters and black marketeers would descend on Montmartre. And with them came the Occupiers, their uniform pockets stuffed with overvalued occupation marks affording them the most valued luxury goods, whether of material or of flesh variety. Nighttime Paris would soon open to the highest bidder.

Ryan followed the familiar path to *la Chatte bottée*. He wasn't surprised to find no doorman at the entrance. It was early yet. He continued past the shuttered storefronts and up the alley to the side door, where a young man in leather jacket and cloth cap propped himself against the wall under the glow of a caged bulb. His right shoe was oddly distorted, a clubfoot perhaps. He'd seen no military action. The stub of a cigarette dangled from his lower lip as he studied a pornographic magazine.

"*Excusez-moi, monsieur*—Mademoiselle Lesney is in?" Ryan asked.

"*Bientôt, monsieur.*" He angled the magazine to the dim light above his head to better focus his attention. *Soon.* At that moment two animated young women entered the alley arm in arm, laughing and talking, and the young man quickly stashed the magazine in his jacket, pulled off his cap to run his fingers through pomaded hair, tossed the butt and assumed a most world-weary smile. He glanced at Ryan at last, anxious to send him on his way. "A little later, an hour, perhaps?"

Ryan thanked the fellow and headed back up the alley, tipping his hat to the two attractive young arrivals as they approached. They giggled in response and shared a private joke. He turned to catch both girls watching him leave, and the saucy brunette with scarlet lipstick called out: "Come back later—you'll enjoy what's on offer!"

"Without a doubt—*un grand plaisir*, I'm sure!" He didn't catch her final reply as he reached the sidewalk.

He suspected Marita would still be at her flat, and if he hurried they could chat in private before she left for the club. On Rue Veron he headed east, remembering walking this street with her when all hope for the survival of Erika and Leo was lost and Marita had encouraged him to carry on despite all his self-blame. The concierge at the apartment house would surely allow him up the three flights to Marita's door, and his long-time friend would give him that surprised but cynical look of hers and then embrace him in delight. He would give her money to make life easier despite the Occupation and deprivation. She had always meant more to him than she knew, but a greater commitment was never in the cards. He had known she carried a long-burning torch for him, but he wasn't willing to break her heart. The timing had never been right.

Heady with anticipation, at Rue Aubran he turned toward her flat, then abruptly changed course and continued on down toward the next cross street. He shook his head and hurried his step, feigning the look of a man nearly making the wrong turn. Once around the corner and out of sight, he slipped into the covered entry of a closed shop to disappear in the deep shadows. He held his breath.

A disturbing reflection in a barred shop window just moments before had caught his eye—a brief memory, and then immediate recollection. A man in herringbone jacket with fedora low on his forehead. Perhaps even the thin mustache, although the light was fading rapidly and the bluish glow of the blacked-out streetlamps prevented knowing with any certainty.

Now he waited in the gloom, breathing shallowly, all senses alert for the footsteps. He extended the short blade of his pen knife, of little use for anything but scraping out the bowl of his briar pipe. But certainly this could work—a stealthy approach from behind, an arm thrust around the neck, a deep plunge, yes, an artery could be cut. He thought of how he had trained in the killing arts in Toronto, and of the Gestapo agent he and Erika had killed on the Koblenz train, the man's struggle over in a bloody flash.

He still hoped his senses had betrayed him. But when the stranger passed, peering intently up the street ahead and unaware he strode within arm's reach of his intended target, Ryan knew there'd been no mistake. The man seen boarding the train at Châtelet was shadowing him, and Ryan would not risk leading him to Marita's flat. Stepping quietly from his hiding place, his eyes glued to the back of the man's head, Ryan took several steps backward, keeping the blade of his penknife extended.

The man sped forward now, aware his prey might have eluded him, and at that moment Ryan slipped back out onto Rue Veron. As he passed Marita's street he glanced down toward her apartment house. Only a young *Wehrmacht* officer strode in Ryan's direction, disinterested in his surroundings, perhaps distracted by personal thoughts.

As soon as Ryan was sure his footfalls would go unnoticed and he was free of the tail, he took off in a run toward the Abbesses subway station.

Who would want him followed, and, more important, why? For God's sake, only those associated with the exchange program even knew he was in Paris! Only a very few at the embassy in Vichy, and, of course, Edward. And, of course, Kohl. That son of a bitch!

Surprising Marita would have to wait until after Gurs.

CHAPTER NINE

Paris, Occupied France
12 August 1941

Rolf von Haldheim had truly found paradise. Compared with the horrors of the Polish invasion and a long year stuck in Krakow with the SD he now thoroughly-despised, Paris was indeed heaven. *Jeder einmal in Paris* was Hitler's slogan, *Everyone in Paris once*, and unlike the steady stream of German enlisted men arriving on leave to experience the Führer's most prized conquest, Rolf was a permanent resident of the lovely city on the Seine. Even now, with the war against the Bolsheviks and troop transfers to the new eastern front underway, he was here to stay, for Admiral Canaris had his back. *Paris for Rolf von Haldheim, forever.*

The summer day was turning warmer as he strolled down the Champs Élysées for a rendezvous with his favored agent. The role of spymaster suited him, especially under the loose leash of the admiral. As long as his people brought interesting information, no one questioned his methods. And for Rolf this assignment could not have been more appropriate. He had spent the last year inhabiting a comfortable suite of rooms in the 16th arrondissement with a balcony view across the Seine to the Eiffel Tower and Dôme Church, courtesy of the Abwehr budget office. Most evenings he made optimal use of the city's renowned nightlife, all in the name of intelligence gathering. When he needed a break he settled in with a glass of champagne and a good book to watch the hazy skies dim to rose and then to black. This was the life.

Canaris had offered him something impossible to refuse—a directive to mingle with those rich or famous, in command or influential. He was to dine at hotspots like Maxim's and Le Pré Catalan on caviar and lobster and champagne before trolling the famed brothels and cabarets of the city looking for recruits. The lovely girls at the officers-only Le Chabanais bordello now called him *Uncle* Rolf, and knew ways to indulge his disparate tastes in pleasure, for Rolf enjoyed life in all its diversity.

His task was to assemble and maintain a small coterie of reliable agents. They in turn would contact and recruit disgruntled, angry, patriotic or just plain avaricious types willing to undermine those standing in the way of German honor and destiny. And honor was the key word, for honor played no role under the current Reich leadership, as Canaris had made abundantly clear before posting Rolf von Haldheim to beautiful Paris.

The admiral believed the Nazi hierarchy to be a great threat to the German nation, seeking self-aggrandizement and personal gain at the expense of all that the German people had struggled for over generations. He knew the *Sicherheitsdienst* and its Gestapo were determined to root out all those who questioned the Reich's means and motives or undermined her political and military successes. And they were very good at it.

Originally the separation of intelligence-gathering powers was clearly defined: the Gestapo and SD would seek out acts of treason within the Reich; the Abwehr would unearth military espionage in foreign countries. But gradually the Gestapo had branched out into every area, much to the Admiral's displeasure. Canaris saw his Abwehr as the last support for the valiant German Wehrmacht, Kriegsmarine and Luftwaffe, protectors and defenders of the German nation when not misused to further National Socialist aims. Hitler's all-consuming war of conquest had become a misguided adventure in hubris destined to destroy the honor and prestige which were Germany's birthright.

So Canaris tasked certain agents with exposing the same discontented, dangerous types sought by Heydrich's minions, but not to arrest, torture and eliminate them. He hoped to empower them to help undermine the regime and work toward a peace with England which would leave Germany a spark of her old dignity. His actions had nothing to do with treason. His maneuvers were the epitome of patriotism destined to restore a strong German nation amongst the other leading nations of the world.

And for the first time in his life Rolf was running great risks for an even greater cause, and enjoying the raw excitement in most pleasurable surroundings. His personal role was to identify well-placed officers who shared his admiral's contempt for the Nazis, and he thought the best way to learn their innermost secrets was to join them in relaxing pastimes, such as consuming the best French spirits in the company of men and women of pleasure in the most beautiful of European cities.

This afternoon Rolf was meeting a Wehrmacht officer he had given the code name "Argent." The name meant "money" in French, but also "silver." Rolf thought the name fitting for such a shining example of manhood. Rolf had stumbled upon this young man—quite literally—in a Montmartre night club. With one too many glasses under his belt, Rolf had pushed through a small group of officers to congratulate him on a promotion. In his fervor, Rolf had tripped over the seated man's extended boot and spilled a drink over his uniform. As the evening progressed and the crowds thinned, Rolf invited the young man for a nightcap at a nearby bar, and they had hit it off from the start.

After sharing a bottle of expensive Cognac, the officer had candidly admitted some dissatisfaction with his current assignment in the quartermaster corps. He found it rife with corruption, as Wehrmacht officers worked hand-in-hand with black marketeers to siphon off the best French consumer goods to resell at great profit. Another casual remark suggested qualms with the direction of the war, and Rolf had seen an opening which he then developed over several weeks until a wide gulf appeared. Argent was deeply troubled by the war with Britain, and Rolf also noted in him a deep dislike of the SS. One day he hoped to learn why.

As always upon seeing him, Rolf caught his breath at the sheer beauty of the man. Striking physique, strong cleft chin, piercing gray eyes above a winning smile—Rolf's type through and through but for one major problem: Argent only loved women, and women couldn't resist him. And now this Adonis had been placed in a position to do Rolf's mission a great good. Hands off was the best policy, even if there had been a choice.

The lieutenant rose to greet Rolf. "How nice to see you again, *mein Herr*, as always." Despite the warm weather they met inside at the back table of a café and ordered Evian alongside a bottle of Sauvignon Blanc.

Once the waiter left earshot Rolf rested his hand on Argent's forearm. "And how goes it with your brunette?" He gave a squeeze of complicity.

"A true beauty, Herr von Haldmann." Argent intentionally misspoke Rolf's name. Should he ever forget and use Haldheim and someone catch the slip, the listener might assume to have misheard. One could never be too careful. "She and her girls are really paying off for us."

Rolf nodded and tasted the wine before filling both glasses. "And you have something for me?" Argent took a folded newspaper from the bench and set it near Rolf's sleeve. The most recent intelligence findings lay within it folds.

"May I suggest a bit of caution in your…shall we say, 'personal' dealings with Mademoiselle Lesney? It wouldn't do to have her know too much about our overall program and goals, just in case the Gestapo gets wind of what she has going at the club and she's interrogated. For our purposes, we need most the information her girls learn from the loose tongues. A mistake to lose track of our mission, *nicht wahr*?"

Finding Marita Lesney had been a stroke of both luck and Rolf's excellent memory, still reliable despite years of drinking and carousing. A decade earlier, young Ryan Lemmon had spoken of his enamored dancer from the Folies Bergères. Her letters pursuing the American across the continent and beyond, often arrived at the von Haldheim manor in Grunewald, and Rolf still clearly remembered the feminine script and memorable scent on the envelopes he had perused before his father forwarded them on to America or France.

Upon first researching which Parisian night spots might provide the best source for intelligence findings, he had ordered a comprehensive list of locales most popular with German officers. The meticulously-researched pages included contact data for the owners of each nightspot, and the name Marita Lesney had immediately struck a chord. In espionage, serendipity was often as valuable as diligent research. After an evening observing her at the club, Rolf had known that handsome young Argent should make the first contact, and the result had proven most valuable, but the assignment had cost Argent his heart in the process. The handsome young fool had obviously fallen for this woman some eight years his senior.

Ah, youth, Rolf thought, *seldom appreciated till it abandons you. Thank God money and a clever mind can prove just as powerful.*

❖

Harry Sperling, the agent known as "Argent," had reason to despise the SS, but the why of it was known to only a few.

His only sister Doro had been his one constant companion as they grew up in the university town of Tübingen. Two years his senior, Dorothea was born to his father's first wife, Greta, a woman widely recognized as a descendent of the Duke of Württemberg and thus of noble stock. Despite leading a bourgeois lifestyle married to the city's mayor, Greta Sperling radiated nobility in all she did. And once grown, her daughter Doro projected a self-confidence and beauty that would have made her mother proud, had she only lived to see it. Years later, when Harry was old enough to notice, he took immense pride in being her only brother.

Their father, Edgar Sperling, had also come from an established, albeit less- esteemed German bloodline. His great-grandfather oversaw the royal hunting grounds of Baden-Württemberg, reputedly having knightly blood flowing through his veins. On a summer day when Doro was barely two, her mother had broken her neck in a fall from her horse. Edgar mourned for six months before singling out the town's most charming and attractive widow as his new wife. Bernice Langenfeld was an anomaly in Tübingen, an Englishwoman who had lost her German husband to a street fight after his customary night of boisterous drinking. As a young woman on Grand Tour of the Continent, Bernice had first fallen in love with this region of Germany. And despite the violent death of her husband, she remained determined to stay in the medieval town.

Nevertheless, she never surrendered a fierce pride in her English roots. She had quickly given Edgar a son, and taught the young Harold to admire British spirit and heritage. After all, wasn't King George III of the House of Hanover, a German through and through? In fact—Bernice told anyone who would listen—the English still pronounced "schedule" with a "sh" sound to emulate their German-born king. Every afternoon she hosted low tea for her friends and encouraged young Harry to master English and value his roots. But she was a cold and disengaged mother in every other respect.

The National Socialists seized power in 1934, and Edgar Sperling joined the Party as a late-comer, primarily interested in maintaining his post as mayor. Young Harry marched off as a Hitler Youth to hike, camp and sing rousing Nazi anthems and learn the Party dogma. His lovely older sister Doro already belonged to the Band of German Maidens, the *Bund Deutscher Mädel*, braiding wildflowers in their hair while singing folksongs, exercising to build strong bodies for healthy motherhood, and marching through the countryside. They learned the values of a National Socialist education and to favor their *Führer* Adolph Hitler and his teachings over the old guidelines and moralities of their parents.

At the 1936 Party Congress in Nürnberg, Doro made friends with handsome young men of the SS, and came home unmarried but pregnant, as did many hundreds of her fellow celebrants. The BDM encouraged unwed German girls of pure racial stock to bear children fathered by the best specimens of pure German manhood.

And that was when Harry first heard of *Lebensborn*, a state-sanctioned organization dedicated to raising the birthrate of children of pure Aryan parents. *Lebensborn*, "Wellspring of Life," an almost mystical-sounding project of Himmler destined to place the future of Germany in the hands of a new "super race." Rather than finding shame in her condition, as the parents thought proper, Doro took pride in her accomplishment and gladly headed off to Steinhöring near Munich. There she resided in a *Lebensborn* home, furnished with the finest trappings from homes liberated from wealthy, Dachau-bound Jews.

Harry's adored older sister returned to visit the family home a changed woman. Gone was the sweet and loving girl who had made his childhood a delight despite an emotional-ly-reserved mother and a stern and distant father. Gone was her newborn, now in the hands of specially-chosen nursemaids and educators intent on rearing a new generation in line with Nazi theory of "racial hygiene." The child would go to a worthy SS family to be raised to lead the masses.

Harry was heartbroken when Doro told him that his breeding was corrupted by his English bloodline, and regretted the fact that her half-brother could never measure up to join the SS and father beautiful, racially-pure children as she would bring to the world. He was stunned by the new coldness in her bearing, felt an immeasurable loss, and heard from his father only later that his formerly kind and gentle sister had volunteered to work as a guard in the concentration camp of Dachau.

This "Fount of Life" had destroyed Harry's beloved sister, and now Argent bore an unrelenting hatred for all the SS embodied and where it had taken both his countries, Germany and England.

CHAPTER TEN

Vichy France
12 August 1941

The first three hours of their train journey to the new and often-ridiculed capital of the French State had proven uncomfortable. They shared the first-class cabin with three Waffen-SS officers and a civilian in a fine gabardine suit. The four Germans had boarded as a group in Paris, giving perfunctory greetings to the Americans before settling in. During the long stretch to reach the demarcation line between the northern and southern zones the colonel read a French edition of Victor Hugo while igniting each new cigarette with the last. His lieutenants sat quietly by and watched the passing countryside. The civilian removed thick files from his briefcase and perused them, marking passages with a leaking fountain pen which gave no end of trouble. Not a word passed within the group.

Ryan and Edward could do nothing but observe the passing countryside and smoke an occasional pipe and cigarette to kill time. Ryan found himself lost in memories of the hectic few weeks which had brought him so quickly to his new role in collaborationist France.

❖

Ryan had not been excited about starting a new career with the new Special War Problems Division at the State Department. Old memories were surfacing, memories of the bureaucratic hierarchies and hidden agendas which had last driven him from Washington. He had agreed to return to State for two reasons only—first, to get his friends out of that infernal internment camp, and second, because his brother's argument had been sound. Sooner or later he would step up to serve his country in the coming conflict, and he preferred to play a role of his own choosing. Once Erika, Leo and René were safely out of France, he had expected to step into a boring program with little personal satisfaction, especially since Ed had warned him that some of the German citizens returned to the Reich might not be anxious for repatriation.

But Ed didn't take him to the massive State Department complex Ryan had grown to hate after the disastrous last encounter with Kohl in 1938. Instead, the government sedan dropped him off at the Bureau of the Budget building. Here Ryan first met David K. E. Bruce, destined head of the secret intelligence branch of the newly-planned COI, Coordinator of Information. Bruce was a well-spoken man, clean-cut with thin hair parted high on his scalp.

"Let's face it, Dr. Lemmon—" Ryan clearly remembered David Bruce's opening words in that cramped, non-descript office. "—you are without a doubt very poor Foreign Service material."

Damn it, Ed, what the hell have you gotten me into now? "Uh, pardon me, sir?"

Bruce had continued undeterred as he read from Ryan's State Department file. "Says here you can be 'bull-headed, self-absorbed, cocky and at times irresponsible' "—he glanced again at the file and added a final comment— "and let's not ignore 'apt to forget official assignments at the drop of a hat.' "

"But, sir, to what purpose—?"

Bruce interrupted again. "Not exactly traits one seeks out in diplomats, especially where delicacy and discretion are paramount, wouldn't you agree?"

"Perhaps not, Mr. Bruce, but I must say in my defense that—"

Bruce held up a finger in caution: "Hear me out—you're also said to be 'quick thinking, resourceful, tenacious, ethically-sound and unafraid of deception and violence to achieve a given end.' " Bruce sat back in his creaking desk chair with the hint of a smile. "And let's not forget 'brilliant in subterfuge and the use of foreign language and custom when undercover.' Does any or all of this strike a chord, Dr. Lemmon?"

"It seems you vetted my file with a very critical eye."

"Dr. Lemmon, both Colonel Donovan and I have read your file many times through, and we've given special attention to your final debriefing. It's true you attempted to spirit a girlfriend out of Nazi Germany under the nose of her Gestapo husband?"

"Yes, sir, that sounds about right. And my boss at State, Richard Kohl, damn him, destroyed evidence that could have saved millions of Jews. Is that in there, too?"

Bruce regarded Ryan directly but ignored the question. "Dr. Lemmon, let's face facts—you're a poor diplomat but a helluva good covert operative. And right now diplomacy isn't worth squat, so let's leave that business to the diplomatic drudges."

"Sir?"

"What Bill Donovan and I are about to launch—what the United States most needs right now—is a centralized intelligence-gathering organization. Our involvement over there is about to heat up whether America likes it or not. We have nothing at the moment but a grab bag of agencies involved in overseas intelligence. Just think of it—eight different fact-finding units, from the Navy's ONI to the FBI to the FCC, believe it or not, and each wants control at the expense of the other. Hell, they treat each other as the enemy, and that'll kill us in a year. Does anyone actually believe Nazi Germany won't have centralized intelligence leadership when they come after us?"

Ryan bent forward.

"Well, it's clear you don't personally give a damn about oversight and control. Just look at your brother's frustrations with you the last time. It's all in here." Bruce tapped the open file. "But two attributes are of unmatched value to us—a proven hatred of Hitler's thugs, and first-hand knowledge of what makes them tick."

"No argument from me."

"So let's put those qualities to work for America."

"Ready and willing, sir, as long as I can first get my friends out of that French internment camp." Now Ryan pointed to the open file. "I'm sure it's all detailed there."

"That shouldn't present a problem, Dr. Lemmon. We'll expedite the process with our people already in Vichy."

"In that case, I'm all yours." Ryan felt a glimmer of mounting excitement.

"We'll need to bring you up-to-date quickly on some skills, a bit of training before you fly."

"The sooner, the better, sir."

"And Dr. Lemmon...those 'negative attributes' I mentioned earlier?"

"Yes...?"

"Colonel Donovan and I would consider them positives for our new operatives, so feel free to be yourself."

❖

And he had. Toronto had been aces, at least the training camp nearby where he'd spent a week, with no time to actually visit the city. COI had as yet no facility of its own, and David Bruce relied on Donovan's UK intelligence friends to get Ryan into the camp for British agents for an abbreviated course in the latest espionage techniques. One week only—nothing more, nothing less—and he would be Clipper-bound for Lisbon with Ed. Ryan zipped through most of the challenges already mastered years before outside Alexandria.

Just as at the camp in Virginia years before, the Toronto trainers had also decided on a code name for the American inspired by his Florentine cameo ring. From that moment on he was "Tuscan." The ring was taken for safekeeping along with all other personal items which might reveal his true identity to fellow trainees. A few hours passed creating a plausible backstory for his newly-minted persona, and he was to memorize every detail for testing within twenty-four hours.

The initial orientation was familiar—the government would deny his very existence if he fell into enemy hands, that sort of thing, all old hat for Ryan after Virginia training. The camp leadership waived the standard assessment of suitability, resourcefulness, and emotional stability under stress—Donovan assured his MI6 friends that Ryan had more than proven himself against the Gestapo. So the demanding week, sunup to sundown, was devoted to jump school, special code and relearned wireless skills, pistol marksmanship, close combat, and, of course, killing with whatever came to hand.

Once back in Washington, having earned his colors at the training school, he finally met Colonel William "Wild Bill" Donovan. A pending executive order from the White House was about to name him director of an integrated spy agency. For the first time in its history the country was to consolidate all aspects of unorthodox warfare under one roof. Ryan already knew quite a bit about "Wild Bill." Anybody who read the newspapers knew of Roosevelt's "mystery man," the unofficial ambassador just returned from a fact-finding mission in Europe, the Balkans and the Middle East. Ryan had listened intently to Colonel Donovan's recent coast-to-coast radio broadcast, where he warned that Germany was "aiming at absolute domination of the world." The stunning conclusion of the broadcast remained fixed in Ryan's memory: "Our only choice is to decide whether or not we will resist. And to decide in time: while resistance is still possible, while others are still alive to stand beside us."

Ryan had been excited to finally meet in person a man he already greatly admired. The colonel had earned the Distinguished Service Cross for valor in the Great War, and Ryan wondered if he would find the war hero arrogant. Instead he felt a soft-spoken warmth and regard, and liked the man instantly at first greeting. "Welcome to our team, Dr. Lemmon."

"Thank you, sir. A great honor to meet you in person, and to play a part in this new enterprise."

"Well, wait until you've been tested a bit in our COI waters and then you may sing a different tune. But for the moment, you're well-trained—my spies tell me you excel at special operations—and David Bruce thinks the world of your potential."

"Means a great deal to me, sir. I'm anxious to get back in the fray."

"In a nutshell, Ryan—I may call you Ryan?—a lot of people in Washington would like to see us fail at this. They think we're going to step on their toes or steal their thunder. Hell, State is afraid associating with us threatens America's "neutrality," so they're already considering refusing cover for our COI agents abroad."

"That could make things tough for me, Colonel—"

"Call me Bill. I like professionals, academic types like you, and our methods and operations around here are going to be a little more relaxed than in the military."

"Yes, sir…Bill. Here's the thing, if I may speak candidly—"

"Counting on it, Ryan. I'm a straight-shooter myself." He chuckled. "No reflection on my nickname, of course."

"Well, you know my brother Edward's helping set up State's new Special War Problems Division. We were intending to use that cover to get me overseas again with few questions asked."

"Not a problem from our end, Ryan. Bill Stephenson's British operation here in Washington is already helping us contact underground organizations behind the lines, so we're off to a great start." He reached for a file. "How do you think we got you into Toronto on such short notice? For what David and I have in mind—for you especially—you won't need much of a cover at all."

"Sounds damned intriguing, sir."

"Intriguing…and dangerous." Donovan opened the file. "But I read here that you don't flinch when the going gets tough, so here's where we're at. I want you in France, specifically Paris to begin with. Your cover is simple, just be yourself, college professor on sabbatical. Or you can be "assigned" to State and that new War Problems Division they're setting up. It's all the same to us…" The Colonel hesitated as he looked up from the file, "because we don't want you working for us."

"How's that, sir?" Ryan thought he'd misheard.

With a quiet laugh Donovan continued. "We want you working for the Germans."

"But, sir—"

"No, Ryan, hear me out, this may interest you more than you think. And it's an assignment fraught with danger, right up your alley." He leaned back in his chair and Ryan felt the Colonel watching for his reaction. "Hazardous, but also immensely rewarding."

"I'm listening, sir."

"We know next to nothing about what the Nazis have in store for us, but you can bet your bottom dollar they're way out in front with an espionage network already in place. Once we abandon that vaunted "neutrality" Lindberg and his ilk keep whining about, we'll need to go 'guns to guns' with the Reich. That means we need to get inside their network, learn what they know about gathering intelligence and how much they already know about us."

"Makes a lot of sense."

"Face it, we're coming late to this game. The Brits have a leg-up on us by a couple of years; the Nazis have been at it since '33 or '34."

"I'm listening, sir."

"Here's what I think—and you tell me if I'm wrong. I know you lived over there from the get-go, '29 to '38, right?"

"Yes, sir, with intervals in France, primarily Paris, Burgundy and the Riviera."

"It says here," he tapped the file, "you used to live and breathe Germany, may even have been a bit of a fan of some things at one time. Judging by your old newspaper clippings, you reported all angles and early on even suggested Hitler might bring the factions together and help the country out of its economic pain."

"Yes…about that, sir, it was before the Nazi take-over, when Weimar was falling to pieces. In retrospect, I was naïve, to put it mildly."

"Not really, Ryan—you actually got it right. He did indeed help their economic recovery. And very few of us suspected that he would go on to enslave his own people and now try to conquer the western world. But your early, more positive read of the movement is exactly how you can be of service to us now."

"Sorry, Bill. I'm still not exactly clear on this assignment."

"We want you in Paris. Enjoying yourself as best you can for as long as you can, at least till we give up this cloak of neutrality. We want you hobnobbing with the Germans, badmouthing the States and Roosevelt, convincing the Nazis you've had a real change of heart and now support the Reich as the world's best chance to stop the Bolsheviks, Freemasons, Socialists and Jews."

"My God, sir, you do know I left the Reich with the Gestapo on my tail and a stolen plan for the mass extermination of European Jews hidden in my tobacco pouch?"

Donovan's face went blank. "How was that again?"

"It should be right there in my file." Ryan pointed to the open folder on the desk. "Just look for the debriefing report, mid-December'38."

"Wild Bill" flipped through the pages before looking up with a shake of the head. "Don't find it here."

"That's impossible, sir. There should be page after page of it, a full record. All the contacts I made with anti-Nazi groups inside the Reich, then meeting up with an old female acquaintance in Berlin married to a top Gestapo leader, Horst von Kredow. She photographed his secret protocol demonstrating intent to annihilate the European Jews, and I sent the film back to Washington by courier."

Donovan had continued to search while Ryan talked. "It's not here. Sorry."

Ryan knew where the blame lay. "It was that damned Richard Kohl! He destroyed the film rather than send it up the line in State, so he must have also stripped all mention from the record." Ryan shook his head in revulsion. "Damn, how I despise the bastard."

"Water under the bridge, Ryan." He closed the file. "Who else besides this Kohl knew of what you did...how you felt?"

"God only knows...Kohl was kicked out—had gotten a bit too cozy with the American Nazi movement, it appears. He may have had some contacts in the Reich."

"Well, I can't see how this will compromise your new role. Paris is filled with Germans on leave, all enjoying the sights, and the possibility of blowing your cover is remote, to say the least. I think you can safely play the disenchanted American fed up with people ignoring the Bolshevik menace and willing to work hand-in-hand with the Nazis. And, if you play your cards right—our cards—you may find a way to become a triple agent right out of the chute."

"Triple agent?"

"We send you in to spy for us, but our ultimate goal is to have them enlist you to gather intelligence in America. You learn all you can about their espionage and counter-espionage structure, so we know what to expect. And in the process you plant false information to undermine their intelligence. As far as they're concerned, you're a disgruntled American scholar willing to support the Reich in the coming war by spying on America. In reality, you bury yourself deep in their intelligence operation. Take your pick, either Sicherheitsdienst for the Nazi Party or Abwehr for military, depending on the lay of the land. Either way, someone is bound to want you, and we gain invaluable intelligence on troop deployments, military and naval bases, anything you think will be useful once we're in this fight for good."

Ryan quietly digested what COI was asking of him. "There is one thing, Bill, and most important to me personally."

"Your friends detained in the camp in Gurs." Donovan nodded toward the file. "It indicates that's priority number one for you."

"Yes, sir, it certainly is."

"Anything to do with this Kohl fiasco?"

"Yes, sir. A great deal, actually."

"Well then, get that taken care of right off the bat. State will fly you over, Lisbon via Bermuda on the Clipper. You and your brother check in once you're in Paris, in case you want to keep the State Department cover alive, then get down south and help your friends out of France. But once they're on their own, you return to Paris and you're all ours, agreed?"

"Agreed."

"We'll have things in order in Vichy when you arrive, so you shouldn't run into any delays."

"That's very helpful, sir."

"And Ryan?"

"Yes?"

"You'll be running blind much of the time, self-sufficient. You have wireless skills, and may eventually need them. But as long as we're neutrals, you can use the mails, cables, that sort of thing, properly encoded, of course. We understand your brother will remain in Paris for the time being as the State Department civilian exchanges shape up. You want to stick with him as your handler?"

"That suits me fine, Bill."

"Just as I'd expect, but this time, do keep him in the loop. We'll make sure he does the same with us. Whether the Foreign Service wants it or not, neutrality in Europe won't be an option much longer, and America needs to win this covert war."

CHAPTER ELEVEN

Occupied France to Vichy France
12 August 1941

Only as the train slowed for the border did the taciturn SS officers and the civilian nod to the Americans in polite farewell and head for the vestibule to detrain.

"Well, that was interesting." Ed took to his feet to stretch. "Such a talkative bunch, I thought they'd never shut up."

Ryan opened the window to freshen the cabin. The brothers leaned out for a better view. Their train sat just shy of the demarcation line between the northern Occupied Zone and southern Vichy France, the "free" zone. Armed German soldiers watched either side of the train while a uniformed contingent moved slowly down the line of cars, thrusting bayonets into every possible hiding spot between and under the carriages. Two large Alsatian dogs lunged on leashes and barked incessantly while an SS officer waited imperiously off to the side, observing the search but obviously bored with the task. The four men who had shared their cabin stopped briefly to speak with the officer, then rode off in a military sedan.

Suddenly, loud voices approached from the aisle beyond their compartment. German soldiers shoved a protesting young businessman past their cabin toward the front vestibule. He clutched a briefcase to his chest and wasn't going willingly. A sullen German lieutenant trailed behind, stopping briefly to demand identification from the Americans.

"Papiere, bitte—vos papiers, s'il-vous-plâit."

A conductor for the French Railways system followed on his heels, clearly subservient to the German and making the same demand with a scowl: *"Cartes d'identité, messieurs."* Ed and Ryan produced diplomatic passports and the Reich-issued transit visas allowing their passage through the Occupied Zone.

"In Ordnung." The officer returned the documents, his manner brusque, his attention already focused on the next compartment's occupants.

"Such friendly chaps." Ryan returned his attention to the exterior manhunt. "Makes me feel right at home…back in the Reich three years ago."

Ed pulled out an embassy-issue map and traced the boundary between the two halves of France. Alsace and Lorraine showed now as part of the Reich, annexed almost immediately after the armistice. The boundary between zones rose from the Spanish border in the Pyrénées to bisect the country west to east between Paris and Vichy. The entire Atlantic coast region and the northern half of the country lay in occupied territory. "The Germans can't possibly patrol this entire stretch; we're talking huge distances here."

"Both sides patrol it." Ryan raised his voice to overcome the barking of orders and dogs outside. "Illegals and fugitives pay a *'passeur'* to guide them across. And I'm told the

Vichy border police can be every bit as dangerous as the SS patrols."

Below their cabin the young man rousted from the carriage lay prone on the gravel, a snarling guard dog hovering above him. A soldier slapped on handcuffs. Ryan forcefully shut the window and the compartment grew quieter.

Ed looked up from his map. "I understand trying to get to the south, but why on earth would anyone sneak north? I don't get the appeal."

"Profits, brother. The black market pays well, especially in Paris. With Germany requisitioning all it can and northern France starving, smuggling has become extremely profitable."

"I know keeping workers in the north is a problem. Hell, two-thirds of the prisoners of war are farmers. The north can't afford to lose a single one to the south." Ed refolded the map. "And I'm sure they're watching for downed British flyboys, escaping POW's, that sort of thing."

Ryan looked pointedly at Edward. "Not to mention spies."

Ed chuckled. "And on the French side, Marshall Pétain's government wants to keep out Jews and political refugees. I assure you, Washington doesn't expect much from this new 'French State,' what with home-grown fascists now in control. No one at the embassy likes dealing with these guys. Pretty much anyone removed from power or influence during the Third Republic is back in charge and out for blood against enemies, real or perceived." Ed took his seat again. "Everyone knows we'll be in this war soon, and all the embassy hopes to accomplish here in the 'Frog Pond" is to keep the Vichy fleet out of German hands."

"So what's Pétain really up to?"

"He may have been the 'Hero of Verdun,' but he's over eighty and rumor has it he sleeps away most of the day. Yet Vichy propaganda is making him a savior, practically a god."

"Where do his loyalties actually lie?" Ryan had seen the glorifying posters of the aging hero.

"Well, up north they think he's just playing ball to spare the country worse, but those in the south suspect he's happy enough collaborating with the Reich. And Vichy wants to show they can be even more ruthless in dealing with 'undesirables' than the German master race. They figure if they're especially brutal, the Reich won't impose Nazi laws on them and they'll retain at least the semblance of autonomy."

"So that's it for *Liberté, Égalité, Fraternité?*"

Ed shrugged. "Gone the way of the Third Republic, I'm afraid."

The barking of the police dogs outside intensified, and Ryan again lowered the window. Ed stepped to his side. The soldiers now held the captured businessman against a wall, forcing him upright. The officer in charge rifled through the leather briefcase."

"Smuggler, you think." Ryan couldn't imagine much of value hidden in the man's case.

"More likely a courier for one of the underground movements."

Even from a distance, Ryan could see the man tremble as three soldiers lined up facing him from less than ten meters away. Each held a rifle, and Ryan and Edward watched them draw back the bolts of their carbines and seat the cartridges.

"My God!" Ed's whisper was barely audible over the commotion.

On an order from the officer the three barrels converged on the man. His legs shook so violently he appeared on the verge of collapse. Two other soldiers encouraged the leashed dogs to lunge at the captive to keep him in place.

"Feuer!" shouted the officer, and the weapons discharged as one.

The young man fell to the dirt as the bullets struck. The projectiles had buried themselves deeply in the side of the shed, a good meter above where the captive's head had been just seconds before. Plaster dust sifted down on the shuddering body of the collapsed man. The officer rocked with laughter and the soldiers joined in the merriment. The devastated young man lay on his side, his body convulsed by sobs of disbelief as a dark stain spread across the crotch of his tan trousers.

With a jolt their train crept past the barbed wire of the German checkpoint and they were once again underway toward the new capital of France. The brothers sat in silence for several minutes, shaken by the cruelty just witnessed, but gradually they picked up the thread of their interrupted conversation. Each sought to complete the other's partial picture of Occupied France.

From Paris to the border Ryan and Ed had witnessed long caravans of vehicles on the roadways, large Wehrmacht and SS contingents already on the move toward the Reich. Only six weeks earlier, Hitler's betrayal of his former ally Stalin had opened a vast new eastern front. Tanks and motorized artillery led the processions, with horse-drawn vehicles bringing up the rear. And leaving Paris, their express had given right-of-way to a number of military trains on the highline toward Berlin and beyond. It was a formidable display of power.

But as they moved into the Free Zone, the roads turned quieter with far fewer motorized vehicles in sight. Instead Ryan noted a pitiful collection of horses working the fields and hauling crops, the younger, more reliable steeds conscripted for war duty, leaving the French to make do with inferior stock. The Reich was bleeding France dry to feed its expansion, either by direct appropriation or by economic pressure and willing cooperation by the ruling clique anxious to impress the Nazi leadership.

As the train neared their destination, Ryan headed for the lavatory at the end of the carriage, hoping to find it in working order. The condition of the passenger coaches reflected the growing impoverishment of the divided nation. Even the first-class cabins showed neglect. He glanced into each compartment he passed before stepping out into the noisy vestibule and coming to an abrupt halt.

It took only a moment to register what he had just seen. For a split second he thought he had spotted the mustachioed man who had shadowed him on the way to Marita's flat. He turned back to make certain, but his eyes had obviously fooled him, for no one even remotely familiar sat in the last crowded compartment. All but one seat was occupied. A movement caught Ryan's eye. At the far end of the carriage the swinging door closed on a man moving quickly between cars.

"Probably nothing but your imagination, but you might as well get used to it," Ed told Ryan upon his return to their compartment. "In your line of work a tail is *de rigueur*, right?"

"So this is what I have to look forward to once things get rolling?"

"Please tread carefully, Ryan. Vichy officially rules the entire country, since it's too big and burdensome for the Reich to manage personally. But the Nazis are very active behind the scenes. Whatever zone you're in, they'll keep a close watch on you. And these Vichy police aren't fooling around. Just think homegrown French Gestapo and you'll be fine."

The forests, fields and meadowlands near Vichy were lovely, and as the train approached the station, they spotted huge old spa hotels draped in the *tricolore* and grand mansions of obvious faded wealth.

"Quite a change from Paris, right?" Ed shook his head in disbelief. "Welcome to the new capital of France. Once a quiet backwater famed for hot springs and colon irrigations, and hardly a world-class center of culture and learning. But they needed something centrally-located once Paris was off the table."

The whole resort town felt remarkably dull to Ryan, better suited to idle, expensive vacations poolside or in the casino, certainly not to the business of governing a venerable European power.

A deep-blue Buick flying American flags brought them to their hotel. After check-in a government aide came to verify their credentials before leading them to the embassy. A slender man in a well-cut suit welcomed them, obviously prepared for their arrival. He handed Ryan a leather portfolio holding three official forms and a letter signed by the ambassador himself. Here in his hands at last were the Vichy warrants remanding custody of the internees into the care of the bearer. And in a smaller envelope Ryan found the identification documents and visas placing René, Erika and Leo under American diplomatic protection and allowing them to leave France.

"So I just present these at the camp and we're away?"

"Nothing's ever quite that simple here—this place is a bureaucratic nightmare." The secretary showed frustration in having to explain. "The warrants are already signed by the Superintendent of Internment Camps, but you'll still need a counter-signature by an Interior Ministry official of sufficient rank."

"And where do we find such a person?" Ed showed his displeasure. "This should have been addressed prior to our arrival." He knew money had changed hands to facilitate the release. Unofficially, of course.

The secretary ignored Ed's perturbed tone. "It should be very simple, sir. Just cross the park there," he pointed out the window, "and ask for Monsieur Delaporte at the pool." The secretary checked his watch. "In fact, your timing should be perfect; Delaporte should be on his third cocktail by now and quite likely very pliable. Just be prepared to grease the wheels with a bit more cash, if needed."

"Charming." Ryan exchanged a concerned glance with his brother.

They passed beneath the canopy of plane trees toward a fountain supported by naked muses and descended to the swimming pool behind a grand but neglected hotel. A waiter in a white jacket directed them to a seated man dwarfing a small table poolside. The man wore burgundy swim trunks and canvas espadrilles, and sported an imposing ring and heavy Rolex. Almost lost on his hairy chest hung a Croix de Guerre affixed to a gold chain. A half-empty whiskey glass rested in his plump hand.

"Monsieur Delaporte?"

"And you are, *messieurs*?"

"Edward Lemmon, American Department of State. And this is Dr. Ryan Lemmon, from the American Embassy. Forgive the interruption, but we have need of a few signatures, *s'il-vous-plaît*."

"More signatures? Can't a man enjoy a moment's leisure on a warm afternoon?"

"But, sir..." Ed prepared his most diplomatic tack.

"*Non,* you're right," the man interrupted, "duty always calls, *n'est-ce pas?* Let's have a look." He took another sip and set his drink aside, then picked up reading glasses and balanced them on his bulbous nose. "One can't be too careful with official paperwork." Ryan removed the letter packet from his coat pocket.

At that moment a young woman of considerable beauty approached from the hotel. Her sleek bathing suit flashed beneath a sheer day robe and her blond hair was cut in a closely-cropped pageboy. However nothing of her remarkable physique appeared remotely boyish. All three men watched appreciatively as she approached the table.

"Is there nothing here for a girl to drink?"

"For you, *ma Chérie*, always."

The minister quickly pulled the eyeglasses from his nose and rose clumsily from the deck chair. He kissed her, as if there were any doubt to whom she belonged. The girl smiled serenely, taking in the handsome Americans with an approving glance before returning her full attention to the portly official. The minister snapped his fingers and the waiter appeared immediately at his side for her order.

"Campari on the rocks."

The blonde spread a towel on a deck chair next to the Frenchman, kicked off her low heels, and exposed her legs to the sun. She took a tube of cream from a small mesh handbag and began to apply it in long smooth strokes following the curves of her thighs and calves.

His eyes glued to the long limbs of his companion, the Vichy minister reached distractedly for the packet of letters in Ryan's hand. Ryan offered his own pen, and the statesman signed each page with barely a glance at its content. The fate of a few foreigners in some distant internment camp was obviously immaterial to a man picturing himself huffing and puffing between those thighs.

"Merci beaucoup, monsieur," Ryan retrieved the packet.

"Pas du tout, monsieur." The minister's eyes remained fixed on his lovely companion. However the blonde raised her lashes and gave Ryan and Edward a wink and a sweet parting smile.

CHAPTER TWELVE

Gascony, Occupied France
12 August 1941

Devon Whitaker knew he was dying. He could still think clearly enough, and his initial injuries had not been so severe as to put him in mortal danger had he received proper medical care. But now he felt his body shutting down, muscle by muscle, organ by organ, cell by cell. He recalled biology lab at the university, the anatomical charts on the walls, the endless memorization of structures and tissues, the dissection of frogs and fetal pigs. He could picture some of the changes taking place within his own body and track the succession of failed metabolic processes which were slowly guiding him to his death. Physiological self-analysis and memories were the only distraction for an active mind in a rapidly weakening shell.

The decision had been so easy when first approached by His Majesty's Secret Service. His marks both at school and university had been strong. He was intelligent, a more than adequate athlete, and one of those men who won—and broke—hearts. Girls simply loved him: dark and curly hair, aquiline nose, pencil-thin mustache, and flashing green eyes. Science was his passion, the law his future, intent on stepping into the legal practice established by his well-regarded barrister father.

But then Hitler rolled into Poland, and the *drôle de guerre*, the year-long "phony war" began, with no further land combat on either side. Devon had signed up for officer training school. They steered him into the intelligence field, at first only a desk job, but his quick mind and decisiveness brought him to the attention of MI6.

Devon had spent the summers of his youth learning to speak French and the Celtic language Breton in the home of his maternal uncle who owned a small Brittany farmstead near Rennes. That ancient stone farmhouse with the musty smell of centuries and the broad terrace that hosted many local families created unforgettable memories. The thought of a jackboot heel on the neck of Devon's beloved France filled him with sorrow and fed his anger. He intended to make a difference, and secret service work seemed an ideal match to his talents.

Leaving Patricia had not been easy. Their romance had been so quick, so passionate. He had seen her chatting up fellow secretaries in the smoky subterranean vaults of MI6. Her eyes met his, and he knew at once she was the one for him. The hint of a smile on those red lips, that dark lustrous hair, and those gorgeous blue eyes cast briefly his way before she rejoined her friends in conversation. The lift had arrived to take the group from sight, but she had remained indelibly fixed in his heart.

That afternoon he tracked down her desk, a solitary rosebud in hand, the bloom pinched from a bouquet his superior officer's wife had brought that morning to brighten her husband's office. The clatter of typewriters hushed just barely as he introduced himself to the girl.

"I'm Devon Whitaker."

"Patricia Wales, but my friends call me Trish." She offered her hand and he kept it in his.

"Then we shall be friends, shan't we, Trish." His shy but knowledgeable grin had won many hearts, but there was more to it this time than just plotting to bed another beauty.

Trish removed her hand from his. "Time will tell, I suppose." She glanced right and left at her friends, who feigned disinterest as their fingers worked the typewriter keys. Her best friend Dottie couldn't muffle a giggle.

Devon acknowledged the friend with a conspiratorial smile and continued unabashed. "Sadly, that does present us with a problem. Time is precious in a country at war, so we really must move things along more quickly, don't you think? Do have dinner with me tonight."

"Thank you, but I've plans already. Perhaps another time?"

"Top-notch idea, my dear—we shall move those evening plans of yours to another time, and we dine together tonight—just the two of us—and become better acquainted, right?"

She laughed at his presumption, loving every minute of it. "So, I should simply give in to every pushy young gent I've only just met?"

"Ah, but that's a different matter, you see. It's you who manipulates me. That first smile this morning did the trick."

She couldn't help but give him another. "Have you plans for that rose you're torturing—or could it be for some other girl here in the steno pool?"

Devon looked at the mangled stem in his hands. He handed it to her with both hands and a deep bow, a knight offering his sword to a queen. "For you alone, Trish."

Happily resigned to her fate, she jotted down her phone number and address, handing him the note with another smile. "Eight tonight, then?"

❖

After dinner they'd taken in Ivor Novello's much-admired "The Dancing Years" in the West End. When the air raid sirens wailed and everyone rushed to the shelters, they ignored the perturbed wardens and hid instead behind a large velvet couch in the lobby, smothering their laughter to avoid discovery. The crump of German bombs shook the building and rattled windows, and anti-aircraft fire responded in the distance. Later at the door to her flat she came into his arms. Roommate, she explained, otherwise he might join her for a nightcap. A few long kisses and he was gone, only to see her almost every night for a month before he proposed. And Trish accepted by covering his face with carmine kisses.

His departure was filled with tears, for he couldn't speak of where he was going and what he was facing, only that he would be out of country and not able to write for some time. And that he would be safe. Only the first part had proven true.

SOE—Special Operations, Executive—had dropped him into the moonless sky over Occupied France with a wireless set, entrenching tool, pistol and false identity papers. And, of course, a potassium cyanide pill hiding in the rollup cuff of the worker's trousers beneath his jump suit.

The landing should have been easy. He had practiced extensively, first screwing up his courage and jumping from balloons at ever increasing height, then tumbling from aircraft by day and night and feeling the upward jerk as his parachute deployed, watching the ground rush up, enjoying the thrill of the moment, and anxiously anticipating doing an important job to help win the war.

The terrain was well chosen for his drop, a level field with a nearby hay barn and a few distant farmhouses. The plane had crossed over his beloved Brittany avoiding Luftwaffe patrols, and kept to very low altitude as it moved into the Loire region. The drop came well after the midnight hour so that few might look skyward and see his chute, and his landing target lay some distance from any urban areas protected by flak guns and spotters. And yet, nothing had gone as planned.

CHAPTER THIRTEEN

Gurs, Vichy France
13 August 1941

The stench assailed him as he neared the gates. Three guards idled at the entrance to the Gurs camp, apparently immune to the sour smell of unwashed humanity and raw sewage, to the reek of despair. He read only boredom on their faces, no curiosity at the approach of a visitor reporting to the guard shack under a stifling, late summer sun. Ryan was just one more tiresome petitioner on behalf of some wasted soul trapped behind the barbed wire.

"*Vous voulez, monsieur?*" Unlike his subordinates, the officer-in-charge standing tall in his police uniform.

"I'm here for the release of three detainees." He pulled the portfolio from his pocket. "And here are the required forms." Ryan handed over the letters one by one, citing each name affixed at the top—*Erika Breitling von Kredow, Leonhard von Kredow, René Gesslinger*. The officer appeared momentarily surprised by Ryan's faultless German on the heels of educated French. *"Votre carte d'identité, monsieur?"* Ryan obliged.

The policeman's curiosity turned to disdain. He returned the American passport and directed his attention to the letters in hand, carefully scanning each in turn. Stepping back into the guard shack, he sat behind a desk to compare the names against a ledger showing line after line of prisoner identities. He reached for the phone.

Standing outside the gate, Ryan stared nervously into the camp, hoping for an early glimpse of his friends. The last twenty-four hours had been especially difficult for him. He knew his undertaking was near completion, but regretted having no means to alert his friends of their imminent release. Now he would finally fulfill a promise made to Erika nearly three years earlier when all had seemed lost. Ed had managed to obtain American visas for all three, and for the hundredth time Ryan felt for those documents, still tucked safely in the jacket he held in his arm.

Into the distance stretched a central street bordered by block after block of identical barracks numbering in the hundreds, each *îlot* of thirty or so separated by barbed wire stretched along wooden posts buried in the heavy clay soil. Barbed fencing about as high as a man surrounded the huge settlement. The ground was rutted and hard, evidence that during the winter months it had been a morass of mud. The individual barracks were uniformly covered in thin wooden planking and frayed, tarred fabric. There were no windows.

The officer returned to the doorway. "Tomorrow."

"Why tomorrow? I'm here, they're here, and my papers are in order." The last thing Ryan needed now was another delay.

"We need time to process the paperwork."

"What paperwork do you need? You hold the required forms, so you've no reason to wait. I take three detainees off your hands and we're on our way." Ryan tucked a wad of tightly-rolled currency into the officer's breast-pocket flap. "Simple as that."

"Procedures must be followed, and for the moment I can't spare the personnel." He pushed the bills farther into his pocket before stepping back into the shack. "Tomorrow at noon."

❖

The small town nearby had little to recommend it. Ryan took a dingy room at the only local inn, reached by a creaking external staircase and surely infested with bedbugs and lice. The frustration in having to wait almost twenty-four hours before reuniting with his friends gnawed at him. After stowing his bag he wandered down to a tavern to while away the afternoon over a beer and the local paper. A small shop actually displayed bread, produce and dairy products with no line of hopeful buyers out front. Unlike Paris and even Vichy itself, this region of southwestern France was not suffering the same degree of economic hardship as farther north.

The tavern was nearly empty. A middle-aged man sat alone, his peasant garb patched and stained, a red beret angled on his head, and an unlit pipe perched between his lips. He faced a water glass and some cloudy liqueur, *pastis* perhaps. He appeared to doze. In the opposite corner a bedraggled couple waited with infinite patience, rarely uttering a word while staring vacantly out the window much of the time. Perhaps they too were hoping to see someone in the camp and had been shoved off until the next day. Ryan considered whether he should have offered a larger bribe. Between the couple sat a plate holding slices of bread and a single fatty sausage already reduced to bite-sized slices. A dollop of brownish mustard left a smear across the plate. From time to time the man speared a piece of meat with his fork, raked it through the mustard, then chewed industriously to extract every last bit of flavor. The woman seemed content to nibble on a slice of bread.

Ryan's beer arrived and he used his handkerchief to wipe the smudged rim. He thought the glass might have escaped a final rinse in a seldom-changed dishpan. The bartender was a stiff-backed woman, her hair bound tightly in a bun, her arms bony to the point of malnourishment, and her whole body shrinking beneath a stained apron touching her shoes. Obviously put off by Ryan's odd fastidiousness, she demanded immediate payment. Ryan obliged. After emptying the glass and exhausting the local newspaper, Ryan decided to return to his room. As he got to his feet, two camp guards entered the inn and seated themselves at his table.

"You're not a local, monsieur." Ryan's clean-cut American suit did appear out of place in these surroundings.

"And certainly not French either," the other added.

"Is that a concern, messieurs?" Ryan's eyes narrowed.

"*Pas du tout*, monsieur. We can only assume our fine detention facility brings you to Gurs." Both guards laughed as they signaled the bartender, who brought them beer in glasses no cleaner than Ryan's had been.

At least I'm not getting any special treatment, he thought.

Ryan relaxed and laughed along. "Regrettably, I must wait until tomorrow to see my friends inside."

The older guard glanced at his partner, who nodded before continuing quietly: "That's not always the case, monsieur. There are ways to gain immediate access...less formal ways, shall we say?" He rubbed an imaginary coin between his fingers and laughed again.

"That might interest me." Ryan sat again in the chair just vacated.

"And how many friends do you wish to visit?"

"A German couple about my age and a small boy. You know them?"

"Our camp is large. We have many couples and many small boys."

"And a fair number of German Jews." The younger guard interrupted, barely suppressing his grin. "Can we throw in a few displaced Spanish Republicans, as well?" Ryan remembered that the camp had originally housed refugees from Franco. Apparently a few still remained.

The older guard ignored his colleague's jest. "Give me some names and we'll see what can be done to speed things up for you."

Ryan wrote on a corner torn from his newspaper and slid it across the table.

"Five hundred francs per head," said the older man, regarding the list.

Ryan pulled out his wallet and placed three bills on the newsprint.

"Did I say five hundred? My apologies, monsieur. I misspoke. I meant a thousand francs each." He winked at his colleague.

Ryan pulled out the additional notes and added a hundred francs for good measure.

The money and names disappeared into the pocket of the guard. "Wait right here—this could take a while." They downed their beers in one long draught, rose from the table to salute the bartender good-naturedly, and gave a mocking little bow to the American before they left the bar, laughing at some private joke.

Ryan nursed another beer while awaiting their return. By dinnertime he knew he'd been had. He ordered a bowl of pea soup, sausage and a bread roll. He didn't want to go to bed hungry, knowing the vermin he'd face in his room would make sleep difficult anyway. The bartender demanded money for the guards' unpaid beers, so he coughed up the additional cash. Back in his room, he opened both windows to draw in a bit of air and prepared for what would likely be a restless night. Noon tomorrow couldn't come soon enough.

❖

Under the searing midday sun the ramshackle buildings seem to tremble in the thick air. The walls showed obvious makeshift efforts to cover holes in the fabric siding with whatever had proved handy, and the open areas between barbed wire runs and camp structures were rutted, dusty and weedy. A washroom platform with a long trough separated the two closest buildings, and Ryan spotted other similar structures farther down the rows. No running water was apparent, and toilet facilities consisted of trough latrines and raised platforms with collection tubs for catching excrement.

Prisoners gathered alongside the structures seeking shade under the eaves. Surely the heat inside the cramped barracks would be intolerable. Makeshift fans of scrap cardboard moved lethargically in many hands, fighting a losing battle against the miserable day. Occasionally heads bent close to share a word, but no murmur came from the crowd as would be expected with a gathering of this size. Instead, the air hummed with the incessant buzz of insects, and he could see internees swatting the pests. A group of children played listlessly with an old bicycle rim, its tire long gone, but they too seemed strangely quiet.

Ryan scanned the faces of the malnourished children, wondering if one might be six-year-old Leo. Guilt overcame him in the face of so much misery. He would only be able to help three, while so many others waited in vain for rescue. *But I can only do what I can.*

A few prisoners stared through the barbed wire to the distant woods and fields, shoulders hunched, alone in their thoughts. He looked from face to face, from one gaunt figure to the next, and wondered what changes he would find in his friends, how severe the toll of their past years.

He glanced back into the guard shack and observed the same senior officer from the previous day, now once again on the phone. The man saw Ryan and offered a nod, then set down the receiver and gestured to the younger guard at the door. He had seen nothing of the two men who had fleeced him of thirty-one hundred francs the previous afternoon. Plus the two beers.

"Take him in, block B, barrack 15."

The gate swung open, and Ryan and the guard walked a gauntlet of listless prisoners before entering one of the passages between two rows of buildings. Women tended cooking pots on portable burners set in the broiling sun, and male cooks in dirty aprons prepared to butcher a small pig carcass. He smelled soup of some kind.

The internees observed his progress, hollow eyes tracking, curious to see a well-dressed stranger enter their closed world of neglect and decay. Any break in the tedium was welcome. "Help us, monsieur, please?" a plaintive request from an old woman, followed quickly by another plea for help from the opposite side of their path. He felt shame for his freedom, for his own health, and his helplessness in the face of such despair.

"*Silence*!" ordered the guard. "Come, monsieur, *vite, vite!*" The policeman pushed forward quickly now as some of the prisoners threatened to approach. One hand went to the truncheon on his belt. He appeared anxious to escape the searing sun and gathering crowd.

Ryan's own pace had slowed as he considered how his own life was once again about to change direction.

❖

Every minute was tedious, every hour unending, each day relentless, and a week, oh God, an eternity. René slumped down in the face of such deadly heat and boredom, rubbing his aching knee.

Life back in Alsace had been so easy. Just ten kilometers south of Colmar, a private road led visitors past the family's thriving vineyards and perfectly-kept bottling barn to reach the lovely two-storied family home of half-timbers, stucco, and steep red-tiled roof. Leaving all that behind had been a serious blow, perhaps worse than abandoning Kehl and the family shipping business in those final disastrous hours under SS attack. For a fleeting second René thought of Ryan, wondering once again if his friend could have survived the night in the Rhine. He supposed not. No word had ever reached them despite the letters René had sent to Washington for so long.

"What I wouldn't give for a glass of chilled pinot blanc right now." René wiped sweat from his neck and brow and extended his legs. The ancient wooden chair creaked beneath his large frame.

"You say something, *Liebling*?"

"Nothing important, just remembering Colmar…and how happy mother was there."

Jeanne had beamed at returning to the town of her birth and her familial home. The abandonment of her mansion on the Rhine and the pre-dawn river crossing to France had shaken her badly. René had waited until safely in Strasbourg before phoning Charles Rothe and requesting he come to the train station to bring them to Colmar. With affection and relief Jeanne had greeted the family who ran the vintner operation left by her parents, and the Rothes in turn treated the silver-haired *grande dame* with a respect bordering on adulation.

"The Rothes are such sweet, caring people." Erika's look mirrored his melancholy. "They treated us all like family."

"I do hope they made it safely away." The extent of their concern went unspoken. René had tried to reach the vineyard manager several times in the past year. An unrecognized voice answered each time. Fearing a wiretap, he'd immediately hung up. With Alsace now part of the Third Reich, there was little expectation the family had been left alone, given the Gesslinger taint.

Leaving that beautiful home and its warm memories for unknown Lyon had been very hard on his mother, and each subsequent move had taken a further toll. "I realize how little the thought helps, but at least your mother's finally safe with Brigitte over at the Morlanne farm now." Erika offered a hopeful smile. "One less thing to worry about, right?"

René only nodded. He had no shortage of worries and was sure the next blow would come soon. The situation in France for Jewish and political refugees from Hitler's Germany had deteriorated rapidly. The influx of Jews only heightened an inherent distrust of foreigners among the French populace. The country had its own long tradition of anti-Semitism. The newcomers flooding over the borders were not just Germans, they were German Jews. Internment camps across the country swallowed up the newly homeless, offering only disease-ridden squalor and neglect.

He removed a bottle from the shelf and took a long swallow from a chipped glass. Good drinkable alcohol was ever more difficult to come by, but having money of any kind helped. René had grown accustomed to being master of his own destiny. But for now—and despite his reassurance to himself and his wife—deep in his heart he questioned whether that opportunity would ever arise again.

CHAPTER FOURTEEN

Gurs, Vichy France
14 August 1941

The guard disappeared the moment Ryan entered B15. The oppressive air was pierced by shafts of sunlight breaching the siding. Ryan's eyes adjusted to the sudden change from searing sunlight to dark interior, and a cold sweat broke across his face despite the sweltering heat.

"How nice we meet again!" Horst von Kredow's voice was cordial, a gentleman greeting an old acquaintance. The man's face was a mask, unmoving and unnerving, his mouth a slit, his eyes pale-blue markers in the lifeless flesh. "Welcome to beautiful France. But enough pleasantries—it's been a long while and we do need to chat."

Nausea welled in Ryan's throat and instinct shouted "run!", but unyielding hands forced him to face his adversary. He'd left the sun's glare filled with the joy of anticipation in surprising long-lost friends. Now Ryan searched the shadows for Erika and Leo, for René. He trembled, groping for words that didn't come.

"Doctor Lemmon, how pale you look! Don't worry about your friends, you'll see them soon enough." Horst directed Ryan toward a wooden chair. "Very soon, in fact." The men at his back gripped his elbows again. "No need for force, *meine Herren*, I'm sure our guest is exhausted from his travels and will welcome our hospitality." For a brief moment the unblemished side of Horst's face caught the scattered light, and Ryan recognized again the handsome Nazi from Marburg. "Gentlemen, do help our guest with his coat."

The taller agent took the jacket from Ryan's arm before retreating into the shadows. He felt certain he recognized this man with the ramrod posture from years past, but couldn't place him. Ryan sat. The chair lacked a leg, forcing him to extend one of his own to maintain balance and avoid falling to the floor. It was meant to disconcert him further, and it worked.

"Where are they?" Ryan found his voice at last. "What've you done with them?"

"We'll get there in a moment. For now, let's consider your immediate position—not ideal, *nicht wahr*? You're back in a game where I control the entire board, and you are merely my pawn."

Ryan seethed with fury at having stepped into another trap. "How in God's name did you find me?"

"The easiest thing in the world, *Herr Doktor*, for you see, it was *you* who found *me*." A chuckle escaped those tight lips. In the mote-filled light Horst's scars shown livid, his jaw tight. "In truth, I sent you a personal invitation and you came of your own free will."

Ryan groped for answers. Here he was again in the hands of Horst von Kredow, the Gestapo sadist who pursued him in '38, tortured him, and would gladly have killed him had Ryan failed to escape. Here was the Nazi who planned the extermination of European Jewry, and wished to destroy Erika and his son Leo and his friend René. Nothing here made sense. Ryan had been in California for years, all ties to Washington and espionage cleanly severed. Who had known of his return to Europe, his trip to Gurs? Who had betrayed him? "They're already dead, aren't they?"

"By no means—at least not yet." He formed the words with great care. "But that touching note in pencil which lured you here was my very own creation. Quite clever, don't you think? You see, your Alsatian Gesslinger may have eluded me for the moment, but his lackey in Kehl shared your friend's code name before he died, so I knew exactly how to bring you back to me."

"Hugo Gerson." Ryan pictured the overcoat spreading in the oily backwash of the Rhine lagoon, the balding skull with the single bullet wound.

"Yes, that was it, Gerson. A weak man—you'd be surprised how talkative he became—but when all was said and done, I did admire his loyalty."

Ryan felt numb. He recalled the signature on the note which had drawn him back to Europe and guilelessly into Horst's clutches, "The Lone Ranger," his friend's *nom de guerre*. Under torture Gerson had sung, unraveling René's anti-Nazi network. "Then you got them all?"

"*Ach*, your 'Lone Ranger' gang, you mean? A childish choice of names, but my Washington colleague recognized it at once, and it didn't take us long to round up that pitiful band. Had my recuperation from that distasteful night on the river been shorter, our three remaining fugitives would never have led such a merry chase. But here you are at last, joining me of your own accord, and a grand reunion is finally in sight. It will be the final game, so to speak, and I assure you I will make it well worth the wait."

"But surely the boy's done nothing wrong! He's your son!"

"The boy was always as weak as his mother." Any pretense of affability was gone. "Her Jew-blood pollutes his veins, corrupting any chance to be a productive Aryan. Witnessing her brat's painful death will make her anguish all the more exquisite, and Leo finally serves me as a son should."

Ryan's fingernails dug into the flesh of his fists. "So they're not here…not in this camp?"

"Ah, the coin drops at last." Horst drew a line in the filthy dirt with the toe of his shoe. "No, I regret they've never experienced this despicable cesspool. My Jew-bitch of a wife hides in the coastal hills, sneaking into Bayonne always one step ahead of my people. She and her fuck-partner spy on our troops, help enemies on the run, dabble in sabotage—that sort of nonsense. They view themselves as partisans, not the anarchist Jews they really are…" he appeared distracted for a moment, "…but difficult to capture all the same. So I placed you back on the game board, and you came willingly as I knew you would. For that I thank you. You always play the role of simpleton so well—once again the bait to draw my enemies to me."

The deception was truly brilliant in its scope. *Horst and Kohl—and undoubtedly Heydrich behind it all.* "So The Group…?"

Horst laughed, for the first time distorting his mask. "You Americans are always so naïve, so ready to believe whatever we set before you. *Die Gruppe* was my invention, created out of whole cloth. Heydrich loved the plan—further engaging your rich American industrialists who saw how the Führer would expand their influence in Europe. Their funding and political influence made The Group a reality, and our man Kohl, buried deep in your own State Department, found do-gooders like you to expose the few in Germany who still opposed us. Worked like a charm."

Ryan's mind buzzed with the implications. "So how did you track me down?"

"Don't you see? Who should appear on Richard Kohl's list of eager future diplomats but your drudge of a brother? Anxious to do his part to fight our Nazi menace, your sibling bragged incessantly to his boss of your vast experience in Germany, and Richard proposed recruiting you to be one of The Group's 'operatives.' Needless to say, I was delighted you wanted to join in the fun. After all, we had left things rather unfinished in Marburg after you screwed my whore of a fiancée."

"So you knew—"

"Every move you would make, probably before you did." Horst made no effort to hide his gloating. "We tracked you across France and through Baden, but then you disappeared on me in Berlin, and the next thing I knew you were running for France with the Jew-bitch and my protocol. And what irony to learn you delivered the photos directly to my man Kohl! But we couldn't let you get away with such impudence, now could we?"

Ryan ran the revelations through his mind, stunned by their complexity and cleverness. "So the note from René…"

"Pure forgery. Kohl's cover was about to be blown. He was setting up the exchange program to repatriate some of our desirable citizens. He knew my need for your services, and your brother wanted you back in the espionage game, so it was child's play using the bogus note alongside real ones Kohl had squirreled away, and now here you are again, literally at my beck and call."

Ryan shook his head at his own gullibility. How royally von Kredow had played them all. Kohl must have reported Ryan finally underway to Gurs. He recalled his shadow in Paris and the stranger on the train. Yesterday's twenty-four hour delay had surely given Horst the time to reach Gurs.

Horst bent down to pry a slender metal rod from the hardened clay of the floor. He creased the air as with a fencing foil, its whistle breaking the leaden stillness.

Damn, what a fool I am! Ryan felt an unexpected calm descend. Neither fury nor fear would serve him now, and neither emotion could help his friends. Only self-control might buy a reprieve, reveal an out. He knew Horst needed him, at least for the moment, so death wasn't on the table. Not yet.

"So where do we go from here?" Ryan's struggle with the off-kilter chair was taking its toll on his cramping leg as he eyed the switch in Horst's hand.

"Well, my friend, let's consider our options. And we can be friends, right? After all, we've been through so much together, *meinst Du nicht*? Horst used the "du" reserved for family and close friends, for children and soldier comrades. It grated, patronizing and degrading. "Now you'll help me draw in the others."

"Well, '*friend*,' what's the intent of that rod in your hand?"

"My dear Ryan, I've learned so much about 'persuasion through pain' that I can assure you—anticipation is more effective than any troubling conclusion." He split the air with the metal switch again. "The end is over so quickly, don't you know?"

"I'll take your word for that, von Kredow."

"I forget. You've never experienced this pleasure—you're far too weak to know anything as intensely satisfying as wielding slow death with every flick of the wrist." The whip snapped again.

The nightmare vision of the Gestapo agent on the train flashed through Ryan's mind, the blood and horror, but he said nothing.

"Effective torture is actually much like sex—control is everything. But interrogation can be vastly more rewarding, what with its unlimited variations on pleasure and pain. And all things are best when taken exquisitely slowly."

"Then let's follow that maxim and postpone whatever you've in mind for me now?"

Horst chuckled before giving his men a nod. Leaving a dust cloud in their wake, they dragged heavy wooden saw-horses across the caked dirt floor, placing them a meter apart before Ryan.

"I've anticipated the coming reunion with my traitorous wife for years, so for the moment I must keep you healthy or the others won't join our game. But this time around I won't be delayed by another of your untimely escapes." He cleared his throat of the rising dust. "You eluded me once in Marburg, and then again in Kehl. Believe me, it won't happen again."

"As a 'friend' you have my word." Ryan swallowed hard. "No escapes."

Horst hesitated, seemingly lost in thought. "Klaus Pabst never learned to swim, you know. Hated the water. Even at university you never found him in the Marburg pools." He refocused on Ryan, new steel in his voice. "My 'dagger' was a priceless asset you took from me." His face hardened. "For that you still owe me, and I *will* collect."

Without warning, the men dropped Ryan on his back. One kicked away the chair while the other shoved a rough-hewn wooden pole beneath his knees. The larger man held a foot to Ryan's throat while the second pulled his arms beneath the shaft and bound the captive's wrists to his ankles with a cord. The pole now separated knees above and arms below, leaving Ryan completely at Horst's mercy.

Both the foot at his throat and the swirling dust forced Ryan to find his voice through a fit of coughing: "France is a neutral country, Horst…" more racking cough, "…and mine is a diplomatic passport. People in Vichy know I'm here—they'll come looking."

"Ah, interesting point—shall we examine those papers?" The taller man slid the passport from Ryan's jacket and handed it over. Horst moved Ryan's photo into a ragged beam of sunlight. "A fair likeness, actually. A shame you'll appear far less youthful when all this is over. But first, let's ease your mind regarding diplomatic status." He bent over to stare into Ryan's eyes. "You no longer exist at all. In fact, you never made it to this hellhole, and those 'neutral' Vichy bureaucrats you trust so much will all confirm that, just as they assured you that your friends were detained here."

A deep chill raced through Ryan, his body remembering the agonies suffered on the Gesslinger docks. "You said you needed me alive." A quick swallow as he steadied himself.

"And alive you shall be! This next little exercise is merely a precaution. I regret I can't go to Biarritz with you this afternoon as I'd first planned. I'd anticipated a lengthier stay for you in Paris, so your premature arrival here threw me off schedule. I must entrust your transport to these gentlemen here, and we certainly can't have you slipping away again, now can we?"

Without bidding they hoisted Ryan from the floor, spanning the sawhorses with the pole. His head dangled toward the floor.

"Comfortable?"

The sharp edges of the wooden rod dug into the back of Ryan's knees as the blood rushed to his head. He knew the pain was coming. "It'll do, though rather hot and stuffy."

"Well then, let's cool you off."

At a flick of the rod the two henchmen tore off Ryan's footwear and tossed shoes and socks aside. He hung upside-down facing the ill-fitted door, its rim framed in sunlight, a mocking beacon to freedom. His entire body recoiled at the first blow to the bare soles of his feet.

"Now then, still bothered by the heat? Concentrate instead on the cramping, here before you know it." The lash bit again. "You won't be walking on your own for some time, I'm afraid."

The following strikes came in steady, measured succession, each more painful than the last. Occasionally Horst broke the rhythm. Ryan heard the passage of the switch, but no blow came, giving him momentary hope that the beating was about to end. Then followed a new series of light, teasing taps to the raw flesh, and abruptly the whip struck again.

LA COLLABORATION

1941

❖

CHAPTER ONE

Gascony, Occupied France
14 August 1941

Only one leisure pastime interested Horst von Kredow. Just as in the pursuit of human quarry, the game of chess demanded forward thinking, anticipating your opponent's moves and potential errors, and calculating the odds of winning or losing by following a particular strategy. Unfortunately, *le Masque* found few willing to sit across from him at the checkered board. He didn't know whether his face alone distracted and intimidated his opponents, or if they were simply unable to concentrate, knowing he held their fate in his hands.

So he normally challenged only detainees, offering freedom from their expected fate if they managed to outplay him. Only one had ever succeeded. Horst was true to his word and let the man live, but first he used pliers to painstakingly remove the winner's teeth, giving each ivory stump its own square on the chess board.

"Looks like I've taken the bite out of his victory," he had joked to his lieutenant Brenner. "And it's perfect! Thirty-two teeth, thirty-two playing pieces back on the board." The man's bloody gums and slack mouth caused Peter Brenner to turn aside and vomit.

Horst hated seeing weakness in his men, almost as much as he hated to lose.

Whenever Horst had time on his hands and lacked a worthy opponent, he played chess against himself, observing his 'opponent' for errors in judgment, vying to outthink himself as he swiveled the board after each move. He had practiced this mental exercise for years. And, though stalemate was the most disappointing outcome, the inconclusive matches honed his game skills and patience.

So it was little wonder he was now taking such pleasure in the moment. His greatest chess game had finally reached the end stage. The foolish American knight was finally under his control. The Jew-bitch Erika thought herself the powerful queen and safe from Horst's attack, but she lived in ignorance. She could only see the few squares surrounding her, a tiny piece of the game. And the lump of a rook Gesslinger would limp beside her right into Horst's trap. In truth, they were all his expendable pieces, lowly pawns. Black side, white side, it made no difference, for soon he would have his win, and the board would run red.

Horst had also assumed Lemmon was dead when he learned Klaus Pabst had washed ashore after the Kehl episode. His closest ally surfaced with his head a pulpy mess and his body bloated nearly beyond recognition. Horst had kept the photos to remind him of the tragic loss. But Richard

Kohl in Washington was only too happy to set Horst straight about the fate of the man responsible for the loss of his most loyal follower. The Jewess and her mongrel American Lemmon had managed to photograph his protocol proposing mass extermination of the Jews, a report destined for first Heydrich and Himmler's eyes only, and ultimately for the Führer's final approval. Lemmon returned home alive, a beaten dog with his tail between his legs, and Kohl had boasted of personally destroying Lemmon's evidence of the potentially damaging protocol.

So typical of Kohl to take credit for saving the day. That man had always been sour over working undercover while Horst publicly enforced Party rule. Still, Kohl remained a capable colleague, and they had worked well together. A shame the man had been ousted from that plum State Department assignment, for there was so much more they might have accomplished. From its inception under Heydrich's encouraging eye, "The Group" had manipulated those naïve fools in Washington to identify foes of the Reich, working the willing American puppets with Horst's invisible strings. "*Die Gruppe*" had been a stroke of genius. Horst's genius. His alone.

❖

The downed mare struggled to rise from the road surface, her hooves kicking desperately, her neck arching against the taut harness. A wagon lay on one side behind her, its cargo of hay strewn across the roadway. The farmer lay half-hidden beneath the overturned cart, his hands to his head, rocking and moaning.

Blocking the opposite lane was a farm truck, skewed on the pavement with its front end jutting over the narrow roadside ditch. Its driver slumped across the wheel, a bloody gash visible on his forehead.

The black Citröen slowed immediately as it approached the accident site. Ryan, his hands in cuffs and his thighs alternately cramping and aching from the hours spent suspended from the wooden rod, hardly noticed the deceleration. The soles of his feet were bloodied and raw, and he wore no shoes.

The Gestapo agent beside him cursed under his breath. This military type about Ryan's own age wore a knotted tie despite the oppressive heat. Exhaustion and aggravation were apparent in his mood. He still seemed somehow familiar to Ryan, but had ignored any attempt at conversation. "Circle around," he ordered the driver, "and make it fast. These oafish peasants haven't a clue how to drive."

"We can't pass, sir," replied the young man at the wheel, perhaps twenty at most, and deferential. He brought the sedan to a halt some ten meters from the collision site.

"My God, such imbeciles we have to deal with!" The Gestapo man loosened one of Ryan's cuffs, ran the chain through the door grip to prevent any attempt at escape, and refastened the link. "Must I handle everything?" Stepping from the vehicle he ordered the driver to follow. "All we needed, *verdammt nochmal*, another delay."

They approached the man caught beneath the cart until close enough to hear his moans. Keeping to any schedule was a challenge in this godforsaken France. They had been late escaping the insufferable heat and filth of the internment camp at Gurs due to engine trouble, had stopped at a garage in Pau when the Citroën threw a fan belt, and now this. He had promised delivery of the prisoner to Biarritz before dusk, and *Die Maske* wasn't someone you disappointed. Ever. "Drag the imbecile out from under that wagon, and if you can't move him, just run him over. His life won't be any the worse for it."

The driver glanced at the Gestapo officer in disbelief, looking for some sign of a jest. The superior's glare and military bearing told him humor played no role in either comment or mood. "Yes, sir, right away, sir."

The younger man grabbed the farmer under the arms and tugged fiercely in an effort to dislodge him. The injured man muttered something incomprehensible—*that damned Basque tongue*, thought the driver—and tried to extricate the trapped peasant, but his feet appeared firmly wedged beneath the wagon. The skinny dray horse whinnied softly, making feeble attempts to stand despite the restraining harness trappings.

"Forget him," the officer said, "go move that damned truck—put it in the ditch if needed. Just get us on our way."

He gently lowered the suffering man back to the roadway and strode over to the truck, its engine idling roughly, the trucker's head still slumped over the steering wheel. The German opened the door, stepped up onto the running board and shoved the unconscious man aside to take control of the wheel.

The first two pops came in rapid succession, muffled by the cab of the truck and the folds of the trucker's jacket hiding the pistol. But the Gestapo officer on the roadbed recognized gunfire and turned abruptly toward the source. The second two shots—aimed with obvious skill—thudded into him from the opposite direction. The first sent his hat flying as the round pierced his skull, the second thumped dully into his side. He wheeled to his right, disbelief flashing across his face as he sank to the pavement. Blood slowly saturated his jacket and spread onto the asphalt.

Summoned by the quick shots, two men in peasant clothing scrambled up the bank from either side to cover the sedan with their weapons. They trained their shotguns into the backseat as Ryan struggled with his cuffs.

"Well done, *copains*," shouted the trucker. He kicked the lifeless body from his cab and resumed his position behind the wheel. Closing the door, he put the truck in reverse to back up onto the roadway and alongside the car. With a handkerchief he scrubbed the "wound" from his forehead.

"Not bad." The farmer pulled his legs easily from beneath the wagon. He went to comfort his horse, which responded to the attentions with a whicker, quickly regaining her feet. She shuddered in satisfaction. The farmer briefly stroked her neck before examining the fallen officer for any sign of life.

"The first shot did the trick." A woman in her mid-twenties emerged from the woods carrying a hunting rifle. "The second was my insurance policy." She strode toward the sedan, her pony-tail bouncing with each step. "Now let's examine our prize."

The young men yanked open both sedan doors simultaneously and Ryan fell to the roadbed, his bound wrist twisted in the handcuffs. *"Américain! Je suis Américain!"*

"Merde!" The woman's disappointment appeared shared by all. "Who the hell are *you*?"

"A prisoner of those damned *Boches* you just killed, and grateful for your help." He struggled to find footing, but the cramping in his legs and the rawness of his feet dropped him to the ground again. He looked up in embarrassment and smiled at the woman.

"What good does an American do us?" She turned away to mutter instructions to one of the shotgun bearers. "Cut him loose and bring him along, though I see little value in it." She turned to the approaching farmer. "One lousy American, impressing us with Parisian French—it's not *le Masque*." She shrugged. "*Alors*, the hunt continues."

One of the partisans retrieved the handcuff key from the pocket of the dead Gestapo officer and removed Ryan's restraints. The other tossed his shotgun into the back seat, slipped behind the wheel of the idling Citroën to reverse direction, and headed south toward the Pyrenées. Ryan suspected the car would bring good money in Spain for the partisan cause. Meanwhile, the other driver pulled the truck forward and helped Ryan into the bed, since he couldn't manage on his own. With great heaves the men tossed the dead Gestapo agents alongside the American and covered all three with loose hay from the farm wagon and roadway.

"Shut up and stay put," the lankier partisan said, "and don't come out until we tell you." Ryan gladly obeyed. It felt good to extend his legs. He rubbed his wrists, chafed by wearing the cuffs for hours, and distanced himself from the corpses to find a crack between the side boards for a better view.

The partisans drew long poles from the far side of the truck bed, using them as levers to right the farm cart. They moved with speed and precision, obviously well practiced. After two heaves, the wagon rolled back onto its wheels as the farmer reassured the nervous horse. Pitchforks quickly loaded the remaining hay from the roadbed. The farmer flicked the reins, and the skinny mare tossed her head, neighing. She put her back to the load and moved the wagon up a rutted dirt path into the woods.

Now only traces of hay and a glistening pool of blood were witness to the scene of the staged accident, and the remaining partisans clambered into the cab beside the driver. The truck headed north, halting a kilometer up the road to allow a lookout to jump onto the running board and join his crew.

The newcomer climbed up into the bed, stepping clumsily on Ryan's tortured feet. He jerked them back and a thigh muscle protested with a painful spasm. "Careful, monsieur!"

"Shut the fuck up," the man said, "or you'll feel as little as the men beside you."

Ryan settled in for the duration, his thoughts racing.

CHAPTER TWO

Espelette, Occupied France
14 August 1941

René downed the Armagnac in one swallow and poured himself another. He held up the bottle to get Erika's attention. She declined with a smile. "Still a bit early for me, thanks."

"We're getting nowhere with all this, you know." He leaned back against the wall, his chair at a dangerous angle, and hoisted his weak leg across the corner of the table. The amber Cognac caught the light from the window. He swirled the dense alcohol round and round against the stark sunlight. "We're in this vicious circle, with never an end in sight."

The farmstead near Morlanne had become insufferably boring after only weeks, but Jeanne had chosen to remain there with her ailing cousin Brigitte. Her age was catching up with her, and she was determined to avoid further sudden and strenuous moves. The farm required little effort from the two old women. The immediate neighbor leased the fields, providing Brigitte a modest income, and only the vegetable garden and the farmyard animals required daily attention. René and Erika had seen them well-provided with cash before moving on south with Leo.

Hardly a soul moved in the sweltering streets of Espelette. They had settled for the moment in this village less than two hours away but overlooking the heart of the Coastal Defense Zone. From this location it was easy for them to slip down to the shore and then disappear again up into the countryside. Below their window spread a still life of glaring white house fronts, green vines climbing rock walls, and shutters nearly as red as the sweet peppers harvested here near the Atlantic.

While the more-heavily populated areas along the coast were regularly patrolled, the *Boches* tended to ignore the small villages in the hills above, hesitant to get off the more heavily-trafficked routes. Partisan friends in Bayonne had provided the family with forged documentation showing residency in Espelette. René's limp was a reasonable explanation for his lack of employment, and Vichy discouraged working mothers. Women belonged at the hearth, cooking and making a home for strong children. Leo had begun to attend the local school. Minor targets for sabotage and disruption this close to the Waffen-SS garrisons were everywhere, but opportunities for acts of significance rare. Several weeks had passed and they were becoming discouraged.

Erika knew the old chair would soon surrender in splinters to René's large frame. Her eyes ran over his face with its newly-acquired mustache and beard, noting the deepening lines and furrows, witness to almost three years on the run—years of worry and care for her. And for their son.

"We've accomplished so much, René, more than anyone will ever know. It's too soon to give in to frustration." She felt it, too, but knew where his thoughts were headed, and it all revolved around Leo's safety.

"All we do lately is relay information rather than put it to use ourselves. What good is helping a few cross the mountains into Spain, or cutting some phone lines, or even crippling machinery down at the docks?" René raked his fingernails down through the stubble of his beard. "But we don't dare break heads around here or they'll take it out on the civilian hostages, and we both know what these bastards are capable of."

"Does it itch?" She thought the new look suited him, but more important, his face was becoming known on the Bayonne docks, and any disguise might help. The limp, though slight, was impossible to hide, and more noticeable when he walked slowly, so he always moved at a brisk pace. And when real speed was needed he could still impress. René had lost none of his agility or nerve. She came over and placed a hand on his shoulder. "What would you have us do, love?"

"Jacques says there's plenty to do up near Nantes and Saint-Lazaire—large military and naval installations, anti-aircraft batteries, submarine pens under construction, and major supply lines to sabotage—opportunities for major disruption and damage, while we're stuck here in this backwater. Jacques can introduce us to an established *groupe-franc*, so they trust us immediately." It wasn't the first time he had broached the topic, and she knew where all this was heading. "The English are bound to return before we know it, the Americans may finally come in, and you and I'll be able to actually make a real difference again. The English value our help, and I want to make a meaningful contribution for once." Just two weeks earlier a British agent had passed through to set up an intelligence communications channel into Portugal and Gibraltar.

"Leo needs something more permanent, René. He's started making a few friends here, but his language and pride still get him into trouble with his classmates and teacher. Think about it—Colmar, Lyon, Morlanne, a few brief stops in-between, and now barely settled in here…he deserves more." She looked him in the eye, pleading without words. "He really does, you know."

René sighed. "It's true, of course." He obviously wished it weren't. "You're right, as always, my darling."

He set aside the glass to massage his knee with both hands. Erika knew the beating he had suffered in Marburg at the hands of von Kredow and his Nazi thugs still plagued him, both physically and with occasional lapses of memory. She saw René's spirits weakening daily. Just too little to do here, too few people in need of his physical help. The tedium of gathering intelligence for others to use went against his grain. He had always been hands-on and she loved him for it, but feared for his safety all the same.

The last years in France had been a trial for all of them. Her French was now strong enough to more than get by, but she occasionally encountered suspicion if not outright hatred. The French knew a German accent when they heard it, and things had gotten worse with the Occupation. Luckily, Leo was a natural genius in picking up the language—Ryan's gift?—but he still occasionally used German, especially when tired or provoked. His teacher reported a week earlier that Leo told a classmate his father was secret police. The young bully had mocked Leo, calling him a foreigner and a Jew. No one here knew his real background, but there were so many Jewish refugees trying to find new homes in France, and most were as little loved by the French as the "Hebrews" who had lived in the country for generations.

"Leo needs stability; he's becoming too much a loner." She removed a Pyramidon tablet from the metal tin and stared out the window, wondering if her child was alone in the woods again. She ground the headache remedy between two spoons and mixed the powder into the white gin. Using a cotton ball, she rubbed one side of the writing paper to roughen the surface before using the secret ink and a sharpened matchstick to record their latest intelligence. Once the invisible communication was dry, she would devote the front pages to innocuous personal gossip in regular ink and send the nonsense off to a "cousin" in Lisbon. The recipient was actually MI6, the agent from whom they'd learned the technique had assured her.

She could see René about to take the final step. "Don't hate me for suggesting this, darling, but what if you and Leo stay on the farm with my mother while I head north. She's well settled there and must be lonely since Brigitte passed, the farm is self-sufficient so food rations aren't a worry, and Leo made some neighborhood friends there. Bringing him north would be a mistake, and considerably more dangerous, especially if I must cut out in a hurry. The best alternative is for you two both to go stay with my mother for the time being."

"You expect me to constantly worry about what trouble you've gotten yourself into? René, we've been through so much together, I owe you too much to let you go north alone!" She lowered his leg off the table to stabilize the old chair before tentatively taking a seat on his lap and burying her face against his chest. "Whether you know it or not, I adore you and I'm not about to let you go it alone."

He stared out at the green hills to the west, and she knew he was once again imagining the Rhine of his boyhood and the call of the ocean, the roll of a boat underfoot, a future filled with distant lands and great adventures stolen from him by the Nazis. Nantes was on a river, Saint-Lazaire, as well.

He gently kissed the top of her head, his beard still short and prickly. "My mother does love Leo, you know. She's now his *grand-mère*, through and through. And he loves her, too—that's why he asked to stay at the farm when we decided to come here." She nodded, lost briefly in the memory of her own dead parents. "Let Leo go back to the farm, we go north, and we'll visit any chance we get. Leo gets a little stability, has his friends and animals, and we know he's safe."

"But I'd miss him so much."

"We're not abandoning him. We're giving him an actual childhood, and we'll never be more than a few days away. Mother has her telephone, you know. Don't you see? It's all for his own good." He kissed her damp cheek. "And we get on with making a difference in this damned war."

Erika heard the truth in his words, but still she cried for an hour.

❖

Leo had been alone in the woods again. A tick hung from the crook of his elbow, and he extended his arm to show it off proudly to René.

"A nice, fat one, Leo. You chose well." René grinned at Erika, then back at Leo.

"I wonder what ticks do when no one feeds them." Leo touched the parasite gently, rocking the swollen body to the side. "I forget—Maman, do we twist it to the left or the right before we yank?"

She reached for her son's elbow and plucked the bug off in one quick motion before crushing it on the porcelain sink. The little splatter of blood spread on the aged white surface, and her tears surfaced again.

"What's wrong, Maman?"

"Not a thing, Leo." She dried her eyes. "It's only that Uncle René and I have business away for a while and we think it best you stay with *Grand-mère* Jeanne at the farm for a bit." She put down the dishtowel. "And I'm already missing you."

"I get to stay with *Grand-mère* and see my animals? *Formidable, Maman, ça c'est merveilleux!*"

She saw a fleeting reminder of Ryan in Leo's broad grin.

❖

René removed the last of Leo's clothing from the rucksack and arranged his few shirts and shorts on a shelf above the cot in the corner near the woodstove. Leo chose to sleep in the kitchen rather than the bedroom so recently vacated by the passing of Cousin Brigitte. The room had not been touched and still carried the faint memory of lavender perfume. He placed Leo's underwear and socks in a separate stack. The farmhouse was small but spotless, its stone walls bearing witness to centuries of family living.

"Hurry it up, Erika. It's getting dark."

"Soon, love." At the window she folded and refolded a small undershirt. "Just a few moments longer."

Leo had run down to help his grandmother feed the chickens, and now Erika watched them coming up through the garden, Leo alternately leading Jeanne by the hand and then leaving her again to pick a flower and ask its French and German name. It was good to see him so involved with someone, so relaxed in his grandmother's company. This would be good for them both, since Jeanne had revealed that morning how lonely she'd been since her cousin's quiet death a month earlier. Exhaustion showed in her mother-in-law's gait. The first thing Jeanne had done after the funeral was to send away the cruel young farmworker who had helped out around the place. He had bullied Leo when they had first arrived at Morlanne months before, and Jeanne hadn't forgotten.

"It will work out fine, won't it, René?"

He stepped behind her and his arms encircled her waist. One of his hands crept up to cup her breast and he bent closer and kissed behind her ear. She wore her hair up just for him, longer now than back in Germany, and he loved the smooth skin of her neck and her soft scent. Erika leaned her head back in appreciation of the caress and gave him a half-hearted smile.

"Don't worry, darling." René lightly bit her neck to lighten her mood. "Just see how happy the two of them are! He'll be fine. We can show him on the map that we aren't really all that far away, and we'll come back to visit in a month or two."

"Or two?" Erika frowned.

"Maybe sooner. But we've work to do."

"I know. It's just so difficult leaving him after all he's been through."

"We're not *leaving* him—we're putting him in loving hands. And don't forget, he gives my mother a reason for living. She's lost all she loved, you know—my father, the shipping business, both homes on the Rhine. And now Brigitte's gone, too, just as they were reunited. My mother has only us now... and our little Leo there." He pushed a strand of hair from her eyes. "And she does love you, too, you know."

A new tear streaked her cheek. "I miss my parents so much, René."

"Why wouldn't you? They loved you and fought hard to spare you this horror. That bastard von Kredow stole you away from them, and then took them from you. But we both have reason to remember the good things of the past as we fight for a better future." He nodded toward the garden. "If nothing else, for Leo there."

She stared out the open kitchen window. Leo sat on a rough-hewn bench, the resident cat's forepaws on his leg as she stretched to rub her face against his cheek. The cat would be purring, and Leo was certainly giggling at the tickle of the whiskers. Jeanne sat beside him and stared down toward the cow pasture, perhaps lost in her own memories. But then she turned and smiled as she stroked Leo's head while he stroked the cat, and Erika was finally satisfied. "Let's go. Night's coming. It's time to finally make these Nazi bastards pay."

CHAPTER THREE

Paris, Occupied France
15 August 1941

Pascal found her. Pascal of the clubbed foot, Pascal of the undying devotion to the ladies of the stage who treated him like a younger brother and not the suave lover he aspired to be. Except for one of them. Except for Colette, who smiled and teased and ignored his limp and foot and left him totally captivated.

Bruised and battered, she lay just beyond his regular post at the side door of *la Chatte bottée*, unconscious beside the trash bins. It hadn't been the kind of beating that breaks bones or does permanent damage, but rather the slow, methodical beating that bruises muscles deeply and leaves the victim laid up for weeks, and prevents her from ever feeling secure again when walking the dimly-lit streets and alleys to the Montmartre night club.

That evening he had first spied a crumpled heap beside the bins as he turned off Rue Pigalle to unlock the stage door and assume his watch in the narrow passageway. He thought someone must have abandoned household rubbish that he might exchange on the black market for a few extra francs or a ration coupon. But as he neared he saw long, lovely legs, except they were now scratched and mottled purple, and as he drew off the sheet of old pasteboard he saw in horror that it was Colette, naked and abused. Despite the dim light he heard her mumble incoherently from swollen and bloody lips, so he knew she still lived.

Pascal carried her into the night club, shocked that anyone could have been so cruel and vicious to this sweet girl. He maneuvered around the tightly-spaced tables toward the curtains separating the dance floor and the foyer. Despite her condition and his better thoughts, he felt himself respond to her nakedness, his hand on one of those lovely breasts he had admired on stage for so long, and he hated himself for thinking such thoughts at that moment. He consoled himself with another thought: at least she lives, and I'm rescuing her, and she'll be grateful when she awakens, knowing I really do care about her.

He clumsily switched on the lights, reaching the staircase to what once was a projection room years before when the night club was a failing movie theater. Taking care not to hit the girl's head on the wall of the narrow passage, he reached the office of the owner Mademoiselle Lesney. He knew she wasn't in yet, but the phone in her office would bring her running. Mademoiselle Lesney loved all the girls who worked for her. She would know what to do.

The door was unlocked as always, and Pascal pushed down the handle with his elbow and clicked on the overhead light. He carried the unconscious girl to the small couch in the corner beside the writing desk where his boss kept her neatly-stacked paperwork. He set Colette down as gently as he could, crossing her legs for modesty's sake, and reluctantly covered her bruised body with the owner's shawl.

He dialed the number, and his boss answered immediately to say she was on her way.

In the short time before the arrival of his boss he adjusted Colette's head on the cushion and looked again beneath the shawl at her perfect body made so dirty and ugly by the beating. And that was when he saw it. The one thing that would never heal completely and disappear—a permanent mark on her young flesh. Artfully etched with a blade into the skin of her belly, clearly legible in the glare of the office light, was a single word, a name: SERGE.

❖

"My God, what utter depravity!" Marita stared dumbfounded at the young dancer's abdomen as the doctor bathed the wound and applied iodine. Out of respect he had placed towels over her lap and breasts once those areas had been cleaned and checked for injuries. Now he carefully examined the knife wound.

"Whoever did this used a very sharp blade, so scarring should be minimal." The girl was now conscious but sedated, and the doctor chose his words carefully, assuming she was listening. He had placed a wet cloth over her swollen eyes and given her homeopathic Arnica Montana to hold down the bruising. "She'll dance again, but you may need a bit of costume to cover the blemishes." The physician looked up at Marita over the rim of his glasses and shook his head in disgust. "Isn't our world ugly enough without this?"

Marita had sent young Pascal away with sincere thanks for his quick thinking and some francs offered in gratitude. She had never had a problem with any of her girls before but now she had a frightening thought to consider: what monster was threatening their livelihood. Was this simply a hot-tempered, jilted lover? A madman? Or, equally possible, was the attack related to the secret work some of the girls were doing at her request, gathering the names and designations of the military units represented by the officers frequenting the club? Marita routinely passed this information on to Argent.

She shook aside those thoughts to deal with immediate concerns as the doctor bandaged the worst of the wounds. "So, where do we go from here? Will she need further treatment?"

"This young lady's going to be mighty sore for a few weeks, but I find no evidence of broken bones or internal injuries. And mademoiselle, there's no evidence of rape. Whoever did this to her knew his stuff. He didn't want to do permanent damage—just send a message." The doctor handed Marita two small envelopes of medication and began to pack away his equipment. "Keep her warm—get her some clothing as soon as possible—and have her rest. Let me know if she starts to vomit or has other signs of distress beyond the obvious. Can you keep her here for twenty-four hours?"

"Of course. I'll stay with her personally, but we'll let her mother know." Marita pursed her lips, recalling Colette's situation. "She's the only breadwinner—her father's in a German camp."

"No charge for my services. Just keep her comfortable."

"Thank you so much, Doctor. And these envelopes?"

"The pill's a pain-killer, the powder a sedative. Use as directed on the envelopes and I'll check in on her tomorrow." He reached back into his black bag. "And here's an ointment for the..." he hesitated, not sure what word to use for the atrocity etched in that beautiful skin, "...for the wound, and have her keep it covered to prevent infection." He shook Marita's hand. "And Mademoiselle Lesney...you may wish to hire a couple of bodyguards to look after your girls. Whoever this 'Serge' is, he may not be finished here."

He let himself out of the office, still shaking his head over the human condition as Marita applied another cool compress to Colette's eyes and forehead.

❖

The line of applicants trailed out the lobby and into the street, and Marita interviewed each one personally. The bouncer Florian, her personal bodyguard, kept to her side, his focus constantly shifting from Marita to each candidate. Florian had already completed the initial sorting in the lobby, sending off those totally disqualified at first sight. Most applicants were unsuited to the task—too frail from hunger and deprivation, too old or weak but longing for this employment, others wounded in the war and unfit for the task. The marginal and the obviously fit waited in line to climb the stairs and meet with the owner.

Marita sat on the Louis XVI chair with the tapestry print and took notes on each applicant. She had placed a small ad in the newspaper, printed among listings announcing the latest rationed food items and schedules of coupon availability, other employment want-ads, and plaintive pleas for information on persons still missing since the great exodus from the city the year before. The Gauloises she had smoked for years were getting more difficult to obtain, even on the black market, so she tapped incessantly with a lacquered fingernail tip on the smooth desk surface to still the nicotine hunger. She missed the comfort of her sister, her parents.

The newest candidate was mid-thirties, of average height but with huge arms and narrow waist. She found him physically suited for the bodyguard post. "So," she gave a friendly smile, "just why do you want this job?"

"I need the money—simple as that."

"Can you fight, if need be?"

"Been a fighter all my life, miss, truth be told. But most recently—before the war, that is—did some prize-fighting, middle-weight." He named a working-class neighborhood in the north of the city.

"Can you keep your hands off the dancers?"

"Got a wife and four kids to feed and love, mademoiselle. Last thing I need right now is for the missus to kick me out, trust me."

Marita turned to Florian, who was eyeing each candidate in turn with a look of pure scorn, just to test the men's reactions. This one seemed immune to his glare. "What do you think, a possibility?"

Florian nodded in agreement.

"Your name and a way to reach you."

"Jérôme Lafleur. 38 Rue du Gaspardin. Got no telephone, but the shoe repair downstairs has one we can use anytime. They practically make their business from us resoling the kids' shoes."

Marita nodded with a smile and rose to shake his hand. "We'll be in touch, monsieur. Thank you for coming."

A full week had passed since Colette had been brutalized, and the entire club was on tenterhooks. The girls had taken to meeting elsewhere and coming to *la Chatte bottée* in larger groups. Most evenings Marita haunted the projection window overlooking the club, her eyes moving from guest to guest, wondering if one of them had been responsible for the terrible attack. All the men on staff were now armed with knives or blackjacks, a few with pistols. Illegal, but a wise precaution they'd been happy to adopt.

Colette was now under the care of her mother and recovering well enough, but she wouldn't soon dance again or entertain the German officers in her current condition. To help mother and daughter make ends meet, Marita was sending money and extra ration coupons supplied by Argent. And because of everyone's concern, she had agreed to the physician's advice to hire two new bodyguards, one to watch the alleyway and another to offer the girls protection on their way home after closing.

The next candidate appearing at the door was a barrel-shaped man with a shaved head and brushy salt-and-pepper mustache. His arms seemed unnaturally long for his body, his eyes intelligent and his smile friendly though cynical. And he appeared to be all muscle.

"Bonjour mademoiselle," he nodded to Marita and then acknowledged Florian's glare, "and to you, monsieur."

The teeth beneath the mustache were long and very yellow, testimony to years of smoking with little attention to brushing. Uninvited he took a seat on the couch and crossed his legs. She noted immediately the man wore clothing of very high quality, surprising for a prospective bodyguard in the Occupation economy. His boots appeared new, the soles of genuine leather and barely marked.

"Monsieur, I would ask you to *stand* should you wish to continue this interview." Marita was in no mood for disrespect.

"Of course, Mademoiselle Lesney." He rose with a smile and straightened the crease of his trousers. "But will it bother you if I smoke?" Without waiting, he drew a cigar from his vest pocket and lit up, releasing an acrid cloud into the close chamber. "More comfortable now, miss?" The amber teeth appeared again beneath the brush on his lip.

"Monsieur, I regret any inconvenience you encountered in coming here this afternoon, but you don't appear to meet our criteria." Marita turned back to her desk in dismissal. "Thank you for your troubles."

"No trouble at all, miss. Glad to pop in. Although I thought you might be gracious enough to at least note my name." His lower lip protruded in a ludicrous pout, a feigned disappointment.

She looked up from the desk. "All right then, what *is* your name, monsieur?"

"Why, thank you for asking—I go by Serge."

Marita's eyes sprung wide and she involuntarily drew back in the chair. Florian took an aggressive step forward with fists clenched.

"Serge Bergieux, but all my friends call me simply 'Serge.' As future business partners, I'm sure we're to be friends."

Marita sat silent for several moments, suppressing the fury which threatened to overwhelm her. "Did you assault one of my girls last week, Monsieur Bergieux?"

"Now why would I do that, Mademoiselle Lesney? I have more profitable uses for my time and energy than assaulting young women, and am insulted you should ask." A flash of yellow teeth, then another drag on the cigar.

"Because the man who did that atrocity signed his work—with your name."

"Serge?"

"Serge."

"A common enough name here in Paris, you realize. But very few bearing it have my special talents—talents certainly of future value to you."

"And what could possibly suggest we might become business partners?" She placed a hand on Florian's arm, her glance warning him to keep his anger in check. His hate-filled glare never left the stocky man.

"Well, obviously times are difficult for you, what with running a profitable establishment such as this. Alcohol is hard to come by, and word on the street is your dancers are running scared. That makes for a less inviting stage performance, don't you agree? You suggest that one poor child may have been assaulted, so can you really blame the girls for having doubts about working here? And soon your clientele may decide to find a club where things are a bit more, shall we say, settled?"

She got to her feet. "Go on."

"I'm merely saying that this world of ours gets rougher by the day—so much so that you're hiring new bodyguards. Suppose you took on a partner instead, a man well connected, someone like me? I could personally oversee the criminal elements hereabouts and make sure your dancers and your operation continue unmolested by those dangerous types. Wouldn't that be worth something to you?"

"I can take care of things on my own. I already have good people."

"With all respect to present company—obviously not, Miss Lesney. What if the next problem with one of your people, one of those lovely young ladies, is something considerably worse, say a mutilation, a missing limb, a death, perhaps? What if the monster capable of such a thing went after your friends, or their spouses and children? Where might all this end? Would you really want that on your conscious, when I am here now to offer you my services?"

Marita sat down again. Her voice remained steady but she shook inside. "What exactly do you want?"

"Me? Not much at all. I simply offer my help, and in return I get...say...fifty per cent of the club's profits?"

The enormity of the situation made her hold her tongue. She raced through the dangers and possibilities. Whom could she call on to help? Her own past misjudgment and fear had already cost the lives of her family. Her German lover might be able to help, but for now she had to buy time.

"I don't make enough to survive on half the profits. I'm barely scraping by now."

She knew Florian was itching to take out this criminal. She caught his eye and gave a slight shake of the head. Better to wait.

"You'll find me a fair man, Mademoiselle Lesney. So let me demonstrate my reasonable nature. I shall accept thirty per cent out of the goodness of my heart, and I guarantee that none of your people run any further risk. Naturally, as your new partner, I will review your books weekly. And to help compensate for my lesser cut, I will also help with your orders for wine and spirits. You'll continue to place the orders, while I oversee deliveries."

Serge stepped over to the desk, his arm intentionally brushing Marita's breast in passing. He extinguished the cigar in her crystal ashtray, then stopped short directly at her side and spoke softly into her ear. "And should the deliveries occasionally come up short by a few cases, I'll make certain that the purveyors take full responsibility so it won't impact our profits."

Marita stepped back to give herself distance. "I need time to think all this through, monsieur. I'm not sure I can run this club and still feed myself on that percentage."

"Take all the time you want, mademoiselle. It's all the same to me. But I can only guarantee the safety of those young girls of yours—or even that crippled boy who haunts the alleyway—once I've become your partner in this charming establishment, clear?"

"Very."

"Then I'll wish you good night. Here's my card. Call when you've made your decision." He gave Florian a jaundiced smile, shutting the door behind him as he left the room.

She sat stunned as she heard the man proclaim loudly from the top of the staircase to the waiting men below: "The rest of you, clear on out. The position's taken, there's nothing here for you."

"Want me to go after him, miss? I can easily take that bastard." Florian's voice dripped menace as he pulled a pistol from his pocket and checked the cartridges.

"No!...no, thank you, it's all right. We'll handle this."

She looked at the calling card in her hand, expensively-engraved with only a name and phone number:

Serge Bergieux, Facilitateur de Commerce.

❖

The club was closed for the night. Florian had been last to leave, his reluctance apparent, but she assured him she was fine and they would work this out. She locked the front doors behind him and double-checked the rear door. A few small lamps still burned on the club dance floor but the stage was dark.

Argent wasn't expected until the following evening, but she needed him now. Marita sat at her desk and lifted the receiver. The number she had memorized was for emergencies only, but when it came to her people she wouldn't take chances. This Serge had proven he meant business. She dialed, and a woman answered, the voice frail and quaking like a grandmother's.

Marita gave her *nom de guerre* followed by his. "Céleste for Argent." He would understand and come as quickly as he could. The woman said only *"confirmé"* and replaced the receiver.

Marita opened the desk drawer to remove the last of her Gauloises and light up, holding the smoke in her lungs as she waited for the nicotine to work its magic. She went to the office door and locked it, something rarely done before. Five minutes later, as she threw the crumpled cigarette pack in the waste bin after double-checking its contents, her phone jangled.

The sound startled her and she almost tipped over the glass of Cognac. Lost in thought, deep in self-recrimination, she had been reliving again the loss of her family.

CHAPTER FOUR

Gascony, Occupied France
16 August 1941

Ryan's fingers surveyed the base of his skull. He winced as he propped himself up on the narrow bed, the soles of his feet raw, his head aching. The scab on his neck broke loose and he sensed fresh, sticky blood. He felt like hell warmed over. Yet in spite of all physical discomfort he was newly energized, having escaped Horst's grasp once again. *Good God, first Marburg back in '34, then Kehl, and now this rabbit out of the hat!*

And most important, he now knew that Erika and René were somewhere close in southwestern France and for the moment safe from Horst's reach. He himself might now do what von Kredow obviously could not accomplish without him—find his friends. The letters and visas to get them out of France had been lost in Horst's trap, but new ones were only a telegram or phone call away.

A breeze tugged at the frayed curtain, revealing glimpses of rolling pasture and a woodland patch below. In the far distance ocean sketched an azure ribbon along the horizon. The Atlantic. It had to be the Occupied Zone, he presumed somewhere near Bayonne. Horst had mentioned Biarritz, the resort town on the Bay of Biscay.

The heavy door creaked and the petite woman whose rifle had taken out the Gestapo officer glared down at him.

"You hit me, mademoiselle."

"True." No trace of a smile in response to his. "Twice, actually. You wouldn't go down."

"A first for me, I assure you."

Her glacial features betrayed no sign of a thaw. His head throbbed and the soles of his feet burned. His fingers left a pale smear of blood as he wiped them on the sheet, and still he smiled. He felt so lucky to be free of the Gestapo.

"So why first save me from the Germans and then knock me out?"

He clearly remembered the removal of handcuffs, the short trip beside corpses with straw scratching his face and an obnoxious itch beneath his clothing. After they picked up a sentry they made a rumbling stop under dense tree cover, and he followed orders to get down onto the dirt road, every awkward step agonizing, only to have this lovely young woman come up behind him and club him with the butt of her rifle. Twice, apparently.

"*Silence!* I'll do it again if you don't shut up. You're disturbing your roommate." Ryan turned with some difficulty, his neck as sore as his feet. A man lay on the floor, a blanket covering his rough straw mattress. Ryan saw a head of curly black hair but couldn't make out his face. The man appeared to sleep, certainly not concerned with them.

"You really found me a threat? I'm surprised you didn't shoot me for good measure."

"It did cross my mind."

"Then why the rescue?"

"We expect to find *le Masque*, we end up with a would-be Errol Flynn. No papers, no shoes, just bloody feet and a smart mouth." She checked his chamber pot before sliding it back beneath the bed.

"The Mask"—von Kredow, of course.

"My apologies for any inconvenience." Ryan attempted his smile again.

"A favorite of theirs, by the way." She pointed to his exposed feet. "The wooden bar, the chairs, the switch." She drew open the curtain and scanned the courtyard below.

"Sawhorses, actually, but otherwise—"

"Sawhorses, chairs, would one have been better than the other?"

"Well, most likely not." He raised one foot to take a closer look at the damage.

"Free advice for you, *Monsieur l'Américain*. It's never the specifics that count, never the details—you might as well learn that—all that really matters is the ultimate goal. In this world we now live in, the end really does justify any means."

"Sorry to speak specifically again, but my goal is to get out of this place, and now." He smiled past the pounding in his temples. "I work for the American State Department. They'll be searching for me."

"*Je m'en fous.*" She showed that indifference by squatting down beside the other man's straw mattress, resting a hand on the man's brow to check for a fever, then adjusting his pillow. She was obviously ignoring the American.

Ryan saw no response to her ministrations. *Perhaps the man's unconscious rather than asleep?* "Miss, please just give me shoes and a phone and I'll be out of your hair." He swung his feet to the wooden planks, only to quickly lift them again. They hurt like hell.

"What brings you to this corner of France, anyway? Shouldn't you be cowering across the Atlantic, debating American neutrality in the European war?"

"I've friends here, old friends who desperately need my help. I plan to find them before the Germans can kill them.

She rubbed her temples and sighed. "You're all alike, you know...you men." Bitterness suffused her tone. "So go ahead—leave now, as far as I'm concerned." Her glance could have melted ice. "You're just one more cocky fool to bother with, nothing to me but unwanted trouble. Go on, get out of here—your 'State Department' is welcome to you!"

Her French carried a southern flair, perhaps a hint of the Basque tongue. Despite the bitter words, the fire in her eyes was appealing, and he liked the upturned nose. She was obviously offended by anyone gauche enough to be born American. The woman was probably only in her twenties and might not find Ryan interesting, but his wit and charm had won over much more difficult subjects. His spirits remained high despite his painful head, neck and feet. After escaping certain death, Ryan wasn't ready to let this woman's disdain kill his enthusiasm for life. Von Kredow needed Ryan as bait, and now the bait was off the hook and had likely learned enough in the process to track Erika and René down first. But until he had recovered enough to walk on his own he might as well make the best of things. The company of this pretty woman seemed a perfect distraction. Besides, her skill with a rifle meant he preferred having her on his side.

"So why *did* you hit me? And twice, yet?"

Her ponytail bounced with the toss of her head. "You're obviously not the brightest of Americans. Do you really think we'd show you how to find this place?"

"Well in the future, please consider using a cloth hood." He touched his sore neck and forced a grin. "It's far less painful to your captives."

She brought in a tray from the hall and set it on the table at the foot of his bed. Ryan saw a wine bottle with a heavy drinking glass, a chunk of cheese, and a crust of brown bread. Everything remained just beyond his reach. He'd have to work for it.

"Since you're going nowhere until those feet heal, here are my rules: do exactly as I say or I'll drop you again. And next time—rest assured—I'll be hitting harder." She raised the iron latch and swung open the door.

"Bien sûr, mademoiselle. I'll count on that."

The door scraped shut.

He knew she had a smile in her. He just had to work at finding the key.

❖

Devon heard the voices. At first they came from very far, but then he felt a gentle touch on his forehead and he forced himself to focus on the individual words, and he became aware that one speaker was close enough for him to reach out and touch. A woman—now he was sure—a young woman, and at first he thought Trish was waking him from a very long and disturbing dream.

But then he knew it was someone else, the voice all wrong and the French—Trish spoke no French—and he could tell the woman wanted nothing to do with the man speaking with her. *A Yank, and he wants out of here.* Good French, Parisian French, none of the Breton accent which colored Devon's own. The American likes this young woman, but tries too hard to be clever. *We're brothers under the skin, he and I,* thought Devon, *I would have tried the same banter, the same double entendre. Before Trish, that is, only before Trish.*

And Devon surrendered again to the lethargy of dying. He was aware of the tears pooling at his eyes, tears for Trish and for what might have been, but he no longer felt pain. He thought back over the last week and wondered at the strange turn of events that brought him to this sorry end. The road to this stinking *paillasse* on the rough-hewn flooring had been long and challenging.

His mind drifted to that painful trek to the first station on the escape itinerary. In London he had memorized the underground route from town to town, ever southward across Occupied France. The plan had seemed so simple. A guide would be there to welcome him, to take the wireless off his hands and bring him to the drop-off point, and provide current ration coupons and any newly-forged identification needed.

Instead, he had the identification papers forged in London, and the would-be guide had died a brutal death in the dark field. And the body of that crazed pig farmer would slowly waste away in the shallow grave Devon had carved out near the road. In his troubled mind he smelled the rich, fresh loam once again. Such a colossal waste of lives over mistaken identity and stolen swine.

Devon had managed only a few kilometers by dawn. Traffic on the back road was light—a heavily-laden wagon, a local farmwife, her basket filled with beets, her dress hitched up to make pedaling easier, and a postal worker on a bicycle going about his rural deliveries. His instructions had been clear. Don't approach anyone unless absolutely necessary, just proceed to your first station. Despite the ache in his chest Devon had forged on. What choice had he? He stumbled for cover in the wayside brush when anyone approached. It felt as if a sharp stone lay buried beneath his ribs.

Some farmers' fields appeared badly neglected—he'd learned that laborers were at a premium—but other crops were reaching maturity, and Devon found an old plum tree with low-hanging fruit. He hadn't had a bite since boarding the airplane—his nervous stomach had prevented keeping anything down—so knew he should eat to keep up his strength. *Hell*, he thought, *if they give me gas it can't be worse than this bloody chest of mine.* He soon discovered he'd been wrong.

His energies had flagged as the sun rose higher and the heat began to drain his reserves. Abdominal cramps only amplified the pain in his chest. By noon he leaned against the trunk of a tree to contemplate a muddy pool of field run-off. *Could I possibly make things worse by quenching this hellish thirst?*

Abruptly a man appeared above him, sweat streaks on his brow and a filthy cap in his hands.

"You need help, monsieur." It was a simple statement of fact.

Devon raised his head with difficulty. "Wouldn't say no, monsieur."

The peasant replaced his cap and helped Devon stand upright, wrapping the weakened man's arm around his shoulder. They stumbled up to a cart where a mule stretched its neck to the grass lining the edge of the roadway. The man immediately handed the Englishman a bottle of water. He drank greedily.

Devon couldn't help wrinkling his nose at the ripe odor, first believing it came from his savior. However, the contents of the cart explained all—a full load of manure ready for spreading on the fields.

"You'll prefer to sit up top by me." The man helped Devon step up to the bench and then took the reins. Devon cast a wary eye at the stinking cargo. "But we'll need a name, monsieur."

"Je m'appelle..." he hesitated, the name of the alias on his forged papers refusing to come back to him in his troubled state.

"Non, non, monsieur, your personal name is unimportant. Few strangers end up on this road without a purpose, and I'm sure yours is very important. You obviously need medical attention, but all I need to know from you is the name of your destination."

"The nearest village, perhaps?" Devon was wary of divulging any unnecessary information.

The peasant smiled. "Here's how I suggest we do this, monsieur. I say a name, and you only respond if it doesn't work for you."

Devon nodded.

"*Alors*, I propose a fine local name—'Charrat.'"

Devon released his breath. "No need for the village, then, monsieur. Let's go find Madame Charrat. And quickly, please."

"Indeed, monsieur, as quickly as Louise here can pull us there."

He clicked his tongue and the mule perked up its ears, reluctantly abandoning the fresh grass. The animal broke wind as it took up the load while Devon bent over double, struggling to hold back his own. With such a rich blend of earthy odors surrounding the cart the driver would hardly have noticed. *Those damn plums,* thought Devon.

CHAPTER FIVE

Vichy, Vichy France
18 August 1941

That week in Vichy had felt like a demotion after working the German Affairs desk in Washington. With all that was happening in Europe, State had hummed as coded cables and overworked couriers shot back and forth across the Atlantic, exchanging latest word on the Reich's territorial expansion and delivering analyses and recommendations back to the field. The war was going well for Hitler, and the discussions and argument on how to get America directly involved in stopping the aggression made for exciting days. Ed had rarely found a moment to relax, and often didn't make it home until well after nine. The late nights hadn't pleased Grace either, with two young boys to look after and her social life gone to hell.

But there in Vichy, boredom reigned alongside *Maréchal* Pétain, and the Foreign Service embassy personnel was fed up with the spa town's mindless *Pétainistes* who drained the place of any semblance of liveliness. The reactionary leaders of the new and prudish French State blamed France's fall on the hedonistic behavior of her people, and they were intent on eliminating the loose morals and liberal education exemplified by Paris which had made that failure possible. Laws now prohibited public dances until the war's end, called for all women to quit the working sector and return home to rear children, and those same children sang hymns of praise to the aging leader as if he were the new king or some god.

In retrospect, troubled Paris seemed a delight despite Nazi occupation. Ed was happy to see his week of meetings nearing completion. It was time to return to the former capital to oversee the incoming arrivals for the exchange program. Even the likelihood of dealing with Kohl was better than wading through this morass of sour, petty bickering and legal repression.

He hadn't overcome his astonishment that Mr. Goldblum, the German-American chemical industrialist who traveled with them from Washington to Paris for the initial exchange, had come of his own accord. Before the three ever left the capital, Ryan had described in horrifying detail the proposal for mass eradication of Jews clearly laid out in the stolen protocol. Goldblum had written it off as anti-German propaganda and hysteria crafted by anti-Nazi factions to rile up the Americans to go to war. "It doesn't matter one bit that I'm a Jew—I am first and foremost a German, and my *Vaterland* needs my services."

After five days and no word from his brother, Ed was becoming perturbed but was not surprised. *Up to his old tricks, most likely.* Ryan would have found some excuse to spend time with his friends before sending them out of country. The health and sanitary conditions in the Gurs camp must not have been as bad as anticipated. And it was typical Ryan behavior not to keep in close touch with his "handler," despite the assurances he had given Bruce and Donovan. *Oh well,* thought Edward, *at least he gets the job done.* Ed figured to just head back to Paris, start getting his own job underway, and wait for his brother to make contact. After all, not much could go wrong for a neutral American in this boring new "French State."

But what awaited him two days before at the Vichy embassy came as a surprise—the mail from Paris brought an expensively engraved note in an envelope bearing the initials "RvH."

My dear Mr. Lemmon –

While I have yet to have the pleasure of making your acquaintance, I did share some lovely evenings with your younger brother Ryan Lemmon back when Berlin was a more cultured and carefree place. I well recall his stories of your shared childhood in the American Midwest.

A review of Vichy embassy personnel turned up your name, a chance find I simply cannot ignore. Might I have the opportunity to learn more about your current interests in France, and catch up on the doings of dear Ryan?

A bite to eat shared in a quiet Parisian locale would be a pleasure, perhaps this coming Monday around two? I shall await your arrival at Chez Claude, a little café just moments from Notre Dame on Île St. Louis. I'm sure you will find the place as charming as it is discreet.

Should you not be able to make it, please pay it no mind. I will contact you again.

You may rest assured I remain

your Rolf von Haldheim

A slip of paper fell from the folded note. Ed stooped to retrieve from the floor what proved to be simply a Parisian phone number penned in an elegant ink script.

The following morning Edward caught the 8:15 for Paris. Before signing out at the embassy a secretary handed him a postcard which had just arrived with a message from Ryan: "All well now. Delayed getting in by a day. Southern France lovely in the heat. R." Ed was furious. Just like Ryan, no explanation, even coded, just more of the same old laissez-faire attitude toward his assignments. *My God, if the man weren't such a brain, I swear he'd lost all his marbles.*

During the nearly five-hour train ride back to Paris he pondered the note from von Haldheim. He vaguely remembered Ryan's talk of the family and the prodigal son who tried to warn his parents of impending trouble. Why would the man want to make contact and what could he possibly offer that might be of use to Ed's assignment. This covert business, espionage and subterfuge, wasn't his cup of tea. Give him straight-forward diplomacy any day, and leave the deception to his younger brother. Ed wanted stability, missed Grace, and hated having the boys grow up without his being a short train ride from Falls Church. But he would keep the afternoon's lunchtime rendezvous, caution be damned, just to show Ryan that he had it in him to step outside the bounds. At least this one time.

CHAPTER SIX

Gascony, Occupied France
18 August 1941

Ryan saw only a wash of pale moonlight, now motionless, now shifting across the plank flooring. Something—some repetitive sound— had startled him from uneasy dreams. His eyes searched for movement but found only a fluttering curtain in the gentle nighttime breeze.

Another day had merged into night and Ryan had slept through it all soundly. He wondered whether the girl might be putting something in his water, a bromide perhaps. Once, when there was still light at the window, he had awakened to loud voices coming from below. Two men in an argument, probably the older farmer he had seen drive off with the hay wagon and one of the younger partisans. He couldn't make out what was upsetting them, but it had sounded as if they came close to blows. Then the voice of the girl, intense and in control. Then quiet again, and he had slept on. A bit later he awoke briefly to find her in the darkened room, ministering to the ailing man on the floor. She had left without a word to him, a fresh tray of food and a bottle of red wine at the foot of his bed.

But now fully awake, he heard something distinctive and very disturbing. The stranger on the straw mattress was struggling to rise, his strained voice like some animal crying from the depths of an abandoned well.

"*Ça va, monsieur?* Ryan regretted the foolish question the moment he spoke. There was no chance the man was doing all right. Now a gurgling rattle emerged from deep in his lungs and Ryan feared the stranger might drown in his own phlegm.

"For God's sake, a little help here, mate!" The man spoke British English, his words almost suffocated by the congestion. Ryan swung his feet to the floor, testing if his own pain would be bearable. It would have to do. He dropped to his knees beside the makeshift bed, slipping an arm beneath the ailing man's back to help him upright, and then braced the stranger against the wall. He lit the kerosene wick of the lantern on the shelf above the mattress, and a sickly yellowish glow reached into all but the deepest shadows. Next he fashioned a back support with the man's filthy pillow and the support of an overturned wooden chair.

"Water...please." The request came in quick troubled breaths. Ryan poured from the chipped carafe and tore cloth from his own bed sheet to serve as a makeshift handkerchief. He encouraged the suffering man to cough and spit while Ryan pounded on his back.

"Better?" Ryan hit him again and bent closer to catch the man's response.

"Easy, old chap, don't finish me off quite yet." The fit of coughing finally came to a spasmodic halt, but his shoulders still heaved. Ryan could see now that the stranger was perhaps ten years his junior. A recent slash to his forehead had scabbed over, leaving only a bruised knob. The man wore a sleeveless undershirt and shorts, and Ryan noted his badly distended belly below the narrow ribcage. The smell of a sick old man, of loose bowels and stale urine.

"More water?"

"Enough for now, but—" He cleared his throat with obvious difficulty and spat thick, bloody mucous into the cloth. "Listen, time is short for me, mate, so pay close attention."

"Listening."

"Yank, right?"

"American, Department of State. Ryan Lemmon's the name."

"We're alone now, just the two of us?"

"For the moment. But it's safe here—they're French partisans."

The man lifted his hand with difficulty and offered it to Ryan. "Devon Whitaker, Secret Service. Remember that…should you make it out of here."

"Consider it done." Ryan repeated the name: "Whitaker."

"And Lemmon, listen up, important matters now…" The lungs of a croupy infant, each word a struggle. "Not all partisans…dependable." Ryan thought of a dog's panting. "Stay alert… people gone missing." The Englishman doubled over and moaned, remaining motionless for an endless minute before straightening his back once again. "What brings you here?"

"Pure luck. These folks saved me from the Gestapo."

The man remained quiet for so long Ryan feared he had passed out or something worse. He sat with his back to the wall beside the head of the mattress and listened closely to the English spy's ragged breathing. And then with renewed energy the man hacked brutally before offering a bittersweet smile. "I'm a goner, Yank, dead by morning." The words rushed forth now as if he feared forgetting something should he stop for breath. "My time's up, and frankly I welcome an end to this bloody crap." He suppressed a shudder by wrapping his arms around his ribcage. "Took a brutal hit a few days ago, something seriously wrong inside and I'm shutting down fast."

Ryan leapt to his feet, ignoring his own pain. "I'll call the girl or the farmer; they'll send for a doctor!"

"Doctor was here days ago. Hopeless he said. Chest topped off with blood, and inner organs damaged beyond repair. All hopeless, mate, so let it go." He loosed a frightening cough and braced himself against the overturned chair. "I know I have."

"What about surgery? Surely there's a hospital nearby?"

"Gestapo watches them all."

"Then what *can* I do?" Ryan squatted down to better catch his fading words.

"Just this…" Devon waved away the offer of more water. "…just a favor, old fellow…look up Patricia Wales, 54 Broadway…London." His shaky voice a rattling whisper.

"You'll see the business sign—Minimax Fire Extinguisher Company."

Ryan bent closer still. "This Patricia Wales…what do I tell her?"

"Tell her I truly loved her." His eyes lost focus in the lantern light. "No, that's wrong—that I do and always will…and I'm sorry…for all this." Devon wrapped himself in his arms to stop the shaking that rattled his frail frame, a chill unsuited to the warm summer night. He lurched over on his side.

Ryan barely made out the man's final words, but etched them in his mind.

Devon's head lay motionless on the scarred wooden floor.

❖

The Englishman was dead, but Ryan still checked for a pulse. He rolled the body back onto the mattress and covered it with the worn blanket. The total silence was strange after all the coughing and gasping for breath. He sat on the floor beside the body and recalled the spy's last words, memorizing the details.

Ryan checked the bare soles of his feet. Some scabs were intact, others oozing, but overall he knew he could walk. Shoes would be a plus. He lowered the wick of the lantern, then stepped to the window and surveyed the grounds below. Across a graveled courtyard flickered a single light, a candle perhaps, glowing from the window of an old stone structure. Nearby a dog barked, then all went still again. Nothing moved. A rooster crowed briefly and cut himself short, another early riser. Ryan guessed three a.m., the yellow moon now low on the horizon. He instinctively looked to his wrist for the watch that had disappeared into the care of the Gestapo. At least the black onyx ring was still on his finger. He watched a lone silhouette move in and out of the candlelight across the way, working on something at this odd hour.

A tall wardrobe against the wall faced the window. His suit jacket and trousers hung alongside some faded and patched worker's garb. More important for his needs—the floor of the cabinet held shoes stuffed with heavy woolen socks. Ryan grabbed the bundle and laid it out on the bed in the moonlight. He would keep his own shirt, dirty as it was, but abandon the suit he had worn to rescue his friends in Gurs. He tried on the blue trousers, the fit satisfactory, the smell less so. Devon's worker's jacket would do just fine.

Ryan sat on the edge of the bed and slipped on the handwoven socks. He then tentatively tried one of the shoes, taking care with his sensitive foot in the process. The heavy-leather footwear was fully adequate if a fraction large for him. *Beats being a size too small,* he thought. His feet now protected from the rough wooden flooring, Ryan searched the shelves of the armoire to find the one item still missing—a felt beret. Under the moon it was difficult to judge, but Ryan guessed the well-worn cap would be red in daylight.

The candle no longer burned in the window below.

From the jacket pocket he pulled a bundle of documents, identification papers held by a tired rubber band. Holding the *carte d'identité* to the moonlight he saw Devon's unsmiling photo affixed to the card with two rusting staples, and beside it name, date, place of birth, and occupation: Hervé Delacourt, *23 novembre 1916 à Rennes*, skilled mechanic. The faux identification was well crafted, the corners bent, the surface stained—coffee?—and the printing, stamps and signatures a bit worn. He found a letter of proposed employment at an aircraft parts factory near Bayonne and a special pass issued by the German occupation authority for a non-resident to enter the so-called Coastal Defense Zone. A statement from a French hospital in the north noted that M. Delacourt had recently undergone treatment for a debilitating illness. Ryan noted that the buttons on the clothing were sewn the European way with a parallel stitch. The jacket also hid a wad of badly worn franc notes and ration coupons issued in Delacourt's name, a map of western France worn through at the folds with brownish stains, and a half-smoked pack of Gitanes. A series of indecipherable letters and numbers had been scrawled in pencil along the margin of the map.

Ryan returned to the agent's body and drew back the blanket to expose the man's face, now at peace in the dim yellow light of the kerosene lantern. He examined the features carefully: dark hair, aquiline nose, a strong chin. But for the narrow mustache and the curl to the hair Ryan could pass for Devon Whitaker, or at least his brother. Or more accurately, for Hervé Delacourt. A mustache would grow quickly; a better hat would disguise the lack of curly hair.

He scanned the room one last time before rolling his own clothes into a tight bundle to leave no trace of his visit. Devon Whitaker was once again a quiet mound beneath the blanket on his paillasse, just as Ryan had first seen him days before. But Ryan would not forget his promise to the English spy.

The house appeared to be vacant, and the creaking staircase to the courtyard unlit. Once out in the moonlight he edged cautiously alongside the high rock wall, aware that the crunch of footsteps on the graveled surface would shatter the stillness of the pre-dawn hour. The last thing he wanted was for any dog to announce him to a sleeping world. At the stone barn he peered through the mullioned window where he'd glimpsed a burning candle, pressing his face to a pane smudged with years of neglect. He saw no movement, only black.

"Anything of interest in there, *monsieur*?"

A chill ran the length of his spine, but he didn't budge. The snout of a shotgun nudged the base of his back.

"No, *mademoiselle*. It's nothing without you."

"Inside, and no sudden moves."

He pushed open the heavy wooden door as hinges squealed in protest and a neighbor's dog barked somewhere beyond the stone wall. The room smelled of old damp stone and rotting hay and somewhere nearby was certainly a chicken coop.

"What are you doing here?" Her tone held no warmth.

"The Englishman's dead. I didn't know what else to do, and saw a candle down here earlier so decided to check it out."

"No surprise the poor man's dead—he was pretty far along when he got here." She lowered the double barrels slightly. "Now turn around and face me."

"With pleasure, *mademoiselle*." Only a faint hint of moonlight entered the space.

"Back up to the table and light that candle so I can see you clearly." Ryan caught a glint off the firearm and knew it was pointed at his crotch. He wasn't going anywhere. "And be quick about it."

Ryan did as told. By candlelight he could see that this was the girl's room. A cot against the wall bore a worn quilted comforter. A small suitcase plastered with ragged hotel stickers was bound with a cord, ready for a hasty departure. Beside the valise lay a handbag.

"You now wear his clothes, *monsieur*."

Ryan liked her flowered sundress cut above the knee, inappropriate perhaps for the new, more modest Vichy fashion taste, but fetching, he thought, despite his less than ideal situation.

"I needed shoes, and the rest of the clothing appeared better suited to fitting in down here. My things were a bit much, don't you think?"

"It's true—we don't see many fine suits in the country."

"Well, then, I suppose I'm now prepared to head back to Vichy."

"And your friends? What about those friends you wished to rescue?"

Ryan hesitated. "I'll still find a way."

"Don't waste your time. You'll be as dead as the Englishman within the hour."

"Why shoot me? We're on the same side, you know." Ryan's mood grew darker.

"Oh, you can forget about me, *monsieur*—I'm out of here."

"Who else, then? Your comrades who helped drag me here?" Ryan glanced out the door to the courtyard, but nothing moved. "No one needs to know—just let me go and I'm gone from here forever."

"You have much worse to worry about, and they're on the way now—Gestapo with SS in tow. They usually avoid our back roads—too exposed—but for special cases they'll always make an exception." Her eyes had turned vacant and her face expressionless, her mind seemingly lost in memories.

"What do you mean? How do you know they're coming?" *Horst. Again.*

The girl lowered her gun a fraction much to Ryan's relief and focused on the situation at hand. "Phone call an hour ago. I'm surprised the ringing didn't wake you. I've people on the coast keeping an eye out for me, so I knew the minute the *Boches* left Biarritz."

"Look, *mademoiselle*, we can get out of here together. You know the area and have local friends. We watch out for each other until we're both safe, then part ways, what do you think?'

Their eyes met directly but he felt no warmth, just practicality. "No time for further discussion, *monsieur*." She lowered the weapon. "Very well, together for now, but don't get any ideas." She grabbed her valise and handbag and turned to leave. "Rest assured, I'll be rid of you as soon as possible."

"Sounds like a plan, *mademoiselle*. You have a name?" He was pleased to see she was leaving the shotgun behind.

She hesitated at the door. "'Mademoiselle' will do."

He blew out the candle and they moved silently onto the courtyard and down toward a corral. In any other circumstance he would have taken her valise and put an arm around her, but he knew better. At the broad sliding doors to a barn she turned to face him.

"You know horses?"

"Of course."

"Good, because the others are away with the truck, and we've no time to waste."

She pointed down into the dark valley. In the far distance the headlamps of three closely-spaced vehicles threaded their way up in their direction, moving as quickly as the country road allowed.

"Then let's saddle up."

❖

Horst sat stock still at the phone, receiver to his ear, every sense on alert. Before him on the wall of his hotel suite hung an oil painting of spotted cows grazing a lush green field by golden morning light. A windmill hovered on the horizon, almost lost in the haze rising from the pasture. His eyes moved across the bucolic scene, but his mind was far distant, his thoughts several steps ahead as he learned all that was known about the staged roadway accident, the removal of bodies and evidence, and the abduction of Lemmon.

Both Peter Brenner and the young driver were gone. No great loss there. Drivers were easy to come by. And Horst had already determined that Brenner lacked the grit and determination to do what was necessary. His days at Horst's side had been numbered anyway. Brenner—always the ramrod-straight military type, even back in the old days of Marburg. There was good purpose in Horst's having chosen Klaus Pabst as his second-in-command, as his "dagger." In Horst's Gestapo you bent with the wind, and Klaus Pabst had bent willingly; Brenner had faulted Horst's methods and refused to bend.

It had started with the interrogations. Brenner had no problem eliminating enemies of the Reich with the immediacy of fist or knife or gun. But when it came to forceful extraction of information, his weak stomach got the best of him. From the beginning Horst had noted his looking away, his finding excuses to distance himself from what should be the most satisfying of experiences, since only by carefully noting the rising levels of pain could the interrogator really understand which methods worked and which merely delayed the inevitable. If secrets were held, or if the subject unknowingly had knowledge which could be of value to the Reich, only the most painstaking techniques would draw them out. Klaus had lived and breathed this awareness, while Brenner had cowered as the interrogations became more thorough. And then he had made the unforgivable error of sending protests up the line to Berlin. Upon hearing of this, Horst had decided Brenner should go. So, good riddance—there would always be others to do his bidding without complaint.

Horst's mask revealed nothing as he hung up the phone. He reached for his morphine kit—the degree of need lessened but the physical craving as strong as ever—and stepped out on the balcony overlooking the broad expanse of beach, now empty of officers and young women. *Let the game play out*, he thought.

CHAPTER SEVEN

Paris, Occupied France
19 August 1941

Marita strode confidently across the Place de la Concorde. In public she always moved as if late to an appointment, alert for anyone showing undue interest in her passage. Serge's visit had cast an ominous pall over an already troubled life, and she hoped to reach a solution by meeting with Argent that morning. She now knew her lover's real name was Harold Sperling, nicknamed Harry by his English mother. But for safety's sake he could only be Argent to her, at least until the war ended. He had investigated this monster Serge and now had news to share with her, but suggested they avoid any place that might be under observation by the criminal.

In her heart she wished never to have learned his true identity. She hadn't asked, but one of her girls overheard him addressed by name by a fellow officer. Should she ever lose this risky espionage game played out nightly, she was certain to face death at Gestapo hands. She hoped she would be strong and courageous enough not to break under torture and reveal his identity, and thus send him to a horrible death, as well.

Since the loss of her family she had taken to heart what Ryan once suggested and trained her trusted girls to extract intelligence from officers on leave in the city. Knowledge of what military units they commanded and where they were heading or currently fighting could conceivably complete a picture of German armed forces and armaments across the expanding Reich and prove valuable to the Allies. She had hoped by chance to run into an English spy. Rumor had it that many hid in the city, but none came to single her out.

Instead, Argent had caught her eye, this tall, handsome young man with the kind eyes. She had sworn to hate all the Boches, for no matter how polite and intelligent, their hearts were dark enough to sanction mowing down innocents trying to flee the horrors of war. And Ryan had told her of the Nazi intent to annihilate all Jews. And then Argent had won her heart while finding an appropriate use for the intelligence-gathering system she had devised.

On this warming August day only a few delivery vehicles and bicycles merged with the military transports and motorcycles. Across the Seine sat the Chamber of Deputies in neoclassical splendor. This former home to the French Parliament and now seat of the Nazi administration displayed a giant V for *Victoire* fronting the pediment and a long banner above the rank of columns proclaimed *DEUTSCHLAND SIEGT AN ALLEN FRONTEN*, "Germany victorious on all fronts." On the square, French police mimicked the robotic gestures of their German trainers as they directed the meager traffic. She noted that the police saluted German officers passing by in their massive sedans. A soft wind tugged at the swastika flags draping balconies and façades, and she shuddered, her disgust never fading.

Marita headed up Rue Royale toward the Madeleine, passing through a group of Wehrmacht soldiers on leave.

She turned a deaf ear to their bawdy comments on her shapely figure. Would their tune change if they knew she was half-Jewish? How many shared the despicable bigotry, and how many others were in the same boat as Argent, merely conscripted into a war ordained by the almighty Führer? Her thoughts returned time and again to her handsome lover, so German in his looks and earnestness, and yet so seemingly pure of heart. He waited for her now, just moments away in their special café near Place de la Madeleine. He always arrived first to be sure all was safe for their rendezvous.

One year had passed since Paris had opened its gates to the Occupiers, since her family had fallen under that rain of lead. She still trembled at night, imagining again and again what they experienced in those final moments. Had they thought of her safety back in Paris? Had they blamed her for making them flee and thus bringing them to that horrifying scene of death and terror? How much better might they have fared if they had all lived to see the relentless grip of racial hatred tighten further? Her fears for their well-being had driven them from the city. She was responsible for those deaths, and now she vowed never to run scared again.

Just as Ryan had predicted, anti-Semitic persecution followed in the wake of the *Boche* hegemony. Obligatory registration of all Jews had begun within months. Vichy authorities seized Jewish property and goods, compulsory yellow posters singled out businesses as Jewish enterprises, and Marita witnessed the desecration of Jewish-owned storefronts by the anti-Semitic fascists. And then followed the first round-up, thousands of foreign-born Jews whisked away to the camps. How long before the educated and wealthy French Jews felt the weight of oppression, persecution and reprisal for daring to be born "Hebrew"?

Marita side-stepped an old woman of obvious means whose tiny poodle in a diamond-studded collar hoisted his leg to a tree. She marveled at the changes in her divided city.

For the vast majority of citizens life had become a constant struggle to find the food needed to survive another day. The long lines before the shops, the steady new release of rationed goods and foodstuffs—butter, meat, cheese, eggs, fresh fish, offal; every week something new, from potatoes to wine to milk. The shopkeepers hovering with their scissors, snipping the ration tickets into the special collection boxes. Special dispensation for those with children, but never enough to fill the stomach, and pity the sick, infirm or elderly who lived alone and couldn't shop the black market, where the price of a kilo of butter rapidly approached the annual wages of an average working stiff. Without soup kitchens whole families would starve. Without fuel for stoves many more would die if the next winter proved as heartless as the last.

But for those with established means and others with new, black-market wealth, Paris remained an oyster with pearls to be had. The finest restaurants offered caviar and foie gras to all who could pay: powerful German officers, high-society Parisians, black-market geniuses, politicians, and celebrities of stage and screen. One only needed money or connections or both. To succeed, one needed only to follow the dictates of Hermann Göring. The *Reichsmarshall* demanded the city be squeezed for all its worth. Using the procurement officers of the German military and intelligence branches, those with means and power hoarded the treasures of Paris and France, packing them off to Germany while lining their own pockets with fortunes.

Argent wore a fine light-weight worsted suit and red tie, and she hated herself for finding his superbly-cut Wehrmacht uniform equally attractive. He sat toward the rear of Café de la Madeleine, his hat placed atop one of the dainty chairs. His broad smile reminded her, as always, of Ryan Lemmon, her first and unrequited love. But now this *Boche* was rapidly winning her heart in an ironic twist of fate.

He had arrived at the club barely an hour after that devastating visit from Serge, and they sat together for hours and discussed what might be done to save her business from the ravages of the gangster. His type of extortion had become so prevalent in a Paris of officially-sanctioned criminal activity that she wondered how her little realm had remained untouched for so long. Shouldn't a club designated officers-only and purveying solely to the *Boches* have avoided this fate? Late that evening, Argent had left her with a promise to investigate and determine what could be done, and Marita implored him to act quickly before another of her people suffered at the hands of this monster.

Now she joined him at the table, kissing both cheeks in an ordinary air-kiss betraying none of the passion in their hearts.

"You have news for me, darling?"

He nodded but didn't speak, sipping his coffee as a young waitress approached to take her order. Marita asked for tea and the uniformed server scurried away, allowing them privacy in the near-empty café. No other customers sat near enough to overhear their conversation.

Marita glanced about the room adorned with pale-yellow tablecloths and matching damask-papered walls. She always found this café so soothing. A glass-fronted display cabinet offered a wealth of cakes and beautiful pastel macaroons, treats for the German guests and the wealthy. Normally out of reach for someone like Marita.

"It's going to be more difficult than we hoped." Argent picked up a sterling silver spoon to stir his lukewarm coffee, a nervous gesture. She could tell he was hesitant to bring her the news. "This man's well-connected and very successful at what he does."

"Give it to me straight."

"His name—his given name—is Pierre Savoyard. He goes only by "Serge." He's a gutter bum from the 11th with a police record as long as your arm—mostly assaults, armed robbery, break-ins, that sort of thing. He sat out a couple of years for extortion at La Santé but walked on all the other charges. The police were very obliging at first but soon clammed up. I asked my superior to look into it further, and it seems that Serge's connections go high up indeed. He's in league with a guy named Lafont, whose ties include the purchasing officer for the SS. They're all in deep with the German military who share in the profit-taking, so we can't just make him disappear or they'd come down twice as hard on you."

"*Mon Dieu*! So what are we to do now?" Marita ignored the tea delivered to the table, instead taking a sugar cube and dissolving the sweetness on her tongue, a rare and welcome distraction to the mess she was in. Although frequently receiving gifts of better foodstuffs from the customers of the club, she shared them and her personal ration coupons with the girls and staff, especially those with children or elderly family. Marita often joined her fellow citizens in going to bed hungry. "There has to be a way to get rid of him."

"Not until we better understand how he works. We know he lifts liquor from club shipments and resells at a profit, then threatens the suppliers if they claim the order was incomplete. He may have an extortion racket with some of the other night clubs, just as he's going for with you. It's all guesswork until we learn more, but word is he's loaded and greedy." Argent looked both apologetic and worried. "I'm afraid you'll have to team up with this guy until we can find a hole in his armor."

"But my dancers will quit in droves—they know what he did to Colette!"

"Make that case to him. Tell him he's a partner but has to visit only when the club isn't open for business. Show him the books, appear cooperative, and all the while you find out all you can about his operations."

"So I'm a spy, once again."

"Come on, *ma petite*, you do it so well." He gave her his best smile.

Marita looked wary. "I hate the bastard's guts. And if he's willing to mutilate a beautiful young girl, what makes you think I'm safe with him?"

"We won't take that chance. Count on it. Tell him you need advance notice anytime he plans to show up—you know, to be sure the girls aren't there. Then call me, and I'll stay out of sight but ready to shoot if needed, all his powerful friends be damned."

She placed a hand over his. "I've a small storage closet in my office for the film reels back in the days when the place was a movie house. The shelves are long gone and I just keep boxes of records there. If we put a hole in the door for ventilation, you can hide whenever he visits and listen in."

"That should work, and if we disguise the opening in the door I can keep an eye on him, as well." Argent appeared dubious.

Marita had difficulty imagining Argent hunkering down in a closet and spying through a peephole. "So, is this our *only* plan?"

"Doesn't seem we have much choice, does it?"

"For the moment, no, but keep thinking. There's got to be a better solution to rid us of this bastard."

❖

On the quiet Rue St. Louis, just across the bridge from Îsle de la Cité and the towering Notre Dame, the French window fronting Chez Claude was open to the street and passers-by. A small blackboard posted alongside proclaimed the day's menu: sausage and kraut, galettes and crêpes, green salad. The proprietor had chalked a diagonal line through the word "sausage," reflecting the vagaries of that day's food supplies.

Ed stepped up from street level into a narrow space lined by banquettes and small cloth-covered tables. Enameled panels advertised the pleasures of various beers and liqueurs. The lunchtime patronage was mostly gone. A young couple at the table nearest the open window lingered over a near-empty bottle of rosé. He spotted a zinc bar at the rear with two beer taps and high shelves of wine and spirits. An older man in rolled-up sleeves busied himself behind the bar, and the pass-through revealed a tiny kitchen staffed by a disheveled woman, an unlit cigarette butt at her lips. Ed placed her immediately as the man's overworked wife. To the right leaned an off-kilter door in red indicating "Toilettes." The proprietor wore a collarless shirt with a red scarf around his neck and a long apron which had seen better days. He smiled as Ed entered and returned his greeting while coming forward to welcome the stranger."

"You wish to dine, *monsieur?*" His best hope was for one more paying customer before closing for the afternoon break. He directed the new guest to a table near the bar.

"Un verre de rouge, s'il-vous-plaît." Ed had quickly decided to wait for von Haldheim. A glass of wine would hit the spot.

The bell over the door jingled anew and a well-dressed man entered. He wore a finely-cut suit and vest with a silk tie despite the warm weather. Though the man's nose was pore-ridden and his complexion flushed, von Haldheim carried himself majestically. He appeared fit and moved with grace toward Ed's table, stopping to greet the owner with a handshake and quietly whisper something before introducing himself to the American.

"Mr. Lemmon, what a pleasure! I would have known you from afar—you bear a striking resemblance to your brother, just not as tall, perhaps?"

"Not quite." They shook hands. "Herr von Haldheim, I recall Ryan's stories. You introduced him to the Berlin nightlife a good decade back. He appreciated having such a knowledgeable guide."

The proprietor interrupted their small talk with a 1921 Château Haut-Brion straight from the cellar beneath the establishment. He carefully removed the layer of dust from the bottle before pulling the cork with a flourish and sampling the wine, then nodded his personal approval and offered it to his two guests to try. Ed knew a little about wine, and was amazed to see this *grand cru* and desirable vintage appear in such a surprising locale.

"Excellent, Claude. As always, you surpass my hopes and expectations." Rolf poured a bit more of the wine into the owner's tasting glass as he withdrew from the table.

"Merci, Monsieur von Haldheim. So kind to grace again our humble establishment." Claude disappeared into the kitchen to huddle with his wife. Ed suspected they would be happily preparing the check for such a well-paying customer.

With the place all theirs after the other couple departed hand-in-hand, Ed asked the obvious. "So tell me, to what do I owe this pleasure?"

"First, please tell me of Ryan. Is the splendid chap doing well and now at some American university, as he had hoped?"

"Ryan does very well indeed. He's now working with our State Department on an exchange program with your government." Ed tried the excellent Bordeaux and wished he were enjoying it with Grace rather than stuck here with this stranger. "Ryan is also here in Europe."

"Really? What luck! Perhaps the three of us might have dinner sometime. The *canard à l'orange* at Le Pré Catalan is superb."

"Well, I don't know Ryan's schedule so can't say when he might be back in Paris. We'll just have to see how things go. But meanwhile, I'm very intrigued by your contacting me—it's a bit out of the ordinary. Are you in Paris in some official government capacity? You mentioned access to our embassy roster."

"My heavens no, Mr. Lemmon. I've independent means so am lucky enough to enjoy myself here on my own schedule. But I do know certain people who have interest in furthering closer relations with your government, and I thought you might help me put them together with the right contacts in Vichy."

Ed found himself in very uncomfortable territory. He knew his German didn't approach Ryan's degree of native fluency and he feared expressing either too much or too little by choosing the wrong words. "I'm not sure I can be of help, sir. My line of work isn't quite at that diplomatic level."

"Please hear me out, Mr. Lemmon. We can be candid in this pleasant setting free of eavesdroppers."

Ed nodded and took another sip of wine, casting a glance toward the kitchen to be certain Claude and his wife hadn't moved.

"Would you concur that your American 'neutrality' in the European conflict will be short-lived?"

"Off the record, I'm certain that's true. We've reached the limits of what we can do as 'neutrals' and we certainly won't permit Great Britain to fall to the Reich. After all, Canada's our own backyard."

"Then we're on the same page, Mr. Lemmon. The people I represent want nothing more than an end to these hostilities, an honorable end. And we feel the way to accomplish this is to hold quiet meetings between the Americans and like-minded Germans who wish to avoid further discord between our nations. Please note that I don't say "our governments." Governments come and go—just look at what our dear hosts the French now have to deal with! But nations abide, and we have a great hope to reestablish some semblance of a League of Nations but this time with American participation and a just and equitable conclusion to this war."

Ed found himself at a loss for words. His eyes shot to the front of the café, then over his shoulder to the proprietor and his wife, their attentive faces just visible beyond the pass-through to the kitchen. If he had understood the German correctly, this man was opening a backdoor into negotiations with powerful Germans interested in undermining Hitler.

But was this an honest feeler or a dangerous trap? *My God,* Ed realized, *speaking of leagues, am I ever out of my own!*

CHAPTER EIGHT

Paris, Occupied France
19 August 1941

Argent turned sideways on the bench to face Marita, keeping her hand in his. They'd chosen a spot just above a riding path, almost invisible to strolling park visitors and the occasional equestrians in German uniform. The morning was passing far too quickly, and he had duties he must attend to. But he would make this stolen moment in the Bois de Boulogne last as long he could.

"You're unusually quiet, darling." She watched him expectantly. Despite the heat, the shade from hornbeam and chestnut trees made their quiet rendezvous spot ideal.

For months he had wondered why she had taken him as a lover but had been hesitant to ask. She was at least seven years his senior, and he felt somewhat in awe of this experienced and worldly woman. He knew she despised Germans for the brutal loss of her family—she had made that very clear, something he could certainly understand. But gradually a mutual trust had developed as she recognized his desire to help end an ill-considered, unjust war, and she worked diligently at his side to weaken the Nazi-driven effort. His willingness to help her cause must surely have touched her, but it certainly didn't explain the relationship which had become so much more to them both. "So why did you choose me?"

She smiled as she traced each of his long, slender fingers with one of her own. "Did you ever want to play piano?"

"Not exactly getting to my question, are you?" He lifted her hand to his lips.

"Isn't it enough to say I find you incredibly handsome?"

"Not even close. I find you incredibly beautiful, too, but I'm German—"

"And part-English, don't forget!"

"But German-born and -raised, and yet you chose to love me despite your hatred for my country and people."

Marita turned away, and when she looked back at him any momentary darkness had passed. Her words came slowly, each sentence carefully framed, as if revealing even fleeting emotion might unleash a great wave of sorrow. "It's true, when your countrymen slaughtered innocent refugees, civilians in trains and on foot who wanted nothing more than to escape your horrible war, I despised every one of you. I lived and breathed that hatred, and was determined to fight you any way I could—" She raised a hand to fend off his interruption. "Let me finish."

"So when you first showed up at the club and made clear you wanted to know me better, I saw you as just another one of them, one of those murderers who impress with their polite manners, all the while planning to destroy the lives of any who cross them. So I intended to milk you of any secrets which could lead to your…" she sought the right way to express it, "…to your country's downfall. And while I did find you very handsome, I never intended to share my bed with you."

Argent grinned but said nothing, happy to have her finally open up to him. He squeezed her hand in encouragement.

"But as we sat and talked, and I learned more of your life and your thoughts, I came to understand that there must be others like you, other Germans who found themselves trapped in a totalitarian system without control of their lives. Helpless in the face of such overwhelming hatred and cruelty, they were doing their best to bring a glimmer of hope for a better future. And that's what I saw in you."

"And that's it? That's why you chose me?" He furrowed his brow, still confused by her motives.

"That, and because of your sister Dorothea, and what her loss meant to you." The warmth in her eyes expressed more understanding than any words she might say. "You see, *mon amour*, "I loved my dear sister Marie every bit as much. We were more than sisters, we were practically twins—even our names mirrored how close we were. She and I shared life's secrets, we stole away from our disapproving parents to dance on the stage, and we built the club together, always knowing we had each other to count on, even if the world didn't agree. So when you told me of your sister…of what became of her…I knew you were a man of compassion and caring, one of the few I have met, and I wanted to share all of me with you."

He bent close to kiss her, one hand on her cheek in affection and understanding.

❖

Ed's superiors were not thrilled with the proposal floated by Rolf von Haldheim. A possible peace feeler from some disenchanted German military bigwigs threatened to upset America's careful balancing act. After modest preliminary investigation, the embassy attaché dealing with such matters determined that von Haldheim was indeed operating at some unknown level within the Abwehr, but the Foreign Service already considered itself on tenuous ground as representatives of a neutral country in Vichy France. There was zero interest in going out on a limb for a matter best left to the new operatives of the COI.

"Look, Lemmon. We think it best you stick to your own field and proceed with negotiating those exchanges in Paris. That work better suits your talents and your assignment." His immediate boss shot him a stern glance over his reading glasses. "Keep your nose out of espionage and undercover negotiations of any kind and we'll get along just fine."

"Yes, sir." Ed regretted having even brought up the matter. "My feelings exactly."

"Your brother, the one with COI, is he still here in the Frog Pond?"

"Yes, sir. Returning to Paris shortly, I expect."

"Then hand this hot potato off to him. You say he has old ties to this von Haldheim anyway, so let the two of them work it out." He waved off Edward, swiveling his leather chair to face the window and reaching for his phone. "And by the way—"

"Yes, sir?"

"If all this goes sideways, let it be on "Wild Bill's" shoulders, not ours, right?"

Edward nodded to the back of his boss's head and left the office. He would wait for Ryan to pick up the contact again in Paris.

CHAPTER NINE

Morlanne, Occupied France
19 August 1941

Leo pumped the red handle, filled the blackened pot, and set it on the stove without spilling a drop of water. The metal door to the firebox creaked as he added kindling and two lengths of firewood before clanging it shut to prevent smoke from entering the room. It was exactly as *Grand-mère* had taught him. He pulled aside the chintz curtains to let in the first rays of sun and looked out at the fields below. It would be warm and clear, ideal for his needs.

He took a moment to scratch Musette between the ears before she abandoned the window sill. The cat purred contentedly and nudged his hand, then jumped down and ran to the door, stretching both paws up against it. He knew she was through with indoors and wanted to spend the day exploring and keeping mice at bay. He slid open the latch and followed on the heels of the tabby, quietly shutting the door behind them. The cat nearly tripped him as she threaded through his feet and rubbed against his ankles. Then she spied something in the tall grasses and disappeared in a flash down the garden path.

The boy followed the gravel path to the animal pens, brushing his hand along the top of the flower stalks in *Grand-mère* Jeanne's garden. He tried to match them to the

German equivalents she had taught him. Leo didn't care for the marigolds, preferring the colorful roses blooming along the rail fence at the edge of the garden. He knew these were also his grandmother's favorites.

The goose pen was the first of his morning tasks. Leo greeted the birds with a click of his tongue as he had learned, and the flock gathered to follow him to the lower gate. He released them to the pond, and they quickly waddled away and took to the water. He left the gate open behind him.

Next Leo went to the stall and greeted the pig. *Grand-mère* had told him only yesterday that the sow was expecting piglets, and she hoped the old girl would be healthy enough to have the babies, since her diet was as meager as theirs. He patted her on the snout, ignoring the stench of excrement which surrounded her. "Good girl, Solange, be a good *maman*." The pig looked in vain for the feed bucket, and Leo, noting her consternation, quickly ran back up to the kitchen to fetch the scraps from last night's dinner. He left the sow slurping at the trough, took special care to leave the pen gate open behind him, and headed over to the rabbit cage alongside the stone barn.

Leo knew what his grandmother had christened the two rabbits, but refused to address them by name. When his family had first arrived at the farm—back when Cousin Brigitte still lived—the young farmhand Louis had taken Leo to visit the bunnies.

"And which one's your favorite, kid?" The surly teenager had told Leo from the start that he would rather be off fighting Germans than teaching *Boches* how to farm. Louis had never repeated that comment in front of the adults, but Leo had told his uncle and mother later.

Leo had regarded the fluffy young rabbits, some a patchwork of colors, others all gray or brown. He'd never touched a farm animal before, and he took them in his hands to examine, one by one. Their whiskers tickled as he held each close to his cheek. It was a difficult decision, but finally he chose the smallest with the longest ears, "the runt," as Louis called him.

"You must name him," the hired hand said.

"Then he's Michel," Leo decided immediately. His best friend during their stay in Lyon had been Michel, and Leo still missed the fun they'd had together before *Maman* announced they would leave again—as always in the dark of night, always without good-byes. Leo took the little male from the cage again and cuddled him, rubbing the soft fur against his face as the bunny's nose twitched inquisitively.

"You're sure he's the one?"

"Oh, yes, he's my favorite."

"Very well—decision made." Louis grabbed the little rabbit by the scruff and held him up to examine. "Scrawny little twerp." In one motion he lifted a cleaver imbedded in the post beside the cage, pinned the squirming rabbit to the wooden shelf and with a single chop removed the animal's head. He handed Leo the twitching body.

"No!" screamed Leo. Horror shook the child while the farmhand laughed.

"Go on, now, city boy, up to the house. Skin it for dinner, or else starve—your choice—I don't give a damn."

Instead, barely able to see through his tears, Leo stumbled down to the creek, scratching his face on the brambles along the way but not caring. He dug a small depression in the soft loam beside the streambed and laid the headless rabbit to rest. "I'm really sorry, Michel. I never meant it," his words disappearing in the sobs. And Leo had never again used the names given to rabbits in the pen.

Now he set the husky buck in the tall grass and reached for the smaller doe, taking a brief moment to stroke her fur before placing her beside her partner. "Shoo! Get going, both of you!" he said, and stomped a foot, trying to scare them away. They looked up in apparent disbelief at both the shouts and the unexpected freedom before slowly hopping off to nibble carrot tops up in the garden beyond the rose bushes. Leo wiped his eyes and headed toward the chicken coop.

The hens already announced the first eggs. The cock had been crowing repeatedly for some time now, but the angry old bird didn't deserve Leo's glance. He had never taken to the rooster who repeatedly interfered with the egg gathering. His beak was sharp, and Leo didn't trust those talons. As always, the hens squawked upon his arrival, and the cock gave him a menacing look but kept his distance. Most of the fowl scattered, but he had to lift two hens from their laying boxes to get at the fresh eggs. He gathered five—fewer had been coming lately—and lowered each brown egg carefully into the pocket of his shorts. Again, he left the door to the enclosure standing wide open.

He looked down across the farmyard to the lower pasture. Monsieur LeBlanc would have to look after the old cow when he made his daily visit to the fields he tended. Her milk had dried up, as *Grand-mère* Jeanne had complained only the day before. For the moment the cow grazed contentedly. He felt he had done his best.

Back in the kitchen half the water had boiled away, and he knew this was wasteful. He lowered the eggs gently into the roiling water and glanced at the old wall clock. *Maman* always said the best eggs are cooked no longer than five minutes. While waiting, he removed his jacket from the peg above his cot and stuffed it into the small canvas rucksack he used whenever they moved. He checked for his pocket knife and the carefully-folded map along with the compass he had taken from the abandoned house across the road.

Leo and two playmates from the LeBlanc farm had snuck over one evening. The big house was obviously vacant, and older kids had already broken windows and scattered furnishings everywhere. They'd also written on the walls—nasty things. *Maman* had told him the place belonged to a Jewish family that had never returned from Paris when the war came. "A summer house," she said. Leo had found the compass in its polished brass case and decided it deserved a good, year-round home. Uncle René had shown him how to use it, setting the compass atop the map and explaining east and west, north and south. Leo learned quickly, and had already explored the surrounding woods. "A young Wild West scout," said Uncle René. Surprisingly, his uncle had never even asked how he came by the compass.

While the eggs boiled Leo opened the case and pivoted the piece to watch the needle track north, then carefully snapped it shut before returning it to his pack. He lifted the hardboiled eggs from the water one by one and set them on the counter to cool. He took a small square of waxed paper to enclose a spoonful of salt, and uncovered the strong-smelling cheese, wrapping a large slice in waxed paper, as well. Finally, he packed the half-loaf of yesterday's bread. Once he was sure the eggs were sufficiently cooled, he rolled them into a dishtowel and his rucksack was full. He would eat well enough, at least for a day or two.

Leo knew it was time to go. As a last-minute thought he reached for the pruners in the woven basket by the door and brought up three roses from the lower end of the garden, being careful to remove the thorns. He knew the peach-colored ones were her favorites. He tiptoed into Grandmother Jeanne's room. She lay on the bed, eyes shut, hands now folded at her chest. He would miss her hugs. Her white hair spread out across the pillow, gleaming silver in the morning light. He gently lifted her hands to slide the flowers beneath and stretched over to kiss her forehead, now cool to the touch.

Leo had seen death before, of course. At first it had frightened and saddened him. But that was when he was little, the first time with the bunnies. Now he was a country boy, after all, and almost seven. It was time to head north to find his mother and his uncle. The farm would have to fend for itself, but at least the animals now ran free.

The rooster crowed as the boy entered the woods. Leo glanced back but kept on walking. Musette followed him to the edge of the trees, then thought better of it and raced back up the path toward the quiet house.

CHAPTER TEN

Gascony, Occupied France
19 August 1941

The ride down from the hills had been a change of pace for Ryan, so different from the beautiful horses and breathtaking Irish countryside he'd remembered from when he'd led the Wellesley girls on a Grand Tour in 1929. He'd cut a fine figure of a horseman in his riding jacket and jodhpurs and a natty Trilby on his head. And the riding tack had been of superior Irish leather and craftsmanship. This young woman's horses were of significantly lesser vigor and beauty, for the Waffen-SS had repeatedly confiscated the region's best, leaving only decrepit or ailing work animals to carry the farming load. And in this one particular case, to transport partisans out of harm's way.

Beyond the planted fields she chose a well-worn deer and boar trail cutting through dense woodland and the occasional meadow. As first light brightened the sky, Ryan got a better view of his companion. She rode with her head high, her dress hitched up over her legs, revealing shapely thighs. From time to time they would cross open pasture and speed the pace, increasing the bounce of her breasts beneath the summer dress. She had stuffed her hair under the broad-brimmed hat and tied it with a lavender ribbon, and the small valise bobbed at the back of her saddle. Ryan was finding this strangely-distant woman increasingly enigmatic yet attractive.

She had left him with the horses beside a field planted in peppers. Ryan watched her stroll onto the country road which led to a small village in the distance. As the animals grazed near a creek, Ryan assessed his damaged feet and decided things were healing as well as could be expected. The pressure on the stirrups had caused fresh blood to dampen his socks. He tugged them off to soak his feet in the stream and some of the scabs remained attached to the wool. The cool water felt soothing, and his thoughts drifted.

He could never have foreseen Horst's manipulations of The Group. Kohl and his Gestapo partners had used Ryan and Ed from the start. Once the bogus program was in play, Horst must have spotted their uncommon family name on the progress reports destined for Heydrich, and further investigation had brought the bastard straight to Ryan. From there it was only a matter of using Ed to draw his brother in. Now that duplicity had worked twice, and Ryan shook his head at the calculated treachery of his nemesis. He had walked into the Gurs trap totally unprepared despite espionage training and awareness of how dangerous Europe had become. He would not allow anyone to catch him off-guard again.

Almost an hour passed before a sharp whistle startled him awake, and he found himself on the receiving end of the lapping tongue of a golden retriever. The dog acted as if she had known Ryan her entire life, bounding around him and trying to climb onto his shoulders. He jumped up quickly to escape that insatiable tongue.

"Down, girl," called his guide, "Lucille, down!"

Lucille ignored the commands.

"A friend of yours?" Ryan raised an arm to fend off another attack.

"They both are." She gestured back to a woman about her own age coming up the path, a leash in her hand. His guide explained Ryan's presence with a simple "*Américain*," which seemed to say enough. The newcomer, shorter and more buxom than his companion, gave him a shy smile. With only a *"bonjour, monsieur"* upon greeting and an *"au revoir"* before taking the reins of the two horses, she headed into the woods they had recently left. The retriever, sniffing at Ryan's trouser cuffs, noticed her mistress gone and quickly disappeared into the trees.

"So what now?"

She gestured to his shoes. "Put those on and get ready to walk."

They followed the tree line to the road and turned downhill from there, keeping an eye out for traffic. There was little to watch for—an occasional horse-drawn wagon, a farm couple on foot carrying a rake and a shovel, and a man pedaling valiantly on a bicycle-drawn cart filled with terracotta tiles. The sun was rising at their backs but the verdant hills kept the roadway in shadow, and they stayed close to the roadside ditch in case a motorized vehicle approached. After a few kilometers Ryan's feet ached, each step a painful reminder of his recent thrashing. "How much longer?"

"As long as it takes."

"Where are we headed?"

"Bayonne."

"On foot? That seems a ways."

"You've made it this far, now do the rest."

Walking alongside this silent woman drove him nuts. One could only admire her physical attributes for so long before the urge to know the person behind them crept in, and after an hour without exchanging a word, Ryan decided to take another tack. "You seem to know your way around a firearm."

"One must to survive a war."

"Your father?"

"What about him?"

"Is he the one who taught you to handle that rifle so well?"

She strode on a ways before replying. "Yes. My father...and my husband."

Ryan couldn't hide his surprise. "You're married?" He'd seen no ring on her hand.

"Widowed. Look, monsieur." She waited for him to catch up. "Let's get one thing settled—I don't want to know you better, I don't share my life story with anyone, and I sure as hell don't want to go to bed with you, so give it a rest. As far as I'm concerned, once we reach Bayonne you're on your own."

They walked on and he began to talk, more to himself, since she gave no sign of listening. He spoke of the harrowing race across Germany with Erika and Leo almost three years earlier—broad terms, no names or details. How his old university friend René had risked everything to help. He didn't speak of the stolen protocol, not knowing her attitude toward Jews. And finally he described the Gestapo trap at Gurs and how she and her partisans had saved him from *le Masque*. He said he had to get his friends out of France. He'd been a reporter, and was now a low-level diplomat. His throat felt tight because he not only wanted this woman's help, he needed it. And because the memories of '38 still haunted him.

She hadn't smiled once, cold even at the description of Leo, and once he was done talking she remained in her own private thoughts.

Within the hour they arrived at a larger village, a few streets of neatly-maintained two-story houses with red shutters and cobbled lanes. They drank from the small fountain in the center of the square, bending low to catch the flow from the rusted iron spout. The mountain water was icy and refreshing. They walked past a tobacco shop, and Ryan waited while the girl parted the beaded curtain to speak with the woman at the counter.

Magazines and newspapers hung in the rack outside the door, to the side a display of postcards with scenes of happier days—a couple picnicking on a hillside of wildflowers, a farmers' market strung with colorful banners, children bathing on a beach while parents watched from bright cabañas. The headlines praised the German progress on the eastern front against the Stalinist menace, and Hitler glared from atop a podium, his arm raised in half-hearted salute. Ryan picked up the subtle aroma of tobacco and longed for his briar, but a glance inside showed the shelves almost bare, and his cash reserves taken from the British agent might have to go a long way.

The young woman—damn how he wished for her name!—stepped from the shop carrying two tickets. "At five past the hour the bus for Bayonne comes through, so we've about thirty-five minutes to wait. I suggest finding something to eat." They took a table beneath a red-and-white umbrella and settled for ersatz coffee with cream, but the baguette was fresh and the butter tasted incredibly rich.

Then, without preamble, she suddenly spoke up. "I'm sure you're a nice guy where you come from, monsieur. But there's no room for anyone new in my life, so just leave it alone. I'll get you to the coast, but then we part ways."

"Of course. I appreciate all you've done for me."

Shouts and laughter rose from the end of the street and they turned to watch young children in smocks race down the slope toward school with rucksacks bouncing. A few lingered behind, those not as anxious to sit in a classroom on such a pleasant morning.

"The boy—" Ryan heard the catch in her throat, "…how old?"

"Three and a half then, now nearly seven."

"And you know he still lives?" She was looking away, her glistening eyes following the backs of the children.

"Yes." Ryan swallowed, his own throat constricted. "At the moment."

She got up abruptly and entered the café and returned in less than a minute. "It's nearly time, we should be going." She reached for the valise.

"We need a watch." Ryan hadn't seen his own since the beating in Gurs.

The bus rumbled onto the narrow square a few minutes early and its engine idled roughly at the stop. A crowd had gathered outside to board, but the seats inside were all taken, and Ryan and the woman would have to stand for the ride into the city. As they joined the queue he gestured for her to go first.

At the step she turned back to him. "You'll never need my full name—but call me Nicole. And no more stories from you. I'll stay with you until you've found your friends. *D'accord?*"

He nodded.

"One more thing—if I were you, I'd run like hell and get as far away from me as possible, and quickly, because I only bring trouble." And then she was up the steps and pushing past the other passengers to put distance between them.

That's progress, Ryan thought.

❖

The *Auberge Royale* in Bayonne was anything but royal. A few blocks from the waterfront up Rue Laurac just north of the Adour River, the seedy boarding house rented beds by day or hour. Five francs, either way. Ryan and Nicole took a room upon arrival, just a short walk from the bus and train stations. No questions asked, no documentation of identity requested.

Nicole immediately claimed the bed, making clear the metal-framed cot with a badly-stained mattress was to be hers alone. A pillow and yellowed sheet with thread-bare blanket came at no extra charge, and the unshaven clerk downstairs with the loose dentures had specifically mentioned that no maid service was available. They weren't surprised once they saw the room. The bedclothes had seldom seen a laundrywoman's touch. Ryan accepted the braided rug as his bedding. Sharing one room made sense, since a man and woman traveling together but occupying separate rooms invited curiosity, the last thing they needed. She rolled up her coat for a pillow and tossed him the filthy one from the bed. Both napped before he headed out to try contacting his friends in the drinking establishments along the waterfront.

The first three he visited proved fruitless, the fourth however more promising. This joint appeared better frequented than the others, and better maintained, which didn't say all that much. The windows had a yellowish cast from years of exposure to smoke, the aging blinds to block the setting sun lacked an occasional slat, and the linoleum tiles on the floor peeled and cracked at the edges. He gave the customers a brief glance before approaching the long bar.

"Something to drink, monsieur?" The bartender was old, at least in his sixties, and missing a substantial part of his right ear. Just enough of a stub remained to help support the thick eyeglasses as he scrubbed down the zinc of the bartop.

"*Une bière, s'il-vous-plâit.*" Ryan scanned the shabby bar, taking in the patrons, mostly stevedores, one with an unlit stub of a cigarette bobbing in his lips as he spoke to his buddies in a quiet voice but with animated gestures. Two Waffen-SS non-coms in field-gray and billed caps chatted by the window, one rolling a lit cigarette incessantly between his forefingers and thumb as he talked. A cleaning woman worked a mop furiously over some stain on the linoleum just inside the door, pointless from Ryan's viewpoint given the derelict condition of the flooring. He turned back to the barman who was drawing beer from the tap and slid twenty francs across the smooth surface. "I'm looking for someone. Maybe you can help?"

"Try Colette's around the corner, her girls aren't all that picky." The bartender eyed the cash. "Head out the door, turn down toward the river, take a left, it's on the left. Purple shutters—you can't miss 'em."

"No, I'm looking for a man—" Ryan added another five.

"Can't help you there, monsieur." He turned back to the tap and topped off the glass. Over his shoulder he added: "Try Biarritz. That's where the foreigners play. You'll find what you need there." He slid the beer in front of Ryan. Another five francs hit the counter alongside two for the beer.

"No, you misunderstand…I'm looking for an old friend, said to be hanging out around here now."

"Have a name, monsieur, this friend of yours?" The bartender opened the till to receive the money for the beer and pocketed the extra cash.

"Likely goes by something new now. Tall, heavyset, quick on his feet despite a slight limp. Right leg. Knows his boats."

"Lots of dock men get themselves a limp. What else?"

Ryan thought quickly, sensing progress at last. "Dueling scars."

"*Boche*, eh monsieur?"

"No, Alsatian, actually…so French."

"Not any longer."

Ryan watched the glimmer in the man's eyes fade and disappear. Alsace and Lorraine had been annexed to the Reich, their citizens made German and subject to military duty by order of the *Führer*.

"Sorry. Can't help you there, monsieur." He turned to remove glassware from the sudsy water and place it alongside the sink on a drying rack, but Ryan had sensed something in the man's demeanor and felt he'd made some progress.

He slid a piece of paper across the counter. "Here's where I'm staying, in case something occurs to you."

The barman nodded, his back still to Ryan, who headed for the exit.

"Monsieur?"

Ryan had barely reached the door, side-stepping the mop still in vigorous motion, when he turned. "Yes?"

"Your order." He gestured toward the beer, now gone flat.

"It's yours, monsieur. Stay in touch."

CHAPTER ELEVEN

Bayonne, Occupied France
19 August 1941

Ryan leaned over the washstand and turned his head from side to side to admire his freshly-groomed face. The photo ID of the English spy Whitaker sat propped up on the glass shelf beneath the cracked mirror. With five days of growth to work with, he'd shaved very carefully to avoid nicks. The shape of the mustache had to be just right. Below his nose ran a pencil-thin, horizontal line of hair with a slight separation in the middle, sparse but certainly giving a dashing look. *Isabel was right,* he thought. He could almost hear the Berlin reporter making some smart-ass remark. Memories of the stunning girl's smile and wit flooded in, and with them came the melancholy of loss, no easier to bear despite a decade since she disappeared into the underbelly of the capital city.

Less impressive than the mustache were the tightly-wound pin curls on his head. Nicole had insisted his appearance must better match the man pictured on the spy's *carte d'identité*, so a permanent wave was the answer. She did not wish to risk his being questioned by the authorities as long as they were together. For a long and boring hour she had wound each lock of hair into a tight knot, the stench of the chemicals overwhelming in the narrow room. Thank God it was summer, the window open to the blackened brick wall facing them across the alleyway. Another few minutes and she would apply the final setting chemicals, and then after washing his hair they would judge the results.

Ryan's wardrobe had measurably improved since their arrival in Bayonne. Nicole had spotted a flaw in his disguise. The tailored American shirt which he had preferred over the smelly, bloody shirt of the injured spy was too stark a contrast to the rough woolen pants and faded blue jacket.

A few hours earlier she had suggested the benefits of a shower for both of them, and led Ryan down toward the wharf and a public bathhouse. A stern woman of middle age guarded a small table just inside the entry. Ryan considered whether winding her hair so tightly in a bun might be what kept her from shutting her mouth. Her chatter was constant from the moment they arrived. For two francs apiece dropped in her tray she promised a few minutes warm water, and for an additional franc each the use of two threadbare towels and slivers of cheap soap. A quarter hour later he emerged from the men's showers to find Nicole waiting, her hair loose and damp in a look he always found sexy. She carried a mysterious bundle wrapped in the damp towel beneath her arm. The bath attendant smiled serenely and for the first time had nothing to say. She patted the pocket of her smock with a wink at Nicole and wished them both a good day as she hurried them out the door.

Along the Rue Neuve they stopped at a shabby drugstore for toiletries—the permanent wave kit with hairpins, dentifrice, toothbrushes, and a razor with a package of double-edged blades.

"Keep your money," she said, as he offered to pay, "The *Boches* always provide."

Once back in their room she had unrolled a decent pair of men's trousers, a tweed jacket, a shirt and better socks. She laid out the clothing and newly purchase toiletries and hung the towel over the window sill to dry.

"And how did you pull that off?" He held the pants up for size. A bit short in length but adequate.

"Don't ask."

Ryan suspected that some poor sap at the *bains publics* would be sneaking out in embarrassment, clad only in a couple of those threadbare towels.

His shaving task done, he wiped the blade and set aside the razor. Removing a new blade from the cardboard packet he snapped it in two against the wash basin. Sitting on the edge of her bed, he slit the lining of the jacket lapel and tucked the half-blade beneath the seam. It would be unnoticeable to any but the most dedicated searcher.

Next he opened a groove along the length of a pencil he had lifted from the front desk. He forced the second metal edge sufficiently into the shaft to be gripped by the wood. Finally, he wound thread taken from the cuff of the old trousers to cinch tight the split in the pencil. The make-shift knife went into the pocket of his trousers. Ryan intended never to be caught unprepared again.

While Nicole went down the hall to the WC to fill the pitcher with water in preparation for rinsing out the hair treatment, Ryan turned his attention to the filthy trousers inherited from Devon Whitaker. Recalling the spy's words, he examined the roll-up cuffs of the trousers and quickly found a tiny cellophane sleeve. Tapping the envelope gently on his open palm, a single brown pill emerged. A standard-issue potassium cyanide capsule, a rubber-encased glass oval about the size of a pea, and lethal in minutes if ruptured. A short if jolting trip into nothingness.

Ryan used his thumbnail to pry open the secret compartment in his onyx ring. The chamber behind the stone had been so artfully crafted on the Ponte Vecchio as to be invisible to any but a trained eye with a magnifying loupe. He eased the pill into the ring's cavity and carefully snapped the lid shut, then opened it again to be certain that the capsule hadn't burst. It remained intact. The black cameo of the Roman gladiator now hid death on demand.

When his newly-curled hair was finally dried, Ryan broke into laughter as he examined it in the mirror. Nicole merely nodded her approval of the change.

❖

The knock at their door came around eight in the evening. They had taken a light meal across from the hotel and given up hope that his potentially promising contact in the bar might actually lead them to René. Lost in separate thoughts and memories, she on the bed and he on the wooden chair, they both started at the sharp rap on the door. Ryan waited to her left behind the door, the cord from her valise quickly knotted, one end in each hand, a garrote if needed.

Her voice remained steady and casual showing no sign of concern or fear. "Who's there?"

A rich, masculine voice answered from the hall. "A friend of a friend, mademoiselle."

"You have a name for me, monsieur?"

"Will Gesslinger do?"

She looked for Ryan's nod, then turned the key and cracked the door. Ryan peered through the opening at the jamb as she revealed a young man in faded dockworker's clothing. He offered her a warm smile, very white teeth hiding behind a full, black beard—the look of a boy playing an adult—and reached out his hand in greeting.

Ryan stuffed the knotted cord in his pocket and stepped into sight, glancing over the stranger's shoulder and down the hallway in the hope of seeing René there. The passage at first appeared empty, but then he saw movement in the far shadows, a man with trousers at his ankles, a woman's pale legs encircling his waist, a pale ass rocking back and forth under the circle of light from the ceiling fixture.

The young man followed Ryan's gaze, chuckled, and handed Ryan a folded slip of paper. "Thirty minutes, monsieur— on time, *s'il-vous-plâit.*" And he was gone toward the stairs in a flash. Ryan shut the door on the pre-occupied couple.

Under the room light the paper revealed an address and a hastily-sketched map with a few notes of guidance. He handed the paper to Nicole. "You know the place?"

She examined it closely and nodded. "I believe it's over near the prison and slaughter house. We can ask along the way, but—"

"No, you stay here—this last part is mine." He didn't want to put her at further risk.

"I'd have no problem with that, but I know my way around the city a bit, and without me you'll never make it on time." Despite misgivings, Ryan acknowledged her logic. "Besides, I said I'd stick with you till you've found your friends. Now shut that window and let's get going."

He consulted his bare wrist. "Will we ever get a damned watch?"

She reached for her handbag and coat. "I'll steal one for you."

He smiled, locking the door behind them. Down the hall, the couple was still actively entwined.

❖

From the Quai de Lesseps they followed the river, stopping for a moment in a shabby bar to ask specific directions before following the Boulevard d'Alsace Lorraine to the Boulevard de L'Abbatoire. The river was spanned by an impressive bridge, and imposing municipal buildings formed sharp silhouettes against the evening sky. But on the north side of the Adour the streets were more neglected and poorly lit with blackout in effect, so street addresses were difficult to read. Ryan's feet still suffered from the beating and he wished for a break, but knew time was critical, so they kept moving.

The high walls of the prison were impossible to miss, looming ominously against the clear night sky. Ryan and

Nicole headed north in the shadows across from the guarded stone structure until they came to the slaughterhouse compound. The stench of blood and offal and the lowing of cattle drove them onwards. Once past, they began to search for the small alley depicted in the young man's sketch.

A derelict truck on blocks marked the spot, waiting to feed the Nazi scrap metal drive. Directly behind number 16 an unlit passageway turned to the left. The glow around the edges of heavy curtains on the upper floors allowed them to make out individual buildings, but the alleyway itself lay deep in gloom. Wishing for a flashlight, they felt their way along with one hand on the wall to avoid tripping on trash and fallen brick. As the passage came to an end the alley took a sharp right. Now they watched for a stoop marked by a solitary candle, as indicated in the note.

A rushing sound came from above and they stopped in their tracks. He instinctively reached for her hand and just as quickly thought better of it. Then he spied the bats—ten, maybe twenty—silhouetted against the sky as they fluttered about, disturbed by their passing. Ryan found his hands shaking. The encounter with Horst at Gurs had finally awakened him to just how quickly danger could appear. He tensed in anticipation, wishing for a better weapon, wishing he were alone and less concerned about Nicole's well-being. He gripped the shaft of the makeshift knife deep in his pocket. It wasn't much, but something.

The flickering stub of a candle propped in an empty beer bottle drew them forward. It sat on the stoop of a recessed back door to a four-story tenement. Ryan lifted the flame to the door, searching for any name or markings, but found none. No one appeared to use this door with any regularity, since trash had piled up undisturbed at the threshold. Gesturing Nicole to stand off to one side, he knocked twice before taking to the deep shadow across from her.

The doorway separated a crack and a shaft of light raced across the narrow alley, startling a stray cat who shot away to escape the glare. Ryan quickly returned his gaze to the door.

"Who is it?" The voice gruff but polite.

"Gesslinger," said Ryan, his voice a whisper.

"You alone?"

"Two of us."

Now the voice called out from the narrow opening, "Robert!" From the darkness to their rear emerged the young man who had delivered the note, only the white teeth of his smile visible against the black of his beard. His eyes remained hidden beneath the bill of his worker's cap. Ryan thought of a Cheshire cat. Again that deep voice belying his youth: *"C'est moi.* Follow me, monsieur, mademoiselle."

The man who opened the door for them was older, perhaps in his fifties, a pistol at his side. He slid shut the bolt once all three had entered. The long hallway was littered with trash, broken bottles, newspapers, a pile of long-discarded political posters and frazzled protest signs still on stick handles. Shoulder-high stacks of cardboard boxes lined each side, reeking of dampness and mold. They passed by a frayed Nazi propaganda poster tacked to the wall—Hitler reviewing the troops—defaced with a large "V" sketched in red on his forehead and a crudely-drawn and miniscule cock hanging from the Führer's fly. A single bulb dangled from a frayed cord above their heads.

Their guide ignored the first two doors and opened the third. The room was cleaner than the hall and appeared recently swept. An older man waited for them in an armchair, its dark-green velvet smooth from years of use. The floor lamp with fringed shade cast a bright halo on his bald spot. Newspapers and books were scattered to either side. Ryan spotted on the man's lap a bold headline boasting of the latest Wehrmacht successes.

"Do you read, my friends?"

Ryan gave Nicole a quick glance before answering. "Of course we can read." He relaxed his grip on the pencil knife but held it ready.

"No, not *can* you read, *do* you read?"

A mystified Ryan proceeded with caution. "Yes, of course. What do you mean— newspapers, journals, literature?"

"Whom do you read…who's your favorite author?"

Ryan tried to make out book titles at the man's feet with no success. "Marcel Proust." A stab in the dark.

"Excellent choice, given your reason for coming here." He looked to the others for agreement, but they seemed as confused as Ryan. *Á la recherche du temps perdu*—remembering past times, of course. Destined to be a classic, if not a particularly exciting read."

Ryan felt impatience rising. "What are we doing here?" He glanced at the two men behind him near the door and thought again of Gurs. His fingers tightened on the pencil weapon.

"Why, exactly that, monsieur—we're remembering *your* times past. You couldn't have chosen a better literary title. You come here seeking to reconnect with an old friend, and you need our help finding him, correct?"

Ryan tensed at the click of a hammer. The smiling young man had trained a handgun on them, an old Colt service revolver. The other man held his weapon to the side, his finger on the trigger.

The older man sprang from the armchair, spry for his age, an agility belying his weather-worn face and drooping white mustache. His newspaper fell to the floor. The man tilted the shade of the lamp to cast light directly on them, then stepped to within a meter of Ryan and looked him in the eyes. Dense brushes of hair sprouted from the man's nostrils and ears.

"We have had several 'friends' come calling here, each with a different story and a different reason for seeking this mysterious 'Gesslinger'." He chuckled. "And each proved a liar, not really interested in friendly discourse." He turned abruptly and picked up his newspaper, folding the sheets and adding them to the pile beside the chair. "So we had to kill them."

Nicole clasped her handbag to her chest and her eyes met Ryan's, but he saw no fear.

"What makes you different?" The question came from the middle-aged man behind them. He now pointed his automatic at them.

"Because he and I are old friends—since university days—I know him well, and this young woman is a partisan, only here to help me in my search for them."

"Them?"

"Yes, my friend and his companion…blonde, tall, long legs, a looker. There's also a boy. Do you want names? You already have 'Gesslinger'."

"You bring us nothing new with that, monsieur. Our previous guests could also describe them well, for all the good it did them. And they, too, knew names. What else do you have for us?"

Ryan's mind raced over his past associations and experiences with René, anything that Horst wouldn't know but a true friend might. They now found themselves where Gestapo lackeys had failed this test and died for it. Ryan's eyes dropped to the cracked linoleum at his feet, momentarily seeking signs of dried blood, imagining the bodies falling.

"Here's a thought, monsieur, since you appear a bit stumped. Rather than asking your friend's favorite book—"

"Yes?"

"Try his favorite color. Yes, your Monsieur Gesslinger must have a favorite color. Do you know it?"

My God, thought Ryan, *our lives depend on this?* Nicole watched him calmly, awaiting his response. Her composure floored him. He couldn't recall ever discussing favorite colors with René, unless it was his preference in wine. Pinot blanc. No, that certainly wouldn't do. *Too much at stake to be wrong.*

And then he knew it, as sure as he would ever be, and willing to gamble their lives on it. It wasn't white, because white contains all colors, and not black, for that's the absence of color. "Orange, monsieur. The color is orange." *Gesslinger Rhein-Fracht,* and René, always so proud of his freighters plying the Rhine—its flag white, black, and, of course, orange.

"Bravo, monsieur…" Ryan exhaled as the man jumped from the chair and came over to shake their hands, "…and welcome! Call me Jacques, and this young fellow here calls himself Robert, whom you have already met, and my brother here likes the name Samuel, since it sounds very Jewish."

The others stuck their weapons in their waistbands and shook hands all around.

"I believe we can now help you find our friend."

❖

Once it was clear that Ryan was truly on the level, things went very well with the Bayonne partisans who guarded René's secrets so carefully.

"Come with us, my friends." Jacques clapped Ryan on the shoulder and directed them out of the room which had come close to becoming their death chamber. "We'll have a coffee, a real coffee, since our republican colleagues the other side of the Pyrénées are still able to get us some very fine beans. And then let's discuss what your buddies are up to now."

Ryan traded glances with Nicole as they followed the men. She appeared remarkably sanguine after the close call, almost as if she'd only been observing and not personally under any threat. Smiling Robert had turned back toward the alley entrance, perhaps to stand guard through the long night. The adjacent room held a wooden table covered in red wax cloth and stacked with newspapers,

Jacques set a coffeepot atop a hotplate. He offered them wooden chairs and somewhat stale biscuits from a tin. "A real shame, but you've just missed your friends by a few days. I'm afraid our Monsieur Gesslinger seeks a more active life than we can provide here in Bayonne, so he's gone north to cause trouble on the Loire. With his knowledge of shipping, he should be a valuable thorn in the side of our Germans, don't you think?"

"Definitely one of his strengths." Ryan couldn't hide his disappointment at the news, having come so close. "So how are we to find him now?"

"First, you must get up there undetected. You haven't by chance a valid travel permit from our dear Teutonic masters?" Ryan shook his head in regret. "No problem." Jacques added coffee to the pot. "I do have a few other ideas to make things easier for you. Our mutual friend goes by 'Rénard' now, by the way. A few of our local people plan to join the fun once he's settled in and taken charge up there, so we agreed in advance how to make that as simple—and safe—as possible." Jacques toasted them with a smile and an empty coffee mug removed from the shelf. "You've just survived step one, by the way."

"You must have heard my sigh of relief back there—we'd come too far to die from friendly fire." Ryan's eyes strayed again to the white tufts at the man's ears, thick as the tips of an artist's brush, and the snowy mustache appeared to sprout directly from his nostrils. A wonder the man could hear or breathe. Ryan unconsciously stroked his own slender mustache. "So first off, can you get us to Nantes without one of those transit permits?"

"Fortunately for you, we're very well connected with the French Railways, so I'd expect no problem as long as luck and timing are on your side."

"And once we arrive?"

"Near the port you'll find a hotel, *Le Brigande*. Nice rooms upstairs," his big smile at Nicole caused his mustache to inflate like a hedgehog, "should you and your lovely mademoiselle choose to overnight while waiting to hear from Rénard." Nicole remained mute.

"And how do we reach him when we arrive?"

"We've all agreed on a watchword, a long one, to be sure—'Two Years before the Mast'." Jacques pronounced the book title in heavily-accented English. "Does the name mean something to you?"

Ryan smiled. "Yes, he had trouble with Richard Dana's nautical memoir at the university."

"Well, guard that password very carefully. I doubt anyone would come upon it, but as you almost learned, wrong answers to identity questions can prove fatal." Ryan was glad the book's title hadn't been the answer needed to save their lives a few minutes before.

"And monsieur?"

"*Oui?*"

"Introduce yourself as 'Monsieur Richard Dana'." And Jacques laughed as he poured the coffee into chipped mugs.

❖

They stood side-by-side on Quai de Lesseps. Down river spread the estuary and the sea, and across the Adour loomed the city center and the confluence with the Nive River. Moonlight danced on the flowing water. Eleven o'clock approached, and Ryan was very conscious of the curfew. He had little enough time left to get a commitment from her.

"Nicole, please hear me out. You can go join your friends in the hills and continue your fight. I'm sure you'll track them down and set up your resistance elsewhere, now that the farm's compromised. I won't try to change your mind." Ryan knew the moment had arrived to present his case. "But just consider another option—why not stick with me a while longer and help my friends out of danger first? Isn't your work the same either way? And once we've found them again, you can pick up where you left off."

A police vehicle raced along the far bank of the Adour, its light flashing and siren wailing.

"Tracking them down will be easier if we travel together, and you know more about surviving in this Occupied France than I've picked up in the last few days." Ryan gave his most charming smile. "My God, without your help I'll probably be in Gestapo hands in twenty-four hours."

"And why should I care?" Nicole faced him directly, her chin jutting. The close call with the local partisans had affected her after all. As soon as Boulevard de L'Abbatoire was behind them she had cursed them all, including him. "You came here knowing the risks." Tears blurred her eyes. "Why would anyone leave America to face this horror, this constant deception and killing?"

"I came because the cause is just, noble even. If we don't fight them, who will?"

"Just? A noble cause, you say?" She bit her trembling lip. "There's nothing noble here—nothing courageous, bold or thrilling about war. War is loss!" One foot pounded the cobblestones. "War is death and innocents suffering, women and children dying." Her nose was a hands-breadth from his, her face inflamed with fury. "Believe me, I've seen it all; I live it every single day and dream it all night long."

She turned abruptly and addressed the river, her voice dropping to an ominous calm. "The only thing that matters to me is survival, to do what I must if there's even the slightest chance of success."

"But Nicole, listen, someone has to carry on the fight, whether on the battlefield or undercover, whether soldier or partisan."

She turned abruptly, the fury back. "You men disgust me! You glorify war to justify destroying lives, if only to prove your point, whether political or religious or simply out of greed. And let's not forget blatant, unemotional cruelty, most satisfying of all, *n'est-ce pas?* You men can keep your wars. Go ahead, consider yourselves bold and courageous. As for me, I do what I must because war's all I've become, and that sickens me."

She stared out across the choppy waters, alone with her thoughts. An SS gunboat throbbed downriver, its searchlight scanning the wharves and warehouses. The beam caught them, hesitated blindingly, then swung away as the vessel chugged on. Raucous gulls cried overhead, disturbed by the noise and light, now hoping for food in the wake of the passing boat or from the two figures below. The propeller wash slapped against the pilings.

Ryan admired her passion but couldn't buy into her attitude toward the war. But more important to him now was that she remained at his side. He was too close and really could use her help. "Then it doesn't really matter whether you go with me or return to the hills, does it? The battle, your battle, remains the same wherever you are. Come on, help me, Nicole—years ago I made a promise to get this woman and child to safety, and now I'm almost there. Help me keep that promise."

She remained still for so long he feared he'd lost her, but when she finally turned to him he saw resignation in her eyes and heard it in her voice. "*D'accord,* I'll see this through with you."

Ryan smiled. "I really appreciate—"

"*Non!* Forget the gratitude. I'll come because I have no choice. Just remember what I made clear—no one wins at war!"

She turned in the direction of the hotel. Ryan shook his head as he hurried to catch up with her. Her strength and conviction would give them more than a fighting chance.

LA RÉSISTANCE

1941

❖

CHAPTER ONE

Paris, Occupied France
19 August 1941

Marita had left a message with the gruff-voiced man who answered the number on Serge's calling card. She said she accepted Serge's proposal, needed to speak with him immediately, and requested a call-back that evening at her private office number. Instead, Serge appeared at the club around nine accompanied by a brooding thug who stationed himself at the curtained door to ogle the nearly-nude dancers on stage. Serge headed up the stairs to the office just as Florian came bounding down, one fist clenched, the other in his pocket with a finger on the trigger.

Serge trained a small pistol on the bodyguard and exposed his stained teeth in a malicious grin. "Wouldn't try anything, buddy."

Florian pulled up short and glared.

"That's a good boy—now let's take it nice and easy." Serge stepped past the bouncer, the barrel leveled at Florian's gut, forcing him against the railing. "Now be nice and go entertain my man Paul. And get used to it. I'm your new boss, so play by my rules—" an ugly smile split his face, "—or not at all." He continued up without looking back, returning the gun to his pocket. Furious, Florian turned to grab the man's collar, but caught movement from the corner of his eye. At the foot of the stairs lurked a tall thug, staring his way with heavy revolver drawn. At the landing, Serge entered the office without knocking.

"What the hell?" Marita half-rose from her chair.

"Why, hello, *ma petite*. And a fine good evening to you, as well." Serge settled in on the couch and adjusted the crease of his trousers.

Marita brought her shock under control. "Listen, Serge—I'll need a phone call before you drop in, and we only meet here during daylight hours when the club's closed, got it? The girls all know what happened to Colette, and your being here will drive them away."

"Nonsense." He puffed a cigar alive and tossed the match to the floor. "My man downstairs will have a quiet word with the dancers and staff and I assure you no one will quit." He drew again on the cigar. "Unless I invite them to, clear?" His face disappeared in a cloud of smoke.

"I can't run a business with you and your associates hovering around constantly. You've got my phone number. Just give me a ring when you must come by and I'll arrange to be here."

"Better yet, you be here anytime I decide to drop in. We're partners, right? Any partner of mine is on the job full-time." He took another drag on the cigar. "And evenings suit me better. I need to get acquainted with the personnel. In fact, I'll use this office to interview each of the dancers individually, up close and personal, you know what I mean? Must be sure their physical attributes reflect well on the club." He laughed while Marita seethed but held her tongue.

"You're welcome to join in, or just watch. Either way, they're in good hands, I assure you." Cigar lodged in his mouth, Serge made a crude gesture with each hand.

❖

Three evenings later Marita faced Serge again as music from the three-piece orchestra rose to a crescendo down below. She knew the girls would be parading on stage for the finale. He had actually called to let her know he was coming by toward closing to examine her books. Now he expressed disappointment at both credits and debits.

"Your booze is too good for these *Boches*; we'll switch to my supplier, and mark up the prices. They'll hardly notice the difference."

"My customers treat me well." She shuttered the former projector window, lowering the volume inside the office. "If I lose the big-spenders to one of those clubs up the street, you lose, too. Don't mess with what works."

"Ah, *ma petite*, still think you're in charge around here?" He rose from the couch to stand so close she could smell rot on his breath. He placed a hand on her shoulder, followed the curve of her arm and her hip and squeezed her ass. He stepped away abruptly as she raised a hand to slap him, then laughed at her frustration. "Get used to it, Marita." He drew out her name, emphasizing the liberties he was taking. "Both you and your little operation are now mine."

The phone on the desk startled them both. She sat and steadied her nerves before lifting the receiver.

"Yes, Florian." She listened intently, her eyes never leaving Serge. The gangster leaned against the door jamb, his arms crossed and eyes narrowed. "Yes, fine, just give me a couple of minutes before you send him up."

Serge arched his brows.

"You must leave—and now! One of my best customers, a Wehrmacht colonel, wants to bring me something and I can't have him seeing you up here."

"Ah, a gift of appreciation? Well, thirty percent of any business is mine, so I won't stand in the way of that. But better yet, why must I leave?"

"I have a reputation to protect." She made no effort to hide her disgust. "You don't fit in."

"Oh, how that hurts. I suppose your clientele's too good for the likes of me." He feigned sadness. "Well, tell you what, I'll just step into that closet there and hear the two of you out. After all, private gifts are off the books, and I can't have you hiding anything from me, can I?"

Before she could protest he was at the closet door. He left it open a crack.

A knock came at the door, and Marita put on a brave smile. "Enter, please."

CHAPTER TWO

Bayonne, Occupied France
19 August 1941

Small points of light pierced the darkness of the rail yard. Ryan spotted the shielded headlamps of a locomotive at rest and the sudden flash from coals as the door opened on an engine's firebox. A brakeman's signal lantern swung a wide arc and then disappeared again. The red marker on a departing train dissolved slowly into the night.

He ran his fingers through the tight curls on his head. The chemical smell of the permanent wave still filled his nostrils, but the new disguise was convincing. His finger reassured him that the pencil mustache was filling in with every passing hour. He had a few years on the dead Englishman, but overall their features were close enough to pass superficial police inspection. He reset the beret at an angle and climbed the staircase, still favoring his sensitive feet.

The windows of the main yard tower gave an unobstructed view of the multiple stretches of track spread out below. The trainman leaned over a slanting display board studded with small lights. The diagram indicated which rails were cleared for through traffic and the positioning of turn-outs. The larger road machines huffed about the yard, picking up their assigned consists. A smaller switching locomotive left billows of smoke in its wake as it shunted freight cars about.

One heavy engine and tender rumbled toward the engine barn, shaking the tower with its passage. It came to a stop as another locomotive rotated slowly on the turntable, preparing to head out in the opposite direction. A long train carrying armaments occupied the center of the rail yard. Ryan assumed it was destined for the Russian front via Germany and Poland.

"What the hell do you want?" The yard master had finally taken notice of Ryan, standing quietly at the open door and surveying the rail activity.

"You're Laurent?"

"Who's asking?"

"Jacques sent me. He said to give his best to your wife, Victoria."

"My wife?" Perplexed for a moment. "Ah yes, V for *Victoire*, eh? Fine, how can I be of help?"

"I need to get to Nantes."

"You can pay?" He scanned the board.

Ryan knew his cash reserves were running low. "How much?"

"A joke, monsieur." He returned his attention to Ryan. "When a request comes from Jacques, there's never a charge." Laurent took his time tamping down tobacco in his pipe while Ryan watched with envy. Rail work obviously kept the man fit, but deep creases around his eyes were etched with black soot making him appear much older. "You're also a pipe smoker, monsieur?"

"Lost mine recently to our German friends."

"*Hélas*, we've lost so much to them." Laurent's face darkened as he checked the status of his yard board.

"A ride north?" Ryan reminded the yard master.

"Ah, yes, of course, monsieur. You travel alone?"

"One companion, a woman."

"A pipe and a woman, all a man needs to be happy, *n'est-ce pas*? His mood brightened again as he reached for a clipboard and scanned the top page, his finger stopping at an entry. "What luck! Here's just the thing for the two of you. Speed and comfort! Out any time now, Paris via Bordeaux. At Poitiers you can hop a train west to Nantes."

"Excellent, monsieur. Whom do I see in Poitiers?" Ryan glanced at the large wall clock. A quarter past eleven. He hoped they'd sleep a little on the road. Exhaustion was setting in after the long and trying day.

"Yard master's Max, password's 'Trocadéro,'" but take care in the Poitiers yards, they're much more heavily guarded than ours. You get in trouble, you're done for." He returned the clipboard to its hook. "We can't have that, right? It would mean our friends in Poitiers would have to dream up a new password."

The tower shook as another heavy freight thundered past. Roiling black smoke and soot engulfed their glass box, forcing Ryan to hack his lungs clear. The yard master didn't even cough. "Here's where we're heading—track six." With the stem of his pipe, Laurent tapped the intended spot on the display. "Your woman's nearby, I presume."

"Down below…out of sight."

"Excellent. Now once you're aboard you're on your own. Last I looked, the SS guards were drinking up a storm, so little worry there, and don't be surprised should the run to Poitiers take longer than expected." His wink darkened the creases to a solid black line. "Normally we expect a few hours transit time with this type of priority express, but we're experiencing some unusual slowdowns getting *Boche* trains out." He smiled. "Just can't imagine why, can you?"

Ryan looked out and spotted track six. The military transport. "My God, monsieur, you're putting us on a troop train?"

"No troops, just armaments. A couple of guards ride up front in the locomotive, but most of the soldier guards camp out in the personnel wagon at the rear. With luck, they'll be as drunk as the dogs they are." He smiled again. "And just think how secure you'll feel with all those weapons around you."

"Another joke, monsieur?"

"Look, my friend. I'll get you safely up under the canvas. A bottle of wine—or worst case, water—a chunk of cheese, and you'll be fine till Poitiers. They never expect us to hop a military transport, so it's the safest passage you'll find—no checkpoints, no controls, just priority freight. But don't miss changing trains in the Poitiers yards or you might end up across the Rhine."

"And how do we find this Max in Poitiers?"

"Go to the yard tower again, the main one. Just take care crossing the tracks. Leave your woman below. Ask for him upstairs, and if he isn't there, he'll come running when he hears you're waiting. Just use the password and you'll do fine."

"Trocadéro." Ryan repeated, swallowing hard. "How soon do we leave?"

Laurent consulted his pocket watch and checked the status on his board. "Is now soon enough? Train leaves in about fifteen minutes. All aboard!"

"Sure, of course, why not?" Now Ryan gave his most ingratiating smile. "And, sir?"

"Yes?"

"I fear we've no time to shop." He pointed to a plate of sandwiches lying beside an open wine bottle. A half-filled glass sat nearby. "I'm sure she'll get hungry…my companion."

"Why the hell not?" Laughing, Laurent re-wrapped the sandwiches in the waxed paper, filled his glass, and handed Ryan the re-corked bottle.

Ryan slipped both gifts into the side pockets of his jacket. "We'll toast to your good health with these."

"Glad to help, now go downstairs and stay out of sight. I've got to get someone up here while I give the guided tour." He reached for the phone.

Ryan found Nicole in deep shadow behind an electrical junction box. Coal smoke and engine oil permeated the air. He smiled at catching sight of her in the darkness, grateful she still waited for him. "Ready to hop a freight?"

"Already?"

"Any moment now."

They heard footsteps cross the gravel and then bound up the stairs overhead. Seconds later, the treads creaked again as someone hurried down. A small tank locomotive approached to their immediate left pushing a dozen or so stubby railcars, the wheels click-clacking across the joints. The engine's shrill whistle pierced the air, forcing them to cover their ears. As the smoke cleared, the yard master appeared before them. He shook Nicole's hand with a "*bonsoir*, mademoiselle" and an appreciative smile.

"*Bonsoir*, monsieur. Thank you for your help."

"Quickly, now. If you think you've been spotted, signal me and I'll do my best to defuse the situation." He revealed a pistol hidden under his coat. "But if I say run, run like hell and get out of the yards anyway you can. Oh, and if I say 'drop,' drop between the tracks and keep low. Any questions?"

Neither Ryan nor Nicole spoke up. She appeared calm, but Ryan found himself stroking his unfamiliar mustache. He buried his hands in his trouser pockets.

"Good. Now hold back a couple of steps until I give the all-clear. Once we're close to your train, I check for guards. When I give a sign," Laurent demonstrated with a wave of his hand, "I cross over first and wait for you beneath the appropriate flatcar. You join me, climb aboard, and you're on your way. And for God's sake, not a sound, even if you break something crossing the tracks."

They moved out, following him past a dozen freight cars before all three climbed over the couplers linking two fuel tankers. The petroleum stench etched his nostrils, and Ryan felt momentarily lightheaded. He could tell Nicole was also breathing more raggedly as they cleared that track. Headlamps appeared down to their left. A train entered the yard, approaching rapidly on the only open rails between two strings of cars. The yard master motioned them to wait beneath an empty cattle car while he crouched across from them.

The moment the arriving train cleared the track they rejoined Laurent, now observing the targeted military consist on the next track over. Heavy armaments lay beneath camouflage which did nothing to disguise the intimidating weaponry. The yard master scanned the length of the train and Ryan followed his gaze. At the far end, two dots of orange light flitted about in the darkness beneath the dimly-lit windows of the passenger car. From their stance the cigarette smokers appeared to be talking with fellow soldiers already aboard the troop car.

At the opposite end two workers lubricated the engine's running gear as a second huge steam locomotive backed into place. The train would be double-headed. The ground shook as the engines coupled, and the cars jolted along its length.

The guards at the front end seemed intrigued by the coupling operation and ignored the rest of the train.

Suddenly, two loud SS men leaned out a window of the troop car at the tail end and tossed their comrades bottles of beer. "Now!" Laurent signaled, and Nicole and Ryan ducked low and crossed the rails to clamber beneath the flatcar. Once beyond clear line of sight, Ryan exhaled slowly.

"You first, *monsieur*, then help the mademoiselle board." Laurent pressed close to the car, loosening a tie-down and opening a gap in the tarp. At his signal, Ryan braced one foot on the axle hub, swung the other atop the wheel, and slipped in beneath the canvas.

Voices approached from the front of the train—two SS men talking and laughing. With his razor knife in his hand, Ryan held his breath, expecting any moment to hear someone raise an alarm. The guards came nearer, their words still indistinct, the men clearly unaware of potential trouble. They passed by without incident and silence returned.

Ryan counted the seconds in his mind. The railcars shuddered as the locomotives drew out the slack in preparation for departure. At last Nicole's hands appeared, grasping for a hold, and he hoisted her up and steadied her in his arms. She remained briefly, then pulled away to find a place on the oil-stained planking, her back to a massive metal tread.

The tarp began to tighten, plunging them into darkness. Unexpectedly, Laurent's hand penetrated their hiding space, set something atop the flooring, and withdrew. His hand reappeared holding the end of the tie-down. "Just yank hard when the time comes and it'll come free." He cinched taut the canvas. They barely heard his final "*bon voyage*."

In the gloom of their cave Ryan crawled over to the edge of their tenting, where his hand found a small pen-knife, perhaps for a hurried release from the canvas shroud if needed, and Laurent's pipe with its leather pouch. Matches lay buried in the tobacco. He inhaled the pungent aroma and sent silent thanks to the yard master.

The train rolled slowly from the yards, pulling north and gradually gaining speed as it left Bayonne behind. The repetitive click of the wheels established a rhythm which would accompany them for hours to come.

CHAPTER THREE

Gascony, Occupied France
19-20 August 1941

Dusk caused Leo to rethink his journey. Two ravens settled in the tree above his head, cawing incessantly. They hopped down branch-by-branch to get a closer look at the stranger entering their woods. A few rocks thrown in their direction only made them more curious. One of the large birds flapped to the ground, perhaps hoping for something edible. He cocked his head to examine the bit of stone more closely, turned it over with his beak, then rejoined his companion with a raucous cry of disappointment. Leo's shouts failed to intimidate in the slightest, but the sound of his own voice in the emptiness of the thicket made him shiver.

During the brief stays on the Morlanne farm and then in Espelette he had often escaped to the woods. His school mates were sometimes mean, ridiculing his accented French and his German family, but he had found a few friends with whom he could share his self-taught "woodsman" skills. There were even wild animals he had won over with bread crumbs and patience. One squirrel had grown so accustomed to him that it awaited his arrival daily. But at the end of the day Leo was always happy to return to the company of his mother and uncle and find something warm to eat on the table.

Leo pulled off his rucksack to consider his meager provisions. Two boiled eggs stared back at him, but most of the cheese and bread had disappeared in the course of the day. He wasn't hungry yet, or thirsty—streams offered more than enough to drink as he'd moved from woods to pastures and back, always carefully avoiding farms and waiting to cross roads until any traffic had passed. But his stomach told him he would have to find more to eat by the next evening, for sure. He figured tracking down his mother and Uncle René shouldn't take more than a few days. After all, hadn't she said they'd only be a day or two away to the north and could come for him any time he wished? He'd used his compass and map all day long, always heading just as the needle pointed.

The leaves in the ravine below trembled and something thrashed about in the brush. A snorting and snuffling headed his direction. Leo couldn't see the creature, but knew he wanted to be off the ground before they met eye to eye. Scrambling up the nearest tree, Leo kept one eye on the movement below and one on the next handhold. Surprised by the boy's sudden climb, the ravens also took to higher branches and watched with full attention as the underbrush near the base of the tree finally parted to reveal a huge, bristly pig snout.

"Go away!" Leo shouted at the top of his lungs, making his voice as fierce as possible. "Go away, get!"

The feral boar stared up at the boy. Its eyes appeared as two black olives, reminding Leo of food again. How he wished he'd stocked up better before leaving *Grand-mère's* farm. The wild pig cocked his head to the side, curious rather than aggressive, before calmly trotting up the trail. Leo sat in his perch for long minutes, making sure the visitor was truly gone. Finally bored with the boy, the ravens lifted suddenly through the highest branches and took off toward the setting sun. Their cawing settled into the distance, leaving nothing but the rustle of an evening breeze. Now he felt completely alone.

I could stay right here till morning, he thought. *But if I sleep I could fall.*

Three deer bound from the brush below, stopped for a minute to graze. Startled, they turned abruptly toward the ravine and bound away. Leo stared into the hollow but spied nothing moving.

He decided to stay put for the night, the risk of falling less frightening than whatever he might encounter at ground level in the deep shadows settling in. He positioned himself in a crotch of the tree and buttoned his jacket. He secured the rucksack to the nearest branch. It would never do to have it drop to the ground and have some creature finish off his rations. With the next cool breeze he buried his hands in his pockets and shuddered. For the first time in years he thought of the stuffed bear Bruno who had been his only childhood friend when he was very young. Now that he was grown he missed his mother, of course, but he did wish he had his bear again, at least for this one night. Bruno always knew how to make everything right.

❖

Leo awoke with a start, instinctively grabbing for the nearest branch as he realized where he sat. It had been a restless night—an owl hooting so close he thought he could reach out and touch it, a fox or maybe a badger rustling around the base of his tree, perhaps drawn by the cheese in his pack, and other noises he just couldn't identify. But at last exhaustion had won out and he had dozed off.

Now he had to pee, so he untied his rucksack from the tree and scrambled to the ground. Sunlight broke through the dense green foliage. Wildflowers rose from the grasses in scattered blues and pale yellows, and he tried to remember their names in French and German as he took care of business. How much *Grand-mère* Jeanne would have loved to see these blooms. They had often walked in the woods together before the fierce mid-day sun brought everything to a standstill, and he wondered how he would tell Uncle René that his mother was dead. Leo already missed her.

The trees overhead rustled with birds flitting from branch to branch. He watched two squirrels chasing about, one dropping several meters and then hanging precariously when it missed a landing. Leo almost laughed, but caught himself, sad not to have someone with whom he could share. Perhaps he would find *Maman* by tomorrow.

He leaned against the tree and opened his rucksack to discover ants feasting on his remaining cheese and bread. He quickly gave up trying to scrape away the insects and tossed the food into the brush. At least the eggshells remained intact. He flicked a few ants from the salt and ate his breakfast.

❖

By afternoon he was under arrest. Or so he thought. Leo was hungry, his provisions gone, and the village farmers' market, while short on offerings, was simply too hard to pass up. So he'd wandered down the row of five or six tables laden with eggs, red peppers, potatoes, tomatoes and other fruit. He helped himself to two small apples when no one appeared to be looking.

"Just what's a little boy like you doing here all by yourself?" The man wore a faded blue uniform. His eyes appeared kind, but he grabbed Leo by the jacket collar when the child made a desperate lunge toward the woods.

"I'm going to see my mother."

"And where does your mother live?"

Leo hesitated before replying. His mother had told him to tell no one of their going to Nantes. "Bayonne. She lives in Bayonne, and she's expecting me there soon, so I must be on my way." He turned to leave, the apples still in his shorts.

"Hold up there a minute, son. The only place you're going is with me, at least until we find out where you belong." The policeman knew many children tried to escape the rigorous discipline of the orphanages. The Vichy government was dedicated to ridding the country of the laxness which led to social decay, and the place to start was in the schoolroom.

"It's really simple, sir. My name is Léonard, my mother is in Bayonne and expecting me, and I can't be late." Again he took a step toward the woods.

That's when the gendarme grabbed his collar again and hustled him over to the old Peugeot sedan parked on the edge of the market. "Come along, kid, let's get to the bottom of this. You don't want me to have to use the handcuffs, now do you?"

"No thank you, sir." Now Leo really needed a way out.

The man put Leo on the passenger side and slid behind the wheel. "Now, Léonard, you told me about your mother. Where's your father? Is he a prisoner of war, perhaps? Are you an orphan?"

"No, my father is a policeman."

"Like me?"

"Oh no, something much more important—he's a secret policeman, and he won't be happy if I'm not allowed to go where I choose."

"Oh really, a secret policeman? Sounds very mysterious, Léo. Does he live nearby, or is he also in Bayonne?"

"Oh, he's all over the place. Maman says he's very busy with his duties, so he doesn't come to see us. But he will come see you when he hears you've arrested me."

"I haven't arrested you, Léo, I'm detaining you. Do you know the difference?"

"Feels like I'm arrested, *monsieur l'agent*." Leo decided it was time to pull out the big guns, as he did from time to time when the bullies in school tried to get the best of him.

"My father's German, he's Gestapo, and I'm sure he's not far away, you know."

The policeman hesitated before speaking again. "Gestapo, you say?"

Leo nodded, his face at its most serious. "And very powerful. My *Maman* always says he's a very dangerous man you never want to cross."

"And what's your father's name, Léo? Your family name?"

Leo hesitated once again. It was a name *Maman* always said not to use. A family secret, *dangerous in the wrong hands*, she said. But a serious situation called for most serious measures.

"His name is von Kredow. But you mustn't tell people that or it could get you into trouble, *monsieur l'agent*. A lot of trouble."

"Well, Léo, I still must take you to the station with me. Bayonne is a long way from here. But we can get in touch with the German Gestapo and I'm sure they'll be happy to track down this 'troublesome' father of yours." He turned the key and the engine rumbled to life. "I'm sure Herr von Kredow is worried sick."

❖

For over two hours he sat listlessly at the village police station, watching people come and go, some with complaints about neighbors, one woman telling all who would listen that Madame Lecroix next-door was surely hoarding foodstuffs or engaged in black-marketeering, since she appeared so much better-nourished than most of the village citizens. A man protested that someone was stealing his chickens, but the two policemen laughed him out of the room when he admitted he had no idea how many fowl he had, just "many." Another citizen arrived to demand help in tracking down a stolen bicycle. Leo constantly watched for any opportunity to escape, but none came.

The desk sergeant had seated him behind the counter, and reprimanded him every time he budged or kicked his legs against the chair rungs out of boredom. At last the officer who had arrested him rushed out of the back office, grasping a sheet of paper off the telegraph wire to hand to the sergeant.

"Better take a look at this." The gendarme appeared worried.

The sergeant scanned the wire. "The kid tells the truth, eh?" He glanced over at Leo, who gave him a look of I-told-you-so. "Unbelievable. They want him in Bayonne, and right away. Seems his father really does pull weight in the Gestapo."

Next came a frightening whirl, one stranger after another. First a policeman came to fetch Leo and bring him to the train station. The nervous young man forced the boy to sit quietly at his side during the entire trip to the city. As they entered the terminal they quickly passed through the papers control, waved through thanks to the cop's uniform. Leo, eyes wide at the hustle and bustle of travelers and uniforms, wasn't prepared for what came next.

A stern matron, her face pinched downward in a perpetual frown, her body rigidly erect, waited beyond the control point and glared directly at Leo as he approached. The police companion seemed to know that the woman was awaiting their arrival and handed her paperwork to sign. Leo gave her a shy smile in the hope of breaking through that cold reserve, but it had the opposite effect. She bent toward him and with no warning slapped him across the cheek. The sudden attack left him angry, frightened and disoriented. Through unwanted tears, he started to protest but was cut short by an angry, pinching hand on his shoulder.

"Listen, young man, and listen carefully. I'm not going to repeat myself. Don't expect coddling around here. You're in my care and you'll do exactly as I say, when I say it. I don't take kindly to back-talk or misbehavior of any kind from my children."

Leo's cheek stung from the blow, and the woman hadn't released her viselike grip on his shoulder. In fact, the pressure seemed to have increased as she stared directly in his eyes. He was at a loss to explain her anger, but he knew enough not to aggravate it further. He nodded weakly, trying to hold back further tears.

"But, madame…" began the young policeman, equally surprised by the woman's brutal reception.

"You're dismissed, officer. I have my orders and they come from very high up. You may return to your village duties—the boy's in capable hands and won't give anyone more trouble. Isn't that right, boy?"

Leo forced himself to nod. He was certain there had been some big mistake. His mother or uncle would hear about this and set these people straight.

From the station she marched him down a long street and across a bridge. Leo slowed to watch the gulls swooping and the boats passing on the river below, but the woman would have nothing of it, shoving his shoulder at any slackening of pace. They entered the heart of the city, passing shops and strolling citizens and many men in uniform, but his guardian looked neither right nor left, her attention focused solely on Leo's posture and some as-yet undetermined goal.

Finally they reached a quiet side street flanked by tall apartment buildings unlike any seen by Leo since his childhood in Berlin. The facades were ornate with carvings, and staircases climbed to leaded-glass entries. The matron pushed him brusquely when he hesitated at the foot of steps guarded by massive stone lions. They entered a long hallway with highly-polished wooden floors that creaked under their footsteps. A stone staircase took them to a second-floor apartment where another woman, this one in a white uniform rather than wool suit, stiffened at the sight of the matron.

"Your name?" The matron was grasping his shoulder again, painfully.

"Léo." He made his voice firm, imagining how his uncle would respond to this new situation.

"Agnès, this is our new charge, and an important one. He gives any trouble, whip him into shape. Don't spare the rod. He'll room with the other children, but don't take your eyes off this one, even for a minute. His father has given direct orders that the boy goes nowhere. He escapes, you'll be on a train headed east, and fast, do I make myself clear?"

"Very clear, madame." Agnès glanced at Leo and back to the matron. "Will he be with us long?"

"That's no business of ours. As long as it takes. For now, get the brat bathed and into some clean clothes—hand-me-downs will do for now—and feed him something. He can start his lessons with the rest of the children tomorrow."

"Yes, madame."

The matron didn't give Leo another look before leaving the room. Agnès squatted before him, taking his chin in her hand and looking the boy directly in the eyes. "Listen to me, Léo, and listen carefully. We all do exactly as ordered here, do you understand?"

He nodded, already planning his escape.

"Any trouble from you, I must use the switch, and I don't like it any better than you do, clear?" Leo had never felt a whip, but he had seen farmers striking their animals and he knew his life had taken a turn for the worse.

Agnès led him down a long, dark hallway with enormous ceilings to a very large room. The windows were tall and opened to the street far below. The other children looked up as they entered, eyes filled with curiosity at the new arrival. Leo saw a boy about ten working a puzzle at a table beside the window, a girl close to his own age playing cards with a slightly younger boy and a toddler dressed in a smock stacking colorful blocks on the rug. The older children did not smile, but acknowledged Leo with nods and returned to their play.

"Children, this is Léo. He'll be with us a while. Madame says he gets no special treatment, so inform me if he misbehaves in any way. Understood?" All but the toddler nodded their understanding. "Now, Léo, it's bath time for you. You look like you've tramped across a wilderness, but you're back in civilized society now."

CHAPTER FOUR

Poitou, Occupied France
20 August 1941

The hours passed, an unrelenting clatter of rails and wheels and whistles. Despite the American at her side on the hard planking, she sat alone with her thoughts. Antonio constantly came to mind. Antonio—with the tall, slender physique of an athlete, so handsome in that moody way, his dark eyes witness to his Spanish blood.

When Nicole first saw him she found his arrogance annoying, his self-assurance so powerful it repelled her. Her final year of *lycée* was coming to an end, and she was about to celebrate her twentieth birthday. She sat over lemonade with her friend Adèle at a café in Mauléon-Licharre. He strutted back and forth before his high school buddies, bragging of some winning goal on the soccer field. He glanced their way, scanning their bodies and legs. She knew immediately he preferred Adèle with her chestnut hair and those beautiful pale blue eyes. Most boys did. Nicole assured her friend she had no personal interest, and advised her to return his flirting gaze to draw him over. They returned to their lemonade and soon Antonio appeared at their table, inviting them to join him and his friends.

For Adèle's sake they accepted, and over the next hour he bragged of his prowess on the soccer field, his marksmanship on the target range, and his feats of endurance swimming the surf off Saint-Jean-de-Luz. Nicole stared out the window and let the words flow past her, while Adèle listened intently and asked silly questions to keep him talking, all the while twisting a lock of that hair around her finger. Nicole suddenly realized he was waiting for her to notice him, and she sensed some vulnerability behind all his braggadocio. With that he became more attractive.

She'd seen him again the following week. She had stayed late after school to visit the local library and spotted him as she came up the road to their farm. Antonio sat on the bed of the hay wagon, his long legs dangling, smoking a cigarette and chatting with her father about boar hunting. She avoided his gaze and headed for the door, but her father called her over.

"Nikki, this young man came all the way out here just to see you."

"Well, here I am." She gave her father a perturbed look. "Let him have his look." She turned in place, her skirt swirling and ponytail trailing, then headed back toward the house. "Thanks for coming," she called back, and was gone.

The next evening he and her father sat outside again, talking and smoking, and every day at sundown for two weeks they discussed hunting, shooting and politics. Nicole hated staying inside the house on such beautiful early summer evenings, and soon she found reason to loiter nearby, feeding chickens or rabbits, or reading a novel that didn't really interest her. The more she heard Antonio talk, the more she found herself drawn to him.

Generalissimo Franco's horrific retaliation against supporters of the Republic had driven his family out of Spain. While the democratically-elected government reeled in its death throes, Antonio's French father had situated his wife and children in France before rejoining his overwhelmed Republican comrades. He fell in battle, his body never returned.

Antonio was a committed Socialist like Nicole's own father, and the two spent hours condemning the fascists. Soon they were practicing with firearms, preparing for the imminent ground war in France. It did not take long before Nicole joined them. She had been hunting with her father from her youngest years, and when Antonio challenged her to outshoot him, she did.

One evening they found themselves alone. Her father had left early to help a neighbor birth a calf. Antonio suggested they take the rifles and go down into the meadow for target practice. The setting sun bathed the fields and woods in golden light, and the air was warm and humid. Antonio pulled off his shirt. She liked what she saw, and soon she lay in those well-muscled arms. They made love in the meadow with her skirt around her waist and her backside itching from the grasses. They became lovers.

By the end of summer they were married, finding a common hatred of bullies and an appreciation of the beauties of nature. Her father was thrilled to have a politically likeminded son-in-law who could run the farm, since his arthritis had made significant inroads. Antonio moved his mother and younger sisters into the stone building across the courtyard from the main house. Sophie was born, a beautiful baby with dark hair like her father and blue eyes like her mother.

And when war finally came, Antonio was granted an exemption from military duty because the crops had to be brought in. The Third Republic needed foodstuffs. And then France fell, and the family farm ended up in the Occupied Zone.

Antonio and her father began to plot resistance against the German occupiers, while Nicole sat nearby with Sophie at her breast and worried. She knew how hot-headed her young husband was, filled with stories of his own father's guerilla battles and untimely death under Luftwaffe fire from the skies, as Hitler prepared for his own war of conquest by assuring Franco's army the victory over the Republicans.

"You keep this up," she had cried, "and you'll leave us just as your father abandoned your family. Doesn't our child mean enough to you to stay out of it? Don't I?"

But Antonio wasn't willing to compromise his honor, even for the sake of his wife and child. Then she had lost them both, her husband and her daughter, and the memories of holding her darling baby in her arms brought tears of sorrow and loss. She hated Antonio for having left her all alone and for what he had made her become, yet she still loved him.

Lost in these thoughts, Nicole cried beneath the canvas tent as the military train rolled on toward Bordeaux and Poitiers. The stench of oil and grease from the massive assault vehicle nauseated her, and the American at her side snored in the growing heat, his head against the metal tread. He had tried to smoke the pipe left by the yard master, but knocked out the ashes when he sent her into a fit of coughing.

❖

Ryan used the penknife to open a small slit in the canvas just above their heads. It wasn't much, just enough to allow a draft of air as the train rumbled along toward Bordeaux. He had dozed off for a while, but now the heat was building as morning dawned and the tenting gave their skin a sickly greenish cast. The planking beneath them became ever harder to endure, and his back was sore pressing against the hard track of the motorized gun.

He thought of offering Nicole his lap, since she moved restlessly as if dreaming, and he knew his own backside was already aching from the hard surface so she couldn't be comfortable. But he also knew she would misinterpret the suggestion, and he didn't want to offend her. She clutched her handbag to her chest and in the growing light of dawn he saw tears in the corners of her shut eyes. He wished he could put his arm around her.

Kilometer after kilometer clicked past, the train braking noisily for occasional unscheduled stops. He once heard a trainman or soldier—he couldn't see which—walk past below their car, complaining to a colleague of a broken turnout ahead. An hour or so later it happened once again, but this time someone spoke of a malfunctioning signal light holding up rail traffic in both directions. Laurent's mention of a slower-than-typical journey began to make sense.

He was getting hungry and longed for a sandwich and some wine, but wouldn't disturb Nicole until she was ready. He hoped they would soon arrive in Poitiers to change trains. Ryan already looked forward to Nantes. Jacques had shared a few details about his friends' resistance activities in the Bayonne region, where René and Erika had earned respect despite their German heritage.

The rail journey seemed to take forever, his traveling partner still shifting about constantly on the planks, and his stomach grumbled from hunger. In desperation, he uncorked the wine bottle to tame a raging thirst.

Nicole cried out in her fitful sleep.

❖

They had come in the night, of course. They always came in the night. A biting winter storm had settled in, muffling sound and fraying nerves. The bitter cold robbed the old farm house of any warmth. Nicole had barely put Sophie in her crib—a head cold had troubled the baby for days—and now the anxious young mother slipped beneath the comforter and snuggled close to Antonio. She wanted a bit of his body warmth, to feel deeply loved by him again.

Lately he had been so distant, his thoughts devoted to a grand scheme to strike hard and fast against the Nazis in the heart of their local operations, the Waffen-SS forces stationed between Bayonne and Biarritz. Their top officers partied nightly in the fine restaurants overlooking the beach in the resort town. Antonio and his partisans would plant a bomb, decapitate the troop leadership, and bring the war back to their enemy, since the Allies didn't seem anxious to return to mainland Europe.

Nicole hadn't been able to let it rest, and she knew her nagging aggravated Antonio and pushed him away. But her intuition got the better of her and she feared for them all. Her father could barely walk now, even with a cane. Antonio's mother had her hands full with his two sisters, eleven and thirteen, who still thought of themselves as Spaniards and ached to return south, an impossibility given the fascist rule. "Why not just be satisfied with what we're doing here?" she asked again and again. The farm was a good, secluded way station to guide fugitives across the border, they shared intelligence with friends of the cause, and they were making a difference. It was never enough for her Antonio.

And then that brutal night. Few vehicles made it up their long drive to the house and farmyard, so the sound of engines shutting down and the boots on frozen gravel grabbed her attention.

She shook Antonio awake. "Darling, there's something going on out there!"

"I need my sleep." He turned away from her, his mind fogged.

Her whisper louder now and insistent. "Antonio, something *is* happening outside!"

"Go back to sleep, I'll take a look in the morning." He pulled the covers over his head. "Probably just some animal—now get some rest."

Nicole climbed from bed and peered out into the dark night, her limbs shaking with cold. Nothing moved. An owl hooted somewhere deep below in the wood. But then she knew something was amiss. Her big Labrador Sasha was a light sleeper. Any unusual noise and she would alert them with a throaty bark. Nicole knew her own ears hadn't betrayed her, and Sasha was quiet. Too quiet.

It was all over quickly. The tramping of boots up creaking stairs, the door to their bedroom giving way as Antonio tried to escape the twisted covers. Nicole lunged for the crib. Sophie awoke to the terrible racket and bawled in terror. She lifted the child in her arms and backed into a corner, cowering before the men in black uniforms and helmets, rifles aimed at their bellies and her daughter.

From the courtyard below rose the screams of her mother-in-law and the two girls rousted from their sleep. Antonio reached for his pants but a soldier prodded him with a bayonet and he raised his hands instead, his hatred gleaming in the dim light as he unleashed a torrent of Spanish curses. The soldier brought the rifle butt down and blood streamed from a torn ear.

Nicole had screamed "No!"

The monstrous night remained a strange blur in her memory, every moment sharply in focus when recalled, and yet as a whole amorphous, bathed in mental fog. Perhaps her mind simply refused to accept the tragedy in its entirety.

The soldiers drove them all into the courtyard dressed in nothing but nightclothes. A tall man waited, his face a terrifying mask, frozen, showing nothing, clearly feeling nothing as he ordered his men to herd Antonio and her crippled father to the stone wall. They fell to the gunfire before they could even say good-byes. She remembered Sasha next to their crumpled bodies, her eyes open and glassy as flakes of snow slowly covered them.

Then one SS soldier clubbed her mother-in-law with his rifle and beat her again as she went down. Two others stripped the nightdresses from the girls and tears streamed down their faces as they sought to cover themselves with their hands. Their comrades laughed at the sport and waited their turns. Another man grabbed Nicole and tossed her to the ground. She fell to the icy gravel with the baby in her arms, but the cruel, stone-faced officer intervened and ordered her baby daughter taken from her. Nicole screamed in protest, but the man in charge said nothing. Gripping her hair, he yanked back her head and forced her into the kitchen ahead of him. He slammed her face-down over the table. When he finally left, blood ran down her legs as she crumpled to the floor.

Her father was gone. Antonio was gone. More gunshots stilled the screams of the sisters. And her beloved Sophie, her most precious love, she too was gone.

Somehow, Nicole survived, but she was not the same. She would play it well or die trying. Hers was now to be cruel, emotionless, and brutal. She would use men as they had used her. She would be like the men she so hated, for she, too, was now a ruthless killer.

As their train left the Bordeaux yards they crossed the Garonne and soon a bridge over the Dordogne River rattled beneath them. She watched through the slit of the canvas as the river waters flowed toward the Gironde Estuary, the Atlantic Ocean, and freedom. When the Allied Powers came at last, would they come from the west, attack here at Bordeaux or perhaps somewhere farther north along the Atlantic Wall? Would they come with planes and tanks and landing craft and huge ships to free France from occupation and tyranny?

Would they please come soon, so she could end this life thrust upon her?

❖

The rail yard at Poitiers was in constant motion, loud and dirty. Engines chuffed by relentlessly in all directions, rolling stock coasted past; shrieking train whistles split the muggy air. Their train finally ground to a halt and they waited impatiently as a group of workers gathered alongside for discussion punctuated by bawdy insults. Once the workers went their separate ways, Nicole tore the slit in the canvas a bit further to sight down the train in either direction. Nothing but smoky sky and constant movement met her stinging eyes. It was time for them to switch trains.

Abruptly she lurched backwards. "Oh my God!"

"What is it?" The American scrambled to his feet.

"Troop train," she whispered, one eye glued to the opening in the canvas. "Next track over…just sitting there!"

He moved to take a look but she put a hand to his chest to hold him back, unwilling to surrender the frightening sight. In either direction stretched a string of drab coaches filled with soldiers. Destined for the Eastern Front, she knew. She could see them inside the nearest railcar, so close she felt she could reach out and knock at the windows, and she feared they might spot her at the peep hole. Most men sat idly, some reading letters or newspapers, others laughing and joking, a few looking out directly toward their flatcar. Others gathered in the aisle, smoking and chatting with comrades.

She allowed the small flap to drop. "Nothing to do but wait." The American took his turn at the spyhole before quickly sitting again. Frustration darkened his features. In the pale khaki light of their canvas canopy she thought of Antonio, and knew a similar fervor drove this foreigner. Then she thought of her daughter and her mind clouded, but she refused to allow the tears.

The minutes ticked relentlessly by. A half hour came and went. Unless the neighboring train moved out soon there would be no escape from their sweltering tent, no control tower to seek out, no "Trocadéro" to buy passage to Nantes, no end to all this. They finished the stale cheese sandwiches and the wine, but remained dehydrated and hungry. She sensed the American's frustration seething beneath the surface, but what outlet could he find for his anger, since who could blame fate and ill-timing? Another quarter hour passed and she checked the peephole once again. The Wehrmacht soldiers next door appeared equally restless, anxious to be on their way, even if toward that great killing field now splitting Eastern Europe into bloody halves.

With a sudden jolt their armaments train lurched forward again and crept out through the yards, signal lights ahead turning green to speed their advance.

Ryan appeared glum. "Forget our connection for Nantes."

"Tours, then?" She distractedly ran a fingernail beneath each of her others, trying to dislodge the dirt and grime. Despite the canvas cover they both wore a dark film of soot and cinders.

"That'd be my first guess." He drew out the heavily-worn map taken from the dead English agent. "Tours, and then on to Paris. I've heard they route all the trains heading east through Paris. But that's the last thing I need—we need—right now." He squinted at the map in the pale light, shaking his head from time to time.

My God, she thought, this does change everything. She sat again and sought in vain any marginally comfortable position. Her butt ached, her legs ached, she found her mind aching with exhaustion and frustration. They had both finally surrendered to the inevitable and taken a turn sidling along the huge armored gun to take a piss on the forward planks of the flatcar. Now the American leaned his head back against the vehicle track and shut his eyes. Over the constant rumble and rattle of the flatcar and the endless click-clack of the rail joints, she thought she heard him sigh.

CHAPTER FIVE

Tours, Occupied France
20-21 August 1941

By late afternoon their train reached the yards in Tours. From a distance he spotted the heavy damage the Allied bombs had wrought on the lovely medieval city on the Loire. He remembered the pre-war beauty of this short-lived French capital. Now the sight of this once-charming river town in rubble saddened him. When their train pulled aside to allow passage of a troop transport, perhaps the very one that had thwarted them in Poitiers, they made their break. Below the track bed lay a wooded gully, and no railway or military personnel were visible in either direction. Ryan yanked the tie-down binding their canvas prison and the cord released, just as Laurent had predicted.

Sore from hours of sitting, Ryan and then Nicole dropped clumsily past the canvas flap to the gravel and scrambled beneath the railcar. When all remained clear, they crouched low and ran down the embankment into the trees, all senses alert for the first cry of alarm or a gunshot. None came. So far, so good.

They waited until the train moved on. Beyond the woods lay a paved roadway and they made themselves as presentable as possible. Nicole still carried her handbag, but they had left the valise in Bayonne, expecting to be in Nantes by day's end to easily replace what little they needed. She brushed out her gritty hair and tied up the ponytail with the lavender ribbon. Ryan used his fingers to rake the cinders from his curls. He desperately needed a shave. Their faces, stained by the grime of rail travel, appeared coarse under late afternoon light. On the trek into town Ryan finally found an opportunity to smoke his pipe.

As they approached the ruined center he spotted the control point and grabbed for her elbow. At a narrowing between two piles of building rubble two armed gendarmes smoked, bored, waiting for someone to harass. The officials hadn't yet looked their direction when Ryan pulled Nicole into an alleyway.

So exhausted and on edge, she hadn't paid attention to what lay ahead. "What the hell?"

"Gendarmes, looking for trouble." His voice low and steady. "I'll go through first. We're bound to face this sooner or later, so let's just get it over with. I'm too beat to look for an alternate route. If there's a problem, head back south. Your papers are good. Mine? Who knows?"

"*Non*, better we stay together. Let them check mine first—you're right, mine are solid. Maybe then they'll be less concerned with yours. Men tend to believe what I tell them." Her look dared him to comment, but he kept silent. "Besides—" she opened her handbag for Ryan to glance inside, "—any problem will be theirs."

He saw the grip of a small pistol. "You'll shoot them?"

"They wouldn't be the first."

He remembered the Gestapo agent lying on the roadway, holes in head and side. "No, leave it be—we certainly don't want a manhunt when they find two dead cops. Let me run the gauntlet. The Englishman's papers should be good, and I look enough like him now. I'll say I lost my wallet so I'm on foot, then once through, I'll wait a couple of alleys farther along until you join me. And keep that damned gun out of sight, okay?"

Calm, her hand in the bag. "They try to arrest you and they're mine." He heard the click of the safety.

"Look, it's my fight, not yours. I won't have you take that risk." Ryan strode out purposefully and approached the gendarme control.

They noticed him immediately and ordered a halt. "Monsieur, your papers, please." Ryan handed over his identity card for the man to examine. "And your destination?"

"Heading south. Work permit and job offer are in here." He gave the sergeant the letter promising employment, but the gendarme snatched the whole packet from Ryan's hand and perused it carefully." Ryan played nonchalant. "Hell of a mess here, don't you think? The Allies almost destroyed your beautiful city."

"I'm from Rennes." He refolded the paperwork. "Says there you were hospitalized. What for?"

"Pneumonia, they think."

"You look healthy enough now, although you could use a bath." He grinned at his colleague. "Our friend here says he's heading south, yet we find him heading north? What a poor sense of direction! Hmm, do you find something familiar about him?" His partner rested his hand on a holstered pistol while the sergeant flipped through a clipboard. "Ah, here it is…" the corners of his mouth wrinkled, "Gestapo bulletin 3442. Unfortunately, monsieur, our German colleagues appear interested in someone who looks just like you. Probably your brother, right?"

Ryan sent Nicole a mental message to stay put. He'd find his way out of this without gunplay. "I'm sure there's been a mistake."

The gendarme nodded. "Agreed, they happen everywhere. Well, now, on the way with you." Ryan reached for his papers but the gendarme made no effort to return them.

"*Mab ar c'hast.*"

Ryan pondered the garbled-sounding words. "What's that you say, officer?"

"*Mab ar c'hast.*" The man's smile grew wider as he nudged his colleague.

Ryan felt his shoulders tense. "Sorry, sir, I didn't quite get that."

"Your identity card says you're a native of Rennes, yet you speak no Breton? Now *that's* something we find suspect." He handed the packet of identification papers to his buddy. "I'm sure you'd agree, monsieur."

At that moment a motorcycle rumbled up carrying two more policemen. The driver pushed his goggles to his brow to address the control guards. "Trouble?" His partner extracted himself from the sidecar.

"None at all. The checkpoint's yours. Our wayward friend here will accompany us back to the station. It's a little matter for the Gestapo. I'm sure the gentleman here will soon be back on his way—" he lifted an eyebrow to his comrades, "—south." The officer in charge turned to Ryan. "By the way, in case you were wondering, monsieur—from one Breton to another—I called you a 'son of a bitch'."

The handcuffs clicked shut and they called for a car. Ryan prayed Nicole wouldn't tackle four armed gendarmes with that pitiful little handgun. Thankfully, she didn't.

❖

Ryan rolled to his side to stretch his legs. One calf suddenly cramped and he bolted upright, grasping the limb, willing away the sharp pain. He massaged the sore muscles and waited it out. For a few precious hours he had actually managed to lose himself in troubled dreams, allowing much needed sleep to push reality from his mind. But now it returned in its all-encompassing threat, and the pain in his calf was the least of his worries. He jumped up and down on the tight leg in the narrow confines of the jail cell, insisting the seizing muscle surrender to his will. The soles of his feet were still scabbed and sensitive, so he quickly sat again on the foul-smelling cot.

As the cramping faded, he thought of Nicole and wondered whether she had made it safely away. He half-hoped she would show up to somehow lend support to his story. No, he realized, better she returns to her friends in the south.

There was nothing more she could do for him here. He knew her self-reliance and had no doubts she'd find her way back to Gascony.

Her intensity reminded him of Erika on that fateful run for the Rhine and freedom. Nicole also seemed always distracted, distant, often unreadable. Nicole. All that beauty, but never the hint of a smile. At least Erika had relaxed toward the end as they sat together in the shack, believing they had escaped her husband's wrath. What a wasted effort over intelligence which had never seen the light of day. Ryan reined in his thoughts again. Nothing should distract him from his current dilemma.

He surveyed his surroundings, as if they might have changed even slightly over the preceding hours. The cell was barely a meter-and-a-half wide and two deep. He could easily reach out to touch both slick side walls when standing at the iron door. The short cot left little floor space, and a small, barred window at the back allowed a slender shaft of light to track across the graffiti-laden walls as the day progressed. At head height he noted a series of smudges. Closer examination convinced him of the source—dried smears from a bloody head slammed repeatedly against the wall. He was now the guest of the Tours gendarmerie, awaiting an imminent visit from the Gestapo.

They had taken all of his papers, but none of that mattered anyway. His adopted identity as Hervé Delacourt had been short-lived. He hadn't had time to rid himself of the home-made razor knife and the trainman's penknife, taken as further proof of his suspect motives if not of some as yet undiscovered guilt. He missed the pipe, too, even though he'd only smoked it once after escaping the rail car. He was thankful to keep his clothes, foul-smelling as they had become in the god-awful train ride beneath the tarp. And he had quickly turned his ring inward and closed his fists as they pulled out the cuffs, so the cameo stone had remained out of sight and the rest appeared to be a wedding band. If all else failed, he still had the lethal pill. With the Gestapo alerted and on its way, it would only be a matter of time before Horst had him in his grips again, and he would never get a third chance to escape torture and death. *Could things get any worse?*

❖

Nicole had watched in horror as they put Ryan in restraints and carted him away in a police van. Losing him now was out of the question. They had come this far together, and she had made a commitment to find his friends in Nantes. And here he was, stuck in police custody. Should he end up in Gestapo hands now, all bets were off. She was at wit's end, but too much was at stake to stop now.

At a newsstand she got directions to the nearest public baths. Once showered and her clothes shaken out as best she could, she applied lipstick and mascara and tied back her damp hair. Nothing could be done about the dark circles under her eyes, but overall she found herself presentable for the task at hand.

A bicycle taxi brought her to the gendarmerie. The reception room was quiet in the late afternoon hour—a disheveled man with scraggly beard snored while cuffed to a chair, a prostitute examined her nails, two gendarmes smiled at some shared joke as they took a resigned-looking man toward the presumed holding cells. And the young officer at the desk rose immediately, clearly anxious to impress her. "Your business with us, mademoiselle?"

"You hold in custody a certain Monsieur Hervé Delacourt, *monsieur l'agent*. He's my cousin, and I wish to speak with him." Had he not been in lock-up, Ryan would have been pleased to see Nicole could actually smile, though no warmth shown in her eyes. The policeman appeared anxious to please the young woman with the full red lips. His finger ran the recent entries in the booking ledger and the corners of his mouth dropped as he read a scrawled notation. "I regret, miss, but your cousin awaits an interrogation by the Gestapo. We cannot allow any visits at this time."

"But I must see him right away—his family deserves to know what's going on." She tilted her head to the side and smiled again. "Is there nothing at all you can do? I'd be most grateful." She touched her hair, her lips forming a pout.

"Let me ask, miss." He disappeared into the back but returned almost immediately, his dejection apparent. "Mademoiselle…it's the Gestapo, you do understand. Were it up to me…"

Nicole turned for the door before he'd even finished, a new plan coalescing in her mind. She would handle things differently. Success remained her only option.

❖

Day two in the tiny cell was a torture of its own. The first night's dinner had been a crust of stale bread and a thin soup reminiscent of beets and onion. For breakfast on the second morning the same watery broth arrived enhanced with shavings of carrot and cabbage. A paltry smear of rancid butter accompanied the morning's bread, and Ryan devoured everything with gusto. An enameled vessel held stale drinking water, a metal cup serving as its lid. His stomach still growled in hungry protest, and his mouth tasted of ashes. His teeth were coated. No one had come to empty the latrine bucket shoved beneath the cot and the stench was becoming unbearable. The lid was missing. Only a few squares of newsprint were provided for sanitary purposes.

His protests to the guard who occasionally strode the aisle between cells brought no sympathy. He learned that the Gestapo would arrive by nightfall, or perhaps the next day at the latest, since an official in Bayonne was very interested in his case. "Once they get their hands on you, monsieur, you'll wish you were back enjoying these fine accommodations of ours."

"But the bucket…"

"Cleaning lady's day off, monsieur. Just shit less often, and tomorrow will be here before you know it." He laughed his way down the hall. Ryan had seen the other prisoners taken from their cells with buckets in hand to empty them in a toilet somewhere, so knew he was getting special treatment.

As the day progressed. he gave more serious thought to the K-pill hidden in his ring. Or L-pill, as others called it. "K" for "kill." "L" for "lethal." Whatever the name, the capsule promised a quick end before Gestapo torture broke the oath of silence they'd all sworn. His spirits were flagging as his body drained of energy.

How his life had changed since '29, and what an idiot he'd been! He had arrived in Germany a naïve dilettante. Life to that moment had been so sweet, and promised to continue down that welcome path—a success at every academic and social endeavor, fêted at aristocratic parties for his linguistic skill and quick wit, mingling with the nobility at the von Haldheim mansion. Behind the scenes, he'd played the foreign correspondent, risking his own life and losing that of his friend, exploring the seediest underbelly of Berlin, posing as Nazi or Communist to get a good story. He had it all—his dashing good looks the women loved, a sharp mind, and the determination that whatever he set his mind to, he would get.

But that light-hearted romp of a life was showing cracks, revealing its own vicious and treacherous underside. As the Nazis consolidated their power, as his beloved Germany opened its arms to hatred and persecution, criminal rule and war, Ryan found himself demonstrating his academic worth earning a doctorate from Marburg, gradually recognizing that his old Germany was no more. Then a careless romance—one of so many—had given him a son he barely knew, his boredom with academia had drawn him back for adventure, and his shortcomings nearly destroyed the friends he tried to save.

God, what a fuck-up I've been! The stolen protocol. His moment to make a real difference in a world surrendering to tyranny and racial hatred. And there, too, he'd failed miserably. In the past years he'd grown wiser about the ways of evil, hardened, and substantially more cautious, and yet his whole mission had been a grand joke, a manipulative play directed by a master sadist.

Had he really made any difference at all, had he affected any lives positively? Certainly not his own.

René and Erika were clearly safe without him, obviously doing just fine on their own, making a difference fighting for the cause of freedom. They had no need of him now. And that meant Leo was well looked-after and as safe as any child could be in an occupied Europe now run by the fucking fascists.

In '29 he had left his family to find his own life. Now his family had moved on. His parents had passed away quietly in '39, a year after his return to teaching. Cancer took his father first, likely from x-ray exposure in his dental practice, since few had ever suspected the necessity of lead shielding. His mother had passed a few months later, either from heart disease or loneliness after their forty-five years of marriage.

Sure, Edward would miss him, but Ed had his own family: a rich wife, an influential father-in-law, and two young kids. He would move on from the sadness and loss, telling himself Ryan never did learn to follow the rules.

How simple it would be. Open the little compartment. Crush the rubber of the capsule between his teeth and hear the crack of the tiny glass vial. Invite death in and escape this hell of a life filled with torture and deprivation. What pleasure in refusing Horst his ultimate personal vengeance, in foiling these sick monsters who take personal pleasure in the suffering of others and destroy an entire people to promote a personal agenda.

Ryan thought of Nicole. *What in hell could she possibly have experienced to drain her life of all hope and beauty?*

She could kill without hesitation or emotion, yet protest vehemently against men and their wars.

But then, from the depths of his depression, Colonel Donovan's speech to the country hit home, his call to fight while resistance was still possible and friends still able to fight side-by-side for the world's freedom. *Am I really a quitter, a gutless deserter without convictions?* He imagined the untold suffering of those already under the bastards' guns, of families torn asunder by rabid hatred and unbound cruelty. His own dilemma, his misery in that cell, paled in comparison. Hitler and his Nazis *had* to fail, and Ryan knew he must do his part after all. Perhaps the pill would come later, but for now, he would find some other way.

He scratched fitfully at the bedbug bites and inhaled the disgusting stench of his cell, and suddenly he knew what he must do. Dropping to the filthy floor beside the cot, barely able to reach into the tight space, he pushed aside the stinking latrine bucket with the crusted rim and felt around in the dark beneath the bed. His fingers rapidly found the stiff carcass he had spotted earlier. It was a rat with matted fur, a fellow prisoner that had found dying the only way out their shared cell. Perished from starvation or lack of water, he hoped, and not from poison. What irony if this rat had met death by cyanide.

Under the pale moonlight he removed from his lapel the slip of razor blade. His trembling fingers worked carefully to avoid the sharp edge. With repeated strokes he sliced off the head and tail and slit the belly lengthwise, then drew the skin back toward the neck to expose the meager flesh below. From gullet to crotch he carefully shaved small strips of meat, adding the liver and heart to the finished pile on the bed. He rejected the string of intestines. The stench betrayed decomposition even before he brought the scraps to his lips.

The dissection complete, he held the tin cup ready and forced down the handful of flesh and organs, avoiding chewing, then chased the wretched mouthful with water. It took all his inner strength not to vomit. When the foul meal was done, he downed a second cup of water, then rinsed out his mouth and spit. He buried the torn cadaver in the latrine bucket where the guards shouldn't immediately look.

And then he waited. Within minutes his stomach churned and he felt coming the response he had hoped for. He fought back the gag reflex, dry-swallowing repeatedly and waiting, mentally encouraging the rat flesh to do its damnedest. His face already felt clammy, perhaps just his mind at work, revolting at what he'd just eaten. A half hour passed before the violent retching began, so fierce he could no longer resist and thought he would die, wished he would die. He held his belly and vomited repeatedly until nothing followed but stringy mucous. His throat was raw, and now the sweat and chills were undeniably real.

"Help! *Au secours!*" His cries sounded pitifully weak to his own ears.

He beat the tin cup against the cell door until a neighboring prisoner awoke and added to the clamor: "For God's sake, guard! Save us from this obnoxious fool!"

They found Ryan collapsed across the fouled bedding. Despite the agonizing stomach cramps and drenching sweats, Ryan felt relief when they conferred and agreed an ambulance should deliver him to the nearest hospital.

Should he survive that vile meal, he would at least find hope again.

CHAPTER SIX

Tours, Occupied France
21-22 August 1941

The night in the ward passed in gut-wrenching agony. A policeman cuffed him to an ancient metal bed, its enamel chipped by years of use. His filthy clothing was gone, his flimsy cloth gown open at the back. The long room housed a dozen other patients, some conscious, some asleep and snoring, others moaning and crying out for attention. The man in the next bed coughed blood into a towel and intermittently demanded pain medication in a shaky voice. Lost in his own misery, Ryan took little notice of his neighbors.

Through the dark hours he continued to retch, even though his stomach had long since surrendered anything of substance. The short, middle-aged nurse, her hair prematurely silver, was solicitous and compassionate, emptying the vessel she held to his lips to catch the bile and afterwards wiping his brow and face with a cool, damp cloth. After he soiled the sheets for a third time she gave up on the bedpan and gave him a sponge bath before wrapping him in a cotton diaper. The abdominal cramping was so debilitating that all he could do was fight through the sweats and chills, hoping he hadn't bitten off more than he could chew.

A gendarme kept constant watch over him, as if Ryan might somehow escape the cuffs binding him to the bed frame. The policeman's face was ruddy and sullen, his hair greasy under the uniform cap. He wore a perpetual sneer and treated the hospital personnel as servants, demanding they bring him coffee and sandwiches. Ryan's nurse had to evict a patient from the bed directly opposite the policeman's prisoner. Once all linens were removed, he claimed it as his observation post. This guard made no effort to hide his anger at having to care take a prisoner destined for Gestapo hands, especially such a foul-smelling, vomiting captive as this one. He made sure that miserable Ryan knew he was a bother. Whenever Ryan drifted into restless sleep, the guard beat his nightstick on the uprights of the bedframe and rattled him awake, much to the aggravation of the nursing staff and other patients on the ward.

"You must let the patients rest." The nurse mustered all the power inherent in her uniform. "This man has a high fever and needs to sleep if he's to recover."

"I'll do as I please, and when I please." He sat back down on the appropriated bed. "And it's all the same to me if this one never recovers. Once the Gestapo gets hold of him he's not going to feel quite so coddled."

"Then think of the rest of these patients. They need their rest, as well." She went to Ryan's side. "Sir? Are you doing any better?"

Ryan's head throbbed from the incessant dry heaving. He had tried to conserve what little energy he still had, knowing the clock was ticking. Any escape would have to come before daybreak, for Horst's men were sure to arrive by morning. But he was sensing that the worst had passed, his bowels no longer clenched, his sweats and chills had abated.

"Madame, a request, if I might?" His voice as weak as possible to still be heard.

"What is it, monsieur?"

"You have bathed me as best you could. Do you suppose I could get a quick shave so I'm more presentable for the interrogation?"

She couldn't help but pity the poor wretch and what he would endure at the hands of these police brutes. Everyone knew what the Gestapo was capable of inflicting; everyone feared the police, no matter which branch. "Of course, monsieur. One moment, please." She lit the metal lamp beside his bed and gathered supplies from the wall cabinet in the corner of the ward.

"What the hell are you doing?" The guard had overheard the exchange and wasn't about to let her pamper this criminal any further. The man rose to block her path back to Ryan. "He gets no special treatment, is that clear?"

"Young man, I've sons your age, interned somewhere as POW's. I taught all three of them to respect women, all women, and especially their mother. Your parents obviously failed in that regard. If you lack the common courtesy to allow me to do my job, I shall report you to your superiors. Now go sit and stay out of my way."

The man scowled and muttered under his breath, but returned to his place on the hospital bed. He watched carefully as she set the basin of warm water and mug of shaving soap on the side table. She propped Ryan up with an extra pillow, lathered his face, and skillfully scraped at his two-day growth with a safety blade.

Damn, Ryan thought. He'd hoped for a straight razor. "Please remove the mustache, too, madame." His pitiful half-smile confirmed his weakened condition.

"You're certain, monsieur? It does look rather dashing."

"I'm afraid there's little use for 'dashing' where I'm headed, madame."

"Very well, monsieur," and she scraped off the remnants of the Hervé Delacourt persona, rinsing the remnants of soap with a warm washcloth.

The guard had had enough. "No more nonsense, now. He's done, and so are you." He consulted his watch. "With any luck we'll be out of this piss pot of a hospital in under an hour."

"Madame, if I might, I'd really appreciate a visit to the WC to get out of this diaper. You'll understand if I can't face interrogation looking like this." He gestured to the gown and loincloth.

"Of course, monsieur. I'll take you there, but first the police agent will have to free your hand." She turned to the sullen guard.

"No way," the gendarme was on his feet, "he goes nowhere without me."

"Then take care of it now, please."

The man grasped Ryan's wrist tightly while he released the cuff from the bedframe. Ryan swung his feet off the bed, but light-headedness overcame him and he fell back to get his bearings. The guard clamped the loose cuff on Ryan's other wrist and chuckled. "Better now, diaper-boy? Must *Maman* here make sure you clean yourself properly?"

Ryan's eyes met those of the nurse and he gave her a quiet nod of thanks. The guard yanked hard on the handcuff chain to pull Ryan to his feet, forcing him to stagger through the doors leading to the hallway. Outside the men's room he put his hand on his holstered pistol and took a brief look inside the chamber. "If you think *I'm* about to wipe your ass, think again. Get your business done, and quickly. If you're well enough to shit on your own, you sure don't need a hospital, and it's back to the station with you."

He shoved Ryan to his knees over the toilet and slammed the door behind him. Ryan got to his feet, reaching for the wall to steady himself, and surveyed what tools were at hand. Despite the queasiness, he was feeling stronger than revealed, hoping his show of weakness would buy a few extra minutes.

The toilet was a square porcelain basin with two footrests for squatting and a drain in the middle. He had hoped for a heavy tank lid to use as a weapon. High on the wall hung a water reservoir with a pull chain, but there was no cover. The window above his head was far too small to climb through, even had the many coats of paint not sealed it shut. Ryan removed the pull-chain for the flushing mechanism. He wrestled off the hospital gown and ended up with the thin fabric twisted tightly around one arm, since he was still hampered by the cuffed wrists. He kicked the diaper into the corner. Free range of movement would be a must for a successful escape. With one end of the chain wrapped around each palm he silently waited beside the door, his hands above his head.

"What the hell's taking so long?" The guard rattled the door loudly.

Ryan's voice was weak and desperate. "Help me! Come quickly, I've fallen!"

The door immediately opened and the guard pulled up short. Ryan waited less than an arm's reach away, but it was enough. With one quick motion, he swung the loop of toilet chain over the man's head, pivoted to the side while kneeing him in the gut, and shoved him to the floor with his face over the toilet hole. Ryan cinched the chain taut as he dropped down heavily on the policeman's back, restricting all movement. The cop struggled to rise but the doorway was too narrow and he couldn't dislodge his attacker. The man desperately sought to break the hold of the garrote which was quickly strangling him. Another minute of struggle, and he went slack.

Ryan slowly released the tension on the chain and found a pulse, weak but present. An angry welt encircled the man's neck. He dragged him into the narrow room and shut the door. Setting aside the police weapon, he used the key to remove the handcuffs. Once finally free of the gown restricting his arm, he went to work, removing the man's shoes and socks. The police cap had narrowly missed the toilet, and Ryan set it aside. He unbuttoned the man's jacket and pulled off the trousers, ignoring the undergarments. Only a few minutes elapsed before he was fully in uniform, the fit adequate if not perfect. Ryan scanned the man's identity papers and badge before stuffing them back into the jacket. Last of all, he belted on the holstered revolver and placed the billed cap on his head.

The gendarme began to stir and cough repeatedly from deep in his throat. Ryan clubbed him across the base of the skull with the pistol butt. It wouldn't do to have him wake up anytime soon. He took the cuffs and cinched the man's hands behind his back.

The nurses might come looking soon so Ryan had no time to waste. He opened the door to peer down the hallway in both directions. A nurse was maneuvering a gurney into another ward through distant swinging doors, but no one else prowled the halls in the early morning hour. Facing him was a closet marked "supplies." He dragged the unconscious guard across the hall, flicked on the light, and closed the door. Using bandages from the supplies shelf, he gagged him with gauze and wrapped his lolling head in linen, then tied the man's feet together with the toilet pull chain. Two roll-away beds sat in the back of the closet, and Ryan shoved them aside to stash his captive against the wall, then rolled the beds back into position and checked that no one would spot the change. Satisfied at last with his work, Ryan opened the door a fraction, saw he was still in the clear, and headed for the exit.

On the street he tossed the handcuff key into a rubble pile and set out to put as much distance as possible between himself and the hospital. His head throbbed, his face shone damp despite the cool morning air. He knew he was running on the rush of adrenaline and that he might collapse soon, but he was free at last.

After only a few blocks the pit in his stomach and his weakened condition demanded a break. He would need something to eat before finding a way out of town. An empty café up a side street appeared promising. In the pockets of his stolen trousers were ration coupons, a few crumpled francs, and a coin or two, not enough for train fare but adequate for a slice of bread, a little butter and coffee with milk. He greeted the proprietor, then took a table close to the front window with his back to the wall and invisible to vehicle or pedestrian traffic. To his great relief the first bite of bread stayed down. Once certain his stomach was done rebelling, he finished off the light breakfast. The street beyond the window remained quiet and he began to relax.

Would they be searching for him yet or even have discovered the missing guard? Had the nurse alerted the police? Should he try to get to Paris now, or make his way to Nantes after all? And where was Nicole—headed south, or still in town? No, gone for sure. He had enough money to phone the embassy in Vichy and leave a coded message for Ed. But what could his brother do, and at what risk to State Department neutrality in the Occupied Zone? He thought of David Bruce's caution: "You get in trouble, you're on your own—we'll have to deny all knowledge of you, understood?" Ryan understood.

A slight man in a herringbone jacket, gray tie and faded beret leaned a rust-red bicycle against the bricks out front. As he entered the shop he greeted the proprietor and took a newspaper from the rack. Ryan received a casual glance before the man abruptly averted his gaze. Too abruptly. Ryan knew at once that the uniform had disconcerted the customer. Certainly fear was justified for those living in a police state, but this man had something to hide and wasn't good at disguising his nervousness. The new arrival fumbled his order to the café owner and then stared straight ahead at an unadorned wall, his eyes avoiding his newspaper, the front of the coffee shop, and the curious policeman staring at him.

Ryan took the seat beside him. "*Ça va,* monsieur?"

"Well enough, *monsieur l'agent.*" He took a noisy slurp of his coffee, his eyes darting nervously, a cornered animal. "And you?"

"*Très bien,* monsieur. But listen—I've a small favor to ask of you." Ryan placed both hands on the table and closed the distance with the anxious man.

"How can I be of help? You name it, I'm yours—I've always been a big supporter of our police." The poor man's hands trembled, a tic pulsing in the corner of one eye.

"I need to borrow your bicycle, but just for a short while. My ride hasn't shown."

The man sighed audibly. "Of course, of course. I regret it's such an old one, but it does ride well." He forced a smile.

"Excellent!" Ryan sat upright again and returned the smile. "Now give me your address—phone number, too—and I'll get it back to you when I'm done. Agreed?"

"No problem, officer, a pleasure. Always glad to help." He spoke quickly, jotting down information on the back of a napkin, his fingers barely controlling the pencil. Ryan knew the address would be false.

With directions to the train station from a passer-by, Ryan pedaled away as fast as his weakened legs would allow. The café proprietor appeared only too happy to have the policeman leave his shop. The same could be said for the bicycle's owner.

The intimidation inherent in his uniform had given Ryan a brilliant idea. He recalled playing the Gestapo officer on the train near Kassel back in '38, and rehearsed his new French role. It seemed unlikely he would even have to pay for that train fare to Nantes.

CHAPTER SEVEN

Nantes and Tours, Occupied France
22 August 1941

The first clandestine meeting with the Nantes partisans did not get off to a smooth start. René and Erika felt very much the outsiders, having to meet with them cold. The contacts provided by Jacques in Bayonne had facilitated this rendezvous in an abandoned warehouse north of the Loire. Two young men frisked them at the door, and Erika suspected one partisan took his job too seriously as he ran his hands over her body. René gritted his teeth but remained mute, understanding the need for security and the necessity of establishing trust in this new group.

A young man code-named Jean-Philippe had closely-spaced eyes and an aggressive attitude. "Why the hell should we need your help? I don't give a damn what you've done elsewhere, you're both *Boches*!" He glared at René. "Just what can you bring to the table that we don't already have?"

René attempted to appease. "Perhaps you don't need our help, monsieur, but you'll never know till you hear us out."

Erika jumped in the young man's face. "Just how long have *you* battled the Nazis? A year? A month, maybe? A week?" The partisan took a step back as she continued unchecked. "Yes, we are Germans—Germans who've been fighting Hitler's bastards tooth and nail for years now."

A middle-aged man with the arms of a blacksmith stepped between them. "Please take it easy, madame." Introduced as the group leader under the name Maurice, he tried to soothe Erika's outrage. "Jean-Philippe may be young and new to this battle, but he is committed to our cause. His father and brother fought at Dunkerque and are still in a prison camp, and now he must care for his family on his own."

Despite René's gentle hand on her forearm, Erika's tirade continued unabated. "The fact remains that the two of us have suffered great losses at the hands of these Nazi criminals. We've already killed for the cause, we've sabotaged and undermined and risked all to help both France and Germany slow down these beasts. And now we offer to share what we've learned, what works and what doesn't. And yes, our being German might just help turn the tables for you, since we've spent years dealing with the Nazi bastards." Her anger calmed as she finally sought common ground. "We understand that you'll also have much to share with us, to teach us, but never question our determination or our skills."

Now the young Raymond, so industrious just minutes before in patting down Erika for weapons, voiced his opinion. "I for one vote we hear them out." His glance suggested hope that the attractive blonde would value his support. "Face it, we can use colleagues who look and sound German—just imagine the possibilities."

René made his case. "Look, we're all in this together, and if our help isn't needed we can simply form our own group. There's plenty of work for everyone. But we do come here with the support of the Verneuil network." Several nodded in recognition at mention of the respected Bayonne group. "Let's face facts—as long as we all operate piecemeal across France and duplicate our efforts, we'll step on each other's toes."

Introduced as Cerberus, a short, balding man spoke up. "We've heard the Communists have just unified under a single banner. Liaising with them might be a good place to start."

René saw his opening. "Come on, my friends—just imagine our strength if we follow that lead, if we share and cooperate across France! Our factory workers sabotage armaments production. Our transportation people misdirect deliveries. Our counterfeiters forge impressive identity papers and our tailors assemble convincing disguises. And most important, our shared lines of communication mean intelligence reaches our Allied friends while it still has some value. Can we ever really make a difference without cooperation?"

Laura, a brunette with intelligent brown eyes, spoke up. "I like what they bring to the table—I say we explore this further." Married to Maurice, the very pregnant Laura received Erika's smile of thanks.

"And I say we *kill* more." The young Henri spat on the floor. "What the hell are we doing here, anyway? I say we take out some leaders, kill some soldiers, make the *Boches* fear our streets! Without firing our weapons, we're just old ladies chatting over tea and biscuits."

"But what of the hostages they hold?" Laura held a hand to her rounded belly. "We start shooting as Henri demands, and innocent people die before a firing squad." Her chin jutted. "It's as simple as that."

"Who the fuck cares?" Henri lit the stub of a cigarette, allowing the callousness of his comment to sink in. "What's war without death? We all face it, some of us even welcome it, whether we admit it or not. I say let's get on with it." He exposed a pistol tucked in his belt. "Let's see how much the fuckers enjoy bleeding France dry once their own blood clogs our gutters!" He closed his jacket and stormed out, Jean-Philippe on his heels.

The others looked after them, a few shaking their heads in dismay.

A slight smile crossed Maurice's face. "Don't worry, they're young and mean well…and they always come back." Laura nodded.

"And they may have a point," added Raymond.

Erika exchanged glances with René. "So?"

René's eyes polled the remaining partisans. "Are we all in the same club?"

❖

At eleven that morning a black Citroën sedan braked to a quick stop before the gendarmerie in Tours and two men in suits and fedoras raced up the steps to the reception room. The young policeman at the desk saluted smartly, knowing

Gestapo when he saw it. His forehead already glistened. He knew the reason for the official visit, and the secret police weren't going to be pleased with his report.

"You've detained here a certain Hervé Delacourt, correct?" A mustache bisected the secret policeman's slender face.

"C-c-certainly, monsieur, but there's been a bit of a problem…messieurs." The young gendarme stared down at his log book. How he wished to be anywhere else, and that his sergeant hadn't ordered him to receive these troublesome visitors. That coward now hid in the back.

"A problem?" The taller agent glanced briefly across the otherwise empty room. "What sort of problem?"

Now the sweat on the young policeman's brow beaded and ran. "I regret to say we've misplaced the prisoner." His fingers trembled.

"Misplaced?" The new arrivals exchanged an incredulous look. The gendarme sergeant hovered just out of sight at the end of the hall, watching, waiting for their explosive reaction. "You misplaced a prisoner—here at the gendarmerie?"

"You see, he became ill, and we sent him to the hospital. And he disappeared along with one of our men."

The agents broke out in laughter, one doubling over, unable to contain himself. The other stifled his glee long enough to say: "My regrets for your loss, monsieur. We'll be on our way now." They turned to leave.

"But, sir—"The young man called out after them, "—what should I tell my sergeant?"

"Tell him we came to have the man released. He's not the one we're after." And the men were still laughing as the door closed behind them.

The young policeman sat to quiet the shaking in his legs. He'd come close to landing on the floor.

❖

The semi-local for Nantes was awash in travelers. Luggage and rucksacks were piled across the aisles and stuffed into every available rack. Small children sat on laps, infants bawled, slept in mothers' arms, or nursed at their breasts. Sometimes even strangers took pity on the long-suffering parents and offered to hold the little ones for a while. Anyone hoping to make it down the aisle stumbled over baggage or the feet of passengers making do with the scarcity of space, their backs against the carriage walls. The windows were all lowered as people sought fresher air, but soot and cinders coated every surface. The odor of unwashed bodies and smoke was all-pervasive. Those lucky enough to have picnic baskets guarded them carefully. They were known to disappear after a single moment of inattention, and occasionally fights broke out—verbal and physical—over what belonged to whom.

Into this morass of long-suffering passengers came a gendarme, wading through the sea of humanity, checking papers as he moved toward the front of the train. Those not too exhausted by their journey might have noticed the man appeared under the weather, his skin pale while the sheen on his forehead rapidly gathered soot. A good-looking fellow in his blue uniform, were it not for that sickly pallor.

Having just endured the nuisance of a train conductor checking tickets, the arrival of the policeman might otherwise have been just another bother for the travelers. But the citizens of the Occupied Zone had grown both weary and wary of anyone in uniform. Spot checks of papers were unavoidable. Suspicion was rampant, since many had lost their money or ration coupons to men posing as Gestapo or gendarmes, only to discover later that this was an increasingly common ruse of crooks and scoundrels. And of the real police. There really was no way to be certain—forged official badges and papers were easily available to those who knew where to look and had the funds to pay. Who would knowingly run the risk of arrest, detention or worse by questioning the "official's" authority, just in case it proved valid? So as this pallid policeman moved along, they dutifully produced their papers for his review with the hope he'd be soon out of their hair.

Little did they realize that this gendarme was equally anxious for the trip to end, hoping that none of his "police comrades" would board the train while he was underway to Nantes. Once he'd fought the crowd the length of the train, checking every identity along the way, Ryan camped in the crowded vestibule closest to the locomotive, standing next to a foul-smelling WC, overused to the point of collapse. With his gut still roiling, he would use the facility if he must, filth and clogged toilet be damned.

As the train rattled over poorly-maintained rail beds in its approach to the Nantes station, Ryan spotted two policemen coming his way up the aisle, obviously in a hurry and looking directly toward the final vestibule of the car where he was hiding. The men moved as quickly as they were able given the jumble of seated passengers with legs extended across the narrow passage and surrounded by haphazardly-piled luggage. These cops clearly had no interest in checking anyone's papers, except perhaps Ryan's should they get their hands on him. Someone had become suspicious. The train was pulling in beneath the massive entry arch with its neo-classical columns when he swung open the door of the carriage and hit the platform running, all sensitivity in his feet ignored.

Racing into the station, he turned a few heads of those shouldered aside, but most kept their eyes forward as they regained their balance. It was always best not to get involved in police business. He passed beneath the triple-arched façade and cut across the park to head north. He ran up an alleyway and found refuge in the back streets beyond. Finally in the clear, he nearly collapsed from the exertion. Drenched in sweat, still suffering from the poisons in his system, he crouched low in an alcove until his breathing steadied.

Regaining some strength, Ryan realized his first job was to find civilian clothing, and quickly. Assuming the same caliber of lodgings as what they'd had in Bayonne, he knew that showing up in uniform at *Le Brigande* would earn him a one-way ticket into the waters of the Loire with a slit throat.

He chose the first shop open for business, a hardware store offering wrought-iron wares, hinges, locks and various building materials, some new, most salvaged from buildings damaged or destroyed by the bombings. The proprietor gave directions to a second-hand clothing store. The man was only too willing to help, even drawing a quick sketch of the neighboring streets—anything to get a policeman out of his store quickly.

The used clothing store lay just off Rue d'Allonville. A bell above the door summoned a saleswoman from beyond a curtain of faded damask. Ryan scanned several tables laden with musty old clothing and racks at the walls holding the somewhat superior goods. The woman appeared to wear half of the store's inventory, perhaps believing it might sell better if seen on a living mannequin. But her short stature forced her to roll up the overlapping sleeves, and the two or three skirts were bundled at the waist to prevent the hems from dragging on the scuffed linoleum.

"*Bonjour, madame.*"

"*Bonjour, monsieur l'agent*, how may I be of assistance?" She smiled warmly. Her pendulous goiter swayed as she spoke.

For the first time in his short career as a bogus policeman he found someone apparently comfortable in his presence. "Madame, I'll need you to keep a secret, an official secret."

"But of course, you've come to the right place."

"Then here's what I need." Ryan double-checked that the shop was truly empty. "I'm going on special assignment, and must have clothes suitable for a man of lower social standing. Can you be of assistance, madame?"

Without a word the shopkeeper began rummaging through a rack of men's clothing directly behind the counter, sliding aside hangers with worn jackets and trousers, intently searching for the ideal solution to his needs. "And shoes?"

She continued to move hangers without turning around. "And a shirt, monsieur?"

Ryan took a closer look at the scuffed police-issues and decided they fit well enough not to chance blisters with a different pair. "The shoes are fine, but a different shirt? Yes, definitely a good idea."

"And here we have it all." She displayed piece-by-piece some dark woolen trousers in a pinstripe, a hound's tooth jacket showing wear at the elbows, and a faded, blue cotton shirt. "Exactly what you need, and all for a mere thirty francs."

Ryan looked disconcertedly at his slender fold of cash. "I regret, madame, I've only ten to spare for this assignment." He shrugged in disappointment. "And I'll also need a different hat—" a sudden thought, "and perhaps boxers? Might you have something of lesser quality?" He caught the sparkle in her eyes.

"Well then, would monsieur consider a trade. Ten francs for all this," her sweeping gesture suggesting the finest of couture, "and you leave me that tired uniform of yours." She tossed a soft-billed cap on the pile, then rummaged through a drawer and presented thread-bare undershorts with a final flourish.

Ryan laughed. "But what shall I wear once I'm no longer on assignment?"

The woman gave a wink. "You appear resourceful to me. You'll think of something."

He placed two five-franc notes on the counter. On one blue-and-white bill someone had typed in red ink "*Vive le général de Gaulle*."

"I believe there's no need for a receipt, monsieur?" She grinned in complicity. "And perhaps you'd like to change in the back room."

"My sincere thanks, madame." Ryan pulled the worn curtain aside.

"Oh, and monsieur?"

He turned. "*Oui,* madame."

"You may keep your pistol. I only trade in clothing."

CHAPTER EIGHT

Paris, Occupied France
22 August 1941

Serge knew he had this in the bag, but still his fingers tapped a soft-shoe on the perfect crease of his trouser leg. The dark sedan lurked in the shadows of an alley opening to Rue Jean Maldives. Blocks distant waited two Gestapo cars, one observing the front gate of the warehouse, the other parked just down the street from Serge's passageway. His Walther automatic rested in his lap. His driver Paul and two best men were also suitably armed. Serge himself would oversee this operation.

The Wehrmacht truck with the canvas cover and the bold V stenciled on the hood was at that moment taking on the load at the Branchot & Fils warehouse several blocks to the north. They had watched it pass by empty just before midnight, the masked headlamps casting a spectral bluish glow on the cobbled pavement. The haul was expected to be at least 500 cases, over six thousand bottles of prime Cognac *Hors-d'Age.* The liquid treasure from the château cellars of a wealthy and recently-uprooted Jewish family was now destined for the Reich elite, thanks to the rival Delfanne gang.

Those bastards won't see a drop of alcohol, thought Serge, *or profit*. The radium dial on his Patek-Philippe glowed faintly, but the watch hands seemed to stand still. He ran a hand over his shaved scalp and groomed his mustache with a comb. One a.m., and loading should already be complete. "What the hell's keeping them?"

Paul shrugged but said nothing, knowing his boss's impatience.

Serge's spies had reported the operation was planned for midnight, with the shipment to arrive at the Gare du Nord freight yards no later than two-thirty. The transfer to a supply train destined for Berlin would be immediate. Experience told him the truck should have passed their position a few minutes earlier. He was anxious for a smooth heist and ready for a large score.

The business arrangement with the Lesney woman was proving valuable. She had shown herself cooperative, if not eager. Although a bit old for his tastes—the younger the better in his eyes—her ass was firm and he would screw her eventually, if for no other reason than he could. And she would know he was boss despite the trivial thirty per cent he'd settled for. *Hell, the Boches take that much from every French transaction!* But the profits were adequate to provide him some minor income, and more importantly, she appeared well-connected to the officer crowd who frequented the establishment. Wherever the Krauts gathered he would find fistfuls of money.

So it had been his good fortune to learn of this very shipment from the Wehrmacht colonel, a fool obviously smitten by the attractive bitch and very drunk. The pompous idiot had promised her several cases of the precious Cognac as a personal gift, and slipped up by boasting of the origin of the prize and the date planned for delivery. Nothing escaped

Serge's attention when a fortune in occupation marks was on the table, and his connections had needed only a day to run down the source of the booze and the people involved. As soon as he learned that his long-time rival Masuy was to profit, he knew he would hijack the load and give that Belgian asshole the finger.

The car radio crackled and the game was on. Within minutes the truck rolled past their alleyway. On its tail came the black sedan that had picked up the target as it left the warehouse gates. The *Boche* cop on the passenger side signaled with a flashlight in passing. Paul's engine failed to catch, and Serge buried both him and the vehicle in a foul stream of obscenities. The engine finally roared to life on the third try. Headlamps off, they rolled into the street toward the lights of the tailing car.

Serge had chatted the previous night with the Wehrmacht corporal who was to drive the truck. The soldier agreed to cooperate with the "liberation" of his load in exchange for a commitment that his wife and children in Pirmasens would go untouched. The man was to reassure his co-driver that the police stop would be nothing but a routine spot check due to the late hour.

The second Gestapo car, also alerted by wireless of their approach, would now be just ahead of the target along the dark stretch between Rue Malinot and Rue de Vence. Suddenly the truck's taillight flared and it braked to a stop. The driver had spotted the Gestapo cars, front and rear.

"Move it—now!" With a surge, Paul accelerated past the trailing vehicle and screeched to a halt alongside the truck. Serge's men leapt out to surround the payload. Unexpectedly, a soldier, machine pistol on his shoulder, emerged from the canvas flaps protecting the load. One Gestapo agent spun around and dropped him before the man's feet hit the ground. The body fell in a spray of blood and brain tissue.

The truck driver and his partner came down from the cab with hands high. "Don't shoot! We're not resisting!" Serge approached the driver and put his automatic to the man's head. The corporal trembled. "My god, monsieur, you promised you wouldn't hurt me!"

"Correction. I said *your family* lives." A bullet pierced the man's skull, and just as quickly the other soldier fell to Serge's Walther. He grinned at Paul. "Back me up on this—I never said *he'd* live to see his family, right?"

Two Gestapo agents strode over for further orders. "Get them out of here, *schnell, schnell!*" The two men dragged the bodies to the forward car and stowed them in the trunk. The corpse of the hapless guard landed in the rear of the other sedan. Another policeman reached for the machine pistol which had fallen to the pavement. Their role completed, the Gestapo cars disappeared into the night.

His personal crew knew the rest of the plan. One climbed into the cab and found first gear as the others piled into the sedan. They followed the truck a block up Rue de Vence to a vacant warehouse, where one man sprang out to unlock the padlock and crank up the heavy metal shutter. A solitary light already glowed in the rear of the cavernous space. Once both truck and car were safely inside, the man dropped the noisy door and secured the lock, tugging at it twice to be certain. He then sauntered up the street toward the warehouse office entrance, lighting up as he went.

Inside, Serge had already climbed up into the bed of the truck, a crowbar in hand. Prying open a crate, he pulled out a bottle and shattered its neck, sending the wax seal flying. He poured out some of the precious liquid to clear any glass shards, then downed a solid gulp before raising the tortured bottle to toast his men: "Job well done, lads!" The Cognac made the rounds as they all congratulated themselves on the haul. Serge was jubilant. "We've fucked him over good this time, that bastard Masuy!"

CHAPTER NINE

Nantes and Biarritz, Occupied France
22 August 1941

Le Brigande belied its rough-and-tumble name. It proved to be a modest but respectable small hotel on a quiet commercial street north of the river and well away from the warehouses, cranes and rail tracks servicing the port. *What a contrast to the seedy lodgings in Bayonne!* Facing the sidewalk ran a row of windows, each adorned with a potted plant encased in dark molding. Heavy burgundy drapes framed the plate glass. The lobby offered guests dated but well-maintained furniture. Two women chatted on a couch. A businessman read a newspaper, the aroma of his pipe difficult for Ryan to resist. A bank of mail slots with hooks for keys showed twenty-two rooms in the house, about half occupied.

The man in striped trousers at the reception looked around as Ryan entered, his eyes betraying more than a trace of skepticism. Without a greeting he returned to his paperwork, turning his back to the newcomer. "If you're seeking work, monsieur, I regret that we have no need for a laborer or porter. Absolutely nothing for you here. Perhaps down the street at *La Lorraine?*"

"I'm not seeking work, monsieur." Ryan thought an old suitcase would have completed his disguise. Bad enough that the only identity papers he carried belonged to a Tours policeman, no doubt freed from the storage closet, an all-points bulletin out for his assailant.

Realizing Ryan had no intention of leaving, the clerk turned to face the stranger. Craning his neck over the counter, he gave the new arrival's unkempt appearance a quick once-over and sniffed in obvious displeasure. Ryan knew his face was heavily soot-stained from the rail journey, and he could see the drawn look to his features in the lobby mirror. The desk clerk finally spoke: "Then how may I be of assistance?"

"You are the manager?"

"The assistant manager, monsieur, fully capable of handling any inquiry."

"I prefer to speak with the manager. He is in?"

"Sadly, no, he is not." The man pivoted back to addressing envelopes.

"If I may, monsieur—the open door there is clearly marked 'Director,' and from here I can see the back of a man's head and smoke issuing from somewhere beyond. From the smell I would say a cigar." Now Ryan stretched his neck to get a clearer view beyond the hinged shelf of the counter.

"I am not about to trouble Monsieur Vaucault with some down-and-outer who won't even state his business."

"Then I shall," Ryan lifted the counter flap, took a step forward and called out: "Monsieur Vaucault!" His voice carried over the stuttering protests of the desk clerk. "*Monsieur le directeur!*"

The manager rose from his desk. His pinched face sported a carefully-trimmed mustache almost touching his thick sideburns, perhaps compensating for the thin strands of hair plastered across his head. He removed his wire-framed glasses. "Is there trouble, Frédéric?"

Ryan side-stepped the clerk. "Monsieur Vaucault, I come directly from Bayonne with a message for you from Jacques." He hesitated, not sure whether to proceed further with the clerk standing there imperiously.

"Jacques? Tell me more about this Jacques."

"Snow-white mustache, fuller than your own, monsieur, and..." Ryan placed a finger to each ear and tapped lightly, "ear mustaches?"

The manager laughed. "Of course, *that* Jacques. And your name, monsieur?"

"Richard Dana."

The manager smiled. "Frédéric, this man has business with me. Please leave us undisturbed in my office. Monsieur Dana, please join me."

They entered a tastefully-appointed office crowded with a heavy Victorian-era desk and two matching chairs. Ryan had correctly guessed the source of the smoke—a lit cigar rested in a ceramic ashtray advertising Grand Marnier liqueur. The manager turned the key in the lock. The smoke twisted upward in an acrid curl. "Please take a seat, monsieur, and tell me how Jacques from Bayonne and I can be of assistance."

"I'm looking for a friend of mine, a very close friend. Jacques tells me that this man recently arrived here in Nantes to work with those who share our passion for France."

"I suppose that Jacques and his *copains* have been through all this with you, but forgive me if I, too, am cautious. The name of the man you seek?"

"Jacques says he now goes by the name 'Rénard.' An impressive man, strong but with a limp, and dueling scars here—" Ryan pointed to his left cheek, "—and here." His finger traced further lines on his forehead.

Vaucault nodded. "And your friend has a favorite book?"

"*Two Years before the Mast*."

The manager dragged at his cigar and exhaled. "Now, were I to reach this man you describe—and I'm not saying that I can—how could I prove to him that you are a true friend and not just here to bring him embarrassment?"

Ryan had given this some thought while the clothing shop proprietress sketched out the port neighborhood and approximate location of *Le Brigande*. Some proof of identity would be needed to convince his friends, something indisputable, and his Florentine ring would do the trick. Both René and Erika knew it well. In the narrow alleyway alongside the hotel he had carefully opened the seam in his right trouser cuff and inserted the K-pill taken from the ring's compartment. In the secret compartment he hid a slip of paper on which he scrawled a few words Erika was sure to recognize.

Now he removed the ring from his finger and set it before the director.

"And what do we have here, monsieur?" Vaucault examined the heavy ring under the desk lamp, admiring the black onyx cameo.

"Should you run across my friend, please give him this. And note my features so you can describe me accurately. I haven't changed all that much since he saw me last. Just a bit more down-at-the-heels, perhaps."

The man smiled as he looked him over with a practiced eye.

"Tell him I miss our conversations while strolling through the Marburg woods." Ryan thought of the duel against von Kredow, where René had fought on his behalf while Ryan seconded, unsure of how to handle the saber. "And his advice to keep my head down and not cut myself…and one more thing, monsieur—" Ryan ran a hand through his hair, "tell him this curly hair is only a disguise."

"Very well, monsieur." The hotel director rose to unlock the door. "I'll do what I can, but it may take a day or two of inquiry. Meanwhile, you're in room twenty, two floors up at the end of the hall. Exit left from the lift."

Back at the reception counter his petulant clerk moved aside, pretending to ignore them both. The manager ran his hand along the rank of keys until it reached number twenty, then hesitated. The key to that room was missing.

"Ah, but of course, monsieur. It's already upstairs. Madame Dana has the key. No need to register—Madame has taken care of everything."

❖

"You look terrible!" Nicole motioned him in. "And you've lost half your curls." She dropped the pistol back in the handbag at her shoulder.

"Rough couple of days, I'll grant you that." Ryan shrugged. "You think I need a new hairdresser?" He tossed his cap on the bed. A wave of nausea hit and he considered a quick run for the toilet down the hall. Instead, he sat on the bed while the queasiness passed. It was becoming routine.

She locked the door and came over to sit beside him. "So they released you without question."

"No damned way—I had to make myself sicker than a dog. Luckily, hospital security is more lax than the jail's. But I still had to do a number on a guard and steal his uniform to get out of Tours."

Nicole faced him, eyebrows raised. "But I'd arranged for your release…"

"What?" Ryan was dumbfounded. "Or more important, when the hell did that happen?"

"Some Tours associates came to spring you, sometime early this morning, I'm told. But they reported you'd already gone."

"My God, Nicole. I ate a rotting rat last night!" Pressing a hand to his gut, he suppressed another wave of nausea. "And it's still haunting me."

"Timing is everything." Her eyebrows arched.

Easy for her to say. The stench of the spoiled flesh still lingered in his sinuses. "Well, I appreciate your efforts anyway." He fell back against the pillow and addressed the ceiling. "So how'd you get here?"

"Watched them haul you away, then worked my way around the checkpoint. If we both hadn't been so beat we might have considered that option and you'd have spared yourself that meal. Got to the train station and made a few calls to see what could be done about you. Our people have connections everywhere, you know. I came here with the next express." From the window she looked down vacantly on the early afternoon traffic. "So what comes next?"

"I've already reached out to my friends through the hotel manager. For now, we just wait until they get back to us."

❖

By nightfall the tedium had become unbearable. Nicole read a magazine dog-eared by previous hotel guests. Ryan napped atop the bed, his sleep as restless as his gut. *My God,* he thought, *how long will I pay for that disgusting rat meat?* With no word from René or anyone else, Ryan decided fresh air might help. "Hungry?" He knew Nicole must also be going stir crazy.

"I could eat."

"Something light for me, and then maybe a movie? Shouldn't cost more than a couple francs."

"A bit risky, don't you think?"

"Worth it to get out for a bit, as long as we're careful." Ryan went for his jacket in the armoire. "The manager said we might not hear anything for a day or two, so no point in becoming hermits. We'll leave a note at the front desk. With luck that imbecile Frédéric will be off for the evening."

An acne-scarred and very pleasant young man had taken his place at the reception. He put Ryan's note into the mail slot when they turned over the room key, and Ryan tipped him two francs. Should René arrive in their absence he would either wait for them or leave word where to meet up.

Ryan knew the risk going out in the streets. His only identity papers were those of the cop he had assaulted in Tours. The cops on the train were only looking for an imposter, so he doubted they presented a problem. More dangerous was the policeman's Browning pistol bulging in his inside coat pocket. He moved it to the small of his back. Owning a firearm was a criminal offense under Vichy law, and now both he and Nicole were armed. They would definitely have to be back before the nine p.m. curfew.

In the early evening light Nicole took a closer look at his appearance. "You sure you're up for this? You're pale as a sheet."

"Feeling better all the time, thanks." He tried a smile.

"Well for God's sake, let's buy pomade for that hair—with half the curls already gone you're looking like a hedgehog."

"And while you're at it, please steal me that watch you promised. Drives me nuts not knowing the time."

❖

The lights dimmed in the cinema and a newsreel began to roll, German tanks thundering across a flat plain somewhere on the Eastern Front, stopping to fire, then rumbling on at great speed, stone structures crumbling in smoke and flame. Next came a long file of captured men, hands behind their heads, Slavic faces showing exhaustion and defeat as they paraded past the cameraman. The SS guards flashed broad smiles of victory. The narrator spoke of the extraordinary valor of the German soldiers fighting the Bolshevik terror.

A catcall came from somewhere in the back of the theater, echoed immediately from the front row. The newsreel came to a shaky halt, freezing a close-up image of the *Führer*, arm lifted in a lazy Nazi salute as his Grosser Mercedes passed through adoring crowds. The projector spotlighted nothing but clouds of smoke shifting overhead. The manager called out from the rear of the theater. "Enough nonsense! People want to see the film!"

A solitary shout from the dark. "No! We want to see a free France!" Scattered but enthusiastic applause. Ryan glanced across the half-full cinema and spotted no one involved in the protest. All eyes remained firmly fixed on the frozen screen as the projector lamp melted the celluloid. A hole opened in the middle of Hitler's face and spread rapidly outward until the frame fell away. The screen went white and now many in the audience whistled and clapped loudly or stomped their feet on the floor. The house lights came up as the manager shouted repeatedly for quiet. Now only a cough or two broke the sudden silence.

"Come on, Nicole. Let's get out of here. If this turns ugly they'll call the cops."

"Good idea. You don't do all that well with jail grub." He had only managed a bowl of chicken broth for dinner. Ryan threw her a quick look, hoping in vain to catch a grin on her face.

They headed up the aisle toward the exit, receiving a few sneers from moviegoers who undoubtedly took them for Nazi-sympathizers. *If only they knew the truth.* Outside the cinema a police car braked to a halt. Ryan put his hand to Nicole's back to hurry her along. Three uniformed men jumped out and raced past the few exiting patrons. The ticket seller in her booth watched with a bewildered expression as the cops entered the movie house. Ryan suspected they would find nothing amiss inside the theater and all moviegoers behaving with propriety. Once the film was spliced and rolling again, the house lights would likely stay on for the rest of the evening's entertainment.

It made no sense to leave the hotel again until he had papers which could pass police scrutiny, so the rest would be up to Vaucault and—he fervently hoped—René and Erika.

❖

"Could he really be alive and here in Nantes?" Erika stared in disbelief at the ring, turning it over and over in her hand. "I'd swear it's his."

"How can we be certain, darling? Von Kredow's been after us for years, and who knows what he's got up his sleeve? The man's a sadist and thoroughly devious."

Erika shook her head. "From Vaucault's description this certainly sounds like Ryan—he knows about your walks in the Marburg woods and the duel. Could he have overheard what you told Ryan about being careful with the saber?"

"His men could have overheard, I suppose. Just like him to have someone spying on us before the contest, looking for any weak spot. And we weren't exactly secret about afternoon walks and beer up on Spiegelslust."

"This could be a fake, I suppose." She ran a finger over the onyx cameo and scratched at the stone with a fingernail. "Horst might have had one made by a jeweler." She sat in the chair by the floor lamp, taking a closer look. "But if it's a counterfeit, it's a damned good one."

"I know Ryan's ring looked just like that. But remember—I saw where von Kredow tortured him and can only imagine what Ryan went through. His coat and your handbag were still hanging on the wall of that shack, and he could have left other personal items, as well. Do you suppose Ryan kept his ring, given he had only moments to escape? Was he wearing it when you were stopped by the gunboat?"

"I was exhausted—we all were—and survival was the only thing on our minds. I couldn't say anything for sure about that nightmare." She shuddered. "It was so dark, and cold, and all I wanted was revenge."

"But why didn't he write if he made it back to America? I sent several letters to him at his State Department."

"Perhaps he never got them? Maybe he never made it back there. We surely would have heard if the protocol had been made public. President Roosevelt would have used that knowledge, if only for propaganda purposes, don't you think? Maybe Horst's men caught up with him and he really is dead, and they took this ring just to lure us in."

"God only knows, but whatever happened, if Ryan is alive and has actually tracked us down, Horst may still be behind it all or on his tail, as well. I wouldn't put anything past that son-of-a-bitch, especially with his resources."

"You're right, of course—it's just such a surprise."

"Well, it's one we can't ignore, but we'll have to be extremely careful." René saw the distant look on her face, could tell where her memories had led her. He put his hands on her shoulders and gently massaged them. "Darling, if it truly is Ryan…there's something I must ask you…"

"Yes, love?" She continued to examine the ring.

"I do know what he did for you, what he meant to you. Will things still be right between us…the two of us?"

She looked up and gave him a lingering kiss. "My big bear, you are my one and only love, and things will always be right between us."

He smiled a look of relief.

"But, darling?" Erika had stopped fidgeting with the ring.

"Yes?"

"Watch this." She held the ring up to the light and pressed her thumbnail against the fine seam in the gold just below the cameo. The first attempt failed.

"Watching..."

The second try opened the secret compartment. She flashed René a huge smile. "It is Ryan! It's really Ryan! Horst could never have known about this." Very carefully she unfolded the tiny slip of paper and read aloud the message, three simple words from their shared past she could never forget: *Just in case.*

❖

Despite the blackout restrictions enforced along the Atlantic Wall, Horst found Biarritz breath-taking beneath the evening moonlight. Who needed man-made illumination when nature provided such beauty? He sat on his balcony at the luxurious Hôtel du Palais, looking out to sea as a distant fog bank gradually rolled toward the shore. From time to time he spotted an SS gunship on patrol. So close to the Spanish border at Hendaye it was common for the anarchists to smuggle their human cargo past Biarritz, or from the harbor at Saint-Jean-de-Luz, so the Germans arbitrarily boarded and inspected fishing craft.

His day had been most productive, finally making real progress with the Bayonne terrorists. Armed with intelligence on the old man working under the code name "Jacques," Horst's reconnaissance team had brought in two of the three known members of that little cell, and Horst knew it was only a matter of time before they picked up the young man known as "Robert."

The old man with the hairy ears had died well. Once this "Jacques" was tied to a chair, Horst held his Sauer alongside the man's head and fired repeatedly until the tuft of white bristles ran red from the ruptured eardrum. The man still refused to speak, but Horst already knew everything, so the play with the gun had been just for fun. The *coup de grâce* came with the barrel aimed into the man's undamaged ear. "So he hears it coming." And Horst's men had dutifully laughed.

The most important thing he had learned over the years was patience. Patience in the care he took with detainees. Patience with his subordinates, at least until they might try to undermine him. Brenner was a fool who should have known better. Patience with his less dominant role in the Gestapo, ever since Heydrich withdrew direct support and spent less and less time in Berlin. His successes would draw Berlin's attention before long and he would be back with the Reich's leaders. And patience in accomplishing his most important life goal, revenge for Erika's betrayal.

Horst thought of the three fugitives. He was pleased they were all headed to Nantes. A lovely city, he'd heard. And he had tired of living and working so far out of the mainstream. It would do him good to see new parts of France, perhaps even Paris. *Jeder einmal in Paris*, right? His car and driver would come round in the morning. His civilian dress and his one uniform were already packed and ready to go. His favorite suit of fine, charcoal-gray worsted hung in the wardrobe, freshly-brushed by the hotel valet.

Horst sat naked on the balcony. He tapped the syringe to clear air bubbles—so ordinary a task he never gave it a moment's notice—and injected the morphine between his fingers. After years of use his arms and legs showed a spidery web of tracks. He drew his dagger from its sheath to admire the edge honed to perfection, turning the blade from side to side in the pale moonlight. Then very carefully he carved three parallel lines in the flesh of his left thigh alongside older cuts already healing. One for Erika, one for the "Frenchman," one for Lemmon. The boy was undeserving of his sacrifice. He cut deeply, watching the blood surface and splatter on the tiles at his feet. He dabbed a finger in the fresh blood of each cut and ran it the length of the scar on his left cheek. He felt no pain, just melancholy at the passing of time and opportunity.

Klaus, my dearly departed 'dagger,' what great times we had together, nicht wahr? He picked at the open cuts with the tip of the blade, smearing the welling blood. *What great things we could have accomplished had you only learned to swim.*

The years had been productive, his "extraction commandos" diligently retrieving German and foreign traitors from within Vichy France, even Spain and Portugal. He ran them to ground and taught them a lesson before sending survivors back to Berlin for further interrogation and disposal. Brenner's knowledge of French had been helpful at first, but Horst soon acquired sufficient language skills to operate on his own. He no longer missed Heydrich's direct oversight in the Gestapo, having created his own independent operation which allowed him to pursue his personal interests.

Horst remained still for a few minutes as another gunship just beyond the crashing surf plowed south. The boat's shielded running lights disappeared beyond the rocky spit as it sought to outrun the approaching fog bank. He rose, finished off the Cognac and flung the empty bottle over the balcony to the terrace walkway three floors below. In the bathroom, his bare feet leaving bloody prints on the stone flooring, he removed suturing materials as he quietly hummed the old Nazi marching song to himself.

Die Fahne hoch, die Reihen fest geschlossen...The flag held high, the ranks firmly closed...

LE DÉNOUEMENT

1941

CHAPTER ONE

Nantes, Occupied France
23 August 1941

The long night in the Nantes hotel had passed reasonably well. With only one bed, Ryan had expected banishment to the polished wooden floor. Instead and to his surprise, Nicole had rolled the spread into a barrier to divide the bed down the middle, warning him not to cross the demarcation line. While she was down the hall at the bathroom, he washed at the room sink and slipped beneath the sheet and cover, feeling stronger with every passing hour.

Nicole returned and switched off the overhead light. Only a faint glow entered the window from the street below, but it was enough to awaken his interest. At the sink she stepped out of her dress and slip. Hanging her bra on a chair, she used a cloth to wash her face and underarms. Silhouetted against the mirror, the curve of her bare breast was enough to make him hard. She put on the slip again and combed out her hair.

This will never work, he thought. He was still erect when the mattress shifted. She now lay beyond the barrier, close but very far, separated by an untold past which made him—made all men—her enemy. For over an hour he chased sleep, finally easing himself from the bed and going to the privacy of the hall bathroom to relieve his tension.

The next day proved long and mind-numbing. Imprisoned in the hotel room, Ryan paced incessantly until an aggravated Nicole ordered him to sit. She had a late breakfast delivered to the room—bread, jam and butter, and a weak coffee made from actual beans with only a hint of roasted barley. At Ryan's insistence, the management sent up recent magazines and several cheap novels, and mid-day cheese sandwiches arrived unbidden. Nicole went out from time to time to break the tedium, but without a reliable identity he was at the mercy of this time and place. In the early afternoon she returned to the room with three items: an envelope, a mesh shopping bag holding bread, salami, and wine, and a paper-wrapped bundle tied off with string. She reported his incriminating police identity had turned to ash in the alley next door and the badge had disappeared down a sewer drain.

First she handed him the envelope received from a scowling Frédéric at the front desk. It had been opened. *Tomorrow. Seven p.m. 28 rue de Graves. E.* Ryan remembered the calling card found in the hymnal in Berlin, the start of this long and dangerous adventure, and recognized Erika's neat script. "We've a rendezvous for tomorrow evening." He smiled and showed her the note. "My friends at last."

"Another long day, then." Nicole's off-hand response revealed her thoughts were elsewhere.

She untied the bundle and handed him a cleanly-ironed shirt, a red silk tie, and a tweed jacket free of elbow wear. "Can't do a thing about the shoes—in short supply everywhere. The rest should fit reasonably well."

He smiled broadly. "What a nice surprise, thank you!"

"And you might like these, as well." She tossed him a new undershirt and boxers. "I'll leave a couple of handkerchiefs on the dresser. Now go take a bath and get out of my hair for a while."

"Splendid suggestion." He gathered up the clothing, noting that she had also improved her own wardrobe. A pale yellow dress now joined a few other items on the bed.

"One more thing, monsieur." She had yet to call him by his given name.

He turned at the door. "Yes?"

A small package flew across the room. "Do something with the hair."

Walking down the hall, he opened the package to find a razor, shaving soap, and a tin of pomade. A toothbrush and tooth powder were a further welcome find. Nicole appeared to have an unending supply of ration coupons and cash. He smiled to himself, unwilling to question where she had done her "shopping."

By nightfall he was fully recovered from his encounter with the rat. In the dark of the room he waited for her to return from down the hall. The strain of living in close proximity to such an attractive woman was affecting him, but her lack of interest had forced him to abandon all flirtation. He kept his frustrations to himself. But that didn't prevent his hoping for another glimpse of her silhouette in the evening light. She didn't return to the room before he drifted into sleep.

Later he stirred as the mattress sagged. She slipped in beside him, her slender body cool against his skin. She was unclothed. As he began to speak she put a finger to his lips. "*Silence*!" Her voice trembled, and he wouldn't disobey the command for fear she'd change her mind. She forced aside his hands as he reached to touch her, to caress her.

"For me alone." A troubled whisper, barely a breath. "Not for you."

He was hard, and she took him to her, moving with a fury borne of anger and frustration he couldn't explain. For him, it was over too soon. At last she was spent, rolling off to the side, sobbing. He tried to comfort her, but she pushed him away and crawled across the bedspread barrier. Her back to him, she cried softly to herself.

His heart reached out, seeking to share in her sorrow. He received nothing in response. The sexual encounter had saddened him. It hadn't been love-making—there was no love there, just animal insistence and physical drive, a release without satisfaction. And still she sobbed. A lump rose in his throat, and he felt tears on his cheeks which he couldn't really explain.

CHAPTER TWO

Nantes, Occupied France
23 August 1941

Rue de Graves, a narrow street bathed in silence. Two dark figures moved along at a steady pace, peering up at street numbers in the failing light, anxiously seeking number 28. A scrawny dog ran loose down the street, glancing furtively in passing, stopping to investigate a trash bin here, a lamppost there, marking each station of his journey with a lifted leg before moving on. Ten minutes to seven. Ten minutes to the reunion.

Number 28. An innocuous tenement in a row of similar structures, all neglected due to Occupation fines on the citizenry. The entry door cried out for a fresh coat of paint. Attached to the peeling surface, another short note in Erika's distinctive script—*Apartment E.* The bell handle turned repeatedly in his nervous hand, but no concierge appeared to let them in. Behind the thick blackout curtains the only sign of occupancy was a window two floors up and to the left, where a thin sliver of light lined the drapes. Someone did indeed await their arrival.

Frustrated by the lack of response, Ryan tested and found the door unlocked. The concierge's office was vacant, its door left open. The vestibule smelled of mold and dirty carpet. Before them rose a well-worn staircase, its bannister creaking in protest as they ascended the uneven treads. At the second landing they turned down the hallway lined by a threadbare runner. The door to Apartment E was slightly ajar, casting a slim bar of light into the dark corridor.

He gave Nicole a quick glance before knocking. First came no response, then the door swung open to reveal Erika standing before them. She threw her arms around him, holding him tight and kissing him enthusiastically. Nicole scanned the room beyond but said nothing. Ryan and Erika drew apart at last, their arms still entwined.

She was breathless. "How on earth did you find us, Ryan? We thought you were dead! It's been so long!"

A lump in his throat. "And Leo?" His voice husky.

"Healthy and safe in the country."

"René? Where's René?"

"Right behind you, old friend." And he emerged from the darkness with that wonderful grin and an unexpected beard, and limping ever so slightly. René slid the pistol back in his belt and engulfed Ryan in a massive hug which lifted him from the floor. "*Mein Gott, Alter*, I think you've lost some weight!"

"Tracking the three of you down has taken its toll on me." Ryan threw an arm around Erika and squeezed her again, then hugged René once more before pushing him away to admire the beard. "Nicely grown, my friend. It suits you."

"And, with luck, hides my true identity." René laughed and stroked the growth as he turned to Nicole. "I think I look like a pirate! And who keeps you company this evening, Ryan?"

He felt strangely uncomfortable. During the day Nicole had made no mention of their nighttime encounter, so he had pretended things were unchanged. The intervening hours had been long and stressful. "Erika and René—this is Nicole, who recently rescued me from von Kredow's clutches. We can trust her completely, and I can personally attest to her skill with a weapon." He rubbed his neck as he glanced at Nicole with a grin—an inside joke the others missed and she ignored. Nicole offered her hand to each, nodding with a simple "*bonsoir*."

At the mention of von Kredow, Erika's face had gone pale and René's had darkened. "Horst? Then you've seen him?"

"Yes, unfortunately. And up close. But that's a long story and over now, thanks to Nicole."

"We must hear the story, and soon. But come in now—we've so much to discuss, my friends." René gestured to sagging chairs, their velvet armrests smooth from years of wear. Erika sat on the burgundy sofa while René fetched a bottle and four small glasses from the sideboard.

The loving look on Erika's face as René stepped out of the darkness had not gone unnoticed. They were indeed now a couple, as he had suspected would be the case. After three years on the run together, it would be amazing had they not found each other.

Ryan surveyed the room, neat despite its age and neglect. "A safe house?" He accepted a glass from René.

"Our new group made it available for this rendezvous." Erika poured the brandy. "So, a toast to old friends, and to your new friend who shares our common goals." Ryan sensed a chill between the women on both sides. Trust would have to be built. He sipped the Cognac.

René wanted answers. "But, come on Ryan, we're dying to know—what brought you back after all these years, especially in such dangerous times?" Ryan acknowledged René's squeeze of Erika's hand with a smile of tacit approval.

"And how in God's name did you end up in Horst's company?" Erika looked worried.

He told of Heydrich, Horst and Kohl's engineering of his espionage career from the very start. How a message purportedly from René had lured him to the internment camp at Gurs, only to fall into Horst's clutches once again. And then he described Nicole's roadside trap. "She saved us all from capture and a horrible death—Horst would have used me as bait to draw you in."

At the first mention of Horst, Erika had caught her breath. Now her eyes shot to René. "We must call Leo, and right away!" René put an arm around her and she shrugged it off. "René, he wants to finish what he started in Kehl, and he's getting closer!" The color was gone from her cheeks and her hands trembled. "What if he knows about the farm at Morlanne?"

"No worries, Erika, we were just on the phone with the boy a few days ago." He grasped her shaking hands. "Leo's happy and healthy in Mother's care."

Ryan remembered the cultured older woman he'd met at the Gesslinger home in '38. "Your mother's doing well?" He thought fleetingly of his own, so recently passed.

"Yes, she's doing fine, Ryan, and enjoying the country life in Gascony while looking after our Leo. Life on the constant run proved simply too exhausting." René turned to Nicole. "So, mademoiselle, you set a trap for Horst von Kredow—the one known as *le Masque*. Your people must know where he headquarters, where he travels."

At first it appeared that Nicole wouldn't answer. She stared at her hands and rubbed her ring finger, and then the words poured forth. "Everywhere and nowhere, monsieur. The phantom is seen, we hear stories of his cruelties, and then he disappears, only to appear at our backs just as we begin to feel safe. Vichy does his bidding, and his extraction commandos are terrifying. Imagine the worst of men, a malicious monster…a demon." She stared through embers of hatred, her words filled with loathing. "No one truly escapes him, you know. He's ruthless and patient and does exactly what he threatens. So we all fear, and he relentlessly uses that fear to make us all just like him…to destroy our souls."

Ryan hadn't heard such a torrent of words from her since the outburst in Bayonne days earlier. But now Nicole withdrew again, distracted, fidgeting with the base of her finger as though she still wore a wedding band. The other three remained silent, deeply affected by the raw emotion and reflecting on the suffering each had endured at Horst's hands.

Finally René broke the awkward silence with a question for Ryan: "And you've come to help us?"

"Any way I can."

"Can you bring America into this war? We could use the help."

"Let's start with money. Tell me what you need and I'll see what my people can do—" he added a caveat, "—although technically speaking, I'm supposed to be in Paris as soon as possible." His tone suggested he didn't really care about technicalities. "Do you already have plans for action here in Nantes?"

Erika answered. "First priority is sabotaging the submarine pens under construction over in Saint-Nazaire. We're going to put our René to work retarding their progress." She squeezed René's hand.

"I'll pose as a high-ranking naval engineer just in from Berlin. I'll screw up the construction schedule, find fault with what's already constructed so they have to rebuild, anything of that nature. And meanwhile get as much information to the Brits as we can. What do you think?"

"Dangerous, of course, and I'll bet that's why you like it. Is your engineering knowledge credible enough?" Concern crossed Erika's face.

"Maurice, our local group leader, got his hands on a submarine tech manual and plans for the pens, and I'll master it all quickly enough. He's a great coach, an engineering professor with arms like a stevedore. The rest will be a breeze. Once a sailor, always a sailor, right?" René shot Erika a reassuring glance.

His bravado didn't amuse her. "Overconfidence can get you killed."

"As can doing nothing. Tell me, Ryan...do you have a good channel for relaying intelligence?"

"What have you got for me?"

"The precise location of military and naval installations along the Loire. A suspected training school for Reich spies near Saint-Nazaire. And, I'm told, a reliable map of industrial installations, all fundamental to wartime materiel production. Shipping schedules, as well."

"And all this is ready to go?"

René nodded. "And yours, if you can get it to the right people. Our networks need coordination, and the couriers aren't yet fully in place. Even wireless contact with London is sketchy. Getting this to the right people should please your handlers in Washington, and we won't be disappointed if more English bombs start falling where they're intended."

"What have the locals done so far?"

"Not that much. Over thirty truckloads of new tires destroyed at the Hippodrome du Petit-Port last year. And, of course, a clandestine newssheet and handbills spread the word about the growing secret army. The *Boches* have assigned local citizens to guard communication, water and power facilities, so we try sabotage, it endangers our own people. But it's time to make a bigger impact, and with luck you Americans will soon step up."

Erika shook her head. "Impact, yes, but not by putting the hostages in Paris at risk, as some are willing to do. The two youngest hotheads here want to start assassinating local Occupation leaders and soldiers."

"Charming. When can we meet this new group of yours?"

"Is tomorrow soon enough? Curfew in Nantes kicks in at nine, so we usually gather right after dinner to get home before the SS patrols come out. Speaking of patrols, what identity are you using? Besides our author Richard Dana, of course."

"Glad you asked. I do have a bit of a problem there. My most recent papers belonged to a policeman whom I left indisposed."

"No worries, old friend. I'll have a young man at your hotel in the morning with his camera, and he promises documents by evening. Highest priority, highest quality." René drained his glass.

Erika handed Ryan a slip of paper. "Here's the address for tomorrow evening." A touch of her fingers—memories of past times, opportunities lost. "We gather at seven." Her eyes shifted to the young woman. "Nicole, you're welcome to join us, of course."

"We'll see. About time I got back home."

René gave Ryan another crushing hug. "So pleased to see you again, my old friend!" Then Erika embraced Ryan and murmured their thanks for having found them again.

"You'd have done the same for me, I know. And I look forward to hugging little Leo soon."

"Not so little anymore, and more precocious than ever," she grinned conspiratorially, "much like his father." Ryan caught René acknowledging the inside joke. "Oh, and Ryan, perhaps you'd like this back?"

He gratefully slipped the Florentine ring onto his finger. "That does feel better." The sudden thought of the K-pill in the cuff of his trousers dampened his mood. Things were sure to get more dangerous, not less. He bent down to retrieve the tiny oval. "You're familiar with these?"

Erika's eyes betrayed her distaste as she handed it on to René. A macabre smile played across his lips as he rolled it between two fingers. "I understand these are quite fast…and efficient."

"A kill-pill. Knowing what Horst is capable of, I suggest everyone also note where I hide this gem." Ryan took back the lethal capsule and opened the hidden compartment of his ring. "We're all together at last, thank God, but let's be clear—Horst won't abandon his search. We should prepare a plan to rid ourselves of his menace."

"Agreed. But if it's all the same to you, I prefer to stick with this." René touched the pistol at his belt. "We'll talk more about all that later."

"Well, it's in here—" Ryan snapped the lid shut on the cyanide, "—just in case."

CHAPTER THREE

Nantes, Occupied France
23-24 August 1941

Nicole had just returned from her bath, and Ryan caught himself responding to her despite a renewed commitment to stay clear of temptation. He'd always found damp hair on a woman appealing, as were the scented soap and her new yellow dress. He wasn't about to fall into the previous night's trap. The woman was too unstable, yet too damned attractive.

"Where exactly do you meet your friends tomorrow?" He handed over Erika's little note. Nicole unfolded a plan of the city and quickly found the location. "It appears to be a warehouse district down by the Loire. Should be easy enough for you to find on your own."

"But you are coming along, aren't you?" It hadn't occurred to him that she would really leave. At least not yet. "You can be just as effective here as down south, right? Your skills would be priceless here."

"Not the point." She stared toward the window. "I agreed to see this through till you found your friends. That's done. I've kept my end of the bargain, now you honor yours." Despite the map spread out before her, her focus was clearly elsewhere, her voice emotionless. "We all make our own beds, right?" He couldn't help thinking of their shared bed, their unsatisfying sexual encounter. "I have my path to follow, one I can't ignore, and staying longer will only make it more difficult for us both."

Ryan wasn't ready to surrender. "Listen, give me one more day. Stick around to meet the locals. That way, you can at least tell me what you think of them. You've had experience with other groups, so you'll have insights into how effective this one might become. Maybe you'll even like what you see enough to help us set a trap for *le Masque*."

Her finger now traced paths through the streets of Nantes, taking her mind to who-knew-where.

"Nicole, consider this. When you freed me, you said you were really expecting to get *le Masque*, this von Kredow. We all four have the same goal, to end that man's reign of terror. So just imagine this—we work together as a team, turn the tables on him, track the monster down ourselves. My God, Nicole…now here's another thought—I'm American, my friends are German, but you're French. That can make all the difference, because we're in your own back yard."

Ryan sat beside her on the bed, his leg close but not touching. "I know you're hurting, and hurting badly. You told me long ago you wouldn't share your story, so I'm not asking for that, but it's clear to me von Kredow's involved. Together—the four of us—we have the chance to bring him down. He won't give up, so shouldn't we all take the fight to him?"

Nicole stared listlessly at the map as Ryan's finger traced the filigree on his ring, pleased to have it back, giving her time to think. At last she spoke: "You told me of your escape from *le Masque* in Germany, how he tortured you, yet all three of you still live. Four, including the boy. I don't believe you really know the power that man wields, the extent of his cruelties. If he wants you dead, you die."

Ryan wasn't dissuaded. "Here's what I do know. I know that he and his leaders plan the mass annihilation of all European Jews. And it won't stop in the east. I know this man has no morality and finds his sole pleasure in the suffering of others. And he may be just one man, but he's a cog in a colossal wheel of Nazi brutality and injustice. If our little group can't single-handedly stop Hitler, we can, at the very least, destroy one dangerous off-shoot. Isn't that enough to justify our working together?"

Suddenly Nicole rose, and Ryan thought she'd come to a decision, that his argument had won her over. Instead, she reached for her handbag. At the door, she turned to look him directly in the eyes. "I need fresh air…to think. Alone." And she was gone.

Ryan remained on the bed, trying to guess where her mind was taking her, where his argument had gone wrong. Minutes later something occurred to him too late to help. She was out after curfew. Then he recalled the pistol and her shooting skills. Running after her would be pointless.

An hour later, as he drifted in that netherworld between wakefulness and sleep, one thought stumbling over the next and rest seemingly impossible, the door opened. He felt the mattress sag as she lay down beyond the barrier. She did not come to him in the night.

❖

By morning light he watched Nicole apply lipstick in the mirror. Their eyes met and she spoke to his reflection, saying she would stay. A sudden knock on the door announced breakfast, and Ryan recognized disappointment in the young clerk when Nicole wasn't the one to open the door and take the tray from his hands.

At ten-thirty the man was back again to announce a visitor downstairs. René's forger friend soon hurried into the room, offering the name "Yves" as he pulled a small Leica from deep within his jacket pocket. He was young, perhaps twenty, and declared himself an expert in engraving and photography. He wore a horizontally-striped shirt of black on white reminiscent of a mime, but Yves was anything but silent. He chattered endlessly as he posed Ryan on a chair facing the window. Without flashgun and bulbs, he had Nicole hold up a bed sheet to reflect light and reduce the shadows on Ryan's face. The task was done in minutes, but Ryan could tell from Yves's care in posing him that he took this job seriously.

"Your new identity will be ready by this evening, and the work will be a masterpiece, monsieur." Yves snapped his fingers at the word "masterpiece," and smiled proudly. "We are experts at this, you know."

"I'm most grateful, Yves. And my new identity—who am I to become?"

"Ah, monsieur, that's the decision of another, but I can assure you it will pass the most rigorous examination at the hands of any authority, French or *Boche*."

He left as quickly as he had come.

❖

Ryan remembered his Kansas University days as a pole-vaulter on the varsity track team. Preparing for a meet, he would focus entirely on the task ahead, devoting his energies to warming up and visualizing the challenge. He imagined gripping the long pole, steadying his breath, beginning the run and planting the stick, and finally the gravity-defying arc through the air before releasing his grip as he willed himself over the bar. And then, when his turn came, he would make the actual run and it would seem he'd done it all before. He never recalled the landing. He was simply there, flat on his back, then jumping to his feet to be sure the bar still rested on its supports and accepting the cheers of his fellow team mates.

He recalled such visualization as he watched Nicole pass their day of boredom. He fidgeted, trying to read and staring out for hours at the passers-by, the horse-drawn delivery carts and occasional automobiles. But Nicole sat as though mesmerized, her focus fully within. On occasion he would ask a question. She would sometimes ignore him, other times give a simple nod or utter a word or two before returning to her thoughts. He first considered she might have some mental problem, but then remembered he had also once found strength in such concentration. Perhaps she was finally conquering her personal demons and would emerge as a valuable colleague in the liberation struggle. He wouldn't force the issue. Tonight's meeting would tell.

CHAPTER FOUR

Paris, Occupied France
24 August 1941

Rue Pétrarque was quiet with not a soul in sight. Serge gave Paul the night off and watched the car coast down to the garage at the end of the street. He relaxed his grip on the pistol in his pocket and bound up the steps to the entry, its massive door opened by the attentive doorman. Serge entered the ancient elevator cage, the uniformed operator drawing the doors behind him. The old man knew better than to engage the building owner in any conversation other than a respectful wish for a pleasant evening. The machine creaked in its ascent five floors to the penthouse apartment, where the butler Pierre waited with a cocktail on a silver tray. He took Serge's order for a light dinner served in the formal dining room.

Yesterday had gone exactly as planned. By dawn the stolen Cognac had been transferred to three utility vans with German occupation plates. Burdened by the heavy load, the Renault trucks lumbered out of the Rue de Vence warehouse, each taking a different route to a common destination. Serge's main warehouse and distribution center lay east of the city. An armed Gestapo car accompanied each of the vans until it reached the facility. A high-ranking patron in the Paris SS paid off in spades.

Serge had arranged to divide the load into smaller batches for re-sale to the highest bidders. The *Boche* leadership appreciated a fine turn-of-the-century Cognac, and Serge loved any profit taken at the expense of his rivals. This apartment block in the 16th arrondissement was a good start, but within a year he would have something truly palatial and a staff of servants to rival the richest of them.

He set down the gin martini in his dressing room to put on a smoking jacket and fresh trousers. Leather slippers replaced his street shoes. Knowing that his dinner wouldn't take long, he cast a glance in the mirror, wiped a damp cloth over his pate, and patted down his mustache. Later he would have one of the regular girls brought up for relaxation. That night he would favor the new one, the young Senegalese with those incredibly long legs, a worthy barter for that load of bicycle wheels and tires.

He found a place setting of sterling silver, fine crystal and linen at the head of the massive oak table. A veal cutlet with roasted potatoes awaited, and Pierre had opened a bottle of vintage Bordeaux to allow it to breathe. As instructed, Pierre had also set the needle to Vivaldi's Four Seasons on the mahogany Victrola in the corner. Serge tried the veal, found it perfect, and took a sip of wine. Reaching for bread to sop up the gravy, he found the plate cool to the touch. The bell for Louise brought no response. In frustration he left the table and peered through the swinging doors to the butler's pantry and the kitchen beyond. He cracked the door and shouted out a vulgar command. Surprisingly, no one responded.

Now ready to bash a few heads, Serge stormed back across the dining room into the hallway. Rough hands grabbed him from both sides and an unseen assailant jerked his legs out from behind, landing him face-down on the Persian runner. In a response acquired from years of street fighting, Serge used all his strength to push off the floor, but he remained immobilized by a strong grip on his arms and a knee in his back. Then came a whiff of stale breath and a voice at his ear: "Let it go, Serge, just give it up."

"Who the hell are you guys?"

"Who we are doesn't matter. It's the big guy you stole from who's calling the shots." The men in suits pulled him to his feet, and the spokesman laid a fist into Serge's belly that left him gasping. The man shook out his hand. "Tough little bastard—almost broke my wrist." He slid on brass-knuckles and buried another blow deep in Serge's abdomen. The men holding him released their grip and Serge sank to the floor to curl up in fetal position. The men delivered several solid kicks, concentrating on his tail bone and head.

"What the fuck do you assholes want?" Serge's voice was practically lost in the scuffle and he suddenly wretched violently, making a mess of the wool runner.

"It's not what *we* want; it's what the *Reichsmarshall* wants." The main assailant now used German. "And what he wants, he gets. You've a concentration camp in your future, *Scheisskopf*."

His staff and bodyguard remained out of sight as the Germans dragged him to the elevator and descended to the street. The geriatric elevator operator said nothing, his hand on the brass control, his eyes glued to the passing floors. The doorman was not at his post. A silent captain in a blue-gray

Luftwaffe uniform had the men place Serge in the car beside him. Aching in every muscle, his head still groggy, Serge slumped forward. His hands remained tightly cuffed at his back as the vehicle left the center of the city. Serge recognized the route toward Le Bourget air field, and given the *Reichsmarshall's* inclinations, a Luftwaffe plane would be waiting to whisk him off to Germany and his fate.

Serge knew he'd been set up. The splendid Cognac prize had nothing to do with Masuy and his Delfanne gang. Someone else had needed him out of the picture, wanted him to step on the wrong toes. They had tricked him into treading on some of the most dangerous boots in the Reich: *Reichsmarshall* Hermann Göring, first in line to inherit Hitler's power, first in line to plunder the wealth of France.

Serge's SS purchasing officer may have ranked highly, but clearly not high enough.

CHAPTER FIVE

Nantes, Occupied France
24 August 1941

Nicole's study of the city map proved its worth. She led Ryan directly down to the warehouse district of the port, first passing through a respectable commercial area of shops and inns. Some businesses appeared to thrive despite the hardships of the Occupation. Others were shuttered and abandoned, casualties of POW camps, emigration, or racial persecution. A vigorous black market had brought others to their knees.

On the fringe of the business district the tone of both enterprises and clientele became rougher—cheap dives, second-hand merchandise, bicycle and shoe repair, and obvious sex traffic. He was pleased it was a Sunday, with few pedestrians out and about. A middle-aged prostitute invited them to join her at a bargain price, but Ryan and Nicole forged on. Within sight of the river large structures serving industrial or shipping purposes were shuttered for the weekend. An occasional furtive figure moved along the streets, only to disappear up one of the many narrow passageways. But in this deserted locale few paid attention to the couple as they searched out their destination.

The target address was a nondescript warehouse building no different than all the others. The long, tall structures stretched back from the street toward a frontage road, the railroad tracks and the docks. The rusting enameled sign confirmed they had found *M. Thierry-Garou & Fils, Expediteurs*. Cobblestone courtyards allowed access to the loading docks now blocked off by wide, padlocked gates. Barbed wire atop the metal fencing kept strangers out and goods in. Just to the left of their building a pedestrian gate hung slightly open, its rusting lock loose in the hasp.

Finding no welcoming committee, Ryan took the lead and they entered the loading yard, leaving the gate as they had found it. They spotted a barely-lit entry some twenty-five meters ahead. Above them ran a long bank of multi-paned windows, those with glass still intact dulled by years of grime. Some showed dark gaps where panes had cracked and shattered under the assault of time and vandalism. A solitary, shielded bulb within a small gabled overhang marked the entry. Ryan knocked once, waited a moment, then thumped twice more with a balled fist before completing the sequence with another solitary knock, the code René had given the previous evening. Now the door swung inward to reveal his smiling face. Ryan was still surprised to see the beard.

They passed through a cavernous storage area divided by long rows of shipping crates. The labels in German as well as French indicated destinations on the Eastern Front. The strong smell of new canvas suggested they encased some sort of tenting materials. He thought of the endless day under the railcar tarp. A room some distance away toward the end of the first aisle of containers cast a shaft of light across the warehouse floor. Ryan could see partisans gathered around a table, hunched over maps or diagrams.

René held them back for a private conversation before they entered the room. "Here, these are for you." He handed Ryan a bundle of papers. "Take a look before we go in. Secrecy is our greatest ally, and also our most dangerous foe, of course. But you should know your own identity, right?"

Ryan glanced through the documents, holding them under the light from the nearby door. His photo was affixed to a standard Vichy identity card with the pseudonym Raoul Diderot, age thirty-two, born in Chantilly. His mother's maiden name was Lenôtre. Employed as a professor of humanities at a secondary school in Nice.

"I thought up the professor detail—should make you feel right at home." René was clearly proud of his forgers' accomplishments. "Beautiful work, *n'est-ce'pas?* And I chose Nice because of all the time you spent down there, so if questioned you should be able to bluff your way through, right?"

Ryan grinned, remembering his failure to understand the cop's *Breton* insult at the Tours checkpoint. He pocketed the identity card. He could at least understand a little *Provençal.* He examined the remaining documents, including a demobilization card worn at the corners, a letter of employment issued by the school in Nice, and a second letter from a school administrator granting him temporary leave to liaise with school authorities in Nantes and Paris. The condition of the paperwork suggested the bearer had already presented the documents many times over. Yves and his fellow forgers appeared to have a supply of government-issued blanks. Ryan tucked away the papers. "Top-notch job. Thank you!"

"No need for thanks. Just use them safely. And now, here's something to advance your espionage career." He handed Ryan a second envelope. "Go ahead," he encouraged, "take a look."

Ryan unwound the string tie on the narrow manila envelope and withdrew a dozen or so papers. A quick glance suggested an analysis of current educational curricula offered in Nantes with emphasis on the new Vichy plan to promote traditional values in education. "Pretty exciting stuff, my friend."

"Ah, but wait until your handlers discover what hides beneath. It will be well worth their troubles." Ryan found the backside of the first few pages blank, but knew immediately that secret ink hid the promised intelligence on regional military and industrial projects. The planners of Allied bombing would be delighted with this information.

"Then I shall take good care of these indeed." He closed the envelope and slid it into the other pocket of his jacket. "Again, my heartfelt thanks, René."

"Just know that Erika and I are deeply touched by all you sacrificed—and risked—coming to find us." He grinned. "Even if Nicole here had to save your butt!" Nicole ignored the tease, apparently anxious to get moving. "But now it's time to do something productive with these newly-found comrades of ours. I'll introduce you as 'Duisberg,' an appropriate code name, don't you agree?"

The friends had first met when Ryan resided in the Duisberg Haus in Marburg during their university days. "I'm happy to use it. Has a more familiar ring than Raoul Diderot!"

"Listen—as you know, I'm now going by Rénard, and Erika's Héloise, got it?"

"Nice choices."

"And you, Nicole? Do you have a code name?"

"Nicole will do."

"Then Nicole it is. Some in the group are a bit rough around the edges, but their commitment is strong. So let's figure out how to take advantage of that."

René led them into the room and made introductions. Ryan and Nicole received a respectable welcome, especially from Yves, who greeted them as old friends. Maurice and Laura came across the room to shake hands. Cerberus and Raymond acknowledged them with quick smiles from beyond the large table. René's two "hotheads," Henri and Jean-Philippe, were no-shows.

"I say we give those two a few more minutes." Maurice wanted the two young men present before finalizing the operation against the Saint-Nazaire submarine project. Ryan knew that Maurice, with the shoulders of a dockworker, was actually the engineering professor coaching René for his coming assignment as a bogus German engineer.

"Are they on their way?" Cerberus looked dubious. "Those two seem fed up with our—shall we say—more reasoned approach to dealing with the *Boches*."

"They're still on board, I'm sure. And their friends over in Saint-Nazaire are needed to get us into the installation." Maurice radiated confidence. "And since we may merge the two groups afterwards, we'll need to work well together." As a discussion of this prospective union with the better-established group downriver gained headway, René heard the faint, coded knock on the warehouse door. He went out to open up for the two absent members of the group.

Minutes later he quietly returned, stumbling back into the room with his one arm wrenched behind his back. Horst von Kredow held a dagger to his throat. Two armed men in dark suits covered the group with automatic pistols. "Let's make this as easy as possible on everyone. Arms up and face the wall!" René made an effort to resist and a narrow stripe of blood rose across his neck.

Most immediately raised their hands and turned toward the wall in surrender. Erika went pale and stifled a gasp. One hand over her mouth, she remained frozen in place. Ryan had been examining the large map of the Saint-Nazaire docks and bolted upright at the sound of Horst's voice, only to lurch involuntarily from the table. Horst smiled serenely. "Our first order of business is to relieve you all of firearms, since I presume you all carry weapons."

The two Gestapo agents searched the partisans, gathering revolvers, switchblades and a knuckleduster. Ryan's eyes cut right and left. Erika's face was drained of all color. Nicole had neither raised her hands nor appeared surprised at the sight of her nemesis. As an agent approached her, Horst spoke again, his eyes bright. "Leave her—that one's mine. Marionette, come stand beside me." Nicole found a place behind him. "That's a good girl."

Ryan's jaw dropped. "But Nicole, how can…?"

"You'll learn soon enough, Herr Lemmon, but for now, "*halt's Maul!*" Ryan shut up, his jaw again hanging open.

Nicole's eyes never left Horst, while Erika glared pure hatred at them both. Ryan remained behind the table, stunned by this revelation. None of it made sense. This same woman who despised men for their violence and treachery, the girl who ruthlessly killed two Gestapo at the roadside trap, this lovely but sullen "partisan" who protested even coming this far with him—this woman was Horst's mole, his plant?

Ryan fell back on his training. He held his breath as the agent frisked him, running his hands under Ryan's arms, down his sides and the length of his legs. The man failed to consider the small of the back, where the police Browning was tucked out of sight. Had he moved that direction, Ryan was prepared to drop the agent and then go for Horst. With luck some partisans would join the fray and take out the other Gestapo man. But the agent turned away empty-handed, and Ryan slowly exhaled.

By his own count Ryan was now alone in hiding a weapon. René would have lost his to Horst and his men at the door. Nicole carried the small pistol in her handbag, but she—inexplicably—was in Horst's pocket. There was no logic to it, but also no time to argue with facts—she was a traitor and he would treat her as such.

Horst gave new orders. "Get them out of here—all except these three," he singled out René, Erika and Ryan with the point of the knife, "and my helpful little Marionette stays, as well. Now make it quick—you know what to do with them."

Horst dropped the blade to the floor without warning and yanked René's arm upward using both hands, nearly lifting him from the floor. René's arm dislocated from the shoulder with a resounding pop. The big man fell to his knees, his right hand grasping the damaged shoulder as a low moan escaped his lips. Erika gasped in horror.

Horst retrieved the knife and returned it to René's neck, hissing in his ear: "The last time we crossed blades you managed to best me, Frenchman. Don't think I'll ever offer a second chance." He slammed the hilt of the dagger down atop René's skull, sending a river of blood coursing down his cheeks and through his beard. René lay unmoving on the floor.

Erika screamed.

Ryan inched his hand slowly back toward the pistol. He would make every shot count.

Now Erika put reason in her trembling voice. "Horst, you don't need this. It's all gone on far too long. Do the right thing—it's not for us, it's for your own son!"

"My dear Erika, I *am* considering the little brat, as should you." He shouted out into the darkness of the warehouse. "*Reinbringen, sofort!*" Erika's eyes shot to the open door. A third agent appeared, dragging Leo by the collar. Adhesive bandage bound the boy's hands and feet, another strip covered his mouth. Leo's eyes shot wildly to his mother, then his downed uncle, coming to rest on the frightening man towering over him.

Erika cried out. "Oh my God, Leo, my Leo—"

"Yes, I've returned your Leo to you. It's time we put our family matters to rest, my dear." Returning the dagger to his belt, he ripped the adhesive plaster from Leo's mouth.

"*Mutti!*" Leo struggled with his bound feet.

"Oh, my baby!—" She lurched for her son, but stopped short. Horst held the barrel of his pistol at Leo's head.

"Don't...touch...the *Mischling*, you Jewish whore!" His fist turned pale on the grip of the pistol.

Tears streamed down her face. "But Horst, he's innocent!"

His rage faded as quickly as it had surfaced, his voice suddenly that of reason and philosophical debate. "Is any one of us truly innocent, Erika?" He placed a boot on René's back. "Here's how this final game plays out. First, your fallen hero here—" he stomped down on René's spine, forcing a groan, "I'll bleed him out like the French pig he is, all for our amusement. We'll watch his life spread out on this concrete floor, knowing your time is still to come. It'll be a treat." Horst lifted his foot to deliver a forceful kick to the ribs. René grunted but barely moved as he struggled for breath. "Next, I'll finish what Klaus and I began back in Kehl with our dear Dr. Lemmon, who didn't have the simple decency to stay put." The barrel end of the pistol now singled out Ryan. "We were just about to roast your prick with a hot poker, as I recall. My darling Erika, your old lover still needs to learn not to fuck another man's wife. And finally, the boy here goes, slowly, right before your lovely blue eyes."

Erika stared in fury, hesitant even to speak again, though she knew she must. "Leo has never harmed you."

"Ah, but that's just it, my blonde Jew-bitch of a wife—our little Leo here must pay for *your* sins. You took my pure Germanic sperm and corrupted a noble bloodline by birthing this half-breed. And now you will atone for the crime. Consider this—I first thought you should die with the knowledge that your child's excruciating pain was yet to come. But now I'm convinced you'll agonize more by witnessing his death. And afterwards, believe me, your own final hours will be memorable."

Erika shook in frustration, her reddened eyes glued to her son as Leo cried out to her again. "Mutti, please don't cry!" Horst ordered the boy gagged again, and at the failure of the old bandage to adhere, he sent his man out to fetch more. The moment the agent left the room, Leo tried to crawl toward his mother and she reached out for him.

"I said no touching." Horst hovered over the child, his pistol again at Leo's head.

Erika cried out, new steel in her eyes. "Stay there, baby, don't move!"

Horst turned back to Ryan, a skeletal grimace passing for a grin. "Once again I've played this fool American of yours. He thought he'd escaped me with the help of my Marionette." Nicole's eyes never left him, her face unreadable. "But in truth, her dramatic 'rescue' was only a brilliant ploy to bring you all together."

Erika, her fear suppressed, appeared fully prepared for whatever was coming.

"You and your oaf here may have unmasked my agents in Bayonne, but I knew you could never resist your old lover Lemmon. And my lovely partisan had proved her commitment to your cause by killing my own men. All I lost were one pain-in-the-ass lieutenant and an expendable driver, and that simple ruse made this reunion possible." A chuckle escaped those tight lips. "What did it cost you? Every partisan in my way, for my girl here kept me well informed—first the Bayonne misfits, and now this gathering of Nantes incompetents will pay for your gullibility."

Dampened echoes reverberated as double bursts of automatic gunfire came from the front of the warehouse. "Ah, there we have it now—a fitting end to your sad little terrorist group. My men will return momentarily, and we'll let the show begin!"

CHAPTER SIX

Nantes, Occupied France
24 August 1941

At the sound of the gunfire, Ryan thought of the very pregnant Laura and father-to-be Maurice, of Raymond and Cerberus, and the cheerful forger Yves. And Jacque's poor Bayonne team who had brought them to this sorrowful end. All fallen to Horst's murderous obsession. Ryan's own trustfulness had led to each of those deaths. Horst noted the shock on Ryan's face. "Did you really believe you could outwit me, outrun me, Herr Lemmon? My God, you're a victim of your own childish compassion."

He turned to Erika. "These Americans are so pathetic it's nauseating, as easily manipulated as you kikes. No wonder your kind flocks to America. Our pure German race has had thousands of years to perfect ruthless power, to succeed through intelligence and subterfuge—it's no wonder we control Europe. Even Ancient Rome knew success comes through manipulation and deception." Horst sneered at Ryan's obvious revulsion. "Re-read your Cicero, Herr Professor!

"Spare us your history lessons, von Kredow." During the long harangue Ryan had turned sideways. Each time Horst looked to Erika, Ryan's fingers edged closer to the pistol at his back.

Horst's diatribe continued unabated: "You fools think America can once again pull the Allied feet from the fire. Think again—that crippled Jew Roosevelt doesn't have the guts." His eyes rolled upwards. "*Herr Doktor* Lemmon, Americans are nothing but mongrels and degenerates. There's no possible way to beat a pure-blooded German at this game."

Ryan recognized one truth in the entire spiteful rant—Horst was his superior at deception, a psychopath without moral or ethical compass. To end this decade-long battle, Ryan would have to think like Horst, become like Horst.

The agent returned unannounced. He prepared to gag Leo again, but the boy sank his teeth into the man's hand, clamping down and holding on as blood streamed. The man pulled back in fury and back-handed Leo, sending the bound child sprawling beneath the table. He screamed, and that sudden disruption was enough.

Horst's rage broke loose again. "Shut that fucking brat up, and now!"

In that moment René sprang from the floor, head-butting Horst in the chin while seizing the Sauer and viciously wrenching Horst's wrist to the side. Horst fell as he lost his footing, and René knee-dropped into the Nazi's gut. The dagger skidded away as René repeatedly slammed Horst's head against the floor, punctuating each slam with a menacing growl: "Never…underestimate…a Rhine boatman!" Horst fought back with a vengeance, his fists and legs seemingly unaffected by the damage to his head.

Lost in self-absorption, Horst had noticed nothing, but both Erika and Ryan had seen René positioning himself for attack. Upon her husband's first move, Erika lunged for Nicole and delivered a rapid blow to the woman's head with a blackjack. She went down for the count. Ryan went for the man mishandling Leo. Too concerned with a bleeding hand and vicious child, the agent looked up too late. Ryan buried a shot in his temple. He turned to see Horst and René still locked in battle, and tried desperately to fire without risking the life of his friend.

"Here, use this." Erika tossed him the shot-filled bludgeon and he felled Horst with one blow. Ryan gasped for air after the furious exertion, still weakened from the hospital episode. Erika checked René for fractures and reported all bones intact. She then freed struggling Leo from his bonds. The child covered her face with kisses.

Ryan handed her back the blackjack. "Okay, where the hell was this hidden?"

She grinned through tears of relief. "Tucked in my bra. Still weighs less than a pistol, you know." Now she laughed. "Dangerous work, fighting these bastards—I learned that from you some years back."

"Glad to help. Now keep an eye on these two." He searched the dead agent's pockets, tossing identity papers and handcuffs on the table and taking the man's pistol. "I'll go handle the other two bastards up front."

A still groggy René shook his head. "Be careful, Ryan. They're surely heading this way by now. Leo, you and your mother get the handcuffs and tape. Gag them, we need them both quiet." They made short work of cuffing Horst and binding Nicole's wrists.

Footfalls approached rapidly from deep in the warehouse, then slowed in caution as they neared. "Everyone down, now!" Ryan whispered as he took cover to the side of the door and peered out into the dark of the warehouse, his finger on the trigger.

"Hold your fire!" It was Henri and his Jean-Philippe, approaching carefully with pistols ready. *Partisans, thank God, not Gestapo!*

Henri entered first, out of breath and flushed with excitement. "*Formidable*, real action at last!" He quickly grasped the situation. "We passed an empty cop car parked down by the river so knew they were on to us. We snuck in the back. Our comrades were already up against the wall so we dropped the bastard *Boches*. The Gestapo assholes never saw us coming." He squatted beside the dead agent to examine the single head wound. "Nice shooting. But all this gunfire's sure to bring trouble, so let's get the hell out of here. Maurice took the rest of the group out the front. He told us to stick around to finish the job here."

Jean-Philippe stated the obvious. "Doesn't appear you needed our help."

René tried out his wobbly legs as Erika helped him to the table. "You two," she indicated the young men, "hold him down, he's a big one. Duisberg, pull steadily on his arm—it should reseat easily enough." She bent close to René's ear. "Might hurt a bit, my love."

"Anything you ask, darling," he lowered his voice so that only she could hear, "I do love what you do with your hands." He grinned through gritted teeth as Ryan held his wrist and flexed the arm at the shoulder, extending it out from his body. Erika applied traction and rotation until the arm relocated with an audible "clunk." René grunted. He sat up, rubbing his shoulder, then ran his fingers through the caked blood on his scalp and beard. He tentatively touched the raised knot where the dagger handle had done its worst. "Good thing I'm so hard-headed."

Erika kissed him. "I'll never complain about it again."

René suddenly noticed Leo approaching the unconscious Nicole. "Leo, stay away from those two."

"But she's so pretty!"

"Still dangerous, Leo. Just do as I say."

Leo pointed to the downed Horst. "And this one's really scary looking, and mean." He looked puzzled, some distant memory tugging. "Is he my father?"

Erika was at a loss. "Not the way he is now, baby. That was a long time ago before he changed." A feeble smile, first to René and then to Ryan. "But now he wants to hurt us, and we have to make sure he doesn't get the chance."

"But why does he want to hurt us?"

"He's a bad man now, sick in the head." She put her arm around her son.

René hesitated after swinging his legs from the table. He lowered his head between his knees, allowing a wave of dizziness to pass. One hand cradled his bruised ribs.

Ryan squatted beside Leo. "Some people become mean, Leo…and we have to make certain they never hurt us, right?"

The boy eyed him closely, a glow of recognition spreading across his face. "I know you! You're *Mutti's* friend from the train."

Memories of that dangerous flight from Berlin flooded back, and Ryan nodded. "That's right, Leo. So you can remember that from when you were only three-and-a-half?"

Leo looked very serious as he bent close to whisper in Ryan's ear: "I'm not a secret policeman anymore."

"Neither am I, Leo. That was a long time ago." He gave his son a hug and broad smile, and the boy hugged him back.

"So, time to tie this up." Erika's eyes held Ryan's for the briefest of moments. "The sooner we're rid of these two, the sooner we're out of here. Jean-Philippe and Henri—go crack open a couple of those shipping crates. Stash this guy and the two you took out up front and seal them tight. No one will be the wiser till they show up somewhere on the Russian front, and we'll have no reprisals against the civilian hostages." Jean-Philippe dragged the dead agent out of the room with Paul at his heels. Erika shouted after them: "And take all identity papers and weapons off them first. We can always use them later."

CHAPTER SEVEN

Nantes, Occupied France
24 August 1941

Oh God, please don't kill him—let him live a while longer. Don't let the bastard die, not yet…not yet…

In her formless world of half-consciousness, Nicole knew *le Masque* still lived. She could hear the talk of what should be done with her and that demon. She willed her hands to move, to somehow draw the others' attention, but the muscles refused to obey. She felt the boy nearby and wanted to tell him of the child she loved, a child for whom she had sacrificed everything, including her soul. Instead she drifted back into the nightmare that had haunted her every waking hour for the past six months.

❖

In the morning light she awakens on the kitchen floor. None of the previous night's horror makes sense. Her brain refuses to piece the events into a coherent whole. The screaming and shouting still resonate in her mind, the loss of all she holds dear is too much to bear.

She opens her eyes and sees nothing, then gradually focuses on the planking of the floor, the individual grooves and scratches carved over the many years. She sees broken knots lifting from the wooden surface. Dust and debris have gathered beneath the iron stove. Sasha's hair. How that dog sheds!

And then it all comes rushing back. She lets loose a long, plaintive cry and bolts upright, feeling searing pain between her legs. She rises and steadies herself at the table, her vision clouded by a torrent of tears. The empty kitchen mocks her. It should be alive with activity at this early hour: Antonio picking at his omelet, planning his next sabotage; his sisters bickering; her mother-in-law bent over the stove; her father chain-smoking as he plots the day's business, political and agricultural. And in her arms, her baby girl.

My God, why? A desperate plea, but no answer comes.

Outside, only silence. Nicole stumbles toward the door hanging askew with its broken hinges, out into the frozen light of the courtyard. No bodies lie strewn about. Only Sasha lies exposed to the cold, rising sun. Nicole collapses beside the dog's body and gently runs her fingers through the frost-covered fur, the animal a surrogate for all she has lost.

And then, through her tears, he comes striding up into the courtyard through the open gate, exhaling cigarette smoke through his nostrils and that cruel slit of a mouth. He stops before her, his scarred face even more frightening by light of day. She scoots back along the icy ground until she hits the stone wall, and beneath her lies the smeared and thickened blood of her father, and of her beloved Antonio.

"From this moment you belong to me," his voice low and free of emotion. "I know you've suffered great loss, but isn't that what life is about? He crushes the cigarette, the toe of his boot scraping in the frozen gravel. "You brought it on yourselves, you know, by defying the Reich. By defying me."

Nicole finds no release for her fear and revulsion. She wishes also to have died in the night. Her head shakes in denial, back and forth, slowly at first, and then ever faster until it seems her neck must break. The man bends down and places his hands on her cheeks, steadies her, speaks again: "Hear me out, young woman. I've special plans for you."

She wants to lash out, to kick him, stab him, bite him, tear his heart from his chest as he has torn out hers, hurt him beyond all imagining, worse than she suffers now. But she is powerless, so she must listen.

"Your child lives." Her eyes spring open in desperate hope. "But only as long as I say she does, and while you do my bidding exactly."

Nicole pulls herself free of his hands, nodding. She knows he's capable of anything, no matter how vile.

"Now listen carefully, *ma petite*." He towers over her. "Your terrorist station here will continue to welcome traitors to the Reich, only now you work with my people, do I make myself clear?

Nicole continues to nod, focused on that flickering hope of Sophie still alive.

"I know you'll wish to harm me and my cause—were I in your position I'd do the same. But you will do nothing to stand in my way, because you now know what I'm capable of. One wrong move, one moment questioning my word or going behind my back believing you know better, and your child dies, painfully. Understood?"

Nicole tries to control her breath, her body racked by dry sobs. She trembles in both fear and hope.

"I've had my eye on you for some time. I know you shoot and shoot well. As any good country woman you can slaughter animals without flinching, so you're accustomed to death. I won't ask anything of you I wouldn't ask of myself."

Nicole bites her lip, her mind blank to all but the knowledge that Sophie still lives.

"You, madame, will be my surrogate. You will kill for me when I say 'kill.' You will betray and lie to those I wish to control. You are now my marionette." His mouth takes on the semblance of a grin. "In fact, from now on, that shall be my code name for you—Marionette."

He touches Sasha's stiffened head with the toe of his boot. "Nature is strangely fascinating, don't you think? This was a living, breathing creature, now gone at my whim. All of them—" he makes a broad gesture across the courtyard, "—the living and the dead, all gone at my command." For a moment he remains silent, savoring the thought, and now he squats down before her, his voice barely a whisper: "Listen carefully—your daughter is mine until I no longer need you, Marionette. Then she comes back to you. Whether I bring her to you alive…or dead…is entirely in *your* hands."

He stands upright and straightens his overcoat. She stares at him, at evil incarnate.

"So…we'll meet again soon. Now go clean yourself up and be ready for my call."

Le Masque strides through the gate and down the drive to a black sedan waiting below. He signals the driver, and the growl of the engine reaches her in the hollow of the courtyard, a space devoid of all life, including her own. He does not look back. There is no need. He holds his enemies in the palm of his hand. And she is forever his tool of death.

CHAPTER EIGHT

Nantes, Occupied France
24-25 August 1941

"I say we kill them both, and now." Erika's finger was on the trigger of the pistol taken from Nicole's handbag. The woman's identification papers had joined the growing collection on the table.

"Agreed, we've no choice, but first I need to know why she betrayed us." Ryan turned to René for support.

He shrugged, flinched, and reached for the sore shoulder. "I don't know about the woman, but the sooner we eliminate von Kredow, the better. And taking the woman with us will only slow us down."

Erika nodded. "Leo shouldn't see this, René. Take him far out into the warehouse. Wait at the rear entrance while the young men are busy up front. Ryan and I will handle these two." René limped out, holding Leo by the hand. The boy looked back in silent protest, hesitant to leave his mother.

Ryan pleaded his case: "Look, let's first find out what she knows. It makes no sense she'd kill Horst's men and then turn around and betray us—there's a piece missing to this puzzle." He shook his head. "Nothing here makes sense—I know she despises men and their wars. Her pacifist tirade I witnessed wasn't a show—no one's that good at acting!"

"Frankly, Ryan, I don't give a damn. Go ahead—get her to talk, then we kill them and get out of here."

Ryan fetched water from the tap at the end of the room, pulled the adhesive from Nicole's mouth and doused her face. Groggily with eyes still shut, she struggled against the tape at her wrists. He pushed her down as she tried to sit up while mumbling incoherently.

Horst also began to stir. Erika kicked him in the ribs, and he groaned. "That's for threatening my son!" She knelt beside him and examined his face. "And to think you were once so handsome..." her voice barely audible, her mind momentarily in a different time and place, "…and I such a fool."

Ryan lightly slapped Nicole's cheeks. "Come on now, wake up, dammit!"

Her words suddenly came in strangled bursts, and he held his ear close. "Don't kill him…not yet! He has my Sophie…the stinking bastard can't die…not till I know where my baby is!"

Ryan looked over to Erika. "She's saying Horst has her child, her baby!"

Erika turned at once, wrenched from her memories by the thought of another child at risk. "Get some details. I don't trust her after all she's done, but I'll be damned if I'll risk another kid's life!"

Ryan sat her upright against the wall, encouraging her to continue. The story emerged in a dull monotone, then gathered speed as the truth tumbled out. "That devil there…he slaughtered my husband, my father, my family…and took my little girl and won't give her back if I don't lie for him… kill for him." Her conviction tore at Ryan's heart. "I want him dead more than you ever will, but first he has to tell where he has my baby." Tears streamed as she pounded her bound hands against Ryan's chest.

"Do we dare believe her?" Erika's eyes moved from Ryan to the bawling woman. "She may be as devious as Horst."

"This would explain what she did, and why, and it all sounds like his evil. Erika, you've done everything to protect Leo. In all honesty, would you take innocent lives to protect our son?"

The sheer brutality and cruelty of the concept released anew her tears. She dropped to her knees beside the trembling Nicole, stared her in her eyes and warned: "You lie, you're dead."

"It's all true…" Her breath came in great sobs. "He's holding my little girl!"

"Wake the bastard, Ryan. Either he tells where he's stashed the child, or I'll feed him his balls. I swear to you, I'll do it! If he gives us the child, he dies quickly, agreed?"

"Agreed."

Ripping the tape from Horst's mouth, Ryan brutally slapped him back to consciousness. Finally focused on

Ryan, Horst oozed disdain. "Can't bring yourself to kill me after all?"

"The child you stole from Nicole, where is she?" He held the dagger beneath Horst's eye and nicked at the soft flesh, each cut raising a droplet of blood.

Horst chuckled. "You fool—you'll never have the guts. You can't stop me." He forced his own head up against the tip of the dagger, encouraging the blade to pierce more deeply. A crimson rivulet ran down his scarred cheek. "I write the rules, and the rules say that little girl of hers is mine forever."

Ryan slid the razor-sharp edge repeatedly across Horst's throat, raising bloody welts with each emphasized word. "Where…the hell…is…she?"

Horst dropped his head back to the floor. "Do your worst, weakling. Pain means nothing to me, death itself means nothing. I've explored its entire morbid scale. You're a neophyte—you'll never know the joy, the slow release that comes of making the killing act a thing of beauty." His chuckle a macabre sound through barely-moving lips.

Henri appeared suddenly at the door, breathless, a harsh whisper. "Douse the lights! Cops everywhere out front—someone's reported the shots."

Ryan looked to Erika, now comforting the sobbing Nicole. "Erika, off with the lights—now!" She hit the switch, leaving the room bathed in a soft glow from the filthy panes high above.

"How many?"

"Two squad cars, seven or eight men, approaching from the street but still outside."

"The bodies?"

"Stashed but not yet sealed."

"Room for one more?" Ryan nodded toward Horst.

"Yes, but no gunfire. Keep it quiet."

"Can we get out of here without a battle?"

"The back entrance, maybe, but hurry! They're checking out the main loading docks now."

Ryan bent close to Horst and growled his demand. "Final opportunity. Sing, or I start with your eyes! The little girl…where is she?"

Horst enunciated each word clearly, raising his voice for Nicole to hear: "In an unmarked trench with the remains of her mongrel family." He gloated, his mask filled with malice. Nicole wailed in heartbreak and Erika raced to keep the horrifying sound of a mother's worst loss from betraying them all.

Erika's whisper was venomous. "Kill him now, or I will!" She rocked Nicole in her arms, her own tears flowing.

Ryan's mind raced. A gunshot would bring the Gestapo and they'd all die, including Leo. But to slit a breathing throat, even that of a monster?

"Do it!" Erika, cold and brutal.

Be as vicious as your worst enemy, he told himself. *Strangle the bastard.* He looked across the room for a wire or cord, then went for the belt at his waist.

"The pill, dammit, Ryan, the cyanide in your ring!" Her eyes cut through the darkness.

Ryan shook the capsule from its compartment. Gripping Horst's hair in one hand, he struggled to force the pill between those detestable lips. Horst fought it with his tongue, and Ryan's fury rose with each attempt. He straddled Horst's chest, beating his head against the concrete floor. The Nazi's mouth opened with the impact and Ryan jammed the pill in and slammed the jaw shut with two upper cuts, then ground his enemy's jaws together to break the rubber seal and glass vial and end that miserable, hate-filled life.

Ryan felt the bucking and jerking as Horst's body reacted to the toxin flooding his bloodstream. His head thrashed from side to side and he gasped for breath, saliva foaming. Ryan held the jaw tightly shut as the poison did its work. Long minutes passed before the body gave a final violent shudder. Ryan leaned back, still straddling the body, drained by the act of killing, relieved to finally end the years of mental and physical struggle. His knuckles were bruised and bloody. "It's done." He looked at Erika, still cradling Nicole in her arms. She had unbound her wrists. Ryan rose and helped them to their feet. "Come on, we have to get out of here."

He dragged the body into the warehouse, calling out quietly to the partisans. Only Jean-Philippe appeared from the darkness. "Here's one more for the eastern front. Where's Henri?"

"With Rénard and the kid out back. I was just coming for you." He pointed Erika down the aisle, her arm around the sobbing Nicole to hurry her along. Jean-Philippe took a closer look at the size of Horst. "Sir, I'll need your help getting this big one into a crate. We stuffed two in one box and gave the third guy one of his own. Hammering them shut will bring the cops, so be prepared to shoot it out."

Ryan felt for the Browning in his belt, mentally counting the remaining bullets in the police-issue weapon. Then he recalled the semi-automatic he took from the first man he'd killed that evening. It was getting easier to do the necessary.

❖

René and Leo waited at the rear of the warehouse. Henri had a pistol drawn and his ear to the door, listening for activity outside. When Leo had first appeared in Horst's clutches, René had feared the worst for his mother. "Your grandmother, Leo, what did they do to her?"

"I'm sorry, uncle. *Grand-mère* Jeanne died. Just a few days ago—she never woke up."

"Died? Before the police came?"

"Yes, uncle, that's why I came to find you and *Maman*. I almost made it but the policeman arrested me."

René nodded without really comprehending. His eyes glistened. The rest of the story would have to wait. He hugged Leo tightly. "Better so—we should all go peacefully in our sleep."

"I gave her flowers before I left. She loved flowers."

"Thank you, Leo. That was the right thing to do." He rose with a deep sigh. "Time for us to go. Just remember how much she loved us." Grieving would have to wait.

With Nicole sagging against her, Erika joined them. "She's to be trusted after all?" René sounded doubtful.

"Why's the pretty lady crying, *Maman*?"

"Her little girl Sophie is dead." She cradled Nicole to her shoulder as a new wave of grief overcame her.

"But *Maman*—"

"No time to talk about it, Leo. Right now we must be going."

"But Maman—Sophie's not dead, she's fine! I was teaching her to spell with colored blocks just yesterday—she's in Bayonne with the other kids, in the house where the Gestapo kept me."

Nicole dropped to her knees before Leo, words tumbling forth in desperate hope. "This Sophie—how old is she? What color's her hair, her eyes." She shook him by the shoulders.

Leo became cautious, sensing the importance of his answers. "Agnès says Sophie's almost a year-and-a-half, though she's not really sure. But Sophie does talk a lot already."

Nicole shot Erika a look of hope. "Her hair and eyes—what color?"

"Brown hair, and her eyes are blue…like yours!"

"Then it's possible! It could be my little Sophie!"

"I think Sophie likes me, she follows me everywhere. Of course, I'm too old for blocks, but it's good for her to start learning to spell early."

Now Erika took hold of his shoulders. "This is very important, Leo…can you find her again? The house in Bayonne?"

"Of course, *Maman*. I won't even need my compass. We just walk across the bridge from the train station, and the rest is easy! We look for the stone lions at the door." Nicole dropped to her knees to embrace Leo. He looked up to his mother in surprise.

Ryan appeared with Jean-Philippe. "Come on, we've got to go—and now!"

"She's alive, Ryan—Nicole's daughter's alive!"

He stopped short. "So the bastard lied a final time." He shook his head. "Come on—let's go!"

"Look what I found on one of the dead guys." Jean-Philippe jangled keys, barely visible in the faint blue glow. "For the car in the alley, I'd bet." He set down the cloth sack heavy with weapons, handcuffs and papers taken from the dead men and handed pistols from the haul to Erika and René. Both quickly checked the clips.

"A getaway car's great—but first we have to get out of here alive." Henri drew the bolt and peered out past the trash bins. Nothing moved under a partial moon.

"The alley gate's down to the left. The Gestapo broke the lock when they came in."

"I'll scout it out." Ryan slid out the door. He had traded the agent's pistol for the Sauer taken from Horst. Releasing the safety, he crouched low, working his way around the bins. With a clear view of the rear yard, he saw the wide gate for vehicles and the smaller one beside it. He edged his way along a storage shed, keeping to the shadows. *So far, so good.* At the far end he could follow the shielded flashlights of the police agents in the main delivery yard, checking every possible entry point. Vichy gendarmes, not Gestapo.

Once back inside he filled in the others. "*Flics* coming—they're almost to our end of the building." He described the layout at the rear of the warehouse and reviewed their troops: four men, Erika, one unknown factor in the distressed Nicole, and Leo.

Another jolt of pain coursed through René's bruised ribs, and his hand went to his chest. "How many cops total?" His voice sounded weak.

Ryan didn't miss the signs. "Only two approaching on this side, at least so far. You going to be okay, my friend?"

"Of course. It's nothing but a bruise or two." He rubbed his shoulder. "Everything still works." Scratching the blood-crusted beard, he added: "But I may need a bath when all this is done."

Jean-Philippe added up the cops in his head. "We counted at least two squad cars. The others must be up front or over on the far side."

Erika already had a plan. "Henri and Jean-Philippe, you two are quickest. Move along the shed on the right side and make some noise to draw them out. Duisberg and I'll hide out on the left beyond the trash cans and mow them down once they round the corner and run past. Just remember to duck when we fire. Then get over to the far side and finish the job. Our shots will draw all the remaining cops and we'll pick them off as they come."

Henri smiled. "Damned good plan, Héloise. Let's do it!"

"Rénard, you've been through the wringer. Once you see the coast is clear, make a run with Leo and wait in the car for the rest of us and we'll get the hell out of here."

Nicole spoke up, newly energized and determined to help. "I'll need a weapon."

"Impossible. I am convinced Horst took your child and stashed her where he had my son, and that we'll find her. But for now, you're still suspect. We can't trust someone who's already cost us lives, no matter how justified in your eyes. You go with Rénard and Leo."

"But—"

"No arguments. We're wasting time."

The two partisans slipped out the door, keeping to the dark side of the storage shed. Only at the corner did their silhouettes appear against the lighter sky. Ryan and Erika moved out in a low crouch. René grabbed Leo's hand, told him to keep quiet, and nudged Nicole through the door. They hid behind canisters and abandoned crates.

Ryan heard police approaching, calling out to one another in low voices. He imagined jumping out and mowing them down at point-blank range. An overturned oil drum clattered into the yard, raising an immediate alarm. "Halt! Halt or we fire!" Two cops raced around the corner of the warehouse, flashlights dipping as they un-holstered weapons. Once the police neared the shed, Ryan and Erika let loose, and other shots answered from beyond. The cops went down.

René's small group burst from shelter and ran across the yard as quickly as his limp and aching shoulder would allow. They were almost through the gate when shouts rose from far up front. Bullets ricocheted off both gates, and more resounded from beyond the warehouse building.

Erika and Ryan dropped to the ground, choosing targets as two more gendarmes raced past with barrels spitting. Shots rattled off the metal sides of the building. Just beyond the gate René fell to his knees. Nicole crouched beside him to take his pistol, then returned fire—single, precisely-aimed shots which picked off the last of the assailants. Nicole had something to prove.

The far side of the warehouse fell silent, and Henri shouted to hold fire. He and Jean-Philippe raced down the courtyard from the front, making sure that each of the downed cops was out of commission. Jean-Philippe made a quick detour for his bag of police paraphernalia taken from the Gestapo.

René had been hit in the right buttock. "Dammit, couldn't they pick on my other side for a change."

Ryan helped him stand. "Learn to move faster, Rénard." Ryan supported him while Erika grabbed Leo's hand and the group followed the partisans to the black sedan parked in the shadows below. "We need to find a doctor, and right away."

"I know one." Henri took the wheel, the others piling in. "A doc just down river who won't mind spoiling his evening—it won't be the first time we've inconvenienced him." René sat sideways in the back seat to take the pressure off his wound, while Erika undid his belt to survey the damage in the dim cabin light. Jean-Philippe offered a handkerchief to cover the wound and slow the bleeding.

They sped down to the riverside quay, heading out of the city. Up front at the passenger window, Ryan kept his weapon ready. Erika and Jean-Philippe also remained alert, in case their speed and the late hour drew the attention of more cops.

They had not asked Nicole for the weapon taken from René. She sat between Henri and Ryan, asking in a subdued voice if anyone carried extra ammo. Jean-Philippe searched his bag and handed over a clip. As she reached for it Ryan spotted blood on her side. She'd been hit.

"Oh, it's nothing. Anyone have another handkerchief?" She accepted Ryan's, wincing as she applied it to the wound.

He gently massaged the sore knuckles of his right hand. Taking a closer look at Nicole, he was floored to spot a soft smile on her lips. "How's it going?"

"Barely grazed me…and well worth it." The accustomed hard edge was missing from her eyes.

"You all right, Uncle René?" Leo sat wedged between his mother and uncle, giggling. "You've got a bloody butt!"

"Who's this René? I'm now 'Rénard,' my little man."

Leo looked at him quizzically. "Uncle Rénard?"

"I'll explain later. And don't worry about me—I'll be just fine. It's worth a pain in the butt just knowing you're home with us again!"

Leo scanned the packed car as it sped through the nighttime city. He put his lips close to his uncle's ear to whisper: "If this is our new home, I think we'll need more room."

CHAPTER NINE

Paris, Occupied France
27 August 1941

"Raoul Diderot" retook his seat in the crowded second-class carriage bound for Paris. The air was rank with sweat and cinders, but the "professor of humanities" took little notice as he sighed in relief, knowing his identity papers were in good order. The police control had just given his documents a clean bill of health, and an inspector had fumbled through his leather valise, acknowledging at last that "Raoul" smuggled no foodstuffs or tobacco into the seat of the Occupation. Neither official had shown the slightest interest in the manila envelope which concealed details of German military and economic lifelines throughout the region.

With his friends safe and his personal mission accomplished, Ryan's true espionage assignment could finally begin. Delivering this intelligence coup to Ed would go far toward soothing his brother's certain frustration at losing contact with Ryan for nearly two weeks. He had no idea how Ed would deliver the intelligence to those higher up in the COI network, an important safeguard for a neutral power in a belligerent environment. Should Ryan be tortured for information, he'd know nothing of Ed's higher connections.

He took great satisfaction knowing Horst von Kredow was gone at last. So many had suffered and died at those sadistic hands, and Ryan recognized his own trusting nature had permitted von Kredow to thrive. Never again would he take things at face value. This world of espionage was much more than simply right or wrong, good or evil. It was every shade and gradation, where someone good could be manipulated to do evil, where finding a path to victory meant compromising one's closely-held principles. He had killed. He might be forced to kill again. He hoped it would all make sense when this war came to an end.

Parting from his friends had been bitter-sweet. He recognized that destiny had chosen René and Erika for each other, bonded by their determination to rid the world of Nazism and by their love for Leo. René had sought out Ryan in the doctor's garden. His injuries were healing well and he could sit again, although uncomfortably. The young partisans had returned to Nantes to get on with subterfuge and sabotage. Nicole's wound had been worse than expected but not life-threatening. The doctor sedated her to remove a slug fragment touching a rib. She had lain impatiently in bed for two days, hanging on Erika's promise that the four of them would head south the moment her healing allowed. Leo was anxious to lead them to Sophie. He described in detail the grand house in Bayonne, the crabby Madame, and the gentle Agnès who watched over the children day and night. Perhaps there would be other kids to return to their rightful homes, now that their kidnapper was dead.

"Well, my dear Ryan, rumor has it you leave for Paris this afternoon."

"It's time, right? My work draws me elsewhere. That intelligence windfall of yours will certainly be a welcome gift for the Allies. I thank you for that." Ryan sensed something troubling his friend.

"Ryan, we've been through so much together, and now again we must say *auf Wiedersehen*."

The American displayed a stubby pipe, a gift from the doctor quitting the habit to calm his lungs. "Share a smoke?"

"With pleasure." René took a seat beside him. The Loire flowed leisurely in the distance, recalling times they spent together overlooking the Rhine.

"I'll even provide the tobacco." Ryan opened the pouch holding a handful of loose flakes, the last of the doctor's monthly ration. He took his time tamping the pipe, and once lit, passed it to René. "I look forward to our next meeting, *mein Freund*. With luck and a bit of courage, it could be we gather to celebrate the Allied Powers' return to France."

"Ryan..." his eyes followed a river boat moving upstream pushing a barge, "...listen Ryan, we must talk about Leo, about your son...how to keep him safe in this insane world."

"You and Erika have done a remarkable job, in spite of all you've been through. You're both excellent parents, far better than I could ever be with what's on my plate." He took back the pipe. "Leo obviously loves you, you've been there for him through thick and thin, and I will never interfere with your relationship. He now has two loving parents to keep him safe in this crazy world...thankfully made a bit less so by ridding it of von Kredow."

"'Amen,' as my believer friends would say."

"So I propose a trade—I shall be his uncle and you his father, his only true father. I'll always love Erika—I make no secret of it—and I love you and our Leo, as well. And someday I'll meet the woman meant for me and have children to love and cherish. Perhaps then all four of us can raise kids in a more peaceful world. But for now, wherever the two of you go, I know you'll find a safe place for Leo. But above all else…keep him away from compasses!"

René laughed and drew again on the pipe. "I thank you, Ryan…for risking so much to come to our aid, and for giving me the honor of being Leo's father."

"Here, take this." Ryan handed him Ed's contact information in Paris, Vichy and Washington. "If you ever need help for anything, anything at all, get in touch through my brother. I don't believe for a moment you'll ever quit this fight—it's just not in the two of you. But know there will always be help when needed."

René folded the paper carefully. "Our life is here in the Loire for now, doing whatever we can to free France. But liberating the French people is just the start. One day we'll cross the Rhine again, heading east with those criminals on the run.'"

"Then it's time for me to be on my way and let the 'Lone Ranger' go make more trouble for those outlaws."

❖

Ten minutes later he headed upstairs to pack his few belongings in a worn bag provided by the doctor. Erika appeared at his door. "Ryan?" He smiled in surprise as she embraced him. "Must you leave so soon? Leo wants to show you the garden."

"I've a job to do in Paris, and yours takes you a different direction." He kissed her forehead, remembering her scent from years past, memorizing it for when he would wish to recall this life-changing moment.

"I know…I know…but I thought I'd never see you again, and then you were there, and all the old memories came flooding back, everything we went through together, and all we survived." He sought to ignore the lump in his throat as she spoke. "It was never truly meant to be, was it? For the two of us, I mean. Have you ever considered where things would be if we'd made different choices back in Marburg?"

Ryan dried her eyes with his handkerchief. He swallowed hard. "We make choices and hope for the best, then live or die by them. But all four of us made it this far despite adversity. Now you have a wonderful, devoted husband, a son we can all be proud of, and my love for all three of you, always."

She pushed him away. "Then get out of here and be safe, and find us again when you can." She kissed him and was gone from the room without looking back.

He found Nicole sleeping peacefully. The doctor had probably given her another sedative, a chance to heal before they all raced south to track down the children. Ryan knew she would finally find some peace once she held her little girl in her arms again. He had a train to catch, so he wrote a brief note and left it beside the bed. Perhaps he would see her again someday when all this horror had passed.

Leo played in the garden, and Ryan listened as his son named each flower he found, first in French and then German. The boy hugged him and waved as Ryan left in the doctor's car for the train station. In his hand he held a small bouquet from Leo, a parting gift. While waiting for the next local to Nantes, Ryan singled out a single wildflower, the one Leo had named as his favorite, and pressed it between the pages of a tiny notebook purchased at the newsstand. The rest of the blooms he left on the wooden bench of the waiting room. He would keep the notebook nearby no matter where his journey might next take him.

❖

The train pulled aside as a military consist heading east took precedence. He knew his Paris-bound express wouldn't keep to its schedule at this pace. Upon arrival at Gare Montparnasse, he would leave a phone message for Ed, and he reminded himself to fulfill the promise made to the dying Englishman Devon Whitaker by getting a message to that girl Trish in London. Ed would contact the home office and make it happen. Once he'd checked into a hotel, a hot bath would be in order, and then—with a bit of luck—he'd head to Marita's club. He would arrive right at closing time and surprise her at last.

He smoked the last shreds of the doctor's tobacco as he watched the farms, fields and woods roll by, deceptively beautiful and showing few signs of Occupation. The little leather-bound notebook with the pressed flower remained in his hand.

❖

At 11 Rue des Saussaies in the 8th arrondissement the agents gathered for the evening's assignments. The night promised to be busy, and German Gestapo and French auxiliaries were in good spirits. After distributing mundane investigative and enforcement tasks, the lieutenant ordered all agents to remain in place for a special guest, *SS-Hauptsturmführer* Theodor Dannecker. Adolph Eichmann's representative in Paris planned to attend the briefing and address his men in person. The agents whispered amongst themselves, wondering what called for such an unusual honor.

Voices hushed as Dannecker entered the room. The agents saw a pleasant-looking man with nothing in his features to distinguish him from any other SS officer. But this man had serious clout with SS and SD leadership, for he held responsibility for handling the Jewish problem in France.

"Gentlemen, I won't detain you long from your important duties. I just want to tell you personally how much the Führer and Reich value the contribution each of you makes daily." The audience rapped knuckles on the tabletops in applause. "Yet, despite your best efforts, our results in rounding up and deporting Jews have been very disappointing. Rather than the tens of thousands which the Reich Ministry of Transport can easily handle, we've settled for a fraction of that capability. But I'm here to tell you now that this is all about to change, and you men will be at the forefront of the effort. Homeless refugees and Jewish foreigners were only the beginning; soon we go after every Jew in France!" Heavy applause rose along with a few enthusiastic shouts of "Heil Hitler!" "With the knowledge that you will soon cleanse this country of the Jewish plague, go out this evening and do your job with confidence. Serve your Reich and your Führer, and make your leaders proud."

The agents and their French counterparts rose, raising their arms in salute. Dannecker, walking toward the rear with his lieutenant in tow, stopped to whisper something in his ear. The subordinate turned and called back two teams leaving through the far doors. Surprised at the unexpected-summons, the four men came over, curiosity written on their faces.

"Gentlemen, we've a special assignment for the four of you this evening." The men waited for Dannecker to continue. "An influential friend of ours here in Paris has encountered momentary difficulties and can't personally handle an important piece of business. We, however, are in a position to help him while he's indisposed, and he's shared with me some information well-suited to our assignment."

The agents, honored to have the captain single them out from their colleagues, nodded enthusiastically.

"*Obersturmführer* Rothe here has the address in Montmartre, a night club named…" Dannecker looked to the lieutenant who already consulted his clipboard.

"*La Chatte bottée*, sir."

"Yes, indeed, 'pussy in boots,' it is." Arched brows and ribald laughter. "I've learned from our friend that the proprietress is a half-Jew, which on its own is not enough cause to arrest her." He gave his men a conspiratorial grin. "At least not yet. But here's the important part—at closing time you will find in her office a wireless transmitter hidden in a closet." The agents traded knowing glances. "Yes, gentlemen, this Jewess is a spy for the English. Bring her in, and arrest anyone you find in the office with her. But hands off her clientele—she caters to some of our most influential military officers." Dannecker smiled benevolently. "And keep your hands off the rest of the girls, no matter how tempting—"

The agents came to attention. "*Zu Befehl!*"

Dannecker couldn't resist adding a final word. "—unless those lovely ladies look Jewish. In which case, an in-depth inspection might well be in order." And with a chuckle and a wink he left the room.

One agent questioned the lieutenant. "What about these other assignments for tonight?"

"Let them wait—this takes priority. And gentlemen—"

"Yes, sir?"

"— do have fun tonight!"

❖

The Florentine Ring

AFTERWORD

Even in the best of times, life is uncertain. But in times of war one finds few happy endings. Brief interludes of relief give way to the shifting winds of conflict, to new obstacles and horrors. That was especially true in Europe of the 1930s and '40's. It is still true today.

Post-war published accounts of the German Occupation of France often disagree. National pride and sometimes personal guilt encouraged some writers to exaggerate participation in the resistance movement, particularly in the early years of the war. Only in recent decades have historians attempted a more accurate portrayal of those difficult times.

The fascist mindset that corrupted Germany found its reflection west of the Rhine, and once French adherents took charge, all of France suffered the consequences. Daily life in the two zones differed in many ways, but overall the authoritarian repression was the same. Many brave people on both sides of the Demarcation Line took courageous actions to thwart their occupiers and protect innocents. Others kept their heads low to remain invisible. In the first years of the Occupation, partisan activity was sporadic and poorly organized. Agents from both the Allied Powers and the Reich operated underground. Secret police and snitches lurked everywhere. Corruption was rampant and reached to the highest levels.

I have tried to put the reader into that time and place in **Beacon of Vengeance**. For those seeking greater insight, please visit *www.beaconofvengeance.com* for a bibliography of books I found most helpful in portraying the complexities of the period.

As always, I am indebted to those who give immeasurable help and encouragement in bringing these novels to life. Foremost among them is my wife Dani, whose sharp intellect and keen eye keep me on target. I am grateful to Roy Leighton Malone III, Gerda Tüchsen Brown, and Alexander Mackey for their thoughtful contributions as readers of the finished manuscript. Admired British writer Frank Kusy helped make an authentic-sounding Englishman out of Devon Whitaker. And as always, I give thanks to my late father, Leonard L. O'Bryon, Sr. His spirit reaches out to me as I craft these stories inspired by his adventures in espionage.

Finally, I sincerely thank all who have expressed enthusiasm for **Corridor of Darkness**. Your thoughtful reviews of the novel on Amazon.com, Barnesandnoble.com, Goodreads, blogs and other sites have encouraged many others to experience Ryan Lemmon's Europe. I look forward to hearing what you think of Ryan's latest challenges. Should you have a question or comment for me, please visit my blog site *www.patrickwobryon.com*.

Fans of Ryan's journey will understand that his story takes numerous twists and turns which sometimes leave the reader hanging, so please do stick around for **Fulcrum of Malice**.

But, just as in real life, I hope you find pleasure in those fleeting moments along the path when love overcomes obstacles, someone demonstrates true humanity, and life hints at hope for these characters and their troubled world.

Patrick W. O'Bryon
Cameron Park, California

Don't miss the final volume in the Corridor of Darkness trilogy

Fulcrum of Malice

A Novel of Nazi Germany

Patrick W. O'Bryon has been a Fulbright Scholar,
a Princeton Ph.D., a college professor, a command
military interpreter, a log cabin builder, a natural health
counselor, an investment property broker, an ad man,
and a rescuer of animals—both wild and domesticated.

Will this writer ever settle down?

For now, he brokers real estate and writes novels,
travels as frequently as possible to Europe,
and shares life's adventures with his wife
and some very demanding cats.

42433323R00256

Made in the USA
Middletown, DE
11 April 2017